Jimmy Thomson is a journalist, author and screenwriter whose credits include the ABC-TV series *Rain Shadow*. He is the author of sixteen books ranging through military history, sports biographies and children's literature. *Perfect Criminals* is his first crime novel.

Perfect Criminals

Jimmy Thomson

Affirm press

Published by Affirm Press in 2018
28 Thistlethwaite Street, South Melbourne, VIC 3205
www.affirmpress.com.au
10 9 8 7 6 5 4 3 2 1

Text and copyright © Jimmy Thomson 2018
All rights reserved. No part of this publication may be reproduced without prior permission of the publisher.

National Library of Australia Cataloguing-in-Publication entry available for this title at www.nla.gov.au.
Title: Perfect Criminals / Jimmy Thomson, author.
ISBN: 9781925584721 (paperback)

Cover design by Design by Committe
Typeset in Granjon 12/16.75 pt by J&M Typesetting
Proudly printed in Australia by Griffin Press

The paper this book is printed on is certified against the Forest Stewardship Council® Standards. Griffin Press holds FSC chain of custody certification SGS-COC-005088. FSC promotes environmentally responsible, socially beneficial and economically viable management of the world's forests.

To Sue and Lily, my two muses.

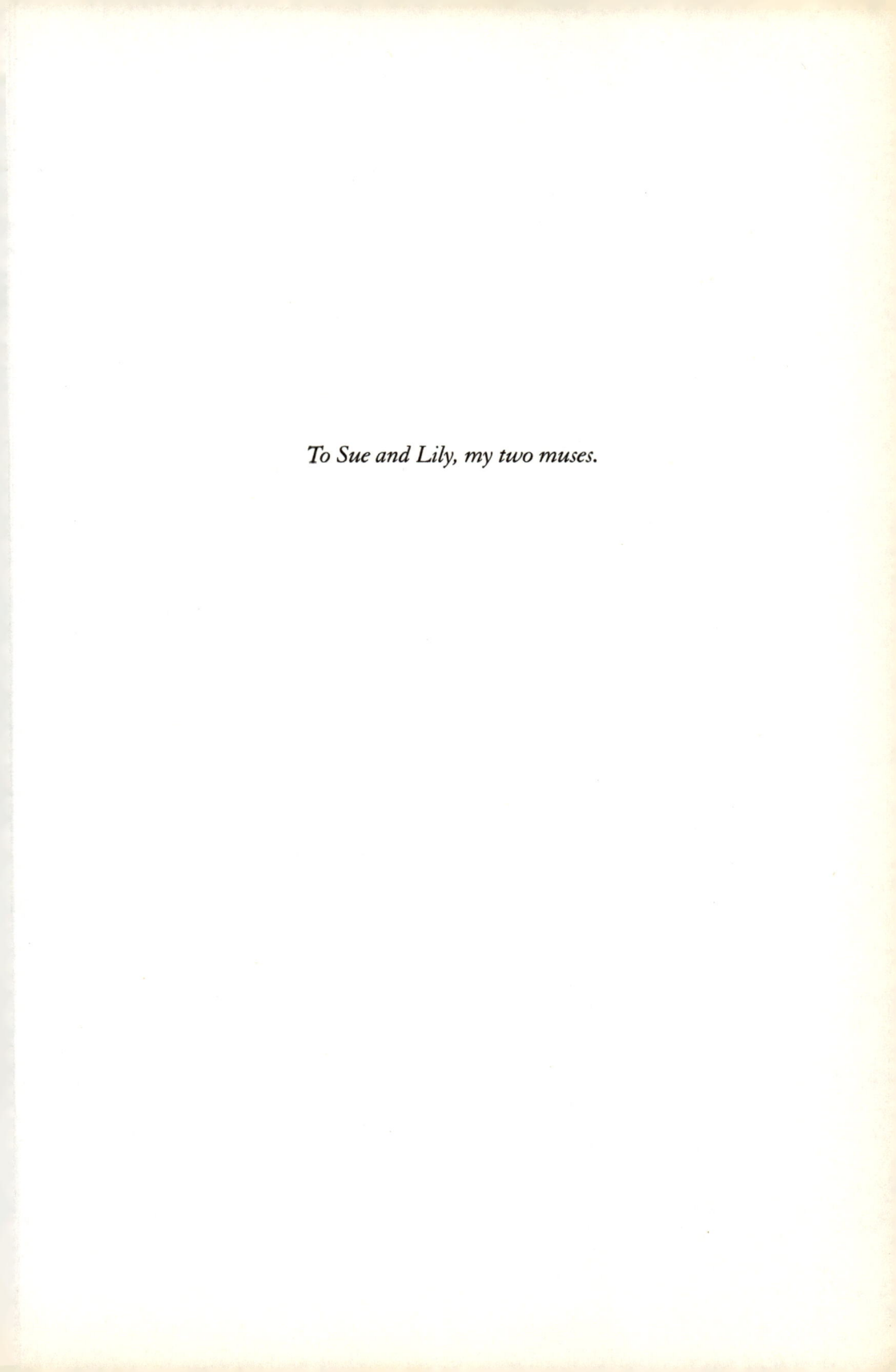

PROLOGUE

The lift doors open with a soft rumble and a clunk, like metal curtains on a tiny stage. A man in his seventies, dressed a little too colourfully for his age, lies on the floor.

His lips, fixed in a pain-filled grimace – or is it a sneer? – are turning blue. His name is Alan Hahn and he has more money than anyone truly needs, but it is of no use to him now because he is dying. On the floor of a lift. Unloved but not alone.

A young Asian woman kneels over him, thrusting downwards on his chest with both hands and counting... *one* ... *two* ... *three* ... *four* ... *five*. Her fingers quickly find the spot on his neck where there should be a pulse but there isn't.

Her name is Zan, at least to her friends. To Alan Hahn she is nobody – a nobody who is now trying to save his life. At least it seems that way to the building's concierge, transfixed by this life-and-death drama as he leans across his desk for a better look.

'Call a fucking ambulance!' yells Zan.

The lift doors close.

Curtains.

1

THE HEAT crackled through the scrub. Sweat filled Danny Clay's goggles and it felt like a river was sluicing along his spine. Along, rather than down, because he was lying flat on his belly, his arms outstretched in front of him as per his training. Explosions, especially those intended to damage vehicles, generally go upwards in a cone. If you are beneath the cone you could be okay. Maybe.

Fuck it, Danny thought. He pulled off the goggles, then his helmet. At least the sweat was drying as soon as it made contact with air. Back to work.

The device was a Soviet TM-72 anti-tank mine. It was connected to a car battery via a folded saw blade buried a few metres away. The different elements were kept separate to make them easier to conceal: a battery could more easily be hidden in a nearby bush than on the dirt road, the firing mechanism was in the wheel tracks, and the explosive device was in the centre of the road, where it would do most damage. The saw blade required the weight of a vehicle, rather than a human or a goat, to complete the circuit and spark the detonator.

Danny had dealt with the firing mechanism using a small controlled explosion. All he needed to do now was neutralise the main device. He'd followed the wires, watching for booby trap bombs laid for anyone who might think the tank-killer was the only threat.

The easiest thing would be to BIP the fucker. Blow In Place. But there was so much intel in every device. Fingerprints on sticky tape can lead you to a bomb factory or – the jackpot – the bomb-maker. Sappers like Danny fantasised about having a print they'd taken from a bomb show up on an immigration screen at an international airport. 'Hello, Aamir, we've been waiting for you.'

More realistically, they could use that evidence to trace the spread of IEDs from a central source. Every bomb had a signature anyway, as clear as if the maker had scrawled his name on the Semtex. Fingerprints were the multi-whorled icing on the high-explosive cake.

Danny took a deep breath. He had quartered the mine, mentally dividing it up like a pizza so he could deal with one section at a time. He used a narrow paintbrush to carefully dust aside sand and grit – like an archaeologist, only with much more at stake than a fragile fossil. He was looking for an anti-tamper switch that he knew would not be there.

As IEDs went, this was pretty crude: a recycled Russian mine attached to a car battery didn't need much ingenuity to assemble. And they had never encountered any hidden complications with similar bodge-ups. If they had, it would have been on the wire in minutes, warning other bomb disposal crews.

'Be careful out there,' the troop commander would have said at the briefing – and not just because he was addicted to re-runs of *Hill Street Blues*.

'Leave it, Sarge. Bip it,' Danny's number two said softly but insistently.

There was a gap under the mine and a tiny rock blocking the brush's progress. Danny took out his probe and, as a voice in his head screamed 'No …!' he flicked it aside.

Click.

There was no *boom*. Danny always woke up before the explosion. It was a dream but the sweat was real. His army-appointed therapist had said that the day the bomb went off would be the day he was finally cured. Danny thought it would be the day he died.

This wasn't even his own nightmare. It had been another sapper in another platoon. They'd met in passing between rotations, and the soldier had survived – seriously fucked-up, but alive. It was his story, not Danny's, but the yarns all got around. The bad luck, the seriously evil IEDs, the casualties, the survivors, and the incidents that ended with a ramp ceremony where you sent one of your mates home, carried up a transport plane ramp in a flag-draped coffin. Danny's talent was his curse; his imagination allowed him to put himself in the other soldiers' boots, right at the heart of other people's nightmares.

It took Danny a little longer than usual to work out where he really was. He was on rather than in his bed. Another army trick: you learn to sleep when you can, where you can. Why had he had the dream? Oh yeah, the meeting at the TV network. He had to try not to think about it. They were only civilians, people who had never sweated under a hostile sun on the Afghan Dasht, where a little mistake could cost you a limb ... or your life.

He rolled over onto his stomach. That was better. He consciously, deliberately, slowed his heart rate and started to drift.

The bushes crackled in the heat. Sweat filled his goggles ...

―

It was an unseasonably hot day as Isaac 'Paddy' Rosenberg waddled briskly down La Croisette: a pink, sweaty ball of frustration in damp, crumpled linen. Although he loved Cannes at night, he loathed it during the day. Daytime meant heat and work, perspiring pure alcohol from the previous evening's excesses while trying to appear cool. Paddy didn't do cool.

He hated the French, he hated France and he hated the whole of Europe. (Except for Israel, which it turns out is not even in Europe – who knew?) He hated all the beautiful people and the (Lord help us) 'artists'. Do me a favour, he thought. If you can't hang what you do on a wall, or stick it on a plinth, you are not a fucking artist! *Capiche?* Writers he could almost tolerate because you could treat them like shit and throw money at them when they complained. Anybody with a laptop that had spellcheck could write, and they knew it. He could write. He *would* write, if he had the time.

But Paddy didn't have time. Paddy was always late for something. It was like his body clock had been synchronised to a time zone that was fifteen minutes later than everyone else's, no matter where he was. Last night he had turned up late for a reception on the beach and the fuckers hadn't let him in. 'Do you know who I am?' he'd said to this stubble-chinned, lank-haired dickwad with what looked like a hearing aid coiling out of one ear. 'Check your underpants,' the guy said. 'Your mother probably wrote your name on a label.'

Fucker.

Paddy spent the whole night trawling the beach and the hotels looking for a familiar face to get him into where all the people he hated were – where he belonged. And now it was 10am and he was worn out already. But he had to get to this meeting. When he'd stumbled home an hour ago he'd found a fax slipped under the door of his hotel room. Who the fuck used faxes these days?

Meet the Australians at the Entrée des Artistes between the Palais and the Riviera market at 10am (your time), it said. *Get this movie or don't come home. Be decisive. Fox and Sony are in too. Take the checkbook.*

Paddy hated Australians. Mel Gibson, Russel Crowe, that chick director who got the Oscar for *The Piano*. For the script, mind you, not for directing. He hated them all anyway, but now they had made him miss breakfast.

Assholes.

2

SITTING IN his battered old Toyota Corolla, Danny was looking at a scene of bucolic stillness. Trees did not sway in a non-breeze, grass stayed bent, a brook that neither babbled nor trickled sat at the foot of a meadow where sunlight had dappled only once, then stayed. Then it all moved at the same time, sideways, as the giant roller door of a sound stage opened its mighty maw and stage hands pushed the backdrop inside.

With real life back in view, Danny watched as workers bustled between an ageing office block and converted cottages at the bottom of a hill, in the shadow of a satellite dish the size of a small apartment block. Crew members strolled rather than walked to and from their tasks, confident that without them nothing could be produced.

Creatives, administrators and junior executives hurried past with the harried look of those who knew the next cull could have their name on it; the next wave of outsourcing could be the rip that left them at sea; the next over-privileged, underqualified scion of an advertiser who 'wanted to direct someday' could be ushered into their seat. Actors walked in through the security gate bright-eyed and eager, and exited slumped and shattered to rejoin the ranks of the unemployed, where ninety per cent of their profession spent ninety per cent of its time. Actors are divided into two groups: those who get everything and those who get nothing.

Danny was thinking, if actors' faces were their fortune, his was his misfortune. Not that he was ugly – far from it. He was reasonably handsome, in a lived-in – make that *slept*-in – way. The ginger eyebrows gave a lie to his much blonder hair, prompting a TV make-up artist to once ask which of them he dyed. The unspectacular moustache looked like it had been chosen from a kit for bank managers. His occasionally unkempt goatee, a narrow strip of bristle travelling southwards from his bottom lip and stopping abruptly under his chin, was his concession to style. His tribute to Frank Zappa, he said, or a sign (now he'd shaved off the rest of his beard) that he had moved from folk to jazz.

Danny had read that jazz musicians adopted the goatee to avoid nicking their bottom lip while shaving, which could potentially ruin their embouchure and lose them at least one paying gig. Maybe. More likely it was just an easy way of being spotted by jazz groupies, and less strenuous than carrying around a tenor sax or double bass when you went out at night.

Danny looked hard at himself in the car's long-unused vanity mirror. He was trying to see what he looked like when he wasn't thinking, because his aforementioned misfortune was that when he *was* thinking, really thinking, it looked like he was angry – *really* angry. The creases of concentration on his brow and below his cheeks formed an X like a St Andrew's Cross, the Scottish flag, making him look like an extra from *Braveheart* – only without the blue paint.

This was one of the many ironies of Danny's life: he was rarely as angry as he was entitled to be. That partly explained how he had managed to sustain a reasonable living as a TV scriptwriter, and before that as an army engineer – a sapper. He had long ago given up arguing with the people he worked for; the only piper who ever calls his own tune is the guy busking at Circular Quay on summer Saturdays, and even then a ten-buck note will turn him into a musical jukebox. '"Stairway to Heaven"? One of my personal favourites, sir ... *There's a laydeee who knows* ...'

Danny didn't mind taking orders, as long as they were clear and concise and didn't get anyone killed: that much he had learned from ten years in the army. But clear and concise weren't part of the creative lexicon: that much he remembered from his first stint in TV, all those years before.

Like it or not, television network executives were the highly paid arbiters of whether or not Danny's ideas would ever make it from paper to picture, so when he disagreed with them, he tried hard not to let them know what he was really thinking. In meetings he nodded his head when he wanted to shake it. He listened when he wanted to scream. He rewrote perfectly good lines, scrubbed whole dimensions out of characters and twisted motivations out of shape to make them fit the latest focus group findings. And smiled gratefully while he was doing it.

But then there was the thinking X, which looked awfully like an angry X. He would be genuinely trying to think of an alternative that would keep the producer happy without completely destroying months of work, but the intersecting furrows on his face would suggest he was about to produce a double-handed broadsword and split the desk like a character in *Game of Thrones*.

That's why, as he looked in the mirror, Danny tried not to think at all and see what *that* looked like. Parked outside a major TV network, preparing for the meeting that could decide the rest of his career, the show that would make his name and allow him to realise all his dreams (apart from the illegal ones), Danny was taking no chances. And, he reassured himself, this was the one place in the world where no one would think twice about seeing someone staring intently into a mirror.

Okay, he thought as he got out of the car. Showtime!

—

One of the last thoughts Bryan Jones entertained was to wonder if the newspapers would spell his name correctly. His Baby Boomer parents had named him after Brian Jones of the Rolling Stones, but that was *totally* too ordinary a name and so, contrarily, they'd replaced the I with a Y.

It could have been a worse Jones: Davy of the Monkees, for instance. Or Tom. At least Brian Jones was still hip, with or without a Y. Bryan used these thoughts to calm himself as he watched the stocky, dark-haired female cop help a befuddled woman in her eighties try to master the intricacies of a parking machine. He savoured the police-issue combat fatigues. There was something about women in uniform – proper, battle-ready uniform – that lifted Bryan's heart rate a notch or two. But he was trying to focus, specifically on her holstered Glock automatic pistol, and even more on the little leather tab that held it in place.

He'd done his research. The Glock was perfect. Its internal safety mechanism meant it could be carried with a live round in the chamber. That in turn meant it could be fired quicker. Or sooner, Bryan thought, being a stickler for precise language. The internal safety catches were there in case the gun was dropped, but a deliberate squeeze of the trigger would override all those hidden precautions. This was a gun made to fire as soon as you wanted it to, but not before. All Bryan's internal safety catches were also switched off.

His research into the gun had been conducted on his computer, and the thought of that made his stomach twist and loop like the blob in a lava lamp. His computer, the perfidious PC, had made him, and now it would betray him. Having contributed to his success as a writer, like a Shakespearean malevolence, it held the seeds of his destruction and would prompt a most theatrical exit. The unforgiving pit of malice called the internet had brought him to this.

The old woman, Edna Sandford, pecked at coins arthritically as she pulled them from the depths of her purse. She handed them one by one to the cop, who fed them into the slot. Bryan smiled: she was fully distracted. Then he sighed. This was the hard part. He didn't want to hurt the young woman, but now that they had tasers he had no choice: they shocked before they shot these days.

Edna Sandford couldn't grasp the idea of the numbered parking bays and wanted a ticket to put in her windscreen. The cop, Jodie, as the next day's newspapers would correctly identify her, tried to explain the difference with apparently infinite patience (a virtue that would be tested to breaking point in the ensuing days of interrogation by her superiors and weeks of enforced stress leave). So she didn't notice the thinly haired, pale, weary and stooped man in his early forties edging towards her, a sheen of sweat forming on his top lip. Jodie's partner, Val, did notice him, but she was busy balancing coffee and muffins as she looked for a gap in the traffic through which to cross the street. In any case he looked like just another civilian about to offer help where none was required. You get that a lot as a female cop.

Bryan, whose name would be misspelled by most of the next day's newspapers, noticed Val approaching and realised he was running out of time. He stepped forward, slammed Jodie's head into a postbox next to the parking machine and said 'sorry' as he unclipped and de-holstered her gun in one smooth movement. His finger had already found the trigger before the Glock was halfway out, and, as expected, by the time he pressed the muzzle to his temple the gun was ready to be fired. Just as Val's coffee and muffins hit the bonnet of a car that had skidded to a halt inches from her shins, fire it he did.

Jodie, Val and Edna looked at the body of Bryan Jones slumping forward in slow motion, already dead, and dropping at their feet. Jodie, feeling her holster suddenly empty but not yet feeling the pain in her head, was more puzzled than shocked. She, Val and Edna looked at each other, then at the little fountain of blood, first spurting from Bryan's temple, then slowing to an ooze as his heart got the message to stop pumping.

Then Edna simply said, 'Fuck me sideways!'

Now Jodie was shocked. So shocked that she didn't see an envelope Bryan had been holding getting caught and kicked along the street by a breeze. Later it would be dropped in a letter box by a passer-by who didn't notice that, rather than an address, it bore only the words 'To whom it may concern'.

3

DANNY HAD made it. Well, not exactly *made it*. He'd made it to the boardroom of The Family Network (aka, The People's Channel, previously known as YOUR TV Station) with an idea that was all his own. He had pitched it to his agent, who had suggested a couple of changes. He had pitched it to the network's head of drama, who had suggested a couple of changes, and the head of drama had pitched it to the head of programming, who had ... you get the picture.

And now Danny was seated in the inner sanctum with an idea for a TV show that was still, to all intents and purposes, his (notwithstanding an age reduction of ten years for one of the leads, the complete disappearance of another and the arrival of a character designed to suit some splinter demographic like twentysomethings who didn't have iPads or men over thirty who lived with their parents and weren't gay). But every hurdle had been cleared and every hoop had been jumped through.

He was so close he could taste it ... and the taste was chocolate. In this particular network, deals may have been signed with names on contracts and cheques, but the pre-deal 'welcome to the fold' was sealed with Arnott's Chocolate Monte biscuits, a stack of which lay untouched on a plate in the middle of the huge oval table. The table, made from ridiculously expensive and probably endangered Javanese timber, wasn't quite the round table of Arthurian legend, but it was a Holy Grail for television writers. The boardroom was decked out in muted pastels and sound-softening (make that scream-absorbing) fabrics. One door led to a corridor lined with executive offices, another was the entrance to the Big Boss's lair.

Huge windows across from where Danny sat were shielded from the afternoon glare by hideously bland vertical blinds. Clearly the usual occupant of the chair at the head of the table liked to be backlit. The other wall was occupied by a concealed wet bar and award-cluttered shelves, built from the same rare, honey-toned wood as the table and the leather-cushioned chairs around it.

A few minutes earlier Danny had been introduced around the table to an impressive array of network executives. There were several heads of department: programming, drama, comedy, reality (bizarrely) and publicity. The last was an encouraging sign, unless they planned to issue a press release about the death of Danny's writing career. He tried to dismiss the thought, but it nudged at him like a determined dog sniffing his crotch.

The buzz around the table was that the Big Boss himself, Jeff Neumann, had decided to sit in on the meeting. This was great news. This meeting – which should have been just to rubber-stamp Danny's comedy–drama cop show development proposal – would be graced by the presence of the man with the golden chequebook. There was no downside to this, Danny had told himself. Don't screw up and it will all be fine. Smile, look as grateful as you feel, don't think, whatever you do, and all will be well. Neumann would not come to commissioning meetings just to say no, however much he enjoyed seeing the tear-filled eyes and quivering lips that signalled another crushed dream.

Everywhere he looked around the table, Danny's glances were met with smiles. The reality department was represented by a small round man with a dress sense that hinted at Target, while the veins on his cheeks and pre-bulbous nose screamed 'problem drinker'. He studiously read Danny's pitch document – not for the first time, judging by the coffee and red-wine rings stamped on it. He knows he's going to be asked something, thought Danny, and he's terrified he won't know the answer.

Drama was a middle-aged, middle-class, middle-sized woman who had clearly abandoned any attempts at corporate couture and embraced 'Bohemian Creative' as her signature style, no doubt hoping this would allow her to identify more closely with her writers (who tended, in any case, towards Tommy Hilfiger knock-offs from the Saturday markets). Wreathed in swirls of silk scarves and gypsy jewellery that seemed to be constantly tangling in her greying bubble-perm hair, her eyes were clear and bright. But the bags under them and the lines beyond betrayed sleepless nights and a level of stress no true bohemian would ever have endured.

Comedy was a worried-looking man who shaved his head to disguise his baldness. Thin as an Italian clown and twitching like a cat in a flea epidemic, he looked as if he lived in constant fear of being asked to say something funny. Clearly having had a weight problem at some time in the recent past, his clothes (Tommy Hilfiger knock-offs) and the loose flesh on his face were both two sizes too big. Being an extreme pessimist, in complete empathy with all his comedic writers and performers, he doubtless thought that despite his best endeavours, his clothes would be fitting him snugly before too long.

Programming looked like an accountant because, somewhere in a previous life at this station, he had been one – and not one of those nice ones on TV ads who give you a hug when it's tax time. He dressed smartly, including collar and tie, but efficiently, like someone who wouldn't open their wardrobe until they had read the weather forecast. Necktie and short sleeves, Danny noted, wondering if he wore socks and sandals on the weekend. Programming's hair, face, eyes and mouth were neutral, as if they were not required to be any more expressive, so why make the effort? He pored over an impressive array of A3 pages. Schedules, Danny hoped, with a big juicy gap for his show, although he admitted to himself it was more likely to be Q scores – the measure of a TV personality's popularity – demographic breakdowns, focus group results and advertising projections, any one of which could kill a project with the click of a calculator.

And then there was Publicity, a little bubble of sunshine in her slightly outdated but colourful corporate suit: a living testimony to the power of surgery and creative matrimony. Over her twenty years with this network she'd had an affair with, married, then divorced a senior executive, and each stage in their deeply flawed romance had entrenched her even further in the structure of the company.

She and Danny had been at daggers drawn a few years earlier while promoting the teen soap that had marked Danny's return to television. She'd consistently misspelled his name 'MacLay' in a series of press releases, and when he made his fourth request to get it right, she suggested he change his name to MacLay because 'the show is bigger than you, darling'. Now Danny smiled at her and she smiled back warmly, clearly having no idea who the hell he was.

Then everyone looked up and smiled when Neumann, the network Head of Everything, strode into the room, proposal in hand, clearly trying not to look as if he had just read the document all the way through for the first time. Danny only just resisted the temptation to stand, as if it were a courtroom, and turned the movement into an exaggerated lounge that almost had him sliding under the table. Neumann watched him arrest his slip to oblivion then nodded at Danny and said, 'Love this. Fucking great!'

Danny tried to project a mixture of delighted surprise and cool confidence, but gave up and nodded and smiled the way you do when the restaurant wine you have just tasted turns out to be better than you had hoped.

'One thing though, mate,' Neumann continued. 'Don't put funny made-up names in proposals. Okay? It's amateur-night and it shits me.'

He smiled benignly at Danny as he sat down. It should have been a passing moment where Neumann asserted his authority and everyone else acknowledged it.

Danny was completely blindsided but, thanks to his car-park practice session, kept his confusion to himself. Made-up names? Me? Funny names were a basic error only the try-hardest writers ever used, and Danny was a few years past that stage. Even so, he nodded, shrugged and smiled apologetically, trying to look as if he was making a mental note of the point – anything to get past the potential quicksand of this moment.

Neumann sat back, suddenly all smiles, and nodded again. 'I'm feeling very good about this, Daniel,' he said. 'Very good indeed. We all are.' Heads around the table nodded dutifully. 'We have a couple of names for the lead roles that we think will get you excited.' Danny tried to look enthused, showing more excitement than was justified by the predictable pool of soapie himbos and bimbos, clip show hosts and retired sports stars they doubtless had in mind.

Neumann beamed, shuffled some papers and frowned, presumably because that's how he thought people looked when they were thinking. He wasn't made Head of Everything for nothing. He was tall, slim and lightly muscled with a swimmer's shoulders and a surfer's tan. He was in his mid-forties but his hair was way ahead of him, with grey appearing like an advance party from a highly stressful future. He was clearly good enough at his job not to need to spend all day doing it – or at least doing it in the office – when he could be at the gym or on the golf course.

Danny was suddenly feeling pretty good about this too, even though, disturbingly, he caught sight of Reality studying the proposal in great detail with concern creasing his forehead.

'All that remains now is for us to nail you to the floor and screw you out of every last cent you have any chance of making out of us.' Neumann laughed. Danny laughed. Everyone laughed.

Everyone except the idiot Reality, who asked, 'What made-up name?' Neumann squinted at Reality, who repeated the question. 'You said there was a made-up name. Which one?'

Neumann scowled and picked up the proposal, flicking through the stapled A4 pages with clear irritation until he found it.

'Ex-anth,' he finally spat. 'Who the fuck is called Ex-anth?'

Danny nodded solemnly as he silently conceded his non-mistake. 'Won't happen again,' his entire body said. 'Sorry,' his downcast eyes concurred.

'It's pronounced *Zanthy*,' said Reality, correctly but, in Danny's eyes, idiotically.

'What?'

'*Zan-thy*,' the network programmer pitched in, smiling supportively at Danny. He was the second-most important person at the table, and Danny allowed himself the slightest flicker of a response in the hope the matter would drop there. 'I've got a niece called Xanthe,' he added. Unnecessarily, Danny thought.

'Never heard of it,' said Neumann. Danny looked at him apologetically and empathically, a complex notion to express in a half-smile, a nod and a semi-shrug, but he gave it his best shot. The moment could pass now and they could get on with the bit where he got to have a glittering career.

'My best friend's called Xanthe,' said Drama. Danny shrivelled inside.

'Yeah. I know a couple of Xanthes – it's Greek,' said Comedy, as Danny contemplated setting fire to something in the hope of creating a distraction.

'Didn't we used to have a Xanthe in publicity?' asked Reality. Everyone nodded their heads except for Danny, who was shaking his ruefully, and Neumann, who was gradually turning red. Shut up, Danny screamed internally. Could you all please shut the fuck up?! Then he realised everyone had stopped talking and was looking at him. He had his thinking face on. He was angry-Xing.

'Look,' he said, trying to force a benign smile onto his features. 'It's just a name. I can change it in seconds with a search and replace. It's not a deal-breaker.'

But there was something in his tone, a sense of suppressed exasperation, that seemed to rankle Neumann even more.

'I'll be the judge of that,' Neumann said. Danny laughed but it was clear from his expression that Neumann wasn't joking.

'It's no big deal,' Danny added, between a mumble and a whisper, forgetting that the first thing to do when you find yourself in a hole is to stop digging.

'Really?' asked Neumann, who had decided to feel insulted. 'So why didn't you get it right first time? Why is it even there? Why are we talking about it?' Neumann rapped the document with a calloused knuckle to emphasise each question, then flicked through the pages and sighed. 'You know what? I still think this is a great concept,' he said, smiling at Danny. 'But I'm beginning to wonder if you are the best person to write it.'

Neumann slid Danny's proposal across the table to Drama. 'See if you can get some fresh writers to make something of that,' he said. 'No rush. Unless, of course, Danny here just wants to take it back and file it in his desk drawer …'

And with that he got up and turned to exit, then paused and fixed Danny with a glare that spoke of unemployment queues. Danny was thinking desperately hard about how to rescue the situation. Too late, Danny realised he was angry-Xing again.

'And don't dare give me that "fuck you" look, matey,' bellowed Neumann. 'Fuck *me*? Fuck *you*!'

He left, slamming the door of his office. There was an embarrassed silence as everyone sat immobilised by the startling turn of events, then began gathering up their notes. Danny took his bag and coat from the empty chair where he'd parked them.

'That's weird, he told me yesterday that he loved your writing,' the programmer said. 'Had only read ten pages, but loved it.'

Drama patted Danny on the shoulder and said, 'Hey, you did nothing wrong.' To his credit, Danny didn't say, 'Great, that really makes up for the nine months of my life I wasted working on this thing for no money.'

'Xanthe Walker,' said Reality. Everyone looked at him. 'The publicist.' They all smiled and nodded as they filed out of the room. Xanthe had been duly remembered, but Danny was already forgotten. He vaguely remembered Xanthe Walker but, in fact, had named his character after his next-door neighbour: a friend, muse and brutally helpful script editor. He was just about to steal a consolatory Chocolate Monte when a secretary appeared and whisked them away. No show, no biscuit. That was the rule.

'Xanthe,' Danny mumbled to himself as the glass-walled lift grumbled its way down the outside of the building. It was the slowest elevator in the world, and he was in full view of all the offices, so the bastard suits got an extra few seconds to savour his pain. 'Fucking Xanthe!'

4

THE SWEET acidity of indigestion rose in Paddy Rosenberg's throat and nibbled at the back of his tongue. He shouldn't have had those biscuits and gravy with his breakfast. Shouldn't have had breakfast. How the fuck could they call that comfort food? Discomfort food was what it should be called. He burped into his hand.

Paddy adjusted his chair. Too low. Aw fuck, too high. What's this lever? *'Aiiee!'* He nearly smacked his head on the almost-empty trophy display cupboard that had been left behind when his predecessor was promoted. 'It was getting kinda crowded anyway,' that blow-ass had said.

Wasn't crowded now, that's for sure, apart from a framed picture of a 22-year-old Paddy in costume as his hilarious former alter ego, Paddy Fields the Oriental Irishman, receiving his award as runner-up in Best Original Solo Comedy Act (Non-stand-up) at the 2002 Reno Nevada International Cabaret Festival. Alongside was the trophy, a silver jester's head on a stick. Paddy had thought the comedy award would launch his career, but that was just before they invented political correctness. Even so, he thought, show business was like prostitution. It didn't matter how you started, once you were in, you were in for good.

The younger Paddy in the photo had more than a passing similarity to the trophy: neurotically stick-thin with a manic grin on his oversized head — all that was missing were the cap and bells. These days his body had caught up with his cranium, and then some. Short and tubby — stubby, his ex-wife had called him — Paddy bemoaned the lunches and dinners he was compelled to attend. While his peers were pumping iron or pedalling spin bikes, he was on the frontline, wining and dining the 'talent'.

The door to his office flew open.

'Paddy, are you all right?' said a panicked Jasmina Hernandez, who, in a strange synchronicity, was Paddy's fifth associate producer that year, while he was her fifth boss. The votes were still being counted on whether they were doomed or destined for greatness.

'What?'

'I heard a scream.'

'What scream?' He looked around his sparsely furnished office to see where a scream might have come from, then realised. 'Oh, this chair. Someone has been messing around with it.'

Jasmina's right eyebrow started to rise but she quickly got it under control.

'Probably the cleaners,' she said.

'Yeah. These fucking Asians. Makes you long for the days when we had Mexicans.'

'Paddy ...' her voice carried just the right level of disappointment.

'Oh, sorry about the foul language.' He smiled. 'And by the way, as my PA, it's probably better if you call me Mr Rosenberg. Only my friends call me Paddy.'

He laughed. Jasmina didn't, wondering where he got the idea that she was his PA, rather than his AP. It was something she would straighten out with him later.

Jasmina also wondered if he was aware that she was half Mexican, or if he just didn't care. It wasn't out of the question, since she often thought she'd acquired the worst physical traits of both her European and Latino stock. Straight brown hair rather than the lustrous blue-black tresses of her cousins, no butt to speak of and no boobs worth mentioning. And unlike her blonde, blue-eyed peers, who would forcefully express their opinions on anything and everything, regardless of the topic or their level of knowledge, she often lacked the conviction that she deserved to be heard.

'I need you to sit on the chair ...' she said, wondering if acting like a PA was just reinforcing his misconception.

'What?'

'The chair, it needs your weight ...'

The ridiculously expensive and spectacularly complicated office chair was one of a job lot, bought cheaply after the GFC had sent the spendthrift twentysomethings scurrying away from their start-ups and back into their parents' homes. It had six principle settings – height, angle, pitch, firmness, lumbar and tilt – so it offered an almost limitless number of combinations. Surprising then that Paddy couldn't find one that suited him. Currently the seat was as high as a bar stool, which, despite being Paddy's favourite piece of furniture, meant he could barely reach his desk with his hands or the floor with his feet.

Paddy sat on the chair as Jasmina leaned over him to fiddle with various knobs and levers. His desk was modern, steel and frosted glass, unencumbered by anything more work-related than an Apple computer and two scripts that Paddy hadn't read (although he had produced one of them).

A framed poster for *Barb Wire*, the Pamela Anderson comic book sci-fi remake of *Casablanca*, adorned one wall for no other reason than the all-too-obvious – and the fact that Paddy had an assistant to an assistant credit that only cinema cleaners would have seen rolling up the screen. An uncomfortable Bauhaus-lite chair in white leather and chrome was positioned on the other side of the desk, defying anyone to sit on it.

The fourth wall of the Century City office had a fantastic view of the Fox lot, and Paddy spent an inordinate amount of time – at least for a showbiz professional – using binoculars to scan the car parks and throughways for anyone famous.

'Your Australian visitor will be here soon,' said Jasmina, leaning across Paddy to reach the tilt dial, the cloth of her shirt accidentally and not quite imperceptibly brushing the lap of his predictably khaki pants.

Paddy felt a stirring, despite his anxiety over his next meeting. The Australian was on his way to seal the deal on *Redneck Airlift*, the movie Paddy had bought in Cannes. This was going to be his crowning achievement, the deal that would elevate him to the ranks of the great movie producers like … well, he couldn't actually think of their names, but those guys. In any case, he was both anxious and excited.

'Have you ever met an Aborigine?' Paddy asked, trying to divert his thoughts.

'Aborigine?' she queried, pushing a lever. 'Sit.'

'People of colour from Australia,' Paddy explained, shifting his weight from his feet to his seat to facilitate the downward height adjustment.

'Can't say I have,' she replied. 'Knees down.' As she reached and twisted the angle control, Paddy was sure he could feel the squish of a boob on his upper thigh.

'I thought they were all like that "shrimp on the barbie" guy … what was it? Paul Brogan?'

'Hogan,' Jasmina muttered through gritted teeth as she wrestled with the lumbar control and tried to ignore the swelling in Paddy's pants.

'Yeah, him. White bread, lightly toasted. Anyway, it turns out they have black people there too.' Why was she leaning over him like that? Were they on the train to Blow Job City?

'What I want to know is, why did the slave traders take them to a place where nobody lived? Huh? Does that make sense to you?'

'Not really.'

'So I have to deal with this guy who is a chromosome away from the Stone Age. I mean, they don't tell you that in the movie course at USC.'

'No, they don't,' said Jasmina who, unlike Paddy, had actually graduated in Film Production from the University of Southern California. Another thing they didn't teach you was how to deal with an unwelcome tumescence in your boss's pants.

'Jesus,' Paddy said, silently congratulating himself as he gently but unmistakably put his hand on Jasmina's neck and pushed.

Jesus, she thought. What a creep! Four bosses down and this one wanted her to toot his flute. Her tactical error was trying to help with the chair. She'd been warned about Paddy. He was a serial sleazebag who was so blatant about it that he had gone ballistic the one time the studio had given him a male PA. Jasmina really deserved better. It was just her luck that she had been paired with a succession of high-flyers and no-hopers. Their rapid ascents and descents had left her stuck in the revolving door before she could establish herself (although she was glad not to have been too close to those who got the Don't Come Monday). Realising she might just have hooked up with another loser, and one who had skipped the sexual harassment classes, Jasmina groaned.

Paddy moaned.

Get your fucking hand off my head, she was about to say when a voice in rich, chocolatey tones – redolent of the subcontinent, rounded by English education and edged with an antipodean twang – asked, 'Am I interrupting something?'

'It's the Aborigine,' hissed Paddy, standing so abruptly that he bumped Jasmina's head against the edge of the desk.

'Just getting comfortable in my chair,' Paddy said, wincing.

'So I see.' The tall, dark-skinned, impeccably dressed visitor tweaked a diamond stud in his left earlobe as he entered from the outer office. 'So I see.'

'Can I get you a coffee … or maybe some water?' Jasmina asked as she emerged from under the desk, rubbing her head.

'I'll have what he's having,' the visitor said, and laughed uproariously.

5

THERE WAS a police car parked near Danny's unit block on Surrey Street, little more than a tree-lined lane that meandered between two of Kings Cross's busiest roads. It was mostly once-elegant terrace houses, gradually having their abominable filled-in balconies ripped out and the iron lace balustrades restored as money moved back into the area and replaced the need for living space with a hunger for style.

Danny and Xanthe, aka Zan, lived in adjoining flats in the slightly better of only two apartment blocks in the street. This was a rare slice of the old Cross, tucked away and forgotten until the yuppies with their interior design magazines and ugly little pugs came to breathe new life into it, God bless 'em. Danny knew the street had changed forever when the laundrette closed and a cheese restaurant opened. A whole restaurant for cheese?

Danny plodded up the steps hoping Zan had already heard the news about Bryan, if only so he wouldn't have to be the one to break it to her. He'd learned about it in a perfunctory voice message from his agent, Rob, but the creative community's jungle telegraph would be running hot, given that most of its members had little better to do than gossip on the pretext of keeping each other 'in the loop'. He could hear voices in her flat, so he tapped on the door. Zan opened it, red-eyed, and threw herself into a hug, sobbing.

'He died,' she said into Danny's chest. 'I can't believe he died.'

That answered the first question, Danny thought. When Zan finally released him she led him to the lounge, only a metre or so inside the front door, where a young woman sat on the sofa.

'Hi, Danny,' said the woman. It was only then that Danny realised he knew her. 'You've heard, huh?'

'Hi, Laura.' Danny nodded. 'Awful. Just ... awful.'

Police Sergeant Laura Revell made room for Danny on the sofa. She was in her mid-twenties with full but natural lips, dark but definitely not natural eyelashes and boyishly short blonde hair that somehow only made her look even more feminine. She was out of uniform, so he assumed she was working a shift in victim support or family liaison or some other non-frontline department that didn't involve occasional hand-to-hand combat with members of the public.

'So you didn't know the guy?' she asked Zan.

Zan was small, even for a Vietnamese woman, but right now she looked tiny, fragile and withdrawn, as if she was trying to disappear inside her own skin. 'Not really. Only to look at in passing.'

Danny chanced a small *WTF?* raised eyebrow in Zan's direction. She responded with a tiny *what's your problem?* shrug.

The exchange was not unnoticed by Laura. 'Am I missing something?' she asked.

Danny and Zan both shook their heads while looking at each other accusingly. Again Laura noticed, but this time said nothing. She was there as a friend more than anything, and the notes scribbled in her Moleskin flip-up were clearly for appearances' sake. She closed the notebook. Danny was surprised; he'd expected to be asked some questions too but wasn't about to volunteer – that's another thing you learn in the army.

'I think I have enough to go on with,' Laura said to Zan as she got up to leave. 'It's been a tough day for you. I'll call you if I need any more.' She hugged them both briefly – more of a shoulder bump, really – and headed for the door. Danny noticed Laura had taken off her shoes when she came in, something he'd been too distracted to remember.

Zan murmured something, and with that Laura was gone, leaving Danny to process what he'd just heard. Zan came back in and slumped on the sofa beside him. They sat in silence.

'Why did you say you only knew Bryan to look at?' Danny asked finally. 'You've been working with him for years.'

'I wasn't talking about Bryan,' she replied. 'Why would I be talking about Bryan?'

Danny was puzzled. It seemed fate hadn't let him off the hook after all, but he wasn't sure how or why.

'So you haven't heard?' he stated the obvious as he tried to concoct a way of telling her that wasn't too brutal. Eventually the expectant look on her face, turning into a worried frown, was more than he could bear. 'Bryan shot himself this afternoon,' he said. 'Took a gun off a cop and did it right in the street.' Danny squeezed Zan's arm. 'I'm sorry. I thought you knew. And Laura. Rob called me earlier and left a message.'

'Bryan ...? He did what? Oh my God. Bryan!' Zan was holding tightly onto Danny's sleeves and staring into his eyes, tears already filling hers again.

A pile of rags, incongruously dumped in the corner of Zan's otherwise uncluttered and sparsely furnished room, suddenly moved and revealed itself to be a large, hairy and unkempt man. 'What did you say?' said the man, staggering to his feet, his voice cracking. 'What happened to Bryan?'

'Hello, Poet,' Danny said, his voice laden with disdain. 'Bryan committed suicide.'

'Suicide? Are you sure?' The Poet demanded.

Danny nodded. 'He did it front of half a dozen witnesses – two of them coppers.'

The Poet sank to his knees and started to moan. 'No, Bryan, nooooo,' he wailed. Zan reluctantly reached out and gave his shoulder a squeeze, while scanning the room for her bottle of hand sanitiser.

'I could use a drink,' the Poet mumbled.

'So, no change there, then,' Danny said under his breath. Zan hesitated for a moment then went to the kitchen.

'Bryan? Are you sure?' the Poet said. He shook his head, answering his own question.

Zan stood in the doorway with a bottle of Monkey Shoulder whisky and a glass. She poured a nip and gulped it down then filled the glass almost to the brim and handed it to the Poet, who took it without thanks and slurped at it greedily.

'Medicinal rather than recreational,' he said between gulps.

'Hey, Zan?' Danny asked. 'If Laura wasn't here about Bryan, why was she here?'

Zan gave a grimace that told him more than he wanted to know. 'I'll get another glass,' she said and disappeared into the kitchen.

—

Danny, Zan and the Poet sat hunched around her coffee table, the Monkey Shoulder bottle now empty and a companion of Talisker Storm well on its way. They had just watched a TV news report on how multimillionaire property developer Alan Hahn had died of a heart attack, despite the best efforts of a young woman, a visitor to his building, to revive him.

And there she was, Zan. On screen, talking about how she'd learned CPR at her kickboxing class. Alan had suffered a heart attack as they travelled together in the lift and she'd done everything she could, but it was not to be. The reporter said Hahn had previously had a quadruple heart bypass and was involved in several disputes with his apartment block neighbours.

Danny looked at her, the question all in his eyes. She returned his stare, tilting her head just enough to say, *don't go there*.

The silent exchange was interrupted when the Poet did several double takes between the TV and Zan before mumbling, 'I'm ashamed to say it's true … you all look the same to me.'

Zan blearily returned the Poet's stare. He reminded her of the illustration on a '70s rock album she'd once found in her parents' garage: a tramp, heavily bearded, tall, shabbily dressed and seemingly bent by an age he was unlikely to achieve. Zan shook her head. Between his looking like a demented vagrant and behaving like an understudy for Falstaff, Zan did not particularly want the Poet in her flat. However, not only was he a paying customer for her transcription and formatting services, he was also an acquaintance of Danny's and, suddenly significantly, a friend of Bryan's.

'Shit,' the Poet said loudly. 'What a fucking waste.' Then he gathered himself, lifted the bottle of Talisker in mid-sway and poured with a surprisingly steady hand. 'As Bertrand Russell said, drunkenness is temporary suicide. I'll drink to that!' he roared

'*Aqualung,*' Zan said, remembering. 'Jethro Tull.' And then she was puzzled. 'Which was the album and which was the group?' she asked no one in particular.

Danny looked at her, then at the Poet, and smiled. He got it. The poet tipped the bottle again until Danny firmly but gently twisted his wrist back 90 degrees and prised the whisky from his fingers.

'I think you've had enough, old son,' Danny said.

'Not even fucking close,' the Poet retorted.

'You have if you want to sleep on my sofa … and you're not sleeping here.'

'Sez who?'

'I thought you would have recognised my voice by now,' Danny said, tiring of this drunken buffoon even sooner than usual. He'd decided to stay mostly sober while the Poet and Zan raced each other to the edge of oblivion, and it had been no fun watching them put themselves outside a litre of very decent Scotch.

'You are going to stop me drinking? You and whose army?' The Poet's breath was now ninety per cent Hebridean peat.

'The United Nations of Fuck You,' Danny said. 'Now, let's get some sleep and we can think about all this in the morning.'

The threat of another day seemed to settle the Poet, who slumped back in his chair and promptly started to snore. Danny had watched these performances a few times too often and was glad when the Poet finally fell silent – or at least stopped declaiming misquotes from Shakespeare and Wilde.

Danny turned his attention to Zan, who sat staring at the table as if willing it to levitate. She suddenly looked up at Danny, but he was ready for her.

'How's your mum?' he asked.

'What?' It wasn't any of the dozen or so questions Zan had been dreading.

'Your mum. How's she taking the news? Relieved? Elated?' Danny paused like a barrister about to nail a witness. 'Shocked?'

'All of the above, I suppose,' Zan said defiantly. 'We haven't had a chance to talk properly.'

Danny had met Zan's mother, Phuong, a couple of times and liked her instantly. She was like an older version of Zan in every way, just one dress-size smaller. However, she had aged terribly under the stress of her battles with Hahn. Danny didn't know all the details, but it was something to do with Hahn not being allowed to do what he wanted with his apartment and Phuong having said something she maybe shouldn't have and it all ending up in court.

Danny did know, however, that this woman was a fighter. She hadn't survived a sea crossing in pirate-infested waters to let an over-privileged bully push her around. She had been working to establish herself from the moment she stepped ashore as a teenage refugee in Darwin in 1979. Six years later Phuong, by then a feisty university student and political activist living in Sydney, married a fellow refugee (and obsessive fan of British rock music) named Jun. Everyone, including Phuong and Jun themselves, seemed to forget they hadn't lived in Australia all their lives.

Phuong had been an impressive force in her only child's life, but right now she was getting close to breaking point. Jun had left her, seeking a less combative existence, and she was about to lose their home to legal bills. Hahn's heart attack couldn't have happened at a better time.

'That thing in the lift …' Danny said.

'Not now,' Zan said, raising her palm to his face before losing herself in her thoughts again.

Letting it go, for now, Danny's thoughts strayed. He was going to tell Zan about the disaster at the TV station, but that seemed so trivial in light of a death – *two* deaths. And he felt sure there was something about Bryan's suicide that he was missing.

Zan looked up, as if anticipating his question.

'You know, when we were talking about Bryan tonight, a couple of times you looked at the Poet …' Danny ventured.

'It's only polite.'

'Nah, there was something.'

'What?'

'Something.'

'Your imagination, Danny Clay. That's what it was.'

'Something you're not telling me.'

'Nope, abshalooly not,' she slurred deliberately and burped delicately.

'Hmmm. Have you got something going on? A little love tryst?'

Zan looked at him with horror that was only slightly exaggerated. 'Me and the Poet?' she said, squirming. 'Euurgh! I just had to swallow my own puke.'

'It's very Mills and Boon,' Danny teased. 'The star-crossed lovers hate each other on page one but by the end, it's dot dot dot.'

'Fuck off, Danny. I think I could do better than this pile of piss in Vinnie rejects.' She gestured towards the Poet, now rumbling rather than snoring while a deeply unattractive dribble made its way down his chin.

Danny laughed. He was always impressed by the stream of gold-standard invective that emanated from this tiny woman. 'So tell me again about the thing in the lift.'

'Nothing to tell. Guy had a heart attack, I tried to save his life, failed, end of story,' she said. 'Well, end of *his* story.'

Danny tried to read her eyes for traces of deception or regret. 'Or part of someone else's story, huh?'

Silence dropped between them like a fire curtain on a stage.

'I know what you're thinking but I'm not a killer. The old bastard had a heart attack,' she eventually said, her eyes narrowing. 'I tried to save him.'

'Why?'

'Why what?' Zan asked.

'Why did you try to save him?' Danny said. 'He wasn't exactly number one on your Christmas card list. Or your mother's.'

'Mum had nothing to do with this,' Zan replied, her tone protective and defensive. 'Why do you keep going on about her?'

Danny looked at her, still not quite buying it.

'Let's talk in the morning,' she said eventually. 'I need to get some sleep.'

'Me too,' Danny replied. 'But tomorrow we definitely talk.'

Zan nodded.

'And what about him?' Danny gestured to the Poet. 'Want me to take him to my flat?'

'No, it's okay. He won't move till morning … if he knows what's good for him.'

The Poet did not so much as flicker an eyelid. Danny pecked Zan lightly on the cheek then exited across the corridor to his own flat.

Zan watched him go and listened for the click of his lock before turning her own key. One day, she was sure, he would change his mind and come back. She wondered why he didn't. She wondered what she would do if he did. But for now she had tomorrow to think about, and the prospect didn't enthral her.

She switched off the light and padded through to her bed. The Poet opened one eye, then the other, and reached for the remnants of the whisky.

6

THERE WAS something wrong. Danny sensed it but couldn't work out what it was. JJ and Dizzy had spotted the IED and the platoon was standing-to, waiting for word from base on whether they should BIP or defuse and dismantle it. It was the last day of a two-week patrol up through valleys and villages about fifty clicks north-east of Tarin Kowt.

They would move by night and search villages at first light, often doubling back and finding even more arms and ammunition in places they had already cleared. The Taliban knew they were coming so they were moving the caches around. The special forces knew what the enemy were up to and were outsmarting them at every turn. The sappers were there to deal with whatever they found.

They were getting results wherever they went and that kept their spirits up, but this was exhausting. Seventeen days and nights with too much action and not enough sleep takes its toll. Danny knew he needed to keep the boys on high alert but he was running low on energy himself.

JJ and Dizzy were talking and smoking, marking their own perimeter around the IED as the SAS boys moved past them. But something was wrong. Every time someone walked past they edged back a little. Danny was already worried that they were getting a bit too close to the bomb when he noticed the man-pack, which JJ had removed when he took off his jacket because of the heat. It was beside the front wheel of the armoured personnel carrier. The man-pack creates a kind of force field or electronic cloud around its wearer, blocking mobile phone signals that could be used to trigger explosives that you're trying to disable. He would put it back on if and when he started defusing the IED. Danny decided not to rip into him, although he should have. At this stage in a long patrol, a quiet word was all that was needed.

Movement in his peripheral vision made Danny look to his right. An Afghani shepherd in a nearby field was taking a mobile phone from deep inside his robes. Danny turned back in time to see JJ and Dizzy disappear in an eruption of dust, rocks, blood and bones.

Danny sat upright in his bed, woken by someone shouting, 'Man-pack, man-pack!'

Then he realised it was him.

He pulled off his sweat-soaked T-shirt and tossed it onto the floor. He fumbled for the remote, switched on the ceiling fan and lay back on the bed. He knew sleep would be a stranger to him, for the rest of that night anyway. Not that he wanted to sleep, not tonight. After a day like today, he didn't want to risk being ambushed by any more memories.

—

Danny held the phone away from his head and glowered at it. Eventually the squawking stopped. He replaced it to his ear, 'Listen, Rob, it wasn't my …'

'Do you know how much work I put into getting you this gig? And then you fuck it up by arguing over a *name*.'

'I told you, I didn't argue …'

'That's not what I heard. Neumann was furious.'

'That's his default condition …'

'Over some girl's name … Ex-something?'

'Xanthe …'

'That's it. So you admit it!'

'I'm admitting nothing. He got all worked up and everybody else –'

'Hang on. Xanthe? Isn't that Zan's real name?' Silence – the sound of another shoe dropping – then, 'Oh, that's great, you blow the biggest gig of your life – *our* life – because you want to get into a girl's pants.'

Danny stewed for a couple of seconds then decided on a cheap shot, by his standards at any rate: 'So you've got nothing to say about Bryan?'

'What about him? I mean, it's a shame for his family and all that.'

'Listen to you, Mr Compassion,' Danny said.

'The guy checked out and left everyone else to deal with the consequences,' Rob said, unemotionally. 'What else do you want from me?'

'He was one of your clients.'

'Was. Extreme past tense. He pulled the plug a couple of months ago.'

'I didn't know that,' Danny said. 'Maybe he was planning this all that time. Clearing the decks.'

'What I heard,' Rob replied, 'he got a big payday and didn't want to share with his hardworking agent.'

'A big payday? From who?' Danny was stunned. 'I never heard about any payout.'

'I thought you and he were buddies?'

'So did I.'

'I hope you're not holding out on me, Danny.'

'Rob? As if –'

'I can't keep doing this for you, Danny. I set these gigs up and then …' Rob trailed off.

'Then what?' Danny challenged.

'Then you find a feeble excuse to lose your temper, and –'

'I didn't lose my temper.'

'Not what I heard.'

'Tell you what, Rob,' Danny spat. 'Blow me.'

'And there you go again,' Rob said.

Danny clicked the 'end call' button and returned the phone to its cradle. It had barely been twenty-four hours since Bryan died, and among the few extraneous interactions he was prepared to deal with right now, a misguided and abusive call from his agent wasn't one of them, even if there were traces of truth in the tirade.

Danny looked at the phone, expecting Rob to call back. Then he looked around his flat. It was a mess. Tidiness was one part of his army training that not stuck. A jumble of books was tumbling either into the sliver of a sunroom or out of it. It was hard to tell. Newspapers – read and unread, some plundered for cuttings, others ring-marked with spilled food – took up most of the empty floor space. Untouched business, property, lifestyle and travel sections were stacked neatly, albeit in teetering piles, sidelined rather than saved, rejected but not removed. There were enough used coffee mugs lying around that, statistically, one of them had to be cultivating a new strain of penicillin.

Unwashed plates were stacked, but in close enough proximity to the sink to suggest they might get washed, some day. The blinds over the kitchen sagged, with one side fanning exhaustedly downwards, the result of extreme string failure. Danny sat on a lumpy, faded chenille chesterfield that had a lever in one arm, allowing it to drop down to form a chaise. He'd thought about getting it reupholstered once but it would have cost more than a brand new and much less stylish sofa – and one that wouldn't accommodate tall friends. Like the Poet, for instance, who had convinced himself that Danny had bought the couch in a premonition of their friendship and his occasional need of a free bed. Poets' incomes don't run to hotel rooms.

Sounds of the street intruded briefly as the front door opened and closed. Danny was immediately on high alert, but relaxed as Zan eased into the room, twirling her key on her finger.

'Coffee?' she said.

Danny nodded, and as Zan was loading up the Nespresso machine – his one concession to modern domestic trends – he allowed himself a lingering assessment. Small, but not for a Vietnamese girl. Twenty-six, slim and fit thanks to a vegetarian diet, yoga and kickboxing classes, Zan had a smooth, round cinnamon-skinned face, and long dark hair that could make her look prim and proper or wild and vaguely threatening depending on how she wore it. She had pianist's fingers but not a note of music in her body, as Danny had realised when he heard her wailing in the shower from across the hallway. Her inability to remember lyrics or hit, let alone hold, any of their associated notes was both frustrating and endearing.

Her birth name, Xuân Thi, meant 'poem of spring' but her parents also wanted her to have an Australian name. Their neighbours in Cabramatta, a Sydney suburb that has housed waves of immigrants from various countries over the years, were Greek – not that Zan's parents cared. And so Xuân Thi became Xanthe, with no more Greek in her than an occasional plate of neighbourly moussaka.

She turned and caught him staring. He didn't turn away and she smiled.

'I hate funerals,' she said, passing him his coffee. Her hand found his and squeezed. His thumb stroked her knuckles. She withdrew her hand gently but deliberately.

'Who doesn't?' Danny sighed.

'All that crying.'

'People gotta grieve, Zan. Give them a break.'

'I meant me, you dickhead.'

'Funerals,' he said, trying to regain the higher ground. 'Plural?'

'What?'

'I thought you might have got an invite to the Hahn funeral – the catering will be better, if nothing else.'

Zan's eyes narrowed. She didn't like the direction this conversation was taking.

'Oh, one other thing,' Danny said. 'Did you hear Bryan got a big payday from somewhere?'

Zan's hairline moved visibly backwards just as Danny's phone rang. She picked it up and tossed it to him. It was clearly a distraction, but Danny answered it anyway – you never knew when that call from Mr Spielberg might come through.

'Y'ello!'

'I forgot to tell you why I called.' It was Rob. 'You're back in at the station.'

'What?'

'The kid they had lined up to play the lead spat the dummy when they killed the project.'

'What kid?'

'Jensen Forbes.'

'Never heard of her.'

'Him. This is why you need me, Danny boy. Young Jensen is the next hot new soap star ready to make the great leap forward into mediocre drama or, at the very least, spack-filler reality hosting. His Q rating is through the roof and the network wants to tie him to a long-term deal.'

'Okay …'

'They offered him the lead in your series …'

'The lesbian detective?' Danny tried not to sound as incredulous as he felt.

'Obviously there would have to be adjustments. Anyway, he loved your script – clearly doesn't have a clue – and spazzed out when he heard it had been given the flick. The network is prepared to talk to you again, if it means getting young Jordan's –'

'Wasn't it Jensen?'

'Whatever. If they get him to sign on the dotted line, we get your series up.'

'We?' Danny asked.

'I gotta get paid for my efforts.'

'As long as you get your cut, huh?'

'Mr Twenty Per Cent, that's me. So I'll set up a meet with you and Jensen … if you promise not to fuck that up too.'

'Understood.'

'One other thing. You needed to apologise to Neumann for telling him "fuck you" in front of his staff.'

'But I …'

'I've already sent the email, so forget it.'

'I hope I was suitably contrite.'

'Don't bother thanking me for saving your arse.'

'I won't.'

'And, Danny, one more thing …'

'Yeah?'

'*You* blow *me*.'

This time Rob hung up. Danny looked up and saw Zan washing coffee mugs in the kitchen area.

'Rob?' Zan asked.

'Yeah. I'm back in with the series.'

'That's great! But I thought …?'

'They had promised the lead to Jensen Forbes.'

'Who's she?'

'*He*, Zan.' Danny sighed. 'See, this is why you need me around.'

—

Barry hated the sorting machine at the central Post Office – it had cost the jobs of so many of his mates. And he hated the fact that he had to wear gloves to empty the mail bags from Kings Cross, Darlinghurst and the City Centre. Half-eaten pizzas, dog shit, needles – you never knew what filth people were going to put in the postbox when they were out on the piss. 'They think they are so fucking funny,' Barry grumbled to himself, wishing he could follow them home and put garbage through *their* letter boxes.

And tonight there was this letter. Was it a letter? Was it a joke? 'To whom it may concern' was all it said on the front. No stamp. No return address. But there was a thumbprint in dark, dark rusty red.

Barry examined his options: the 'unstamped/return to sender' box or the 'insufficient information' tray. There was no stamp and no sender, and there was certainly no information.

Out of the corner of his eye Barry saw Little Miss Fat Bitch Supervisor waddling towards him with that look in her eye. He tossed the envelope in the 'insufficient information' tray and got back to removing burger wrappers and used condoms from the next day's mail.

—

Paddy Rosenberg stared at the phone. Like wartime telegram boys, it only ever brought bad news. It would ring, a voice would say 'my office', and he would toddle up to the top floor for a ritual reaming. Then he would come back to the same phone and have to use it to crawl up some new ass to fix some problem that wouldn't exist if they'd just stop telling him what to do.

The current problem was that crock *Redneck Airlift* he had bought in Cannes, a coup he had mentioned – okay, trumpeted – on his Facebook page. The studio was getting cold feet and he'd been ass-fucked from the boardroom to the mailroom for paying too much for the project. The National Rifle Association had condemned the movie as gun control propaganda before a single frame had been shot. A coalition of Southern state governors had protested that it depicted Southerners as hillbillies, and a prominent TV pastor had condemned its 'pro-Muslim' sentiments. None of them had so much as read a word of the script. But then, neither had Paddy.

Now Paddy had to undo the contract he had signed with the Australian producers and persuade them to give the money back. He hoped they were as naive as they seemed. Nobody gets a cashback guarantee in the movie business: you put your chips down and roll the dice. End of.

Paddy mulled over his usual get-out-of-jail strategies. He could say the studio was insisting on a star that the creators would find so unacceptable that they would walk away of their own accord. But what does an Aborigine find unacceptable? He had no idea. Jews and Muslims were easy. Socialists and fascists were a breeze. Feminists and anyone with a dick. If he got it wrong and pitched, say, Matt LeBlanc, and it turned out every Aborigine in Australia loved *Friends*, he would be even more screwed.

Then there was the option of suggesting a ridiculous and unacceptable plot twist, but how would they even know? They were Australian: they probably didn't know a plot from a plant pot. The 'budget constraints' tactic wouldn't work because they already had the money. Endless delays and rewrites, ditto. He had to find a way of getting them to put the studio's money back where it belonged.

Paddy closed his eyes. He gingerly picked up the telephone receiver, as if it was coated in something toxic, and punched zero on the keypad.

'Paddy?' Jasmina's voice said. He sagged. How many times did he have to tell this idiot girl to call him Mr Rosenberg?

'Get me Mr Corea,' he croaked, the thought of the impending humiliation already choking him.

'Right away,' she said with what sounded like a smile.

Paranoia, Paddy told himself as he replaced the receiver. You can't hear a smile. He breathed in though his nose and out through his mouth, like they had tried to teach him in the tantric sex class for which they still owed him money after throwing him out for inappropriate touching. How can touching in a sex class be inappropriate? He narrowed his eyes and stared at the phone.

'Don't ring, you fucker,' he hissed. 'Don't you dare fucking ring.'

It rang.

7

THE SHOOTER tried to control her heart rate. It was hard. The adrenaline pumping through her veins demanded action, however much her mind called for stillness. This was the first time she had used her new Rap4 T68 Extreme Sniper in earnest, but it had performed beautifully on the range, and the silencer – counter-intuitively – had increased the accuracy by lengthening the barrel (although it did little to reduce the sound).

The bi-pod gave her the stability she needed without having to rest it on the edge of the building – a protruding barrel would increase the risk of discovery. Even the laser sight was frighteningly spot-on, after a few standard adjustments. Often they were little more than gimmicks on these imported weapons; this was the real thing. All she needed now was a target.

PBA, as she called herself, adjusted her position slightly to avoid cramping. She'd taken extra magnesium powder for that very reason and sucked down a carbo-shot to top it up. No point lying in wait for three hours only for a muscle spasm to ruin your aim. Knee and elbow pads – black and non-reflective like her combat pants, skivvy and ski mask – made the wait tolerable. She was keeping herself awake with high-carb snacks and had a jar to pee in, if she needed to, which she'd take with her to avoid leaving clues. She'd done this before.

Below, in Victoria Street, restaurants had long ago disgorged their well-fed patrons into the wholly unnecessary nightclub queues – there was plenty of room inside the clubs, but a queue signalled demand and desirability, so people joined it. That was hours earlier. Now some of the denizens of the clubs were disgorging their undercooked meals and overpriced drinks into the gutter. A young woman tottered behind her friends in shoes that should have come with an altimeter, and a red cocktail dress that was so short and tight on her generous thighs that it threatened to roll up her torso like an out-of-control window blind. She held back a few paces then looked around suspiciously before squatting between two parked cars. PBA could only see her face in her night sight, but the woman's expression of blissful relief said more than she needed to know.

The door of the Soho Bar opened briefly to allow a momentary escape of crump-crump dance music, like mortars being fired in four-four time. Three girls, draped over one another in such close desperation they could have been sharing one dress, tumbled into the steamy, sticky street. They gathered themselves up, wondered collectively where they were, and staggered off in unison to find a bar whose idea of 'drunk' would defy the definition as well as the intention of any responsible service of alcohol laws. The Soho Bar was the trendy incarnation of the Piccadilly Hotel, the faux-Deco frontage of which had survived decades of fashion follies and economic ebbs and flows without skipping a beat. The Divinyls were launched there, in the days when it was owned and run by Mr Sin, Abe Saffron, and it was rumoured there was a door from the cellar directly to the Golden Apple brothel next door.

Now the most venal sin at the Soho was the non-stop ear-pounding of what passed for dance music. The art of conversation – even a half-decent pick-up line – was trampled underfoot by eccied-up backpackers and underclad Westettes along with their charmless, tattooed, wannabe gangster geezers. More ink on their arms than they'd ever have seen in a book, PBA thought. She clicked on the laser sight and watched the dot fall on the T-shirted pecs of Reuben Fata'a, possibly the largest bouncer in the Cross – not the nastiest, but definitely the scariest. Good, she thought, a clear shot. She clicked the dot off before Reuben noticed it. She was 30 metres away, across the road on the third-floor roof of a modern block of four apartments with an uber-trendy restaurant at street level.

The building used to be a Chinese restaurant until ill-fated financier Rene Rivkin, along with the proprietor of his favourite cafe, bought it with plans to turn it into a nightclub. Local residents put paid to that. Depression and overwhelming (entirely justified) guilt put paid to Rene, and the cafe owner built flats and a restaurant that ended up doing better business than the club ever would have. Result.

The nightclub door leaked a brief cacophony, but the noise kept coming after the music had been sucked back inside. It was a basso profundo braying that had PBA releasing the safety and breathing deeply but steadily through her nose.

'So I said, what did you expect when I asked you back to my place, darlin', a cup of fucking Milo?'

The owner of the voice was tall, olive-skinned and formerly muscular. Even in the street light you could see there had once been regular trips to the gym and frequent applications of steroids. But now booze and inertia had combined to make him soft around the edges. The tight pants were stretched around the thighs, but not under strain. The sixpack had inflated to a hint of inner tube over the belt. The biceps didn't quite fill the sleeves of his T-shirt, where they had once extended them. But the voice was undiminished.

'My fucking bedroom, my fucking rules, I told her,' he brayed, and the two smaller men with him laughed. The young blonde behind cracked the thinnest of smiles, and PBA wondered if she was the woman in his story. 'On your fucking kn–'

PBA had heard enough. The *N* sound was extended as a red rose appeared in the centre of Motormouth's chest and the impact knocked him back slightly. He looked down and saw the patch of red spread. His first reaction was horror, then puzzlement as he noticed the red laser dot that, a moment later was replaced by another spreading red stain.

'Oh my God. Oh my God. I've been shot.' Motormouth slumped to his knees as a wet patch appeared in his crotch. The girl screamed and stood back. Mate number one ran and hid behind a car, while number two ducked back inside the doorway.

'Help me, help me ... I'm dying here,' wailed Motormouth, clutching his chest as red oozed between his fingers. The girl stepped forward, reluctantly, then ducked back in the doorway, fumbling in her tiny bag for her huge mobile phone. Motormouth was crying. 'Help me ... it hurts ... it hurts so much.'

Reuben Fata'a ambled over with the urgency of a mortician on a slow Friday. He looked down at Motormouth and poked a finger into the stain on his chest. He examined the liquid closely and rubbed it between his fingers, then laughed. Motormouth, who realised he wasn't dying after all, looked up, puzzled.

'Paintball, mate,' said Reuben. 'It hurts but it won't kill you.' Reuben looked up at the roof opposite, but PBA was long gone. Motormouth's friends reappeared, giggling. 'Paintball,' said one. 'Awesome!' The girl rolled her eyes and walked off down the street alone.

Motormouth, his hands now covered with red, fronted Reuben. 'I want to see the manager,' he shrieked in the taller man's face. 'I'm going to sue you ... all of you. I have witnesses.' He looked around, but his witnesses were holding on to each other, helpless with laughter.

'Step down, brother,' Reuben growled. 'And go home.' Motormouth seemed to briefly consider pushing the issue, but timidity prevailed over tequila and he stepped back. 'Good luck getting a taxi covered in paint and stinking of piss,' Reuben said.

Motormouth turned on his heel and exited alone, his 'bloodstained' shirt earning swift *don't look* glances from passers-by while his former

NBFs, still convulsing with laughter, were in serious danger of wetting themselves too.

The Paintball Assassin watched all this through binoculars with the satisfaction gained by a good night's work. When Reuben shielded his eyes from the streetlights and scanned the rooftops, PBA ducked out of sight and started to collect her gear. Pride comes before a fall, she thought, and she had a long way to drop.

—

The stink of cigarette smoke made Zan push the accelerator a little too hard and the brakes only just in time as she merged into the airport traffic on the Eastern Distributor. Not that she allowed the Poet to smoke in her car: he had enough accumulated fumes in his clothes and beard to set off a smoke alarm.

Dealing with the Poet was a series of trade-offs and compromises. She'd been seriously considering getting an early night when he had called, pleading with her to take him to the airport to get the last plane to Melbourne before the curfew closed the flights. The idea of getting the Poet on a plane and out of her life was so appealing that she barely noticed he hadn't begged a loan to cover the cost of a ticket, as he usually did.

His problem was that taxis tended to slow down then speed off once the driver had a clear sight of the dishevelled drunk outside the pub. The Poet disavowed Uber on moralistic grounds, but in fact rarely had enough credit on his mobile phone to merit taking it anywhere with him. And so it was an emergency call to Zan with his flight due to leave in less than an hour. Luckily for him, she had decided to have an early night and so hadn't had a drink.

Neither spoke for a while. Zan had nothing to say to the Poet that wouldn't sound like a lecture. She switched on the radio for a distraction only to hear a report on how, as a result of Bryan's suicide, the police were considering buying guns with an electronic device that meant they could only be fired by their owner.

'Guns don't kill people,' the Poet muttered. 'People kill people.'

'Shut the fuck up, Poet, or *I'll* kill *you*,' Zan replied. The Poet looked at Zan then at her white knuckles gripping the steering wheel, and they sat in silence until they were kerbside at domestic departures.

'Just get straight on the plane, okay?' she said with a firmness that brooked no response – except the Poet always had a response.

'Occasionally vague and frequently distracted I may be, my dear,' he protested, 'but I can find my way onto an aeroplane.'

'Don't go to the bar. You'll forget and miss your flight.'

'Splendid idea,' he boomed. *'I cannot rest from travel: I will drink life to the lees.'*

Zan almost pushed him out of the passenger door. He turned and leaned back in. 'Tennyson,' he announced, the words laden with smoke from both cigarettes and single malt. She leaned back as he tried to plant a caustic kiss on her lips. As he lurched off then stopped to wave her away from the kerb, Zan was tempted to park up and make sure he got his flight. However, she didn't want to be there when he went through security – that was a tragicomedy of operatic proportions that you could only watch so many times before wanting to run yourself through the X-ray machine in the hope of inducing a brain tumour.

Zan waved, but the Poet was already straightening himself up for a pass through security, knowing that if he looked too drunk they wouldn't let him on the plane. She gunned the engine, merged back into traffic with a squeal of rubber, opened the windows to let the fetid air out and turned around back towards the city. She pulled out her mobile and hit speed dial number one.

To hell with an early night: she and her mother had some serious celebrating to do.

Marcus was feeling woozy, but in a good way. Whether it was the booze, the cone he'd just shared in the street or the girl from the bar who'd shared it with him, he was feeling absafuckinglutely great. Was it his imagination or had she positioned herself exactly so he could see down the front of her shirt? Whatever. For once in his uptight, guilt-edged near-fifty years of life, he didn't care if she caught him looking.

The bar, a converted storage space under a strip club, was pumping. Ceiling spots reflected off stainless steel and shiny, piano-black shelves, while lights behind an array of brightly coloured cocktail liqueurs made them glow invitingly. Those who'd accepted that invitation – apparently enthusiastically – lurched, swayed and shouted at one another above the music. The room was long and narrow, and disappeared into darkness beyond the end of the bar at which Marcus and his lady friend were perched.

Marcus appreciated the darkness. Over-age, overweight and overdressed (who wears a business suit to a nightclub?), he was glad everyone was too close to see him properly. You didn't walk so much as wade through the tightly packed crowd if you wanted to get from one end to the other, where the space opened up into … who knew? Marcus couldn't see and didn't care.

In the receding gloom, neckless football players were redefining the term 'babe magnet', with barely clad young women attached to them like cat hair on velour. The sports stars were aloof from the crowd and amused by one another's macho posturing, but the other men in the bar were too wrapped up in themselves or their equally attractive companions to give them more than a second glance.

Chita, the girl with Marcus, nudged him and pointed across the room, where a plumpish woman in her early twenties had clambered onto a table. Judging by her accent he guessed she was an English backpacker, and she required zero encouragement to pull off her top as she danced. The pallid, spotty skin and her enthusiasm for exposing it indoors at night rather than outdoors during the day confirmed both her nationality and the fact that she had only recently arrived. Within forty-eight hours her blistered epidermis would be peeling off her as she discovered that the warnings about the Bondi sun were less exaggerated than she'd allowed herself to believe. One week per year in Ibiza does not prepare you for eight hours on the beach under Australia's ozone-free sky.

Marcus smiled at Chita. He felt warm, fuzzy and a bit horny. And for once in his mostly disappointing life, it seemed, the latter wasn't a taunting fantasy. Chita wasn't what you'd call busty, but that only meant she didn't need a bra. And Marcus knew for a fact she wasn't wearing one.

He caught her eye and Chita looked down at her chest. She offered a disapproving little frown and leaned back, removing the view. The shirt, white and what they used to call 'cheesecloth', was embroidered, with a vaguely Indian look to it. It was loose, but as she straightened it immediately clung to her damp, almost conical breasts. She shrugged, as if to say she had no choice. If she was going to be comfortable, Marcus was going to get an eyeful. She leaned forward again and Marcus smiled with lowered eyes. Two more shots of tequila appeared on the bar. Chita's tongue appeared between her perfect teeth in a cheeky grin. Her equally flawless urchin-cut purple hair – a wig that would be found in a bin three days later by a befuddled streetie – matched her turned-up nose (which was real). She was a picture of mischief.

A few words that managed to penetrate the thumping din, enhanced by some entry-level lip reading, revealed that Chita was an actress: one of the army of unemployed thespians around Sydney in general and Kings Cross in particular. She'd done a couple of commercials – third angel on the right in the cream cheese ad, she said.

For the first time, an attractive young woman had seemed genuinely impressed when Marcus told her he was a scriptwriter. No, impressed didn't cover it. Fascinated, maybe. Excited, even. Predatory? Who cared? All he knew now was that she had her hand on his thigh and he was looking down at what, all tricks of the light aside, had to be a perfectly pink nipple.

Marcus, suffering a short frisson of guilt, pulled his gaze away and wished the Poet had stuck around long enough to witness his romantic success. They had set out on their own private pub crawl-cum-wake for Bryan – not that the Poet needed an excuse to have a drink – but they had lost each other somewhere at the Three Weeds in Paddington.

Marcus had bumped into Chita there – literally. He'd spilled her drink but had no issue with buying her a replacement. Instead of thanking him and being on her way, to his amazement she wedged herself between him and the Poet and seemed genuinely interested in what he said.

Eventually, feeling ignored and excluded, the Poet had enveloped him in a huge and teary hug and stumbled out into one of those steamy hot nights, now so common in newly sub-tropical Sydney summers.

Marcus couldn't even remember accepting Chita's invitation to join him in her favourite club in the Cross, nor the short cab ride there, the nervous driver switching off his 'for hire' light, locking the doors and speeding off into the night the minute he had deposited them outside the Greek and Italian takeaways on Bayswater Road. Marcus steadied himself against the bar and sat back a little to better appraise Chita, shirtfront notwithstanding. High cheekbones with a hint of Asian grandparents around the eyes. Or Northern European, perhaps. Latvian or Ukrainian.

'Where you from?' he yelled.

'Melbourne,' Chita replied without a hint of irony, as the half-naked Britpacker fell into the fumbling hands of her new chums, and the other drinkers surged and ebbed around them.

Melbourne. That figured. The Poet was from Melbourne and he had style, of sorts.

Marcus looked at her again. This was it. This was the first moment in the life he'd always dreamed of – okay, fantasised about – and he wanted to remember where and when it had really started. This must be what it's like in Hollywood, he thought. Who cared if she was only interested in him because he had signed a deal with a genuine, bona fide Hollywood studio. Once she got to know him, they'd be fine.

—

Paddy Rosenberg almost skipped into the office. He held up his mobile phone triumphantly, as if it were the head of a vanquished foe. 'Paddy Rosenberg does it again!' he said.

Jasmina looked up from her computer screen and tried to smile expectantly.

'The Australians have walked into my trap,' he said, laughing. 'They agreed that if the project didn't move forward, they had to give us the money back.'

'I know they said that but …'

Paddy chortled. 'They're doing it. The money is as good as in the bank. The contracts are in legal as we speak.'

'You're kidding.'

'It's true. The Aborigine wanted to lock it down ASAP.' He pronounced it *ay-sap*. 'Full refund minus agreed expenses. He was worried about expenses. The guy has no clue.'

As he walked into his office, Paddy reread the email on his iPhone for the tenth time to see if he had missed something crucial. Jasmina followed him in.

'You know what this means? I have done something no one has ever done – I got the money back from a bad investment. Well, not bad … just not good.'

'Of course,' Jasmina asked. 'Are you sure they've triggered the rescission?'

'The what?'

'The clause that allows you to get the money back and tear up the contract,' she explained.

'They already sent our first set of script notes back, with a "No Way José" attached. When I said it was a deal-breaker, they paid up.'

'Oh my God,' she said.

'They've even gone public. I just got a call from *Variety*.'

'*Oh my Gooooood*!' Jasmina, for the first time, had a feeling that Paddy might not, after all, be the biggest loser she had ever encountered. A feeling that lasted for as long as it took him to refer to himself in the third person.

'Paddy Rosenberg will be the talk of the commissary.'

'He sure will …'

'I will be promoted, headhunted. I am a solid gold fucking movie legend.'

'Congratulations, Mr Rosenberg.'

'Call me Paddy.'

Paddy looked at the email again, then looked at Jasmina, beaming at the news. He thought of the last time they were in here together, when the Australian had interrupted them. A missed opportunity. That was his life, summed up in two words. Or had been, up till now.

It started in his teens with Naomi, the nice Jewish girl his parents had introduced him to. Both her parents were in the business – a producer and a film editor. Both! Paddy's were an accountant and an excessively houseproud mother who expressed her frustrations with her lot in life through cleaning products. Naomi wasn't particularly attractive – a bit too Middle Eastern for Paddy's tastes – but she was the golden ticket. And he had treated her with total respect, especially when she told him he could do it anywhere except *there* – that was strictly reserved for her future husband. Paddy had set his heart on that exalted role, wooing her, her parents, her grandparents, even her smartass brat brother who called him Paddy the Poodle. But try as he might, he could never get her to play house like they were already married.

Then came the kicker: Naomi got pregnant to some cracker stagehand from Nebraska. Paddy was blamed initially and banished for having betrayed the family's trust. Naomi disappeared to 'finishing school' in Switzerland and shortly after the stagehand, who claimed he was a rabidly pro-life Born Again Christian, revealed himself to be the real father. He had his conscience assuaged and discretion rewarded with non-speaking henchperson roles in a series of action movies. Paddy might have been invited back into the fold had he not already described to Naomi's parents, in great detail, exactly how far their sexual adventures went.

From that moment on, Paddy had felt cheated by life in general and women in particular. When this unfortunate experience was followed by a disastrous and short-lived marriage to a woman who was smarter than him (not hard) and even more ambitious (almost impossible), he came to the conclusion that he could never trust a woman again. Paddy decided to dispense with relationships and just concentrate on sex – that was, he reasoned, the only purpose of having a relationship in the first place, so why not cut to the chase?

Of course, you had to go through the motions – the whole hearts and fucking flowers stuff – but give me the wham and the bam and forget the thank you, ma'am, thought Paddy. But for some reason he could never quite fathom, the closer he got to women the less chance he had of 'closing the deal', as he often put it. There was a window, a sweet spot, and if you didn't make your move at the right time, you might never get another chance. 'Hey, how about you get the door?' he said after a pause, leaning back on the edge of his desk, flashing his eyebrows. Jasmina's expression changed gears, from a smile of genuine curiosity to one of pragmatic enthusiasm as she turned and locked the office door.

'You know, I really need to relax,' said Paddy. 'If you know what I mean.'

The smile stayed fixed on Jasmina's face. 'Let me switch this off so we aren't interrupted,' she said, fumbling with her iPhone. 'Now, what exactly *do* you mean, by "relax", Mr Rosenberg?' Jasmina asked, pitching her tone carefully to avoid sounding too provocative.

'I told you: "Paddy". Solid gold fucking genius Paddy Rosenberg.' He leered at her. 'And as for relax, I think you *know* what I mean.'

'Perhaps. But I would like you to spell it out for me,' she said, licking her lips. 'You're a surprising man, Mr Rosenberg. I need to know exactly what you're thinking.'

Paddy's heart raced. He didn't know where to start.

8

'SO TELL me about this movie,' Chita shouted in Marcus's ear, although the touch of her breast against his bicep was what truly captured his attention.

'I haven't actually got a movie yet,' he said, his innate honesty like a rifle aimed at his big toe. 'I mean, we haven't ...'

'What?'

'We've got the money but ... well, there's a bit of confusion over the script.'

'Who's we?'

'The Poet ... and me ... and Bryan – the guy whose funeral we were at.'

'Cast of thousands. Anybody else?'

'Nope. Just the three of us. Shouldn't even be telling you: it's all a huge secret. Huge.' Marcus hesitated. He was saying too much.

'It's okay,' she purred in his ear. 'You just met me, why would you trust me?'

'Four, if you count Zan,' Marcus blurted, worried that he was losing her over a secret that wouldn't make any difference. 'She's like our script editor.'

'So what's the confusion?'

'The producer wants us to pull out. Says the Yanks are going to screw up the project.'

'That's too bad. And if the money's no good ...'

'The money's not a problem – it's great, in fact, but we have to pay it back if we don't agree to kill the project. Don't ask me how that works; I never understood the money side.'

'Money for nothing.' She smiled. 'Sounds like a good deal to me.'

'Too good to be true,' Marcus said. 'But, you know, this was our chance at the big time. It's like asking a boxer to throw the biggest fight of his life.' He threw a couple of imaginary punches that almost propelled him off his stool. 'I'm tempted to hang in there and make a few compromises – just to see my name on a screen in a cinema.'

'It's that important?' she asked.

'Uh-huh. And you might only get a chance like this once in a lifetime. Some writers would do it even without the money.' He paused. 'But it's a lot of money and it will keep me going for a long, long time,' he said eventually, ruefully. 'And it means I can write other stuff. And maybe someday …'

'I get it. I really do.' Chita smiled, a thought passing as she kissed Marcus on the cheek.

'Bryan took the money. And the Poet. If I don't sign the contract, they'll have to pay it back. And now that Bryan's gone … Emma could really use the cash.'

'Emma?'

'His wife. He's got two kids.' Marcus's brow furrowed. '*Had* two kids. I don't get it; he had so much going for him, and then to take his own life – and do it so publicly – but not tell us why. I'm completely baffled. We all are.'

'I'm sorry about your friend,' Chita said. 'But he's gone, and you're still here. What do you want?'

Marcus was thrown by Chita's bluntness, at first. But then he was flattered to be the centre of attention – a rare pleasure for him. 'What do I want?' he said.

'What have you decided?' Chita asked. 'About the money?'

'I'm keeping it.' He shrugged. 'I'm sorry, I mean, if you were hoping for something else.'

'Why would I be hoping for anything?'

'Well, you're an actress and I just sold my ticket to Hollywood.'

'You think I'm that shallow?' Chita said with a teasing rather than angry pout.

'Fuck, I know I am.' Marcus laughed. 'But not keeping the money would just be selfish and stupid now.'

'But, you know, now that you mention it …' Chita pouted. 'This could be my big break too.'

Marcus looked at her, tempted to tell her the joke about the naive country girl who went to Hollywood and slept with the writer.

'I would be very, very grateful,' Chita continued, nibbling Marcus's ear. 'I could show you how, right now.'

'Tempting … oh, so tempting,' he said, gently pushing her away. 'But I'm not going to lie to you. My mind is made up. Show me the money!'

'Okay.' Chita smiled and shrugged. 'Wanna get out of here?' she asked, as much by gesture as in her half-heard words.

Surprised that she was still interested, Marcus swayed alarmingly on the bar stool. While the honesty and guilt departments of Marcus's brain were working efficiently enough, the motor function section was seriously underperforming. This is the bit, he thought, where she realises I am too old and drunk to be any fun and leaves me anyway. Marcus swayed again and Chita grabbed his arm to steady him.

'Come on. Let's go,' she said, allowing him to push against her as his feet slid to the floor. The evening's possibilities were turning into racing certainties.

Outside an oversized doorman, bristling with steroids and simmering from an earlier confrontation with one of the club owner's wanker mates, glanced at them contemptuously. A sad old fart and his sugar-baby. He hoped she was worth it.

Marcus and Chita squeezed past into Kellett Street. The humid night air hit them like a warm damp towel as they staggered out, beyond the doorway where they'd shared the dope. Kellett Street had a right-angled corner in it, and a kink – in more ways than one – with a lane called Kellett Way hooking off the corner and taking you down behind brothels, bars, flop-houses and around the back of where Barons used to be. Now the friendly old bar with backgammon tables had been replaced by an uber-trendy restaurant that was, they said, an homage to Gaudí. Gaudy, more like, Marcus thought.

'Where we going?' he mumbled, fresh air having brought a moment of clarity.

'My place, unless you've changed your mind,' she whispered in his ear. 'Or we could do it right here.'

Before Marcus could think, her mouth was on his, one hand on his crotch while the other guided his fingers under her shirt and onto her left breast. After what felt like a lifetime, she pushed him away and he allowed himself to be steered into a dark corner behind a rubbish skip.

Suddenly Marcus was face to face with a young guy, dark-skinned in his early twenties, in a red tracksuit top with a hood over a Yankees baseball cap – standard dance club gear, Marcus supposed. He'd make a note of that for a future character profile. The kid was short and skinny with an exaggerated, jerky swagger, like he was trying to fill the space in clothes that were at least one size too large.

The other thing Marcus noticed was that the guy was carrying a golf club. In the half-light Marcus couldn't quite tell if it was a wood or an iron, and the alcohol and drug fug in his brain had him obsessing on that, rather than the more urgent thought that golf clubs had replaced baseball bats as the modern urban thug's weapon of choice – at least before they graduated to guns.

'So?' the golfer asked Chita.

'Nope, he's going to take the money. Nothing I can say or do …'

'What is this?' Marcus blurted. 'What's going on?'

'I got a message for you, Marcus,' the golfer said.

'A message?' Marcus asked. 'From who? Whom? And how do you know my name?'

'The message is, pay the money back and don't sign the contract, Mr Whom,' the golfer replied. 'Or you'll get more of this.'

With that, he took an almighty swing, aiming for Marcus's upper arm. But Marcus heard the threat in the young man's voice, ducked and turned away just enough for the club to catch him on the back of the head. The momentum of Marcus's sudden turn meant that, as he dropped to the ground, his skull hit the kerb.

Marcus's lights had already gone out before the golfer took several hefty swings to his body.

Chita materialised from the shadows and grabbed his arm. 'Enough, I think.'

'Sure. I only really got him the once. He'll be okay.' He took a piece of paper out of his pocket and checked an address scribbled on it.

Chita looked and nodded: 'Yep, her too.'

They walked to the end of the lane, and she pointed along Ward Avenue towards the brightly lit tunnel overpass at Kings Cross Road, but then they headed off together in the opposite direction. No point in being too obvious. They had time to kill.

—

The Paintball Assassin had abseiled quickly down the blank side wall of the building and used the cover of an unused backyard to change into something less suspicious. She'd removed her ski mask to avoid attracting attention, and the gun was safely dismantled and packed away in her Anytime Fitness gym bag, which provided both a convenient holdall for her weapon, ropes and other equipment, and a reason for being out late dressed in what passed for sports gear.

She stood on a wheelie bin, checked the wall for broken glass or spikes embedded in the concrete, scanned the laneway of Earl Street for pedestrians, then tossed the bag over, following it with a practised vault.

She had parked her bike at Springfield Avenue – just off the Strip – but as she turned the tight corner into Earl Place, out of the sudden streetlight glare came an elfin girl with purple hair, and a young bloke in a baseball cap and red hoodie. PBA stepped out of the way of the girl but bumped into Baseball Cap, who swore and hefted a golf club that he'd been holding down his side, tucked under his arm.

'The fuck?' said Baseball Cap.

'Leave it, babe,' the girl said. Her accent was much more modulated and refined than PBA had expected to hear at this time of night, in this part of the city. 'He's just a random …'

'Not he,' said PBA.

'Whatever,' said Baseball Cap, and went on his way. No threat, no danger, just three night people whose paths had crossed. They were out of sight around the corner by the time PBA caught her breath. She made it to her bike, a modest step-through electric bicycle with solid panniers on the back. She opened a lid, removed a high visibility jacket and helmet, and replaced them with her sports bag.

—

Half a block away, outside the Soho Bar, its owner was being debriefed by Reuben on the 'shooting'.

'Why us?' he asked.

'Not just us,' Reuben replied. 'And it's not the club, it's the customers – the loud and stupid ones. The ones we don't want to come back anyway.'

'And what does this joker call himself, again?'

'The Paintball Assassin,' said Reuben. They barely noticed the DMZ

Dumplings electric delivery bike as it swished past, because they were distracted by a woman's screams from a couple of streets away, cutting through the noise and the night.

Marcus had been found. And he wasn't okay.

—

'So she says, "How many episodes do you think this makes in a series?" and I say six – the standard BBC sitcom format. And she says, "Really? It definitely feels like thirteen to me …" Thirteen? Hello!' Danny slurred into his computer screen, his face glowing in an odd bluish light that had been projected halfway around the world from a kitchen in London where Liam, his best friend in the business, also sat looking at his computer.

Danny watched as a slightly watery version of Liam took a sip of his afternoon coffee. Danny raised a large glass of sangiovese – his third – in salute.

'I'm thinking, here we go, thirteen episodes, you beauty! I say, okay, yes, it's an open-ended traditional sitcom format, and there's no series arc, so yes, definitely, it could be thirteen. "That's a shame," she says, "we're not looking for thirteens right now."'

'Away with you!' came the lightly Irished accent.

'You want to say, well, how about when that shit you've got running at the moment curls up and dies of shame?'

'But you don't …'

'No, you don't. But at least I'm getting meetings with these dimwits – still get in the door. Eventually I'll meet one who has a clue.'

'Ah, that's what I love about you, Danny: you're the most optimistic cynic I know.' Liam laughed. 'Now I have to get on and write a script nobody really wants for a show starring someone nobody's really heard of.'

'Paying gig?'

'Is there any other kind? *Sláinte*.' Liam pronounced it the Irish way, *slawn-shuh*, raised his coffee cup with one hand and clicked off the connection with the other.

Danny must have taken an hour out of Liam's day. Through his scrambled blinds, the only light in the sky was the jaundiced glow of street lamps; the noise of the day's traffic and night's carousing had reduced to an irritable murmur. It was 2am – even Sydney had to snooze at some point. Danny was determinedly working his way through the last of his red wine as he turned on cable news, the only thing he'd been able to bear watching on TV for at least a year … okay, a week.

Just then he heard the outside door slam and familiar footsteps come up the small apartment-block stairs. That would be her now. Danny pulled himself to his feet, swayed slightly and lurched to the front door. He opened it in time to see Xanthe fiddling to get the key in her lock while a young guy, dark-skinned in his twenties in a red tracksuit top with a hood over a Yankees baseball cap – 'standard dance club gear,' Danny would later tell police – stepped out of the shadows and began the backswing of a golf club aimed at her head.

'Zan!' Danny shouted as he grabbed the business end of the club. The freestyle golfer tugged it from his grasp and took the stairs to the street, three at a time. Oblivious to her departing assailant, Xanthe turned and saw a shocked Danny standing in his doorway.

'Hey, Danny,' she said, brightly. 'What was that?'

Looking at the blood smeared over his hand, blood he quickly realised was neither his nor Zan's, Danny asked himself the same question.

—

Tony Cufflinks wasn't initially known for extravagant tastes in shirt-cuff closures. When the police found a body that his crew was suspected of having buried in the sands at Kurnell, the victim had been restrained with cable ties inserted through, rather than around, his wrists. 'Tony's cufflinks,' one of the cops had said. When Tony got wind of the nickname he bought his first pair of the real cufflinks that became his trademark.

He turned to the four monitors that formed an arc on the return of his impressive desk. One showed the feeds from a dozen closed-circuit cameras in the club in a four-by-three grid. Another had the 24-hour news, muted, so he could watch the trailer at the bottom of the screen. The third had a desultory hardcore porn movie running on a loop, just so Tony could make sure the feed to the private rooms was still working – he had seen it all before so it only interested him when it wasn't there. The fourth had an online poker game that was in a ten-minute recess (or 'pee-cess', as the regulars called it).

Tony's spotted the headlines on the muted news channel and grimaced. Two unexplained violent deaths on his patch within a couple of days of one another – one 'look-at-me' suicide and one body that had just been found with its head bashed in – were not good news. Well, not for him, anyway. The reptiles would be on the streets by daybreak, beating it up for all it was worth.

He knew who deserved to be beaten up. The TV news would be trying to outdo each other with their exaggerations and conspiracy theories, and the tabloid arsewipes would follow it up with 'think pieces' (now *there* was a contradiction in terms) about the terror on our streets. Nobody would mention that violent crime was on the decrease. When did journalism become about 'mislead and scare' rather than 'inform and entertain'? Oh yeah, when every tosser with a mobile phone became a 'citizen journalist'.

Dead bodies were bad for business: they scared away customers and attracted too much attention to his less-than-legitimate enterprises. The suicide loony he couldn't do much about, but the other stiff sounded like trouble. He needed to find out who was killing civilians on his streets, and stop them.

But for now, the poker game had pinged back to life and dealt him two jacks with a third and a pair of nines in the flop. He bet all-in and watched as the other players hesitated and scrambled, trying to work out if he was bluffing. Tony hoped one of them had a nine, and smiled – he never bluffed.

9

'OF COURSE they'll want to talk to you. Two of your mates have died in, let's face it, seriously weird circumstances, and you claim Zan, who just happens to be your next-door neighbour, was almost attacked by a golf club-wielding thug, *and* you literally have blood on your hands.' Laura sipped her coffee and shook her head in disbelief both at Danny's naivety and at the fact he had no milk for her coffee.

'Claim?' Danny yelped. 'Claim? That's what happened ...'

'Get used to it. So far the only thing linking the two deaths and a possible murder weapon is Danny Clay. You know how it works.'

Danny did know, better than most, and immediately regretted having given Laura the tissue, neatly preserved in a zip-lock sandwich bag, with which he'd wiped the blood from his hands, acquired when he grabbed the golf club aimed at Zan's head. That was the trouble with immersing yourself in crime stories, he thought. You start acting like either a cop or a crim. He knew that police first look at the likeliest possibilities (in murder, nine times out of ten the perp, as they said in the best cop shows, was someone the victim was related to — or at least knew well), then they eliminate the suspects who have alibis or no obvious motive until they have a prime suspect. Then they pursue that angle with unwavering focus bordering on blinkered obsession, until they either get a result or hit a brick wall.

When the cops did get it wrong it was almost always because they had set out on the wrong path for the right reasons but couldn't let it go, even when it became clear they'd screwed up. But a process where every conceivable possibility was given equal weight until all the wrong theories were eliminated would be too time consuming and wasteful. Danny knew this 'single focus' approach worked because it was also a very convenient process for the writers of TV and movie drama, who only canvassed alternative possibilities when it suited their dramatic needs. If the blood on the tissue was Marcus's, then Danny's name would be at or near the top of the detective room whiteboard.

'So where *were* you when Marcus was killed?'

Danny realised what he was about to say, so the words were whispered. 'Here … on my own … drowning my sorrows.'

'Great.'

'Shit.' Danny looked at Laura. 'Hey, *you* don't think …?'

'Mate, we've played golf. I've seen your swing – more of a lunge. The vic would still be walking around.'

'The *vic*? He had a name!'

'Sorry.'

'Poor Marcus,' Danny thought aloud.

Dark thoughts seeped into Danny and Zan like winter cold. Danny stared at the hole that was starting to form in the toe of his right sock. An untrimmed nail peered through worn and spread threads: the cotton inevitable. Nylon makes your feet sweat but lasts longer. He winced at his own lack of focus and tried to think about Marcus.

Zan entered from the bedroom, fastening her jeans. 'Hi, Laura.'

'Hi.' Laura smiled, surprised. 'Anything going on here you don't want to tell me about?'

'Zan stayed overnight,' said Danny, quickly adding, 'I slept on the sofa.'

Laura gave him a look that was somewhere between *yeah, right* and *more fool you*.

'Hey, Zan,' Danny said, avoiding the issue. 'Laura says I'm a prime suspect.'

'In the attack on me?' She bit her lip involuntarily. Danny and Laura looked at each other. 'You saved me – at least, according to you.'

Ignoring the implied doubt, Danny realised Zan wasn't up to speed with the previous night's events.

'You'd better sit down,' he said. Zan seemed about to refuse, but the looks on Laura's and Danny's faces must have convinced her otherwise.

'Look, Marcus was killed last night,' Danny ploughed on, no more adept at passing on bad news than he was a week before. 'In the Cross. Looks like a mugging gone wrong. But it could be the same person who attacked you.'

'Marcus?' she said, struggling to process the information. Tears sprang to her eyes. 'Bryan, then Marcus? What the fuck is going on?'

Danny and Laura looked at each other and then at Zan. They had nothing.

'Wow!' she said, her voice and expression a jumble of emotions. 'And I was supposed to be the third? And you are a prime suspect?'

'I didn't say you were a prime suspect, drama queen.' Laura prodded Danny's shoulder with her index finger. 'I said someone will want to talk to you. And you too, Zan.'

Zan looked up, then away. Then something occurred to her: 'Didn't you say you were Skyping Liam just before I got back?'

'Oh shit, yeah. Of course. I was online to Liam for about an hour, maybe more.'

'That's good,' said Laura. 'There will be computer records at both ends. If you're lucky the Yanks at the Pine Gap electronic monitoring station will have been listening in.'

'Poor bastards, listening to me moaning about life,' Danny said, relieved.

'I'd better get back,' Laura said, hauling herself out of an armchair that was more saggy than easy, and heaving herself to her feet with a grunt. 'You know how it goes, evidence to plant, bribes to take, innocent people to …' she stopped suddenly, interrupting herself. 'Sorry about Marcus, by the way. Only met him a couple of times but he seemed like a nice guy.'

'He was.' Zan sniffed into a tissue. 'They both were.'

Laura picked up her satchel, put the Ziploc bag with the bloody tissue inside it, dusted it off and looked around the room.

'You need to hire someone,' she said gravely to Danny.

'A lawyer?'

'No, mate,' Laura said over her shoulder as she exited. 'A cleaner.'

Danny and Zan sat unspeaking, listening to the door click shut and Laura's footsteps growing quieter on the stairs. Finally …

'What's going on, Zan?'

'I don't know, I really don't.'

'It's just, two of our friends have died and I reckon you were about to be the third.'

'According to you …' said Zan.

'What's this "according to you"? You don't believe me?'

'Of course I do. But you're the only one who saw this guy. I just heard someone running down the stairs, so it's all according to you.'

Danny thought for a moment. 'Maybe I do need a lawyer.'

'Why was Laura here? Is she investigating us?'

'No, we had a meeting. She was dropping this off.' Danny pointed to the coffee table where a neatly bound script bearing the words *CROSSFIRE by Laura Revell (with Danny Clay)* lay on top of a stack of discarded newspaper sports sections. 'She hadn't heard about Marcus – or you – till she got a call on the way. So much for …' he turned the script and read the subtitle, '*A feisty female cop's finger on the pulse of Sydney's mean streets.*'

'Too many Fs. But hey, at least she's given you a credit. That's nice.'

'Wait till you read it.' A thought … 'Hey, you wouldn't consider maybe …?'

'No way. You're the one who agreed to trade information for a crash course in screen writing.'

'And help with my computer,' he said.

'And assistance with her pants,' said Zan with a smirk.

'You know that's not true,' Danny said, wondering if it was. 'Anyway, she doesn't tell me anything I don't already know.'

'Whereas you can impart everything she needs to know about being a frustrated TV writer.' Zan raised a mocking eyebrow.

'Aw, gee, thanks,' Danny muttered.

They both fell silent and Danny guessed Zan was processing the same troubling thoughts as he was. 'Marcus and Bryan?'

'This is scary shit that isn't meant to happen to people like us,' Zan said.

Danny took a deep breath. 'Be honest with me, is there any chance this is related to the thing with Hahn?'

'What thing?' She was suddenly brusque and defensive.

'In the lift. It's a bit like the perfect crime, isn't it?'

'What do you mean?'

'You know *exactly* what I mean.' Now it was Danny's tone that conveyed irritation and frustration. 'The perfect crime in my script.'

'Did you research that?' Zan challenged. 'Properly, I mean. Not just looking it up on Google.'

'Research?' It was Danny's turn to sound defensive.

'If you had, you would know how hard it is to hit someone in exactly the right spot, at *exactly* the right time to make their heart stop.'

'Still, it's kind of convenient, right?'

'Not convenient, a coincidence,' she said. 'Co-inky-dinky, that's all.'

Danny was not convinced.

'And Bryan and Marcus? Co-inky-dinky?' Danny said. 'If you have anything you need to tell me, Zan, now would be a really good time.'

Zan pouted as she knelt on the sofa and put her arms around him.

'Danny, I want to thank you for looking after me last night. And for letting me hang here.' She kissed the side of his head. 'And I know how to repay you ...'

A strand of her blue-black hair brushed his cheek and he felt a faint stirring, wishing he'd worn jocks instead of boxers. 'Yeah?' he croaked.

'Yeah.' She grinned and kissed his cheek. 'I'm going to be your cleaner.' And with that she slid off the sofa and started gathering mugs.

—

PBA stared at the screen. The report, written with the vocabulary of an eight-year-old and the calm recollection of a crack addict in the middle of a panic attack, detailed another sighting of the Paintball Assassin, following an incident in Kings Cross the previous night.

It had been phoned in by a nameless (and probably unregistered) migrant bar worker who'd been hanging out of a first floor window having an illicit smoke when he saw the suspect sneaking down Earl Street. Having just witnessed the far-from-fatal shooting across the road from the front of the building and hearing police and ambulance sirens nearby, the bar worker had been wondering if they were connected.

Punched in by a semi-literate duty constable who probably thought spellcheck was something Harry Potter did (although that assumed he could read), the report referred to a 'giza' in a baseball hat, carrying a silver walking stick, who confronted the alleged paintballer briefly before moving on.

PBA noted the reference to an 'Anyway Gym' holdall, a black 'skivviie' and the removal of a 'baklava'. Those Greek sweets stick to everything, she thought with a smile. PBA looked over her shoulder to check she wasn't being watched, deleted a couple of details of the description, saved the file and closed the screen.

—

It was seven in the evening when Chita woke up and realised Weezl's side of the bed was empty and cold. She'd have rolled over and gone back to sleep, but hunger nipped at her stomach, overcoming the lingering fatigue of the eleven-hour run from Sydney. They'd taken turns driving, but you can't sleep in the passenger seat, not properly. She pulled on a sloppy, oversized white T-shirt that proclaimed 'Vacuums Suck' in huge black letters and moved through their rented apartment to see where he was.

As she expected, Weezl was in the library — at least, that's what they called the small, windowless room that had at various times been a walk-in wardrobe, a study, a storeroom and, early in its life, a bedroom. That was back in the '40s when the high-ceilinged Carlton abode had been home to the nine-strong family of an Irish grocer — unique for that area in being neither Jewish nor Italian — whose shop was on the ground floor. The shop space had evolved through many iterations, from restaurant to real estate office, and was currently a would-be bohemian coffee shop.

The library was basically floor-to-ceiling books covering three walls, albeit with Chita's cello leaning against one corner. An experienced eye would have realised immediately that the books were all of a type: crime and more crime. One shelf was entirely filled with Elmore Leonard's lively work (but not the early cowboy yarns). Another was packed with James Ellroy. Then Michael Connolly, George Pelecanos, Don Winslow (the crime writer, not the porn author), Walter Mosley, Ian Rankin, Robert Crais, Jake Arnott and Leonard's son, Peter. Local true crime had colonised a sizeable corner, while the section devoted to Peter Temple's novels was virtually a shrine, displaying covers rather than spines.

On a side table lay some A4 print-outs, held together by black metal fold-back clips. Some were a couple of hundred pages thick, others comprised less than forty sheets. They all had titles in a variety of exotic fonts in the larger type sizes, with by-lines in smaller, simpler lettering below. *Crime of My Life by Aruna Gunawardena* read one. *The Killer Kid by Aaron Gunnar* proclaimed another. *Shooting Pains – a criminally funny sitcom by Aruna Danushka* said a third, slender manuscript.

Weezl was standing with his back to the table staring at a small whiteboard that occupied a gap in the middle of the shelves. In thick black capitals across the top were the underlined words *THE PERFECT CRIME*, and beneath that, in alternating lines of red and green, Chita's bold but neat hand had written:

No motive
No connection
No clues
No witnesses
No loose ends

Sensing Chita's presence behind him, Weezl tapped the whiteboard and said, 'We need to go back, babe.'

10

TONY CUFFLINKS looked at his phone in disbelief, as if the black plastic had somehow insulted him personally: 'Some *sticchio* with a golf club? That's all you've got?'

'No,' came the nervous voice, tinny on Tony's cheap burner mobile phone. 'Dark-skinned, baseball cap.'

'Who are we looking for here, Tiger Woods?' Tony laughed at his own joke, but there was silence at the other end of the line. 'What else?'

'The dead guy was seen in the Sapphire with a girl no one knew. She was small and skinny and had purple hair. But then she's gone – disappeared off the face. Then some bloke with a golf club turns up later at a flat in Surrey Street, takes a swing at an Asian chick but gets interrupted by the next door neighbour.'

'Don't tell me: he sliced. Hate it when that happens.' Again, a moment of nervous silence. 'So what then?'

'The mad golfer legged it, but it turns out the sheila's neighbour knew the dead guy.'

'Where are you getting all this?'

'Here. At the station.'

'Cops?' Tony snorted. 'Not a reliable source, then.'

'You might know the neighbour. Danny Clay?'

'Danny Clay's the neighbour?' Tony was surprised. 'I do know him. He was snooping around a while ago, wanted to make a TV series set here. He was asking so many questions I thought he was some kind of undercover cop. Then another mob made *Underbelly* and he said he'd missed his chance.'

'That figures. The guy who died was a writer too.'

'Vicious pricks once they get started, aren't they? So it was Clay?'

'Nah, he's got an alibi.'

'We've all got alibis, mate, doesn't mean we're innocent.' Tony sat back and thought for a moment. 'Okay, sounds like this has nothing to do with us or our business. I will give your esteemed colleagues any help they need … Can't have people despoiling the reputation of the great game on our doorsteps.'

Tony was silent for a moment. 'Dark-skinned?' he eventually thought aloud. 'You familiar with Jackie Jazz?'

'Jackie Jazz? Not really …'

'Well, get familiar. His real name is Jackie Corea. I need to know where he is and what he's doing.'

Tony clicked off the phone and sat back in his chair.

'What are you up to, Jazzman?' he said to the TV screens and the wall. He returned to a spreadsheet of the weekend's takings on one of his computer screens. Bad news on the streets was bad for business in the clubs. He needed to put a lid on this ASAP. More importantly, he needed to know if Jackie Jazz was making money without cutting him in.

Weezl and Chita were already tired from the 250 kilometres, forcing down fast food and bad coffee and bickering to keep themselves awake.

'Did you call your guy?' she asked in a low murmur, and not for the first time.

'Twenny? The phone's dead. A burner, most likely.'

'What about your uncle?' she cajoled.

'Call him direct? About this shit?'

'You must be able to get to him somehow.'

'Actions speak louder than words, babe. I gotta get his respect first.'

They fell silent, becoming one with the other night travellers in the Formica-topped feedlot at Glenrowan, just off the freeway between Melbourne and Sydney. On the way they'd talked about Ned Kelly – the town over the hill was where he had made his last stand. Chita had said it was weird that a thief and cop-killer should be a national hero. Weezl had wondered if killing some cops would get him a statue too.

Now Weezl looked into Chita's faraway eyes, and they simply stared at each other for a while, their smiles cross-infectious. Chita's faded first.

'Do we really need to do this?' she asked, a slight plea in her voice.

'I fucked up, Cheets. I gotta put it right. It's business.'

'But a ... gun?' she whispered. 'That's like taking it to a whole new level.'

'I killed someone, babe. There is no other level.'

'That was an accident.'

'Yeah, well, he's dead now, so ...' Weezl shrugged, as if to say he had no choice.

'You going to kill the girl too?'

No response.

'Why don't we just quit while we're ahead?'

'Are we ahead?' Weezl asked. 'Did the girl see me? The neighbour? Probably.'

'So what's the plan?' Chita asked, wondering if there was one.

'Look, I'm going to get to the neighbour. Scare him into telling me how much he saw, and decide what to do then.'

'You mean kill him?' she whispered intently.

Weezl waggled his head in that very subcontinental way.

'No witnesses, no loose ends.' He smiled. 'But a witness is only a witness if they're prepared to talk. Maybe I can persuade him he saw nothing.'

Chita could see Weezl fingering the gun, tucked in an inner pocket of his parka. He'd told her it was bulkier than he would have liked, a Browning

Hi-Power automatic pistol souvenired from the civil war in Sri Lanka by his fleeing father, who had succumbed to heart disease before getting around to telling teenage Weezl what or who he had been fleeing from.

The Browning was nothing special, and as ubiquitous as an AK47. It was called Hi-Power because it held more rounds than most weapons its size, and that was enough for the Third World's military and police. But Chita knew Weezl loved its polished timber grip and the cold efficiency of the steel body. He'd often taken it out of its oil cloth wrapping and wondered if he would ever use it. Now he could, even if it turned out to be only for show.

Chita asked herself if this was another one of Weezl's bullshit and bravado trips, or if he really had decided to kill these strangers. Looking at the shape in Weezl's pocket she frowned, considering the consequences and wondering exactly how she had got here. Just a few months earlier she had been frustrated by the fact that her life was plagued by First-World problems: her parents' four-wheel drives were too big for their two-car garage. Her local health food store had stopped selling her favourite soy milk. Uniqlo had sold out of Peppermint Patty hoodies in her size. Her irritation turned into a realisation that her priorities were seriously out of whack. So she took a semester off uni to change cities and get real, and that led her to wannabe criminal Weezl.

It was a writers' group meeting, of all things, in a Melbourne cafe. She'd wandered in looking for nothing more than a cappuccino with a bit more froth – like they do in Brisbane – and was about to leave when she realised most of the people there were exactly the kind she'd been trying to escape. But then Weezl stood up and started reading from a novel he was writing and she was entranced by this wiry, high-energy creature spitting out violent fantasies that seemed to brutalise grammar as much as the fictional victims in the prose. And while he said it *was* fiction, there was something about the rawness that made Chita think that it was, at least in part, real. When Weezl grabbed another writer by the throat for gently mocking his misuse of tenses, Chita decided this was her entrée to the real world she had been seeking.

It had been fun at first, and the sex was great, but she had taken great care to protect her other life – her real life – so that she could fully and enthusiastically explore this new and exciting detour. Which was fine until Weezl, possibly inspired by her and definitely frustrated at his lack of progress in getting published, had decided to step up in the criminal world, hoping to prove something to his uncle who, he told her, was a serious crim.

The first job was easy – some low-level computer hacking that Weezl could do in his sleep. Result, one dead writer. Then there was the pathetic guy in the bar. He was supposed to put a scare into him. Also now dead. Turning to the reflection of the room in the darkened windows, she again checked the positions of the security cameras, making sure she never looked directly at any of them. Instinctively, she rubbed the small tattoo of a weasel on her inner left wrist. She'd had trouble getting that. The tattooist had thought she wanted a weevil and then offered her a possum. She'd had to download a picture from the internet. Even then it looked more like a meerkat by the time it had been inked into her skin. She smiled at Weezl but he was off in another world: a world of guns.

'You know there's no turning back after this?' she said quietly.

'Why would we want to turn back?' He grinned. 'We're on the Yellow Brick Road.'

'What about your writing?'

'This is research, babe,' he said. 'If we get caught, hey, plenty of time to write in jail.'

We, she thought. If *we* get caught.

'What does your uncle think about you teaming up with me?'

Weezl thought for a moment.

'Look, I didn't really tell him about you, babe.' Weezl looked apologetic. 'He's old-school. I wanted to wait till it was done and dusted.'

Chita pouted but couldn't suppress a smile. Weezl, feeling forgiven, smiled too.

11

TONY CUFFLINKS looked at the phone's screen and shook his head. He didn't like texts. He thought they were for teenagers and illiterate fucks who were trying to hide the fact that they couldn't spell by making a virtue out of it. But this one was both fascinating and frustrating, like a good puzzle.

JJ not seen for wks here but Feds hv hm flyng nto Venice, Berlin, Toronto, Edinburgh, Nice (sth France).

'I know where Nice is,' Tony said angrily to his phone and himself. Then, 'Is this some terrorist shit?'

He read the last line of the text: *They dnt knw wht hs up to ithr.*

That was the part that annoyed him most. Jackie Jazz was allowed to do his own thing in the Cross, provided he kicked back a share of the profits to Tony. But if Tony didn't know what Jackie was doing, he couldn't ask for his tax.

And that was a situation Tony could not allow to continue.

—

Danny stood out on the streets of the Cross, not because of the way he looked, but because of the way he walked. Upright, confident and alert, it was in stark contrast to the eyes-down shufflers, the texters and headphone listeners, loud phone-callers and, especially, the chest-out, manic, elbow pumping, double-time march of the ice addicts on their way to their next score. Danny stood out because he was normal.

That made it all the easier for Zan to spot him as she erupted from the front door of the Kings Cross police station where she had just spent an awkward twenty minutes trying to explain that she hadn't seen the guy with the golf club while steering the conversation away from anything to do with heart attacks or lifts. Zan intercepted Danny at the nearby fountain which, in full flow, looked like a giant dandelion clock, and led him to a table at an outdoor cafe.

'How was it?' Danny asked, looking at his watch. His own interview was fifteen minutes away.

'Awkward,' Zan replied. 'I told them everything I knew and they seemed to accept it.'

'And that is awkward how, exactly?'

'They didn't mention the Hahn thing,' Zan said in a whisper, gripping Danny's arm. 'I think they're trying to wrong-foot me.'

'I think they've succeeded,' he replied.

Zan had been distracted throughout the interview, knowing she had a confession to make to Danny and wondering which of her tried and tested misdirection techniques to use. There was 'this is all your fault', but it clearly wasn't, and there was 'I'm the victim here', but that didn't pass muster either. There was always sex, but Danny invariably saw through that. What was he, a fucking monk? The one thing she was sure of was that it couldn't wait.

'Danny, I have a confession to make,' she said, then realised as he sagged in his chair that this was the best misdirection of them all.

—

Danny's interview was even shorter than Zan's, thanks to a message from Liam confirming that they had indeed been indulging each other's misery via Skype at the time Marcus was killed. The embellishment that Danny was 'droning on' when there was cricket on TV that needed watching was unnecessary, Danny thought, but it had clearly done no harm. He was lucky to be let off the hook so easily, because throughout the interview he had been distracted by thoughts of Zan's confession.

'Danny, I have a confession to make,' she'd said

Danny had grabbed her wrist and squeezed gently, trying to think of a better phrase than 'I'm here for you'.

'He deserved it,' was the best he could come up with.

'Who?' said Zan, abruptly pulling her arm away.

'The guy you killed in the lift,' Danny said.

'*Shoosh* the fuck up,' Zan replied in a loud whisper, glancing at the police station. 'I was trying to save him, right?'

Danny blinked and shrugged – whatever she said …

'No, it's about Bryan and Marcus,' she said, adding as an afterthought, 'and the Poet.'

'The Poet?'

'There was another script, Danny,' she said, her eyes fixed on a crumb of old biscuit that had welded itself to the table.

'It was a piece of nonsense called *Redneck Airlift*. It was about gun nutters in America who go off to the Middle East to shoot Isis members – like they were going duck hunting – but it all goes tits-up and they have to be rescued by special forces.'

'How come I wasn't involved? I could have …'

'That's exactly why. You having been a sapper and Special Forces and all that.'

'Special Ops,' Danny corrected her.

'Whatever,' Zan said dismissively. 'The Poet thought you would get all experty and take over.'

'Well, pardon me for knowing shit,' he'd said, not bothering to hide his bitterness.

'Look, it had zero chance of ever getting up, so there was no harm done.'

'So what changed?'

'It got up.'

That had been the joyful kick in the nuts that set Danny's mind racing. A project getting up is a lottery win. It means the twin mirages of fortune and fame have taken solid form, even if they are just as far away from being fully realised. Somewhere in there, there's a motive for someone, Danny thought. He needed to talk to the Poet ... that's if he could get any sense out of him.

Danny briefly thought about going home from the police station the long way, via the strip, where it was busier and, ironically, the abundance of streeties, spruikers, druggies, dealers and alkies made it safer. The Coke sign on the hill immediately east of the city, the gateway to Kings Cross, was like the Statue of Liberty for the lost souls of Sydney – and the rest of Australia, and New Zealand too. *Bring me your poor and huddled masses*... and your drunks, junkies, hookers, would-be heroes, wannabe hustlers, bent cops, straight shooters and broken-hearted fools, thought Danny. The Cross scared strangers but, like most people who lived there, Danny wasn't cowed by unnamed threats, even when two of his friends had recently been attacked.

He dropped down behind the police station into Ward Avenue and was crossing Royston Street, a narrow clutter of fast-food restaurants and convenience stores on one side, with the Empire Hotel, former home to Les Girls drag queen cabaret, a backpacker hostel, a trendy hipster barber and the almost legendary Piccolo coffee bar near the other. Danny was still thinking about Zan – less about the script she'd hidden and more about her pre-cleaning hug – when he was suddenly aware of a late-model black Mercedes with heavily tinted windows rolling quietly alongside him. Danny stopped and the car did too. The rear door opened and a hand waved him forward.

'Danny,' said Tony Cufflinks. 'A word?'

Danny thought for a moment of walking on but he could feel the beginnings of a rush, so he got in. He closed the door and was pushed back into the shiny soft leather seat by the acceleration as they took off from the kerb.

'Where are we going?' Danny asked.

'Wherever you'd like.'

'I was going home.'

'We can do that.' Tony leaned forward and spoke to the driver, overweight and wearing black wraparound Ray Bans. 'Mr Clay's residence, Bam. But take your time.' He turned to Danny. 'Been to see the cops?'

Danny nodded, wondering if that was a mistake.

'Not that they've got much to go on,' Tony said. 'Girl with purple hair, the blood sample from your hands – it's definitely your mate's by the way – dark-skinned guy with a golf club. That's about it; no motive, see. They need a motive.'

Danny was briefly silenced by Tony's knowledge. He'd got those details fast.

'You know I *had* to speak to the cops?' he finally said.

'Of course – you were a key witness. In fact, for a second or two you were a suspect,' Tony said, reassuring. 'Why wouldn't you talk to them? That would just seem suspicious.'

Another silence.

'So tell me, why exactly did my name came up?' Tony asked.

'Did it?' Danny said dismissively, trying to remember exactly what he had said.

'Let's say it did.' Tony laughed, but then got very serious. 'So why would you mention my name, Danny? I thought we were friends.'

'Oh, you know, they wanted a list of people I know who include violence among their business methods. I gave them the Australian Armed Forces ... and you.'

Tony nodded and half-smiled. 'I like your sense of humour. Always have. So what the fuck is going on?'

'Writers topping themselves is, sadly, not that unusual,' Danny mused. 'But then a friend getting their head bashed in a week later …'

'Coincidence?' Tony smiled, his buffed teeth almost glowing in the gloom of the car's interior. 'I don't believe in coincidence. Do you?'

'Depends.'

'On what?'

'Simple mathematics. The chances of the numbers in Lotto coming up 1,2,3,4,5,6 are exactly the same as any other random set of numbers. But if they did …'

'You'd be having a long hard look at the machine,' Tony offered.

'Exactly,' Danny said. 'Anyway, I told them I met you a while back when I was researching that TV series …'

'Why would you say that?' Tony asked, grimly.

'What can I say? I was being honest. You should try it sometime.'

'I'm honest with the people I need to be honest with,' Tony said. 'And this guy you saw outside your front door. He was dark-skinned?'

'I think so. It was hard to tell. It's not that well-lit, and I'd had a drink. A bottle, in fact.'

Tony nodded, thinking.

'So, you had nothing to do with it?' Danny asked.

'Danny!' Tony protested. 'Why would I? These guys didn't owe me money, they weren't muscling in on my territory and they didn't have anything I needed. Right now you are more of a suspect than I am.'

Danny noticed that they had just rolled past his front door for the second time.

'In fact, that neighbour of yours is well up the list,' Tony said.

'Zan?'

'She is smack in the middle of this clusterfuck. And she was there when that guy in the lift died.'

'Coincidence,' Danny said, as the car turned from Victoria Street into the surprisingly suburban Surrey Street. 'Co-inky-dinky.'

'Let's drop Mr Clay off,' Tony said to the driver. 'So, Danny, I don't want you pointing the cops in my direction again, okay? Don't even say my name, whether you think I'm involved or not. Now I have to go to the police and tell them I had nothing to do with this, and that will just take time out of my busy day.'

'Why don't you just get your snitch to pass on the message?' Danny said with a little too much *fuck you* in the tone.

There was the merest hint of annoyance in Tony's expression. 'You're a funny guy,' Tony said as he tapped rather than slapped Danny's cheek – almost affectionate, mostly patronising. He was about to do it for a second time when Danny grabbed his wrist. Tony's eyes flashed surprise, then anger.

'Newton's third law,' Danny said. 'Every action has an equal and opposite reaction.'

Danny knew he had crossed a line, but he felt the adrenaline bubbling in his system and it was as righteous as a fix. He let go of Tony's arm but held his gaze. The driver looked in the rear-view mirror and slowed, in case he had to stop.

'Hey, soldier boy,' Tony purred. 'Don't think your SAS shit is going to save you if you get into a war with me.'

'I wasn't SAS,' Danny said, matter-of-fact. 'I was a sapper – an engineer.'

'Really?' Tony seemed almost disappointed. 'I heard you were special forces.'

'Yeah, I heard that too. But the truth is, Tony, the only way I could be a threat to you is if someone tied you to a bomb and I decided not to defuse it.'

Tony snorted, pretending not to give the fuck he was giving, but the heat had gone out of the moment.

'I am not doing or saying anything that need concern you,' Danny continued. 'You are just a fact of life around here, that's all.'

'A fact of life?' said Tony, flattered and insulted at the same time. 'Is that what I am?'

The Merc pulled up right outside Danny's front door. He realised this was Tony's way of letting him know that he knew where he lived. Danny opened the car door and started to get out.

'Hey, Danny,' Tony said, gently tugging at Danny's sleeve. 'You're a smart guy. What do Berlin, Venice, Toronto, Edinburgh and Nice have to do with each other?'

'Is this a joke?'

'No, I'm serious. Is it some sort of terrorist shit?'

'Berlin, Venice and Nice …?'

'And Edinburgh and Toronto.' Tony completed the list.

'Beats me,' Danny said.

'Yeah, me too,' Tony said, his tone almost friendly.

'So why did you ask?'

'Two reasons. I wanted to know –' Tony smiled '– and I wanted to know if you knew.'

'Yes, but why?' Danny asked, but Tony let go of his sleeve and waved him away.

'Hey, try not to end up like your pals, okay?' Tony said as he leaned over to close the door. 'And watch your back, especially in lifts. Women can be unpredictable.'

Danny watched the Merc as it pulled away with the slightest squeak of expensive tyres, more of a gentle protest than a squeal. He stood for several minutes, letting the juice subside, breathing deeply and tapping into what he guessed was a form of self-hypnosis, the trick he used to bring his heart rate down at the shooting range. He smiled. That felt good. But he wondered if Tony knew more than he was saying.

Okay, that was a given.

Danny thought about heading for the locksmith's to ramp up his defences, but changed his mind.

'Fuck them,' he said aloud. 'Let them come.'

12

THE POET realised he must have passed the Galle Fort restaurant a hundred times and not even noticed it was there. It was tucked in a lane off St Kilda Road, in a tiny converted shop with a menu and dusty lace curtains barely visible in the window. The tables were small but covered with clean white linen cloths. The aromas drifting from the kitchen — half-hidden behind the kind of bead curtain from which you expected a movie gangster in a white linen suit and a fez to appear — suggested exotic spices laced with generous amounts of chilli.

The Poet liked his curries but he wasn't too familiar with the Sri Lankan version. They tended to be hot, he knew, and favoured seafood and fruit. A small brown man in his twenties with a wispy back moustache approached with a menu, but turned away when an older man, peering through the curtain, berated him in a language the Poet would not have known from Martian.

He felt uneasy and was seriously considering walking out. One phone call telling him to be here, alone, informing no one, seemed a risky proposition on reflection. In fact, it was stupid. Suicidal. But there had been the implied threat that if he didn't come, he might end up like Marcus. Jesus! Bryan and now Marcus. Was it too late to pull out? Go home? Hide? The older man was halfway through the beaded curtain when the doorbell pinged and a man in a motorbike helmet and leathers walked in. The Poet tensed. The newcomer looked ominous, especially when he didn't remove his helmet. The Poet's guts turned to water. This was it. The motorbike guy was between him and the door: there was no escape.

The older waiter retreated to the kitchen then appeared with two bags carrying plastic containers filled with aromatic food. The motorbike guy exited. It took the Poet a moment or two to regain his composure, long enough for the older man to come out from behind the curtain and over to the table.

'Are you the one they call the Poet?' he asked in an accent as thick as a crab curry. The Poet nodded, somewhat reluctantly. 'Then you need to come with me.'

The Poet watched him clatter his way through the beads, then stop, pull a gap in the strands and look back at him. The poet realised that this could be a turning point, but which way to turn? He could duck out now and go back out the way he'd come in, back out onto the street and his former life, or he could go through the beaded curtain to what was going to be, one way or another, a life-changing moment.

'Where are we going?' the Poet asked, his mouth dryer than the morning after a two-day binge.

'Just come,' the older man said, pulling the curtain even wider.

'You know what,' the Poet said, 'I'm having second thoughts ...'

'Too late for that, I'm afraid, Mr Poet,' he replied with a smile.

It was then that the Poet noticed the man was holding a gun, and it was pointed straight at him.

13

A FEW hours later and a thousand kilometres away, Tony Cufflinks sat in the garden of the Caffe Roma on Kellett Street, suddenly aware that he was just a couple of metres from where, only a few nights before, the writer had been beaten to death with a golf club. Alone in the shadows, the other tables having been vacated because of some ridiculous curfew on having fun, Tony sipped on his montepulciano and reflected on how much the street had changed since he first came here all those years ago, in the back seat of his older brother's souped-up Valiant. His brother was long gone, a casualty in the turf war with the Hong Kong crew – but then so was the Hong Kong crew.

Kellett could be entered from Bayswater Road where the Mansions Hotel, once a twenty-four-hour bar, stood sentinel on one corner. The security guards used to wear polo shirts with 'We don't call the police' embroidered on their pockets – a warning that Mansions dispensed its own instant justice. But what had once been the roughest pub in the Cross was now an empty shell with apartments above it. The bar had been gutted just in time to be left high and dry by a change in laws that saw bars, clubs and restaurants close by the truckload.

Opposite was the entrance to the Sapphire, then stairs leading upwards to a strip club that was called, counter-intuitively, the Velvet Underground, then an old-fashioned gents' hairdresser, still going strong after sixty years, although there were a dozen hip imitators around the Cross. Just goes to show, Tony thought, if you stay the same for long enough, eventually you will come back into fashion.

However, that hadn't worked for the old New York Grill, a plastic-tabled greasy spoon cafe that used to serve steak and chips or pie and mash for less than ten dollars, and had been a lifesaver for actors, musos and even gangsters who were down on their luck. Maggie's, a couple of doors down, still offered a selection of mostly sad girls for whatever took a man's fancy.

Around the corner a run of elegant 1930s townhouses accommodated a brisk turnover of restaurants on either side of Caffe Roma. These new kids on the block popped up then sloped off as the economic realities of the restaurant trade bit them in the bum. Even one of the brothels across from the Roma had closed and the other had become a rub'n'tug. As a taxi driver had said to him recently, you know things are bad when the knocking shops are closing.

Three doors down the Iguana Bar, once a twenty-four-hour drinking den much favoured by visiting rock stars, had evolved into a burlesque showroom. Burlesque, Tony thought, all tease and no strip.

Across the road, architects had taken over one former brothel, and what had once been a thriving pole-dancing club was now an organic cafe. Tony wondered if sex had finally gone out of fashion. Danilo, the owner of the Roma, approached as apologetically as a man can when he is carrying an uncorked bottle of wine.

'We have to close soon, my friend,' he said as he filled Tony's glass. 'Or they might never let us open again.' On cue, a switch killed the fairy lights that spiralled around the tree which surged from the courtyard, through the fence and across the footpath. Tony nodded and smiled. He checked his watch. It was shading 2am.

Tony came here when he needed to think, and right now he was thinking about Jackie Jazz and all those visits overseas. What the hell did Berlin, Toronto, Venice and Nice have in common? What was Jackie Jazz up to there? And more to the point, should Tony be getting a piece of the action? Fuck it, he thought. He took out his phone and found Jackie's number under 'Jazzman'. He pressed the button and there was a long delay, but eventually the phone rang.

Jackie's real surname was Corea, common in Sri Lanka, his home country. He'd earned his nickname from unwarranted associations with Chick Corea, the jazz pianist. Jackie Jazz accepted the reflected cred this gave him, despite never having heard a single note that his very, very distant relative had played. Jackie was a good fifteen years younger than Tony, who already had a half century in his rear-view mirror. He was a sharp dresser where Tony was smooth, gym-fit where Tony was naturally strong but tending towards fat. Jackie had an eye on the future, whereas Tony's eyes had seen a bit too much in the past to retain their sparkle. Both men knew that someday Jackie – or someone very like him – would be running the Cross. But until then, Tony was the man, and Jackie wouldn't want to create any unnecessary grief by forcing the issue. Not yet, anyway.

The ringing stopped suddenly and Jackie's voice was as clear as if he had been standing next to Tony – although he was panting. 'Hello! Who is this?'

'Jazzman?' Tony asked, surprised that he had got through. 'Are you shagging?'

'Walking, Tony. Uphill in snow,' he said, before a momentary doubt. 'That is Tony, isn't it?'

'Yeah,' Tony replied. 'It's snowing? Are you in Europe?'

'Utah,' Jackie replied.

'Utah? Where the Muslims come from?'

'Mormons, Tony. The Muslims come from ... I don't know. Not here.'

'What the fuck are you doing in Utah?'

'Skiing,' Jackie answered after a momentary hesitation.

'Bullshit,' Tony said. 'Is this business? And how come I don't know about it?'

'It's nothing to do with the Cross, okay?'

Tony was silent.

'Are we done, Tony? I'm freezing my nuts off here and I haven't had breakfast yet.'

'A guy got himself knocked near here,' Tony said. 'Beaten to death with a golf club. Sounds like the killer was one of your lot.'

'My lot? A nightclub owner? A Catholic?'

'Dark-skinned …'

'There's a lot of dark-skinned people around, Tony, although I'm dealing with one fuckwit who thinks I'm an Aborigine.'

Tony laughed despite himself.

'Look, I've been told about it. As far as I know it wasn't any of my boys, and it was nothing to do with me,' Jackie said.

'Okay it wasn't you,' Tony conceded. 'And it wasn't me. So we need to know who the fuck it was and get them off our patch.'

'I'll let you know if I hear anything,' Jackie said.

'You do that,' Tony replied.

'Hey, Tony, one more thing …'

'What?'

'You want to buy a brothel?'

'Call me in the morning,' Tony replied. 'My morning. We can talk then.'

They hung up and, halfway across the world from each other, both men looked at their phones as if their screens might reveal the answer to the same question: 'How much does he really know?'

—

Danny carefully prised Zan's fingers from the whisky glass. She'd tried to match him glass for glass, but her size and DNA had let her down. She could go from giggling flirt to slobbering mess in less time than it took to drink 35 millilitres of decent Scotch. Zan reached for the glass but Danny downed it in one. Game over. Zan scowled then smiled. She knew she'd had enough. Some guys mistook intoxication for infatuation and Danny had rescued her from too many ugly encounters for her to put up a fight.

Instead she threw her arms around him and snuggled up with a sigh, hugging Danny more like a teddy bear than a lover. Danny wriggled a little to fit her better and replied with a sigh of his own. It had been a long day and they had run out of words. They soaked up the silence gratefully.

One bottle of chianti and a half-litre of whisky earlier, they had been anything but silent. Every how, what and why of the past few days had been discussed at length and in detail, pulled apart and put back together like a corner of a jigsaw sky with one piece that just won't fit.

'Berlin, Toronto, Venice and Edinburgh?' Zan had asked, tapping the names into her laptop.

'And Nice,' Danny added.

'Film festivals,' Zan said.

'Nice doesn't have a film festival, does it?'

Zan tapped away again.

'Nearest airport to Cannes,' she announced.

Danny went very quiet. Zan stared at him, like she was awaiting a computer to reveal the results of a complex calculation.

'Tony Cufflinks asked me what they had in common,' he said. 'But I think he knew. He knew something, anyway. He was testing me.'

'And?'

'And he's made a connection,' Danny said. 'And film festivals would connect with writers, right?'

Now, as Zan drunkenly cuddled up to Danny on the couch, they both retreated to silent thought. For the past hour or more they had picked at the threads of Tony Cufflinks, the Poet, *Redneck Airlift* and what had happened to Marcus and Bryan. But the elevator was taboo, neither willing to lift that particular rock and see what wriggled beneath. Not tonight.

Sadly, having a friend take his own life wasn't so unusual for Danny these days. A lot of guys he'd known in Afghanistan had come home and taken a long drive without leaving their garages, or finally found a use for the pistol they had smuggled out in their kit. It was sad, but the saddest thing about it was that it was no longer a surprise.

'Okay, so how do you reckon Bryan's suicide is connected to attacks on you and Marcus?' Danny asked for the fourth or fifth time that night, as exhaustion and alcohol finally took their toll. 'And film festivals. And Tony Cufflinks. And "Redneck fucking Airport".'

'"Airlift".' Zan released him and sat back on the couch, biting her lip.

'This is the key,' Danny said. 'Tell me everything.'

He looked for a reaction but the alcohol had blurred her body language as well as his focus and he couldn't be sure. She caught his glare.

'The Poet was the go-between.'

'And Marcus, Bryan and him were writing it on spec?'

'No, they got paid, up front and good money.' She raised a shaky finger to emphasise her point. 'That much I know, cos I got paid in advance too.'

'Who by?'

'The Poet. Everything came through him.'

'Okay,' Danny said patiently. 'Who paid the Poet?'

Zan thought for a full twenty seconds and then looked puzzled. 'You know, I don't have a clue. I gave my invoices to the Poet and he turned up with the cash a few days later.'

'Cash?' Danny was getting the picture.

'Yeah, very old-shool,' she slurred. 'Everybody got paid, cash money. Let's talk about it tomorrow.'

'No, tell me now.'

'That's all I know,' she protested. 'I felt guilty about leaving you out and even worse when we got paid so well.'

Zan reached defiantly for the bottle of whisky and topped both their glasses close to the brim. It was both a deliberate distraction as well as a declaration of intent.

'Well, now it makes sense,' Danny said. 'Who pays in cash? Gangsters. Like Tony Cufflinks.'

'Yeah. I guess,' she said. 'Never heard his name mentioned, though.'

'Even so, I think it's time he and I had a little chat,' Danny said, mostly to himself.

Zan reached for her glass but Danny lifted it away and gently pushed her back. She sighed theatrically and used the momentum of his gentle pressure to slump back on the sofa. Within seconds she was out, breathing softly but deeply. Gone.

Danny looked at her in the russet light of the faded shade on an incongruously fussy side lamp. Her blouse had ridden up a little and he could see a slash of pale cinnamon skin above her belt. Over the years, Danny had probably seen enough different parts of Zan naked to create a composite nude. She was neither prudish nor shy. Truth be told, she was probably a little too proud of her near-perfect body. But that unintentional exposure of a fraction of her midriff was a turn-on.

Danny picked Zan up and carried her through to his bed. It was easy: she weighed less than his backpack had on some operations. He threw some blankets over her, kissed her on the forehead and pushed her hand away as she reached sleepily for him. Danny switched off the lamp and looked back at her, her face catching the streetlight from the window, then closed the bedroom door. They still had another night to get through.

He went back to the front door and checked the locks. Despite being an immensely practical man, Danny also worked on instinct, especially when he thought his life was in danger. He did now. There were too many loose ends, too many unknowns. One thing he did know was that there was a killer out there who had offed one of his friends and tried to do the same to another: the one who was now snoring delicately in his bed. He and Zan – Zan especially – were someone's unfinished business.

Danny went to his odds and ends cupboard, as he had every night since the attack on Zan, and took out a couple of tin cans he used for storing loose screws and the like, now connected by a length of fishing line. He placed the cans on either side of the hallway and propped a large-format book against each one, dangling the line loosely over the top so that it drooped between them just above ankle height. Then he tied off the line to the other can. Danny stepped back, satisfied.

There were two kinds of tripwire alarms. One made so much noise it usually scared your attacker off. The other made just enough noise to let you know it was party time and maybe bought you a couple of seconds while the intruder tried to work out what was happening. This one was the latter.

Danny poured himself another Scotch. There were two essential survival skills that he had retained from his army days: the ability to sleep wherever you could, and the power to wake up, fully alert, as soon as you needed to. He switched off all the lights, sat back in his armchair and closed his eyes.

14

PADDY ROSENBERG was not a happy man. He leaned back in his perfectly adjusted Aeron chair, turned to the window and watched the city light up in its daily defiance of the darkness creeping in from the mountains and desert. The Fox lot far below was aglow with a night shoot on the New York streetscape. Paddy was so pissed off that he couldn't even be bothered getting his binoculars out for some casual star spotting.

The day had started well, then rapidly gone downhill. First the Aborigine had called to confirm they were paying the money back. Three million US dollars, minus expenses.

'I am gold,' Paddy had said to himself with a grin as wide as the new Merc he was thinking of treating himself to.

Then his day – no, his whole life – turned to a big steaming pile of dog crap. His mind went back a few days to when he'd thought that conniving bitch Jasmina was going to give him a celebratory blow job. Then she had suddenly gone all coy on him, no matter how much he begged or threatened.

And finally tonight at about 6pm, just when he was dreading the drive up Santa Monica to the 101, she hit him with a demand for a promotion to a different department – or at least a wage rise and 'a little respect'.

Respect? Paddy was about to have her thrown out of the office when the email arrived, sent from her computer just before she walked into his room. It contained an audio recording of his recent demands and her apparently shocked refusal. She told him that these iPhone recordings would form the rock-solid basis of the mother of all sexual harassment suits.

Shit, he thought now, you couldn't trust anyone these days.

He was fucked every which way till Tuesday. How was he supposed to find a job for an evil troll who played like a sophomore at spring break but operated like a CIA spook? He should have seen it coming. But hey, it was entrapment, right? Anyone listening to the recording might think *she* was the one hitting on *him*. He turned back to the computer and pressed play again, listening for the nuances that would betray her evil intent.

'What do you mean by relax?' she said on the recording, her voice sounding frostier than it had seemed at the time. He remembered her look, all pouty. Then, *'Do you mean you want to have sex with me?'*

Again, on reflection, her tone sounded more shocked than enthusiastic.

'A blow job will do for now,' he heard himself say.

'And if I don't, will that affect my career prospects?' she asked.

Paddy was sure he could remember her fluttering her eyelids. That's when the alarm bells should have started ringing, and probably would have if all his blood hadn't already raced from his brain to his dick. She was role-playing, right? Naughty secretary (one of his personal favourites). Wrong! Paddy switched the recording off before he had to listen to the phrase that, if he remembered correctly, included the words 'good spanking' and which surely now meant the end of his career. Jeez, they had nailed Weinstein on less evidence.

There was a time when Paddy could have bluffed and blustered his way out of this. Hell, he'd done it often enough before. But there was this irritating new wave of political correctness sweeping Hollywood and even BJF Studios, his employers, were jumping on the 'respect' bandwagon – which, Paddy thought, was hugely ironic given their origins.

BJF was one of those studios that had grown out of the indie film explosion of the '70s. Using friends and film-school students, a couple of college kids called Chuck and Jeff produced a soft-porn spoof horror movie called *Haltergeist*, about a poltergeist that removed the halterneck tops from well-endowed girls. While younger kids were watching the first *Star Wars* movie and savvy adults were being blown away by De Niro in *Taxi Driver* (and every other movie he made before he discovered comedy), teenage boys were firing up this new machine called a VCR and sitting down with their buddies – or alone in the dark – to drink their parents' beer and watch attractive young women be undressed by a ghost.

BJF didn't take its initials from its founders – that would have been CJF – but from Blow Jobs Forever, their stated intention to maximise the amount of oral sex they received, presumably from budding starlets anxious for a role in *Haltergeist 2* and *3*, not to mention the franchise's final outing, *Haltergeist: The Boob Stops Here*. In fact, they were so instantly successful they had neither the time nor the energy to take advantage of their dream coming true. In any case, it would prove to be a short-sighted joke as they grew up, spread their creative wings and became much more successful than they had ever imagined.

The studio's growing profile, their knack for picking low-cost, high-grossing projects and a creeping desire for credibility meant they were reluctant to reveal the true inspiration for their name, so they took the only possible option to protect their brand and save their blushes: Chuck changed his name to Brandon.

Meanwhile BJF (Brandon and Jeff Films) was involved in a series of takeovers of other even smaller studios, and grew fat on the growing appetite for edgy, non-Hollywood movies. Every time there was a shift in the market, they seemed to be just ahead of the curve (one of their favourite clichés). Cable TV? They had a catalogue of movies that free-to-air stations wouldn't or couldn't show. Then they started creating their own TV series just in time for the streaming revolution. Chuck and Jeff were smart, for sure. They were also lucky and, if they needed to be, ruthless. BJF was the Apple of movie-making and TV production. By trading on their anti-establishment credentials so successfully, they had become the establishment. And, as a result, they were now ready to go postal at the first hint of anything with a whiff of sexual impropriety.

Paddy kicked his desk, causing the chair to roll back, crash into the display cabinet and dislodge his trophy, which felt to the floor and snapped in two.

Paddy could feel real hot tears stinging the corners of his eyes.

It was 2.37am on Danny's Casio Pro Trek when he heard a clumsy click of tumblers, the sign his door lock was being inexpertly picked. He rose slowly from his chair and was met by a brief flash of light and a gust of cold outside air as the door was opened and quickly closed. Almost immediately there was the thump of the books, the rattle of the cans and the muted cursing of someone whose legs were tangled in something they couldn't see.

Two strides got Danny into the hallway, the third got him close enough to see his visitor had a gun, the fourth took him past the business end of the weapon, with his left hand grabbing the gunman's wrist and pushing the muzzle down while his right elbow moved the intruder's nose a couple of inches up his face.

Danny had three or four highly efficient methods for getting the guy to drop his gun, but he didn't need any of them: it clattered to the floor immediately as the gunman yelped in pain. Danny moved quickly behind the man, who was surprisingly small and skinny for a hitman, kicked the back of his knees and, as he dropped, slipped him into a choke hold. The gunman gasped and wriggled but eventually stopped struggling as the flow of blood to his brain was turned off and he slid towards oblivion. Danny checked his watch. It was still 2.37 on the digital display – nice. He breathed in deeply through his nose to make the most of the buzz as the body in his arms went limp.

When the gunman awoke, his wrists and ankles were gaffer-taped to the arms and legs of Danny's old wooden writing chair. He tried to speak but there was wide metallic tape over his mouth too. Danny ripped the tape off, pulling a thousand tiny whiskers with it.

'Ow! You fuck. You fucking fuck. You are a dead ma—'

His threat was cut short when Danny reapplied the tape.

'You couldn't have just called the cops like normal people?' Zan said sleepily, clearly halfway to a decent-sized hangover when the commotion had woken her.

'I need some answers first.'

'Isn't that their job?'

Danny's look was disappointment laced with scepticism. 'They have a snitch in there, remember?' He turned to the gunman.

'Now, I'm going to take the tape off and if you make any noise or refuse to answer my questions, I'm going to put it back on again, then take it off slowly. Every time, tape on hard, then off slowly.'

He peeled back a few inches of tape.

'What? Why?' asked the gunman, scared but mostly confused.

'Because we don't have the facilities for water boarding,' Danny replied, unsmiling.

'You could use my bath,' Zan said blithely.

'There you go.' Danny grinned. 'We have options.'

The wild look in their captive's eyes told him everything he needed to know. Danny reapplied the tape then ripped it off again. The skinny, dark-skinned kid yelped.

'Okay, now let's talk,' Danny said. 'You killed my friend and I want to know why. But first, let's get to know each other – who the fuck are you?'

The prisoner shook his head. Danny reached for the roll of tape and tore off a fresh strip.

'Weezl!' he said.

'Did he say "weasel"?' Danny asked Zan, surprised.

'Sounded like weasel,' Zan replied, similarly taken aback.

'Weezl,' Weezl said in exasperation. 'W.E.E.Z.L. It's my street name.'

'You need to start hanging out in a better class of streets,' Danny said. 'Real name?'

Weezl looked at him balefully. 'Your friend. It was an accident, okay?'

'Not okay. Not even close. Why did you kill him?'

'I wasn't supposed to kill him, just hurt him. Scare him.'

'Why? Who wanted to scare him?'

He shook his head. Danny picked up the roll of tape again but Weezl simply shrugged. There were worse things to be afraid of.

'Listen, sonny,' Danny said as patronisingly as he could muster. 'You are a fucking amateur. Did you learn this from a book? I mean, are those the same clothes you wore the night you killed Marcus?'

'Course not.'

'No, you burned them because they had Marcus's blood on them – am I right?'

Weezl shrugged again, but Danny could see he'd been right on the money.

'But then you went out and bought exactly the same gear. You know, you kids are just way too brand-conscious for your own good.'

'I like Asics, is all. They rock. What difference does it make? Millions of people wear this stuff. It's not like it's unique.'

'Really? So if I ever called around sports goods stores and asked them if they had any record of someone who bought a full Asics tracksuit, Yankee's baseball cap and a single golf club in one hit, how many names are going to come up?'

Weezl's eyes widened. Danny smiled.

'You are so clever and cool,' Zan said, starting to wake up properly now.

'I try,' Danny said, turning back to Weezl.

'Okay, now that we've established you are more amateur than an *Idol* rejects show, and you are in a shit storm that you can't control, how about you tell me who sent you and why?'

Weezl shook his head.

'Hey, Zan, got any smokes?' Danny asked with a sigh.

'I don't smoke,' she said. 'You know that. And when did you start?'

'I haven't. I'm just working my way through the standard low-cost torture techniques before we start stripping wires off side lamps and shit like that.'

'What the fuck?' Weezl was starting to look truly scared now.

'Danny was in Afghanistan,' Zan explained. 'He used to do this stuff for a living.'

'*I have skills*, as Liam Neeson impersonators might put it,' Danny said with a manic grin that was, in truth, more Jack Nicholson.

'Mother fucking bitch, when my uncle hears what you done ...'

'Your uncle?' Danny smirked.

The look on Weezl's face was almost comical.

'I said my people – *pee-pul* – you deaf or what, you old shit?'

'You don't have people. All you have is that purple-haired girl who lured Marcus into your nasty little ambush ...' A thought struck Danny. 'And where is she, while you're all trussed up like the last turkey at Christmas?'

—

Chita didn't have to go all the way down the hall to see what was happening in the impromptu torture chamber. The reflection in a TV screen revealed Zan leaning on the back of a chair and a big guy bent over a third person that she took to be Weezl, who was sitting down. From the conversation, and Weezl's occasional yelps, she deduced that he had been restrained. That meant, apart from anything else, that the odds were stacked against her – one versus two. The thought that her next best move would be a hasty exit surged through her. But Weezl was her man, and she didn't get into this to run away at the first sign of trouble. Chita peered at the TV screen. She thought she could see the outline of Weezl's gun on the table. Maybe it was just wishful thinking, but if it *was* the gun and she could get to it ...

She needed a distraction.

Then she realised that every so often she could see Weezl's face, which meant he could also see *her*. Zan and the guy had their backs to the TV, so Chita started to wave as frantically as she could without making the floorboards creak or sending gusts of disturbed air into the room. A couple of times Weezl seemed to be looking through her, but finally she saw his eyes widen, even in the dim reflection, and he started yelling.

'Help ... police ... someone call the police ... heeeeeelp!'

Chita hefted Weezl's golf club, which she had brought thinking she might have to use it to prevent him needlessly killing someone else, marched quickly into the room and hit Danny over the back of the head. Danny slumped over Weezl, and their combined weight sent the chair crashing backwards to the floor.

Zan stood, clearly too shocked to move. Chita knew she was quite a sight, wearing a black jumpsuit, orange bubble-perm wig, lime-green Skullcandy headphones and a surgical mask.

'The gun. It's on the table.' Weezl's voice was muffled by Danny's bulk on top of him.

Zan looked over at the Browning and Chita hefted the club. 'Don't even think about it.'

Without taking her eyes off Zan, she calmly walked over to the table and dropped the club. She picked up the gun and racked the slide, putting a bullet in the chamber, just like she's seen in a thousand movies. In fact, she had only ever seen this in movies, so Chita was pleasantly surprised when it seemed to have worked. Then she pointed the gun at Zan.

'Get your boyfriend off my boyfriend and cut him loose.'

'He's not my boyfriend.'

'Whatever.'

'I'm just saying ... he's a friend.'

'I don't care. Just move him.'

'I'm going to need help.'

'Fuck off, lady. You gonna get me in close and wrestle the gun off me? Really?'

Zan was momentarily lost for words; that was exactly what she had been planning to do.

'Great hair, by the way,' Zan said. 'You looking to get a rep – the wig killer?'

'Can't do beanies. My face is all the wrong shape.'

'Really? Show me.'

From her eyes, Zan could tell Chita was smiling ironically.

'Can you bitches stop yakking and get this fucker off me?' grunted Weezl.

'Grateful type, your boyfriend, eh?'

'Just fucking move him, right!' ordered Chita, her tone very much back to business. 'Don't forget, we have killed before.'

'Yeah ... by accident.'

'Honey, do I have your permission to shoot these fuckers?'

'Sure, babe. Just be careful how you do the guy. I don't want to get caught in the follow-through.'

Zan raised her hands in surrender then rolled Danny, who was out for the count, away from Weezl. Chita took a butterfly knife from her pocket, whirled it open and cut the tape around Weezl's wrists, handing him the gun before seeing to his ankles. Weezl gave the gun back to her as he struggled to his feet, rubbing his wrists to get some circulation going.

'Babe, go into the bedroom and see if you can find some pillows,' Weezl commanded as he gestured for the gun.

'Why?'

'Well, you know. The noise.'

Zan looked up. Shifting her weight as she prepared to dive at Chita. If they were going to start shooting anyway, she might as well go down fighting. Chita spotted it and waved the gun at her, shaking her head.

'I don't think so, sweetie,' Chita said to Zan, then turned to Weezl. 'I'm sorry, babe. There is no way I am going to let one fucked up beating turn into three murders.'

'Give me the gun, Cheee ...' his voice trailed off as he realised his mistake. 'There's no going back now.'

Oddly that was exactly what Chita had been thinking as she'd waited in the hallway. That would be certain when they had another two dead bodies on their hands. A wave of disappointment swept through her. It had been a fun ride, but Weezl was a one-man disaster zone. Who could guarantee that he wouldn't mess this or something else up and take her down with him? This might be Weezl's shot at gangster stardom but she had another life, a real life, waiting for her to pick up its threads.

'Give me the gun,' Weezl ordered. 'They've seen us. They can identify us.'

'They've seen *you*,' Chita corrected him, gesturing to her own elaborate cover-up. 'Did you tell them anything? Apart from the first part of my name, I mean?'

'Nope.'

'You sure?'

Weezl wondered how much Chita had heard before he'd spotted her. Time to change the subject.

'Gun ...' he said, holding out his hand.

'I don't think so,' she replied, in a 'whatever' tone.

'Give me the fucking gun. You are my bitch and you need to do as you are told,' he moved towards her but she raised the gun and pointed it towards him. Weezl paused, his voice changing to a low growl. 'Don't defy me in front of people.'

'I'm your what?'

'My ... um ... woman, is all.'

'I am not your bitch, you fucking moron,' Chita said, her fury palpable despite her mask. 'And even if you meant "woman" you don't get to tell me what to do. I mean, what the fuck are you? A wannabe crime writer who can't write a fucking email? A wannabe crim who couldn't take candy from a baby without accidentally killing it?'

'If you two want to continue this outside ...' Zan said from the floor, where she had Danny's head in her lap. 'Danny's breathing is really shallow and I need to get him to a hospital.'

'Shut the fuck up,' Chita snarled, then half-relaxed. 'Know what this is like? On TV?'

'*The Walking Dead?*' Zan offered.

'Cute,' said Chita. '*Celebrity Apprentice,*' she explained, sounding like a TV voiceover.

Zan was none the wiser and shook her head. She didn't watch much TV.

'*Three contestants are in the boardroom,*' Chita continued in her TV announcer voice. '*Tonight, one of them will be fired. Who will it be?*'

'Babe, we gotta waste these two and get going,' Weezl protested. 'Or ... or ... let's just tie them up and go.'

'Gook girl ...' Chita seemed oblivious to Weezl's words.

'Hey?!' protested Zan.

'You're a pain in the ass but, you know, gotta look after the sisters,'

Chita said. 'Lover boy there, also a pain but he takes care of his woman so that gets brownie points.'

She turned to Weezl and sighed deeply. He was the only person who could lead the police to her.

'Weezl, you fucked up a simple beating after I had done all the hard work. You ID'd your uncle – yes, I heard you blabbing about that – so you just lied to me too. You got yourself captured when you didn't even need to be here. And yet, and yet, I would have given you the benefit of the doubt. But then you disrespected me, in public, in the worst possible way. This is not East Compton, you are not a gangsta and I am not your bitch,' she said, raising the Browning.

'*Babe*,' Weezl hissed, still not quite appreciating his predicament. 'Stop pissing about …'

'Weezl, you're fired.'

And with that she popped the headphones over her ears and shot him twice: once in the eye, although aiming for his forehead, and once in the chest. It was only when Chita dropped the pistol on Weezl's body as she passed him on the way to the door that Zan noticed she had been wearing yellow rubber kitchen gloves.

'You take care now,' Chita said to Zan, whose ears were still ringing from the gunshots. 'Mixed-race relationships often don't end well.'

'He's not my boyfriend,' Zan shouted after Chita, then she scrabbled for her phone and dialled triple-zero.

'You have called an emergency number,' a recorded voice said. 'Please hold for an operator.'

'What? I'm in a fucking queue …'

'Emergency services,' said a different voice. 'Which service do you require?'

'Ahhh … police and ambulance,' Zan said, then looked from Danny to Weezl. 'Ambulance first … then … fuck it, just send everyone.'

It was after 3am and PBA was packing up, dispirited. A website called www.PBA_Save_Us.com had been set up where members nominated clubs and their patrons who deserved a faux-assassination. It was chancy at first: they could have been setting her up to be ambushed. But now there were so many 'nominations' she might as well have been picking her targets at random.

Even she had to admit this was all getting a bit out of hand. It had started when she was kept awake every weekend after midnight by the same yahoos hanging around the same pub doorways shouting, singing, fighting and dispersing when the cops arrived, only to return when they had gone.

She had fantasised about the paintball gun, then she'd spotted one in a second-hand shop and, well, it worked. And she loved it. But she couldn't do it from her own balcony every night, so she started to spread her wings.

Now here she was, perched on the top of an eight-storey block on the corner of Kings Cross Road and Ward Avenue, awaiting the arrival of a group of mostly British backpackers who, whenever they walked home after midnight, seemed intent on waking every local person who lived between their favourite pub and their hostel.

It was a perfect set-up. If the post on the website was right, they would come out of Surrey Street, cross the half-arsed park over the entrance to the Cross City Tunnel (vandalising a few trees as they went) then disappear down Kings Cross Road. Except they didn't. Two hours she had waited before she heard them one street over. It sounded like they were singing 'Screw you, PBA' to the tune of The Pet Shop Boys' 'Go West'.

PBA had just finished packing away her rifle when she heard what sounded like gunshots, two of them, coming from Surrey Street. Or maybe it was a car backfiring. Or firecrackers. She was trying to decide what she had heard and what to do about it when she saw a slim girl in

PERFECT CRIMINALS

a tight-fitting body suit, with a surgical mask over her face and orange Afro hair, walking briskly from the same direction as the shots.

PBA whipped out her mobile phone and started taking pictures at first, then video. When the girl was right beneath her, she removed the wig, the mask and a pair of rubber gloves and put them in a charity clothing bin. PBA never got a look at her face.

PBA thought about it. There was enough going on down there to justify a stop and search, but then questions would be asked. This was Kings Cross after all; people were expected to behave strangely. She had already deleted information about what the migrant bar worker had seen the night Marcus was killed. If that came out ... it's always the cover-up that gets you, not the crime.

By the time she looked over into the street her internal conflict was hypothetical. There were two very different sirens converging on the junction: police and ambulance. So it *had* been gunshots.

The girl had gone up the laneway behind the Crescent apartments. Time for PBA to disappear too.

———

About forty minutes later Zan was being helped into the back of an ambulance by a cop and a paramedic. Danny was already in the vehicle, still unconscious but stable according to the ambo, and in a moment of impressive clarity, Zan had managed to grab a bag of Danny's clothes that were sitting by the door to take to the hospital before the police ushered her out of the apartment. A journalist using his mobile phone as a voice recorder pushed past the paramedic who was closing the rear door.

'Miss ... miss!' the reporter said with the urgency of a pre-schooler needing a toilet break. Zan turned. 'Was there a terrorist element to the shooting? Or was it a drug deal gone wrong?'

Under the noise cloud of police radios, cops holding back the small pyjama- and bathrobe-clad crowd of neighbours, their animated chatter and the fact that her ears were even now still ringing from the gunshots, Zan misheard the question.

'Yes, I was terrified.'

'And the victim ... was he the terrorist?'

'What?' Zan replied, lacing the one word with as much contempt as she could muster. 'He was special forces, you clown,' she said, Danny being the victim in her mind.

As the policewoman climbed into the back of the ambulance with Zan and the ambo shut the doors, the reporter looked to see another gurney, this time carrying a body bag, emerging from the building. Shots fired, one injured, one dead. He scuttled off to his car where his laptop lay, already fired up and ready to file a bona fide scoop that would be online before the hour was out.

As for the 'interview' he would have to clean that up before he could sell it to radio. He could already hear the electronic dollars clicking into his bank account as he mentally composed the headline. At least some outsourced overseas subeditor would find it hard to change this one: 'SAS hero killed in terrorist revenge shooting'.

Hmmm, he thought, that *sings*.

15

DANNY WOKE slowly to one of those blinding headaches that makes you want to retreat to your worst nightmare. Even his. One eye open: more pain. Other eye: pain plus confusion. Where the hell am I?

'Would you like something for that?' asked a nurse with short red hair.

The room swam as she helped Danny to sit up and placed two pills in his hand.

'What are these?'

'They're for whatever ails you,' she grinned as she handed him a plastic beaker of water. 'Take them. They're just painkillers.'

Danny swallowed them greedily and finished off the water.

'You've missed breakfast,' she said as she placed a menu on the side table. 'Fill that in and you'll get some lunch. Probably.'

'So where am I?'

'St Anthony's Emergency.'

He looked up and as his eyes refocused he could see he was in a massive room with maybe twenty hospital beds radiating out from a central nurse's station. A few beds away a man was screaming.

'Give me something for the pain, you fucking bitch.'

'First you have to tell me what you've taken and how much,' said a voice that was more controlling than consoling. 'And I'd ask you to moderate your language.'

'Just give me a painkiller! Aaaaargh!'

'What happened? How did I get here?' Danny asked the nurse.

'You tell us,' said a voice next to his bed. Danny turned his head, sending another lightning bolt of pain through his cranium. It was Laura.

'Aaargh! Aaaaaaaaargh! I will fucking sue you. I'll have your fucking job!' roared the near neighbour.

The nurse rolled her eyes as she took Danny's blood pressure. 'Sorry. We get a lot of that.'

'Excuse me for a second,' Laura said and walked out past the curtains at the end of the bed.

'Who the fuck are you, bitch?' the voice demanded.

Laura's voice was too quiet to make out the words, but whatever she said had the desired effect. Silence, followed by a mumbled apology. She returned to her seat.

'Now where were we?'

'What did you say to him?' the nurse asked, looking up from filling in Danny's charts.

'I showed him my badge and told him that I had a cop van outside ready to take him to a place where they actually enjoy the sound of scumbag druggies screaming in pain. So he should just tell the nurse what she needed to know …'

'I must remember that line,' the nurse said and turned to Danny. 'Doctor will be along later to explain where we're at with you.'

'Why am I here?'

'Doctor will explain.' She smiled and moved to the next bed.

'Okay, Danny boy, let's get to the bottom of this …'

'Where's Zan?'

'At the bottom of this …'

'What?'

'She's helping us with our inquiries.' A thought. 'Did you know a man was shot dead in your apartment last night?'

'What?! When?!'

'About 3am we reckon. You were there.'

'I was?' Danny's headache was receding and memories were starting to surface.

'You were about a metre away from him – dead too, at first glance.'

Danny gingerly fingered the bandage covering the wound at the back of his head, a jolt of pain in response to the pressure confirming it wasn't there for show.

'The dead guy, was he Indian?' Danny asked tentatively.

'Something like that. Who was he?'

'No idea. Except I think he was the same one who did Marcus.'

'Probably. He left his golf club – a rescue three. You will have the name "Titleist" forever engraved on the back of your skull, if not your heart.'

'Jesus ...'

'So walk me through it, up to the point where chummy catches a bullet or you cop a golf club to the back of your neck, whichever comes first.'

'Is this an official interview?'

'No, this is a mate trying to find out what's going on. CID will be wanting a chat eventually. And a word of advice, don't skip the bit where the victim got the same tape wrapped around his wrists and ankles as was attached to the arms and legs of the chair.'

That brought Danny's memories into sharp focus and he told Laura the whole story, except the tape, in this version, was only used to restrain the assailant until the police could be called, not to facilitate the homemade facial waxing torture method. When he got to the part just before the lights went out, he remembered nothing.

'What about the girl?' Laura said.

'What girl?' Danny asked.

'Zan said you were hit by the dead guy's girlfriend,' Laura explained. 'Probably the same girl who was seen with Marcus.'

'Oh fuck,' Danny said. 'Of course. The golf-club killer's offsider.'

'Did you see her there?'

'No, but … fuck, this is basic stuff. You secure your perimeter, you *always* secure your perimeter. Shit.'

'Yeah okay, Rambo,' Laura chided. 'You didn't actually see her?'

Danny shook his head, and winced at the pain and nausea that induced. 'Why?'

A phalanx of young doctors, shepherded by a consultant and with a nurse on point, was heading their way.

'I'd better give these guys some room. I've probably said way too much already.'

'Laura … mate?'

'I gotta get back to work. By the way, Zan could really use a lawyer. Like, now!'

And with that, Laura pushed past the doctors and disappeared beyond the curtains.

A distinguished looking man picked up Danny's charts. He was greying at the temples and had half-moon spectacles that made him look older than he probably was – although he was no doubt the eldest of the lab-coated crew by at least a quarter century. 'Good morning, Mr ummm …' He glanced at the top sheet. 'Mr Clay. How are we feeling?'

'I'm feeling like shit but I really can't speak for you.'

The doctor handed the chart to one of the juniors.

'Note that the patient is delirious … delusion of humour.' Danny rolled his eyes. 'My name is Dr Truscott, senior registrar in Emergency, and we are going to do some tests on you to see if your brain is still talking to your body. Some may tickle, some may hurt, but trust me, after a head injury most pain is good.'

With that he lifted the end of the bedsheet and jabbed his pen into the sole of Danny's right foot.

'Yowww!' Danny yelled as he almost jumped out of the bed.

'Excellent start,' said Truscott with a supercilious smile. It was a smile that reminded Danny of Tony Cufflinks. And, as the examination progressed and Danny flinched and yelped in response to the doctors' overzealous probing, Tony and what he had to do with this violent interlude in Danny's life was his only thought – apart from Zan. Tony Cufflinks and Zan? What was the connection? Co-inky-fucking-dinky?

When the swarm of doctors and students had filled in their forms and moved on, Danny caught the eye of a passing nurse. 'Excuse me, could I use a phone?'

'I think there's one in your locker.'

Danny looked confused.

'It's your phone … your friend brought it with your stuff. Asian girl, very cute,' the nurse said, smiling with her eyes. 'She brought you a change of clothes because the police took what you were wearing.'

'How long have I been here?'

'About ten hours.' She glanced at the clipboard on the end of the bed. 'Twelve according to your chart. We sedated you to let any swelling on your brain die down,' she added as she took a plastic spring-shaped band from around Danny's wrist. It had a locker key attached. She opened the cabinet beside his bed and pulled out a bundle of clothes as well as Danny's mobile. He groaned.

'Need a charger?' she asked.

'Nope,' Danny replied, holding one up from the pile in front of him. Zan was smart with technology. 'It's just these clothes. I had put them aside for the charity bin.'

'Don't you think the homeless have enough problems?' the nurse asked as she held a garish Hawaiian shirt up to the light and winced.

But Danny was already scrolling through the contacts on his phone.

16

ZAN LOOKED at the mirror on the wall of the interview room. It was a blessed relief from the regurgitated pea soup colours on the other three walls, even if she strongly and rightly suspected it concealed an observation room. She made a face at the mirror, and another for the camera tucked into the corner near the ceiling. She was bored.

The door opened and a chubby, red-faced man in his forties whose wispy hair had taken early retirement walked in, followed by a uniformed female officer who immediately sat in the corner and stared at Zan impassively.

'How's Danny?' Zan said before the door had closed.

The man grunted as he shuffled through the folders. 'Sitting up and taking nourishment, by all accounts.'

'I've been here more than four hours,' Zan said, standing up and taking her jacket off the back of her chair. 'So you have to charge me or let me go.'

'No, you haven't, and no, I don't,' the man said, his finger poised over the digital voice recorder.

'I got here about four this morning. It's now 10am. I know my rights.'

'Like most people who say that, you clearly don't. Your four hours does not include time-outs for things like getting here, being processed, forensic tests, calling your lawyer …'

'I don't have a lawyer, so that doesn't play.'

The man sighed. 'I can always apply for another four.'

'Are you going to?'

'Depends how helpful you are in the next ten minutes. Now, please sit down.'

He pressed the button and the machine beeped a little longer than really necessary. 'Interview commencing at …' He glanced at his watch. 'Ten-eleven am. Present are myself, detective inspector Bill McCue, and …' He looked at the female cop.

'Senior constable Karen Pratt,' she said, leaning forward slightly to make sure her voice was picked up.

'And …?' said McCue to Zan. 'For the tape.'

'It's not a tape,' Zan said.

'What?'

'It's not a tape,' she repeated. 'It's a solid state digital recorder. No moving parts. No tape.'

McCue sighed the sigh of a man who did not need any extraneous shit in an already shitty day. 'For the digital recorder, please,' he said through the thinnest of smiles.

'Xanthe Tran,' Zan said. 'People call me Zan.'

'Zan Tran,' said McCue, as if testing it out. Pratt snorted, but her face returned to its stony default when Zan and McCue both glared at her.

'You've had an eventful couple of weeks,' said McCue as he opened a folder.

'You think?' said Zan. 'Let me see, two good friends have died in horrible circumstances, I have been attacked outside my home, and last night the same psycho broke into the place I was staying, with a gun, and then his fucking nutbag girlfriend turned up, bashed my best friend in the whole world senseless – literally – and then shot her boyfriend in front of me.'

'So you said in your statement.' He looked at her slightly askance. 'Forgive me, but you seem very calm.'

'I'm sorry, Detective Inspector, what is the appropriate response?

Slobbering sobs, rigid terror, catatonic non-communication? Is there a pamphlet you could point me to?' They say sarcasm is the lowest form of wit, but coming from Zan, only the witless would agree. 'You know there's a word to describe me. I'll give you a clue. It starts with V.'

'Vietnamese?' McCue was no slouch in the sarcasm department either.

'Victim. Victim, you fucking moron.'

It was only when McCue asked her to sit down that Zan realised she had been standing, leaning against the table and gripping its edge so hard her knuckles were nearly visible under her skin.

'Okay, Xanthe, why did you tell the media that Danny was an ex-SAS man and he had been shot by a terrorist?'

'I didn't,' Zan replied, trying to piece together the fragments of what she had said.

'Not according to the *Daily Mail Online*, the *Telegraph*, the *Herald* ...' advised McCue as he leafed thorough printouts of news stories.

'Where did they get that shit from?' Zan said, then immediately remembered. 'Oh ...'

'And by the way, this media attention prompted a phone call from the Hahn family,' McCue continued.

Zan tried to cover her surprise but she could feel her cheeks reddening.

'You left that incident out of your rundown of your recent activities. Did you forget that an old man died in a lift of which you were the only other occupant?'

'Slipped my mind,' said Zan, not even convincing herself.

'Just like it slipped your mind to mention that your mother and Mr Hahn were involved in a long-running legal dispute,' said McCue. 'Something to do with the body corporate in their building.'

Zan's expression was concern trying to mask itself as confusion.

'*I don't have time for stupid rules,*' McCue read from a document. '*I've had a quadruple bypass. I get what I want, when I want it, and pity anyone who tries to stop me.*' He looked up from the papers. 'Does that sound familiar to you, Zan?'

Zan shrugged. Alan Hahn had wanted to enclose a balcony on the penthouse apartment of the stylish, modern building where both he and Zan's mother lived. Her mother had roused other residents to block his plan, saying it would be an act of architectural vandalism. 'Vandalism' was the word with which Hahn's obscenely remunerated special counsel was slowly beating her to death in a Supreme Court defamation action. Hahn would probably lose, but by then Zan's mother would be bankrupt. The law favours the rich over the right.

'According to this deposition, you were a witness to that statement by Mr Hahn.'

'So?'

'So you knew Mr Hahn had a weak heart.'

'So?' Zan asked, her temper rising. 'You know there's security footage of me trying to save him?'

'Yes,' McCue nodded. 'From the lobby, but not in the lift.'

McCue turned another page in the file.

'Can we just check the detail on the alleged assailant, please?' McCue continued. 'This "nutbag girlfriend" that you told the responding officer about ... orange bubble perm hair?'

'A wig.'

He looked at the paper and nodded. 'Surgical mask?'

'Like Japanese tourists wear.'

'Yoga pants?' he asked sceptically.

'Lululemon. They're the best, although the style she had is too high-cut for me.'

'You seem very sure.'

'I know clothes. The jacket was Running Bare, League of Her Own, with the grey spots on the sleeves. The bitch has taste ... and money.'

'Anything else?' McCue had his pen poised expectantly.

'Marigolds.'

'I'm sorry?'

'Yellow kitchen gloves. She was wearing Marigolds, but the weirdest thing was her playing out this TV reality show thing: "You're crap, you're crap, you're fired." *Bang bang.* Now can I go? Are we done here?'

'Ms Tran, in the past two weeks there have been two sudden deaths at which you have been the only conscious witness,' McCue said quietly. 'How do you think that looks?'

Zan's face crumpled slightly as she absorbed the simple logic behind the question. There was a sharp knock on the door, it opened and Laura Revell's face appeared.

'Sorry to interrupt, boss, but …'

The door was pushed much further open and a dapper middle-aged man shimmied past Laura and into the room.

'Hope I'm interrupting something important,' sang the roundish face, with thick, dark-framed glasses. The visitor was a trim though not quite slim late-middle-aged gentleman in an Armani suit, highly polished Oxfords and a bow tie that was trying desperately to be unpretentious.

'Excuse me, who the hell are you?' McCue demanded.

'Stephen Godman,' he said, handing him and Zan a card each. 'Ms Tran's lawyer.'

'No, you're not,' Zan protested, reading the card.

'Trust me, I am,' Godman replied. 'Danny sent me. Called me from his sickbed, no less. You must be very important.'

He twirled rather than turned to McCue.

'Now, I think your time is up.'

'I'll decide that,' he replied.

'Let me see, was there any gunshot residue on my client's hands?'

'No, but –'

'Any of my client's fingerprints on the murder weapon?'

McCue shook his head.

'Or on the golf club?' Godman adopted a smug little pose with a thin smile to add to the infuriation factor. He was smart, assertive, competent and as gay as a Judy Garland karaoke night.

McCue started gathering up his notes and pressed the stop button on the recorder. This was clearly over.

'We might need to talk to Xanthe again –'

'My number's on the card,' Godman said.

Zan took a crumpled piece of till roll from her pocket and tossed it on the table.

'You know they're from Melbourne, don't you? The couple?'

McCue, the uniformed cop and Laura looked at her blankly.

'Please ...' Godman sighed.

'We found it in the dead guy's pocket.'

'Careful ...' whispered Godman.

'Before he got shot. When we were searching him for weapons. It's a receipt from a roadhouse in Glenrowan, night before last.'

McCue lifted the receipt with the end of his pen and looked at the female cop in the hope she had an evidence bag.

'And if you want to find out who the bloke was, try calling sports stores in Melbourne and asking if anyone recently bought a full Asics tracksuit, Yankees cap and a golf club. According to Danny, you'll probably get a result. He's quite the detective.'

'Okay, Zan, that's enough for now,' Godman said as he ushered Zan into the corridor.

'Thanks.' Zan smiled with genuine relief as the interview room closed behind them. 'How much is this costing me?'

'It's a favour for Danny.' Godman smiled. 'And I haven't had so much fun in ages.'

Zan looked at his card. 'It says here you're a strata lawyer. Isn't that apartments and stuff?'

'I met Danny when he was buying the flat next to yours. But I'm spreading my wings,' he said with a flourish that was a sequin away from jazz hands. 'Oh, by the way, you'd better brace yourself. There are TV news crews outside.'

'Really?'

'Apparently some idiot told the media that the deceased was killed in a terror revenge attack against an ex-SAS man.'

'Oops.' Zan caught Godman's accusing look. 'Oh well, maybe it will put them off the scent.'

'Off the scent?' Godman laughed. 'That's blood in the water.' And he gently steered Zan through the baying picket line of cameras and microphones.

17

BACK HOME, having braved the minor media gauntlet, Zan was on her computer, checking the breaking news to see how much damage she had done. All the online versions of newspapers were running with variations on the 'SAS man foils terror revenge attack' angle. At least they had moved on from the idea that Danny had died in the shooting. There was a knock on her door.

She looked out the window onto the street. A bored-looking uniformed cop, a photographer and a video cameraman were chatting amiably. A cluster of people she half-recognised as neighbours had run out of speculations and were just staring up at the windows. One of them, a ridiculously thin woman dressed from neck to ankle in black gym gear, saw her and waved, then stopped guiltily and looked around as if she might have just become an accessory to a crime. In Sydney's Kings Cross, no bystander is entirely innocent.

There was another knock, and Zan opened the door cautiously. Danny was leaning against the jamb, the bandage around his head and the garish change of clothes she had left for him making him look like a reject from the E Street Band.

'Aren't you going to invite me in?' He gestured to the 'scene of crime' tape barring the door to his own flat.

Zan threw herself at Danny, hugging him, kissing his face and saying 'Sorry, I am so sorry!' over and over as her tears wet both their cheeks. Then, just as suddenly, she remembered herself, pushed Danny away and walked into her flat, leaving the door open for him to follow.

So there are bells that *can* be un-rung, Danny thought but said nothing.

Zan's flat was the 'after' to Danny's flat's 'before' in an extreme makeover. Surfaces were uncluttered and clean. The furniture, mostly white leather, glass or stainless steel, was sparse but functional and, it seemed, precisely positioned. A large computer screen on a small workstation took up one corner and there was no TV.

The only decorations, on one wall, were four framed prints, replicas of revolutionary posters on handmade paper, all showing Vietnamese women defiantly brandishing AK47s. Zan had bought them from a small shop in Hanoi on her last visit 'home'. 'Women with guns and no babies,' she had told the assistant, who efficiently led her to one pile of posters, among dozens, that fitted her specifications precisely. In a perfect illustration of how Western capitalism had outstripped the communist victors of that conflict, when she got them back to Sydney, the posters had cost 20 times as much to frame as she'd paid to liberate them from the little shop of pop propaganda, even at tourist prices.

'Coffee?' Zan asked, popping her head around from her equally pragmatic kitchen.

'No,' Danny answered, pointing to his head. 'Still a bit woozy.'

He scratched under the bandage and, frustrated, started unwrapping it.

'Here, let me do that,' Zan said, guiding him to a chair. She checked the bandage to make sure it was just holding padding onto the dressing on the back of Danny's head, then carefully started to unwind it.

'Shouldn't you still be in hospital?' she asked.

'People die in hospital,' he said, smiling weakly. 'It's only a mild concussion. They can't wait to get you out before you catch something worse than you came in with.'

The last wrap of bandage came off to reveal a surgical bandaid sitting in a square of trimmed hair.

'Hope that grows back,' she said, 'or you're going to look like a cyborg. Can I get you anything? Water?'

Danny shook his head and immediately regretted it as the room briefly swum before his eyes. Zan sat on her chrome and leather sofa, an awkward distance away considering her recent show of affection – or maybe because of it.

'Your lawyer friend was a major help,' she said. Danny looked at her to see if she was being sarcastic. 'No, really,' she continued. 'That DI McCue is a real hard-arse.'

'Just doing his job, I guess,' Danny said. 'The question is, what are *we* doing?'

It was Zan's turn to shake her head.

'A couple of days ago, we were just stumbling around, making an average mess of our lives, but not so much that we couldn't survive,' Danny said. 'And now we have, what, three dead bodies?'

'Four,' Zan corrected him, and immediately wished she hadn't.

'Yeah, we'll get to that,' Danny said grimly. 'Firstly, Bryan kills himself and leaves no suicide note. I mean Bryan, of all people, would have said something funny and profound, especially if he was thinking of topping himself.'

'He did choose a fairly theatrical exit,' ventured Zan.

Danny shrugged his wry agreement. 'Then Marcus gets clubbed to death –'

'Literally.'

'Then the guy who did it gets shot in my house by a person only you have seen.'

'Meaning?' If Zan had had hackles, they'd have been bristling through her retro *Never Mind the Bollocks* ... T-shirt.

'Meaning there have been two deaths in the past week at which you were the only witness.'

'What?' Her voice filled with outrage and betrayal.

'It's a fact, Zan. Weezl and Hahn. How do you think that looks?'

'It looks like bad luck to me. How does it look to you?'

Danny spread his hands in that gesture that says, *try to see things from my perspective* but means, to the other person, *I don't believe you.*

'Fuck you, Danny.'

'I'm just saying, all I know for sure is that you didn't bash me over the head.'

Zan thought and swallowed for a moment, sucking in a deep breath to calm herself.

'I think you should go.'

'Zan? We both know exactly what that looks like. Let's be honest with each other. We owe each other that much, at least.'

'I've got nothing to say to you. Go and say what you've got to say to your lawyer boyfriend. Or Laura.'

She stomped to her front door and held it open. Danny could see one end of the crime scene tape across his own door. No chance of a change of clothes. He sighed, gathered up his jacket, and walked out to the hall.

'Go back to the hospital. Get your head examined,' she said, before slamming her front door closed.

Danny was halfway down the entrance hall before he remembered the gawk squad outside. He decided to leave the way he'd come in, through the backyard and across the wall before ducking along a service lane – built for access by 'night soil' collectors in the days before sewerage – and out into a street at the other end of the block. As he crossed, using a turning car as a shield, he glanced across its roof to confirm that his flat was still under siege.

Cutting back up onto Victoria Street, Danny took his phone out and started searching again. He found Tony's number just as he reached the Latteria, a cafe as thin as a drunk's excuses and slotted between a hairdressers and Coluzzi's coffee bar, which had been there since Moses put a centre parting in the Red Sea. Danny sat precariously on a narrow stool. The Indian waiter acknowledged him and took his order – long black with a shot of hot milk on the side – with a single nod.

Danny pressed call and the number rang twice before a gruff voice, thick with last night's olive oil and chianti, came on the line.

'Clay?'

'Hi, Tony, I was just …'

'You still have my number? And you are using it?'

'Sorry, Tony, I just need …'

'You need to get off the fucking phone, Clay. Somebody just got shot dead in your apartment and you are calling me on an open line? Is someone recording this? Are you?'

'Tony. Those cities you named. In Europe … they all have movie festivals …'

But there was a click and the line went dead. Danny stared at his smartphone, as if it might be smart enough to explain why Tony Cufflinks had just hung up on him, but too smart to do so. The phone rang. Danny smiled; Tony must have had second thoughts. But it was Rob.

'Danny. Mate. How are you?'

'Meet me at Lowes on George Street in about twenty minutes,' Danny said, foregoing any niceties.

'Lowes? I can't be seen at Lowes,' Rob protested.

'Bring your credit card,' Danny added, before hanging up.

―

Laura checked the coding and signatures for the fourth time. She leaned back in her chair and sighed, then dialled Danny's number.

'Hi, Dan, it's Laura,' she said when Danny picked up. 'I've got some good news and some bad news.'

'Give me the good news first, then I'll decide if I can handle the bad.'

'I've got some video footage and stills here that pretty much confirm what Zan said about the shooter.' She was looking at her computer screen displaying badly lit images of Chita, walking from Surrey Street towards the camera.

'Pictures? Where did you get them?'

Laura clicked onto a video of Chita, above and from the back, taking off her wig to reveal short blonde hair, removing the kitchen gloves and stashing them in a recycling bin.

'The Paintball Assassin website. You heard of him?' Laura clicked another couple of keys and a larger, top-down image filled the screen.

'The guy who shoots drunks from rooftops?' asked Danny.

'That's the one. He has his own fansite now, but they say they have no idea who uploaded these videos. They probably wouldn't tell us even if they did know.'

'So, does this let Zan off the hook?' Danny asked.

'It won't do her any harm, that's for sure,' Laura said.

'Okay, what's the bad news?'

'Listen, I ran some checks on Bryan Jones's laptop.'

'Bryan's computer? Why?'

'It's one of those things,' Laura said. 'You use a cop's gun to shoot yourself and they turn over every possible lead trying to prove there was a connection, just so they can say for sure that there wasn't.'

'And?'

'They picked up the laptop the other day and asked me to see if I could find any connection between Bryan and the cop whose gun he used.'

'And?' Danny said again, a little more insistently this time.

Laura tapped away again and a report came up on the screen. She looked at it briefly to remind herself, then grimaced.

'And?' Danny prompted.

'Okay, most of it was just the usual stuff: emails, scripts – lots of them, most of them old and in several versions – what looked like a half-finished novel ...'

'But?'

'Well, there are two things that stick out. First, there was a locked section on the hard drive that took me about ten minutes to crack open.'

'Only ten minutes?'

'That's quite long, actually, with the software we have. Anyway, it had some pretty dodgy stuff in it.'

'What kind of dodgy?'

'I would call it ... Lolita porn.'

'Oh God!' Danny exclaimed, shaking his head. 'Kiddy porn?'

'Yes and no,' Laura ventured. 'Pictures of girls who looked a bit too young to be in pictures like that. But no actual sex. And young but not *kids,* if you get my drift.'

'Well, that's something,' Danny said. 'So this stuff wasn't actually illegal, right?'

'Oh, I wouldn't go that far,' Laura said, grimacing. 'Some places he'd be in jail for it, and on a sex offenders list.'

'Okay,' said Danny, expecting the worst. 'What else?'

'That was in a locked and heavily secured file. But there was also an open file with some really nasty kiddy porn images in it. I mean, really, really nasty.'

That information rocked Danny a little, then he saw where this was leading.

'You're wondering why he would lock the less awful stuff away and have the other, really bad stuff where anyone could find it?'

'Exactly,' Laura replied. 'Also, judging by the dates, all the archived stuff had been collected over several years. The folder containing the really ugly stuff was created two nights before he died.'

There was an aching silence as Danny calculated the possibilities.

'Got any thoughts?' Laura asked, mostly to check Danny was still there.

'Someone puts the squeeze on Bryan, loads kiddy porn onto his computer, with a plan to blackmail him?' Danny offered.

'Possible,' Laura concurred. 'In fact, if you knew how easy it was to put porn on someone's computer without their knowledge you'd never go on the internet again.'

'But Bryan is already into that stuff, thinks he's been sprung and takes the easy way out?' Danny said. 'Is that too far-fetched?'

'Sounds perfectly logical to me.'

'So, we're dealing with a blackmailer?' Danny suggested.

'It all fits,' Laura replied.

'What are you going to do with the computer?'

'I'm going to copy all the family pictures and videos onto a portable hard drive and give that to his wife,' Laura said. 'Then I'm going to tear the hard drive apart looking for something that will point us in the direction of who's behind all this.'

'Tony Cufflinks?' Danny suggested.

'Not his style,' Laura said after a moment's hesitation. 'Bryan didn't have the kind of money that Tony goes after.'

'Okay, keep me posted,' Danny said. 'And thanks.'

'I have you on speed dial,' Laura said as she hung up.

—

They say one difference between men and women is that if a woman turned up at a party and there was another one there in a similar dress, both would go home and change. If a guy turned up at a party and there were three other men in identical clothes, he'd relax and feel he's in the right place. Lowes clothing chain was where those guys would shop.

Football shirts, work shorts, T-shirts and, in winter, checked flannel shirts all in sizes that soar to XXXL and beyond. This was a shop for working men, as well as those who aspired to at least look like they occasionally got their hands dirty. The true uniform of the Australian male could be found here: Blundstone boots, stubby shorts, 'wife-beater' singlets and bucket hats – all sizes of beer gut accommodated.

Danny was standing pale-faced between the work socks and sensible underpants stalls in the George Street outlet when Rob found him. Laura had just given him the good news about the video of the assailant and the very bad news about Bryan. He owed an apology to Zan.

Rob got his attention, hissing like a small-time drug dealer as he snuck between racks of no-name polo shirts and cargo pants.

'Danny! Can we go somewhere less working class?'

'Hi, Rob,' Danny replied, smiling at Rob's furtive snobbery. 'I need to buy some clothes. My flat is off-limits and Zan grabbed the first things she could find.' He stepped out from behind the sock stand to reveal the eclectic mix of styles and colours Zan had chosen for him.

Rob winced. 'Point taken.'

Danny hefted a pile of clothes he had already chosen and made his way to the check-out. The woman behind the till looked at him slightly askance in that *I know you from somewhere* way. Danny smiled but Rob ignored her as she returned to the customer ahead of them in the queue, a man buying a multipack of blue vests and several pairs of work shorts.

'Do you want to hear the good news or the very good news?' Rob asked.

'Plenty of both would be ideal.'

'Okay, you are hot. Trending like a Kardashian butt shot on the internet, thanks to the SAS thing.'

'I'm not SAS.'

'Whatever. Now *60 Minutes* and *Sunday* are both offering serious money for an exclusive.'

'On what?'

'On "how I killed a terrorist and saved Sydney" yadda, yadda.'

'But I didn't and he wasn't.'

'Details, my boy. Mere details. They'll fill in any gaps in the story.'

'And that's supposed to reassure me?' Danny protested. 'One of them will make shit up, and the one that doesn't get the story will tear me apart – and rightly so because it's made up.'

'All publicity is good publicity.'

'Tell that to Louis C.K.'

Rob realised this wasn't getting the unfettered enthusiasm he had been hoping for, so he changed tack.

'Okay. You're right. Why sweat the small stuff when your future is in … *drrrrrrrrr*.' Rob mimed a drum roll.

'A circus?'

'Hollywood, my friend. Glitter city. Los Angeles. The big apple.'

'I think that's New York.'

'Yeah, well, your biggest fan, Jensen Forbes …'

'The actor? And weren't you supposed to be setting up a meeting?'

'That's the one. Young Jensen is going to Hollywood and he wants to take your show.'

'Really?'

'The kid loves you. He wants to be you … or something. And when he read about how you killed that terrorist –'

Danny was about to correct him but was silenced by Rob's raised finger.

'He called me today. He has just been offered a First Class ticket to La-La Land. Now he wants to take you along for the ride.'

'As what?'

'I don't know. His writer, his muse, his minder … his knob polisher. I don't care,' Rob said. 'Either way, this is the break you've been looking for.'

'No, it isn't.'

'Okay, it's the break *I've* been looking for,' Rob said with unaccustomed honesty. 'Just go there, be brilliant, spend their money and get away from all this other shit.'

The check-out woman raised an eyebrow just as Danny spotted a blue workman's coverall, high-vis jacket and a hard hat on nearby racks and tossed them onto the pile of clothes. He added a beanie, not just because it would cover his injury, but because a hat is one of the simplest, most effective ways of disguising yourself. People who know you well will pass you in the street when you wear a hat they haven't seen before.

'I love this "everyman" look you're going for,' Rob said nodding at the pile of clothes as he passed over his credit card. 'But if you are trying to go unnoticed, the hi-vis vest and hard-hat ain't gonna help ... unless you're joining the Village People.'

Zan was pale, wringing her fingers. Laura had just called her about a couple of 'developments' in her cases. Firstly, the police now had evidence that backed up her story about the girl in the orange wig and rubber gloves, which they had retrieved from a wheelie bin in a lane near her flat. There was gunshot residue all over the items, and if they ever did arrest a suspect, they would probably have good DNA samples with which to make a match.

Thanks to Zan, the shooting victim had been traced to a service station near Glenrowan. Security video footage, already on police computers, showed him and his girlfriend. She may or may not have been the girl in the orange wig, but the complete lack of any images of her face suggested she might have spotted the cameras and actively avoided their gaze. This 'nutbag' was turning out to be a smart cookie.

The shooting victim had been identified thanks to pictures run in Melbourne newspapers and on TV news. And thanks to the recovered golf club, he was now the prime suspect for the fatal attack on Marcus.

'Thanks for letting me know,' Zan had said. 'I appreciate it.'

'There's something else,' Laura said, trying not to overdramatise the moment but failing. 'The Hahn family's lawyer are asking for a forensic autopsy on his remains.'

'Forensic?' Zan protested. 'Are you … I mean, can you?'

'Ordinarily, under the circumstances, we would say no,' Laura said.

'But?'

'But DI McCue is getting pressure from the powers that be,' she explained. 'Hahn was connected.'

'Tell me about it.'

'And, hey, you didn't hear this from me, okay?'

In the ten minutes since Laura had hung up, Zan had canvassed every catastrophic possibility out of this latest development. She had gone from anger and fear to frustration, and now she was feeling very lonely and wondering if she had been too harsh with Danny. She thumbed his picture on her phone and thought for just a second before she hit 'dial'.

18

DANNY'S PHONE buzzed in his pocket just as he reached the reception desk of the Perfumed Garden brothel on Victoria Street. In what was once known as the 'Paris end' of Kings Cross, the tree-canopied avenue had almost survived being maimed by new apartment blocks and the creeping backpackerisation of the remaining buildings. A plaque set in the sidewalk reminded passers-by of Juanita Neilsen, a local woman who had disappeared after proving a little too successful in campaigning against high-rise developers' destruction of rows of terraced houses. Reputedly, she had been accidentally shot while being threatened by a butter-fingered thug and her body was now entombed in the foundations of one of the tower blocks she so loathed.

But thanks to her, the street was still a mixture of three-storey townhouses and only the occasional small apartment block – notwithstanding the cluster of multi-storey monsters that crowded together at its most northerly point. Between them and the actual Cross, there was a scattering of cafes, restaurants – both cheap and classy – convenience stores, backpacker hostels, brothels, bars, massage parlours – both legit and less so – and pizza and Thai takeaways. One end of the street housed the commuter railway station, the other a Catholic girls' school. The whole world was in between.

The Perfumed Garden was tucked back off the street, its entrance reachable only via a bush-lined pathway and stone steps. It had been, since ending its original function as a two-storey secluded dwelling, a gourmet restaurant, a Thai massage day spa, and a less salubrious rub'n'tug' parlour, it was now a fully-fledged brothel – thanks to its previous proprietors' misconceived determination not to pay any tithe to members of the local criminal fraternity, specifically Jackie Jazz. Restitution, when it was demanded, was complete and absolute, and the property was now 'managed' by Tony Cufflinks in a newly forged arrangement with the Jazzman.

It had taken very little in the way of detective work for Danny to establish that Tony was inside. Both his Merc and its driver were fairly obvious. Danny ducked behind one of the street's many giant fig trees and clambered into the coverall, ditching the high-vis jacket and hard-hat but hefting a toolbox purchased en route, into which he had placed a brick to give it authentic weight. Not earning so much as a glance from Tony's driver, who was peering in puzzlement at his mobile phone as if he had just seen the alphabet for the first time, Danny marched up the steps. He ignored both the vibration in his pocket and the buzz surging through his veins as he spoke calmly to the receptionist, a small, busty bottle-blonde in a tight leopard-print blouse.

'Is Tony here?'

'Tony who? I don't know any Tonys.'

'Tony Cufflinks? Heard of him?'

The receptionist rolled her eyes.

'He's very busy,' she mumbled and started intently reading a duty roster.

'That's okay. I'm here about the security system,' Danny said with a bored sigh.

'Really?' she replied. 'Nobody told me there was a problem.'

'Happened last night,' Danny said, correctly assuming the fifty-something garishly dressed gatekeeper was on the day shift. 'Tony asked me to check.'

Her pursed lips suggested she was unconvinced.

'Like I said, Tony's in a meeting right now ...'

'Thing is, I need to get onto this right away,' Danny replied as he slipped his Samsung out of his inside pocket. 'Before you get too busy.' Danny switched on the phone and showed her the screen. It was an email he had sent himself earlier.

Jeff,

Urgent job. Can you check the security cameras at the Garden? I think some fucker has hacked into them. ASAP, mate.

Tony.

The woman donned her reading glasses, which hung on a cord around her neck, and peered at the screen. She looked up. 'And you're Jeff?'

'The one and only.'

'Never seen you before.'

'Never been here before – for either business or pleasure. Just got this contract. Keen to make a good impression.' He smiled. 'You know how it is.'

She did, and in ways Danny preferred not to imagine. She nodded towards a door and pressed a buzzer to unlock it.

'Any rooms I should avoid?'

'We're quiet, so just the spa suite on the top floor. Tony is ... um ... "interviewing" a couple of new girls.' Her eyebrows supplied the quote marks.

'Keen to make a good impression, huh?'

'Well if they're not, now's the time to find out,' she said with a hint of a snort.

Danny laughed and pushed the door open.

'The spa suite's right at the back, upstairs. You'll hear it before you see it.'

Danny smiled his thanks and exited to the corridor. The subdued lighting seemed intended to mask the faded décor rather than enhance the ambience. The carpet may have once been luxuriant, but too many impossibly high heels and guiltily shuffled shoes had compressed the pile and worn patches at the doorways.

Female voices enjoying a good-natured argument drew him to an open door. Two women were trying to identify the professional footballer who had disgraced himself just the previous weekend, but not in ways he'd hoped.

'What a tool,' one voice said. 'Like, if you can't get it up for one girl, how are you going to get it up for three?'

'I know the guy you mean,' another, more mature voice replied. 'He's an islander ... or a Kiwi ... heaps of tatts.'

'All ink but no lead in his pencil.'

Danny followed the shrieks of laughter. Inside were two mostly naked young women, one of whom, a skinny brunette with short hair, pulled her towelling bathrobe around her in a touching display of modesty. She was about twenty years old, with fine features that hadn't yet been hardened by her career choice.

'Can I help you?' she asked in a tone that was friendly but professional.

Her colleague, who could have been aged anywhere between twenty-five and thirty-five, had one foot up on a stool while she used a safety razor to carefully trim her pubic hair into what looked like a lightning bolt. She looked up briefly but resumed her task with nonchalance. Like the other girl, she was thin, although with fewer ribs showing, and a skimpy silk dressing gown hung from her shoulders. Her breasts, which she didn't bother to cover up, were also smaller than the stereotyped image of the hooker, although that's undoubtedly what she was. The scene was like a sad parody of a Degas painting.

Danny quickly took in the room, which had an odd familiarity about it. Clothes hung on racks or were draped over the back of chairs, ready for the next costume change – although the majority of the garments were underwear of one sort or another. A Formica worktop was strewn with cosmetics, perfume bottles, and a range of brushes for face powder, eyeliner and hair. Two big mirrors with bare bulbs around them on the wall behind made the space look like what it was: a place where performers got ready for the next show. In that respect, if no other, it was home turf for Danny.

However, on further appraisal, this was clearly no theatre dressing room. That half of the light bulbs around the mirrors were spent or missing wasn't that unusual, but the stack of unopened tissue boxes and the note stuck to one of the mirrors reading 'Condom and lube packs available at reception' was. A menu taped to the flaking paint on the wall listed sexual services and what should be charged for them. It took Danny a moment to work out the difference between 'oral wc' and 'oral w/oc', but the latter being flagged 'Not approved' gave a clue. The words 'No undercutting' were underlined at the bottom of the list. In this theatre, most of the shows were clearly one-on-one, and the action was a mixture of tried and tested routines and improvisation. But every story had a happy ending. Danny realised the first girl was still staring at him inquisitively.

'Maintenance,' he said hurriedly.

'Maintenance? Hey, did you bring child support from my old man?' the pube shaver asked, looking up with an infectious smile.

'Is it the flush on our toilet?' the first girl asked. 'It's still not working.'

'Electrical,' Danny added with an apologetic shrug.

'Great, you got any batteries for my vibrator?' the older woman said, laughing.

Danny made a show of looking at the ceiling and around the cornices. 'No cameras in here?'

'Fucking better not be,' she replied, following his eye line upwards.

'No worries, just checking.'

'Do I know you?' she asked.

'Not professionally,' Danny said defensively, as it occurred to him that however far down the food chain sex workers may be, the men (and women) who used them, abused them and exploited them, were even lower.

'No?' she said, looking him up and down with a lasciviousness normally reserved for appraisals in the opposite direction. 'Shame. Jeez, I'd even give you a discount.'

'No undercutting!' Danny warned, wagging a finger. The woman laughed. Danny noticed a hairdryer on the dressing table.

'You using this?' he asked, picking it up.

They both shook their heads.

'Just a routine safety check,' he explained as he headed for the door. 'I'll have it back with you soon as …'

The older woman shrugged then yelped as she nicked her skin with the razor.

As he exited, Danny heard the younger woman murmur that he looked like the SAS guy who had killed the terrorist. The other woman said if he was, she'd have given him a freebie, let alone a discount. They both laughed.

―

At precisely the same moment, almost 1000 kilometres away in Brisbane, Maria Cietta DiLivio knocked on the door of Professor Alwyn Sylvester's office on the third floor of the Queensland Arts and Music College (Qamco, to its students). The relatively modern building looked like an office block that had known better times – which in truth was exactly what it was. There may have been money to be made in selling education in South-East Asia, but that was if you were offering degrees in commerce or computer skills, not composition, conducting and concert piano.

Sylvester looked up and called out, 'En-ter,' in descending E to C-sharp. Maria walked in wearing a skirt that would have been too short for school but had to be tolerated by those educating the 'young ladies' of the college. Accordingly, he tried not to notice that her otherwise plain white blouse was a little too tight over what was clearly a black lacy bra. She seemed to have filled out since he last saw her, and in all the best places.

The crowning glory was her long, lustrous black hair which he had advised her to keep in anticipation of the day when it swayed and flared as it caught the spotlights during her cello solos. It could be her weapon and her shield, he'd told her. Her signature, her trademark, her 'USP' – but to have a unique selling point you first need something to sell, and that required a few more years of dedication, study and practice.

'I see you have conquered your issue with punctuality,' Sylvester said with a genuinely warm smile, gesturing to the empty chair across his desk. Slim and stretched, Sylvester had pickpocket fingers and arms too long for his tweed sleeves. His office was his own personal rebellion against the concrete and glass of the building. Pot plants, old-fashioned dark wood bookcases, and a fluted and scrolled walnut writing desk all spoke to nostalgia for a time neither of the room's occupants had ever known. Framed impressionistic pen portraits of Pablo Casals, Yo-Yo Ma and Jacqueline du Pré dominated the wall behind Sylvester.

'I'm a different person.' She smiled. 'I needed to experience life ... real life.

'Glad to hear it,' he said paternally, unconsciously feeling the emerging bald patch in the crown of his wispy, unkempt salt-and-pepper hair. 'We thought we had lost you.'

'Well, I found myself. In so many ways.'

'Excellent, excellent,' he said, steepling his fingers in a half-hearted parody of Mr Burns from *The Simpsons*. 'That's what deferred semesters are for.'

He smiled at her and she beamed right back at him, breathing in deeply, consciously straining the material of her bra even tighter against the cotton of her blouse. She was enjoying this a little too much.

'And have you been keeping up with your practice?'

Maria nodded but blushed.

Sylvester frowned. 'Show me your left hand.'

She leaned forward, hoping a flash of cleavage might distract him, and reluctantly turned her left hand palm upwards. Sylvester took it in both hands and examined her fingertips. Where there should have been callouses there were red grooves. Maria had clearly played recently, but not for a long time before that.

'Let's make that your last lie for this semester.' He smiled benignly before noticing a dressing about four centimetres long on her wrist. His brow expressed concern rather than curiosity.

'I hope that's not what I think it is.' Self-harming could spread like a virus among the less emotionally stable of his female charges.

'A tattoo,' she explained. 'I had it lasered off.'

'A fluffed note in a duet?' he asked, relieved.

'Something like that.'

This seemed to satisfy Sylvester. He pored over the documents in front of him, signing some papers, initialling others, completing the bureaucratic process that marked Maria's return to formal study.

And as she watched, parking a grateful smile on her lips in case he looked up, all Chita could think was that this new wig was making her head itch like a bitch and she couldn't wait until her hair grew back.

19

DANNY FOLLOWED the faint tinkle of more distant laughter and the telltale rumble of a spa bath's pumps until he reached the foot of some narrow wooden stairs that disappeared upwards into an even gloomier corridor. A small angled door under the stairs was slightly ajar. Danny peered inside and saw an array of fuse boxes and electric meters. He smiled. The heavily carpeted treads creaked as he made his way up to the next floor, but not so loudly that they would alert anyone who was otherwise distracted.

He was drawn by the thrum of the spa bath to the end of the corridor, where a door with 'spa room' on a curiously flowery ceramic plate stated the obvious. Outside the door Danny gathered his thoughts and luxuriated for a second or two in buzz. Then he breathed deeply through his nose and down past his diaphragm. Once, twice and a third time, each breath expelled slowly and completely through his mouth as he felt his heartbeat ease to an elevated but steady rhythm. He was locked and loaded.

Danny could have turned the handle and entered the normal way, but he felt that kicking the door in would have more of the effect he desired. In any case, he had the brick from the toolbox in one hand and the hairdryer in the other, so his hands were pretty full. But there was the noise to think of, so he compromised: he tucked the hairdryer under his arm, turned the handle, then kicked. In the instant between his entry and the occupants of the room registering that they had a visitor, Danny absorbed the scene. Tony was lying back in the spa with a blissful smile on his face. Beside him, a young Asian woman sat with a look of distracted anxiety, her expression betraying the fact that she had not anticipated her day turning out this way, even before Danny made his entrance. She didn't scream; instead her eyes said *just when I thought my life couldn't get any worse*, and she sank back into the water, up to her nose, to await whatever the fates had in store for her.

Tony Cufflinks did scream – or roared, to be precise – partly in fury at the intrusion, partly in surprise, but mostly because a second woman whose head had just appeared above the foaming water had ended her underwater blow job a little too abruptly for comfort. She screamed too. Danny waved the hairdryer at them.

'Calm the fuck down,' he said.

The threesome sat back in the spa, in silence.

'Girls, sit on the bed,' Danny ordered. They needed no second invitation as they almost climbed over each other to get out of the spa, slipping, tripping and grabbing at towels and clothes to cover themselves on the way. The pair sat on the bed and pulled a sheet around themselves as they huddled together for security as much as warmth.

'Is that you, Clay?' Tony asked.

'Yup.'

Tony leaned forward and screwed his eyes up against the backlight from a spot behind Danny.

'Is that a fucking hairdryer?'

'Yup.'

'You are a fucking dead man,' Tony said as he started to climb out of the spa. Danny swung the brick to within a nasal hair of Tony's face, and the big man lurched backwards defensively. His momentum, coupled with the lack of purchase on the spa's base, sent him slipping back into the water, his head connecting loudly with the rear wall.

'Okay, I need to explain a couple of things,' Danny said. 'And you need to listen. It's a matter of life and death.'

'Yeah, yours,' said Tony, one of whose legs had folded under him, making sudden movements impossible as well as inadvisable.

'Maybe. Maybe not,' Danny replied, plugging the hairdryer into a wall socket near the spa.

The women were whispering frantically behind him. Danny looked at them and took a punt on them being Hong Kong Chinese.

'*Zhu kow*!' Danny barked, recalling a phrase he had employed in a chopsocky script that had gone nowhere. He hoped he got it right and it meant 'stop talking', as it was the only Cantonese phrase he knew. It did the trick and the women fell silent.

'Okay, Tony, do you know where your electrical power board is?'

'What?'

'Doesn't matter. The important thing is that I do, cause I've just been working on it. It's under the stairs, for future reference. Now, do you know what a power overload switch is?'

'Fuck, Clay, I was just going to kill you – now I'm going to kill you slowly.'

'It's a safety measure that automatically switches off the electricity when there's a short circuit. Like when someone sticks a knife in a toaster or, say, drops a hairdryer in a bath.'

Danny switched the hairdryer on and dangled it by its cord over the water. Tony's expression changed from disbelief to alarm.

'Remember, I'm a sapper,' Danny said. 'I make and I break. And I just broke the safety switch. If I drop this in the water, the fuse won't blow and you will be electrocuted.'

'Fuck do you want, Clay?'

'Just tell me who's trying to kill me and my friends, and why?'

'I don't know and I don't care, and if you don't put that thing away –'

'You'll kill me? You've just told me I'm already dead. Now, talk or I will fry you in your own fat.' That one was a line Danny had written for a short-lived and largely unlamented all-female cop drama called

Cop It Sweet. He was partially interested to see if it worked in real life.

Danny lowered the hairdryer so it was just above the water. Tony's eyes said, *dare you*, but then they changed. His brow creased, his face crumpled and he started to howl.

'Cramp. Jesus H Christ! I got a cramp in my leg.'

'Names,' Danny said.

'Let me up. *Fuuuuuck*.'

'Name, Tony. And I want some explanations.'

Tony shook his head and gritted his teeth. Danny turned the power on the hairdryer to maximum. Its whine doubled in pitch and volume. He knew this would have zero impact on the outcome if he did drop the hairdryer in the water, but the psychological effect was immediate.

'Okay, okay. Let me just move my leg.'

'All right. But be careful not to touch the hairdryer.'

Tony gingerly moved his leg out from under him, stretched it, sat back in the spa and sighed with relief. As he did so, Danny pulled aside a window blind and saw the brothel receptionist standing on the street below, talking animatedly to Tony's driver and glancing up a couple of times at the window. She must have heard the yelling.

'Okay, talk,' Tony said. His new position made him even less able to get out of the spa in a hurry, so Danny switched off both the hairdryer and the spa, better to hear anyone coming up the stairs.

'Those places you asked me about? Berlin, Toronto, Nice, Venice?' Danny ventured.

'What about them?'

'Movie festivals,' Danny explained. 'They all have big movie festivals.'

This silenced Tony as he tried to compute the connections.

'So why did you ask about them?' Danny insisted.

'Jackie Jazz,' Tony replied.

'What?'

'Jackie Jazz. The cops have tracked him to all those airports. If it's any consolation, they don't know what he's up to either.'

'Where is he now?'

'Utah,' Tony said with a shrug. 'Skiing – at least, that's what he told me.'

'Sundance,' Danny thought aloud. 'Another movie festival.' He shook his head as he sat down on the end of the bed. 'There's a connection, but I can't work out what it is.'

Tony started to laugh.

'What's so funny?'

'That kid you killed – the word is he's related to Jackie.'

'I didn't kill him.'

'Save me a couple of ringside seats for when you're explaining that to the Jazzman.'

Danny heard a creak on the stairs. He noticed from the flicker in Tony's eyes that he had too.

'Tell your muscle to piss off,' Danny said.

Tony was clearly about to deny all knowledge, but there was another creak and the faint sound of cursing.

Danny looked at Tony. 'Hard to get good help these days, huh?'

'Bam-Bam,' Tony yelled. 'It's all good. Just wait in the car.' He added something in a foreign language that Danny didn't quite catch.

'Very cute, Antonio.' Danny waved the hairdryer over the water. 'By the way, it doesn't have to be switched on … just plugged in. He comes in here and so much as bumps into me, you get 240 volts of jolt, 50 times a second.'

Tony seemed more bewildered than scared by the technicalities, but it was clear Danny knew shit that he didn't.

'Bam!' he called out. 'Back down, buddy. It's all cool. Wait in the car.'

'Okay, Boss,' came a faint reply, followed by the retreating sound of creaking stairs.

'Bam-Bam?' Danny asked incredulously.

'It's a long story that I've never heard all the way through.'

'I'll bet,' Danny said. 'Now, what about the Poet?'

'Who?'

'The Poet, the other writer. The one who didn't get killed. It sounds like he was the go-between.'

'I hope he has good health cover. Jackie isn't the smartest criminal, but he tries to be thorough.'

'What else?' Danny hissed.

'That's all I got,' Tony replied. 'Really! I honestly couldn't give a flying fuck about you and Jackie and your pissant writer friends.'

'So how come you heavied me?'

'I don't like disorganised crime on my patch and this was getting very messy,' Tony said. 'And every finger pointed at you.'

'It has nothing to do with me.'

'Look, your friends got mixed up with the wrong people. Maybe they got greedy. Maybe Jackie wanted to do something about it, and you and your girlfriend got caught in the middle.'

'That's a lot of maybes. And she's not my girlfriend.'

'Well, tough shit on both counts, soldier.'

Realising he wasn't going to get any more useful information out of Tony, Danny checked the street. There was no sign of Bam-Bam, in or at the car. He lowered his voice and leaned in towards the spa bath.

'Okay, Tony, this is how it's going to work. Both Zan and I are being watched by the cops and the media so if you want revenge, you are going to have to wait.'

'I can do that,' Tony said, matter-of-fact. 'I am a patient man. And maybe Jackie will get to you first.'

'Anything happens to me, you are going to have more heat than even you can handle,' Danny threatened. 'But if you so much as look at Zan ...'

'I'm quaking.' Tony sneered. 'Oh, and a word of advice: you go after Jackie Jazz, you better take more than a hairdryer.'

'Good point,' Danny laughed and tossed the hairdryer towards the spa. As it arced through the air Tony yelled and the girls screamed, and when it hit the water all the lights went out.

Danny ducked out of the room and crept down the stairs.

'I will fuck you, I will kill you and I will fuck you again,' Tony yelled, splashing loudly as he tried to slither out of the water in the darkness.

Danny quickly made his way down the stairs, stepping on the outer sides of the wooden treads so they didn't bend in the middle and creak. It was too dark to see clearly, but below and to Danny's left a shadow moved and there was the faint glow of a mobile phone screen, dimmed by the cloth of a shirt pocket.

Danny smiled to himself as he felt his heart rate rev up. He still had the brick.

20

THE PROBATIONARY constable wasn't sure, but his sergeant insisted: 'Just put your shoulder through it, son,' the older man said. 'The Sydney cops said we might be looking for a body and it does smell a bit iffy.'

They were at the back door of a terraced house in Frankston, Melbourne, having waded through the long grass of an unkempt yard that had so many hidden obstacles – garden tools, beer bottles, milk crates – it could have been landscaped by a Vietcong booby-trap squad. The PC was about to do as instructed when he thought for a moment and tried the handle. It turned and the door swung open with the slightest of squeaks, pushing aside a small pile of unopened mail and fliers advertising pizza delivery and real estate agencies, evidently the two main industries in that area.

'Anybody home?' the sergeant called as they crept along the corridor, linoleum crackling beneath their boots. They heard the flies before they saw them and followed the sound into the kitchen, where a half-drunk glass of red wine sat on the table beside a half-eaten pie crawling with maggots. That explained the smell. The sergeant quickly donned rubber gloves and the constable followed suit.

The rooms were remarkably tidy, considering the description of the house's occupant that had been emailed to them. However, in a corner of the lounge there were definite signs of a struggle. A writing desk had been tipped over, a computer screen was smashed on the floor and there was a pile of books and papers. The sergeant prodded them with his foot and a leather wallet slid into view.

He lifted it with his pen and looked inside. There was no cash but the credit card slots were full, although the cards were functional as well as financial – a frequent flyer card, a points card from a Mexican takeaway and membership of Hawthorn Football Club tucked beside Visa and American Express. In the space on the floor where the wallet had been was a passport. Next to that, a deep red stain and the neck of a broken bottle. Closer examination revealed that the computer's hard drive had been removed.

'I think we'd better let CID take over,' the sergeant told his junior colleague as he reached for his mobile phone.

—

Danny and Laura leaned on the same side of the cafe table staring at a photocopy of a handwritten letter. There were a couple of beads of sweat just south of the first hints of Danny's hairline, but they were evidence of recent exertions rather than harbingers of a stress attack.

First he had shown Bam-Bam that in the rock-paper-scissors of real combat, brick beats wrist every time (even if the hand it's attached to is holding a weapon). Outside the Perfumed Garden he'd called Rob to see if he had heard anything about a movie deal that Jackie Jazz might have been involved in. Rob said he would look into it. Danny was about to return Zan's call when his phone rang. It was Laura. The post office had sent over an undelivered letter that appeared to be a suicide note from Bryan.

Within minutes Danny was at the little French cafe opposite the police station, almost sprinting up Orwell Street and sending a cluster of Danish backpackers scattering.

'We're checking the original for fingerprints, inside and out,' said Laura. 'See if they're his.'

'We used to do that,' Danny said. 'In the field.'

'Sorry?'

'IEDs. The reason we didn't just blow them up was because they had heaps of intel. There's nothing like sticky tape for holding a fingerprint.'

'I never knew …'

'I reckon between us, the Yanks and the NATO guys we must have fingerprinted every fighting-age male in Afghanistan,' he said wryly, 'for all the good it did us.'

'The handwriting?' she said, trying to get the discussion back on track. 'Does it look like Bryan's?'

'Yeah, it looks familiar. It's definitely his verbal style.'

He shifted slightly so he wasn't casting a shadow over the sheet of paper and read it again.

> *To whom it may concern,*
>
> *This is not so much a suicide note as an apology. If this has gone as planned, I probably need to say sorry to a police officer.*
>
> *I also need to apologise to my wife and daughters for any hurt I cause them now and in the future.*
>
> *If you don't know already, you will soon find out that I have been very stupid, selfish and sick. There is only one cure and I have taken it.*
>
> *Please forgive me.*
>
> *To my friends, you need to know that apart from my own pathetic weakness, the person who has driven me to this pitiful exit is the Poet who has stolen my dream.*
>
> *His producer mate has worked out a way of making money by not making the movie. But the Poet says if I don't do what he wants, he'll tell the world all about me. And somewhere in this tangled web, my sad obsession has been exposed.*
>
> *It's all about the dollar, my friends. If you need another clue, watch The Producers.*
>
> *Goodbye and good luck.*
>
> *Bryan*
>
> *XXXX (that's a clue, by the way)*

'It had been lying in an unaddressed mail basket at the post office,' Laura explained. 'Somebody finally opened it and brought it over.' She watched Danny puzzling over the paper. 'Those comments at the end are a bit ...'

'Cryptic?' Danny offered. 'Well, that was Bryan. He felt it was his job as a writer to make people think. Nothing too deep, mind you, just enough to exercise the brain cells. He wouldn't have signed off without a flourish.'

'Even so, it's pretty obvious,' she mused. 'The Poet wanted to cut Bryan out of a deal, he blackmailed him and, we think, didn't realise Bryan was already into the stuff he was threatening to frame him for.'

'That's how it looks,' Danny ventured, slumping back into his chair and trying to collect his thoughts. 'But the Poet could barely send an email let alone hack into someone's computer. And the wannabe hitman said killing Marcus was an accident. They just wanted to put the frighteners on him too.'

'They?' asked Laura.

'The Poet was working as the go-between with a producer,' Danny said. 'And guess what? Jackie Jazz has been racking up the frequent flyer points travelling around film festivals.'

If Laura's eyebrows had shot any higher, she'd have needed to scrape them off the ceiling.

'Jackie Jazz is the mystery producer?' she asked, pointing at the suicide note.

'Looks like it.'

'Where are you getting all this?' she asked.

'You just have to ask the right people the right questions.'

'Well that explains it,' Laura said. 'Jackie Jazz hired them then ripped them off – because it's what he does – they complained and bingo! We have two dead writers on our hands. One suicide and one beating gone seriously wrong.'

'Yeeeeeah,' said Danny, meaning 'no'. 'Thing is, they were all paid, and really well from what I hear. And in cash. No complaints.'

'How about this so-called "clue"?' she said. 'Four Xs.'

'Four-X,' Danny said. 'Queensland beer? And that comment about the Poet?'

Laura and Danny looked at each other for a moment, their brows like matching ploughed fields.

'Have you heard from your friend the Poet recently?' Laura asked.

'No, I haven't,' Danny said. 'I was just thinking the same thing.'

'The Vic cops are going to visit – hold him till we get there.'

'Fair enough, but it all seems a bit organised for him,' Danny said. 'You're talking about a guy who thinks he's having a lucky day when he puts matching socks on.'

Laura smiled and went back to staring at the suicide note.

—

Paddy hated reading, that's why he paid interns to do it for him. Okay, he didn't actually pay them, but he allowed them to be in his office, get his coffee and generally be around him, which was more than the over-privileged, entitled brats deserved. They should be grateful to breathe the same air as him. To be fair, some of them were.

But this was a reading he couldn't duck. If they were going to take the money back from the Australians he had better make sure the script was as big a piece of shit as everyone said. He couldn't even get Jasmina to read it for him. She was coming in late, leaving early and having long lunches in between. And all the while she'd been hinting that time was running out for him to find her another job.

'You'll never work in this town again,' he'd told her.

'And neither will you,' she'd replied. 'Anyway, the money I get when I sue, I could open my own studio.'

Paddy couldn't afford another screw-up. He glowered at the script. He always suspected that whoever he was dealing with knew more than he did, and this was no different. Whenever he let that paranoia subside and his guard came down, something like Jasmina happened. So he needed to know what was in the script. Okay, he had post-it notes coming out of the thing like confetti, but there's nothing quite like actually reading the thing yourself, even if these Australians were strictly amateur night. He had briefly fantasised about getting all the interns in and having them read it aloud, but then he would have to take notes, and he hated taking notes more than he hated reading.

So he flicked through the pages, forcing himself to stop and absorb every line. He had to admit that these Aussie assholes had done a good job, as far as he could tell. It would be a shame not to see it once it had been polished by real writers.

But getting that development money back was crucial. There was a shit storm brewing around this thing and a rumour circulating that one of the writers had killed himself, or been killed by terrorists. Whatever. Every instinct in his body told him he was right to ditch the project and get the money back. But first …

Paddy mumbled his way through *Redneck Airlift* at triple speed, but then something caught his eye, although it took his brain a few seconds to catch up. He flicked back through the pages and found it again. This time he read it slowly and carefully … and smiled.

There were all these references to a 'perfect crime'. One of his buddies was producing a TV show called just that. Except every time they came up with a perfect crime, someone spotted a hole through which you could drive a monster truck.

'Damned writer couldn't make it work,' Saul Lootkin had growled over lunch. 'Re-writer couldn't make it work. William fucking Goldman and Robert McKee locked in a room together for a year couldn't make it work. How can you have a TV drama called 'Perfect Crime' with a crime that could be solved by a five-year-old on a Ritalin binge?'

Paddy started reading again, this time making notes.

Laura had just got back to her office when she noticed the virus alert from her malware filter. She'd gone to meet Danny while her computer finished copying all the personal files, family pictures and videos from Bryan's PC to a portable hard drive.

A few clicks later and Laura was looking at an email from the Poet to Bryan with 'Redneck Airlift' in the subject line. The message was innocuous enough: just an acknowledgement that Bryan had made up his mind and a request to meet 'the team' to discuss it. But an alert in the corner of the screen said a virus in the email had been quarantined and the email was now safe. Laura scrolled up and down through the other emails. There were no other messages about *Redneck Airlift* and none to or from Marcus, Danny, Zan or the Poet since about eighteen months previously.

She checked the trash folder. Nothing. She ran her own retrieval software. All it told her was that there had been 257 emails fitting that description and that they had been erased using military-grade triple deletion software. She realised she was lucky to discover there had ever been emails at all, and suspected that finding out who they were to or from, and what they contained, was beyond her or anyone else's capabilities.

However, somewhat ironically, the one with the virus – a variation on a nasty called *backdoor.vinderfulg* – had a built-in protection from simple deletion. It would copy itself into a folder that had been deleted and hide there until reactivated. Laura checked the virus. As she thought, it was a Trojan that allowed the sender to take over the target computer. The Poet had sent an email that opened a back door into Bryan's computer, from which he could upload, download and delete anything he wanted.

Laura's own computer *pinged*. She had an email from Victoria Police with 'your search requests' in the subject line. It was virus free.

21

'WELL, WE have identified the victim,' Laura told Bill McCue, who could not have looked less interested if she had asked him to watch while she flossed her teeth. 'Aruna Danushka Gunawardena, aka Weezl – with two Es before the Z and none after it.

'*Weezl, according to his friends, was a promising IT student who fantasised about being a criminal mastermind,*' she read from an email printout. 'Apparently he dropped out of university when he met a new girlfriend whose name was something like "Cheetah". But that, according to our chums down in Melbourne, is where the trail of the killer girlfriend ends.'

'So the annoying Asian girl is telling the truth?' McCue said rhetorically.

'According to this, Weezl was a bit of a loner, and his friends were only vaguely aware of his girlfriend,' Laura continued. 'Nobody had spoken to her, very few had seen her and even then only from a distance. She was European looking with short spiky hair – that's all we've got. They say she just arrived on the scene and the pair of them promptly disappeared into their own little world. No parties, no selfies, Facebook snaps ... nothing. Very unusual in that age group. They can't make a piece of toast without photographing it and sending it to their fifteen thousand very closest friends. Some of his mates speculated that she was an undercover cop. Apparently she almost made one girl eat her phone when she took a picture of her. Deleted it, of course.'

'Christ,' said McCue. 'A cop?'

'The Vic police say no, and she's not one of ours or the Feds.

According to the Vics the killer girlfriend is a ghost.'

'The ghost who walks,' McCue mumbled as he swivelled around in his chair. 'You know what this is, Laura?'

She shrugged, assuming any guess would be wrong.

'We have one simple suicide and one fatal assault by a perp who is now dead, killed by a girl who doesn't live in Sydney, if she even exists,' he summarised. 'So she is not our problem. It has all the hallmarks of a classic clusterfuck, but in fact it's a giant nothingburger with a mountainous side-order of paperwork.'

Laura nodded, wondering what she was agreeing to.

'And just saying that has made me hungry,' McCue added, taking his jacket from the back of the chair. 'By the way, what do you make of the Asian chick?' McCue asked as he got to the door.

'Zan?' said Laura. 'I think she's telling the truth. The bubble wig killer shot Weezl.'

'Yeah, not that,' said McCue. 'The other thing. The rich guy in the lift?'

'What about it?' Laura said. 'She tried to save the guy. Couldn't. We've all been there.'

'Yeah, but his family are wondering if she's the hero she claims to be.' McCue swung his jacket over his shoulder. 'You know, no one else knows about this bubble wig killer. It's not like we can put out a description or circulate a picture,' he said.

'No,' Laura agreed, not sure where this was heading.

'But if Zan thinks we still suspect her … that little bit of extra pressure might work in our favour.'

'I'm not with you, boss,' Laura said.

'Let's just keep the bubble wig killer info to ourselves, okay? Get that paintball arsehole website to take those images down.'

'Okay,' Laura said hesitantly.

'And, yeah,' said McCue, warming to an idea. 'Let's find out who this paintball arsehole is. He's starting to give me the shits.'

'What about the two murders?'

'Like I said, a nothingburger,' McCue said as he exited, leaving Laura to ask herself how much more she could tell Danny and Zan without turning her career into a nothingburger.

—

'Young Weezl is connected to Jackie Jazz,' said Danny after Laura had told him about the report from the Melbourne cops. 'As in related by family, according to Tony Cufflinks. Sorry, I was distracted by Bryan's suicide note.'

There was a long pause, and Danny briefly checked his phone screen to make sure they hadn't been cut off.

'Interesting,' Laura finally said, coming back from a thought. 'And our friends down south paid a visit to the Poet's gaff.'

'How is he?' Danny asked.

'Gone. As in *Marie Celeste* gone. Half-eaten meal on the table, a half-drunk glass of wine beside it, signs of a struggle, his computer had been gutted — hard drive stolen — and there was blood and a broken bottle on the floor.'

'Bloody hell, not another one,' said Danny. 'Unless he's just taken off.'

'Doesn't sound like it,' said Laura. 'All his cupboards were full. His suitcases were still in his closet. His passport and credit cards were on the floor.'

'And he didn't finish his wine?' Danny mused. 'Now that's a mystery.'

'And I found a Trojan on Bryan's hard disk,' Laura added.

'A condom?' asked Danny, making a face no one could see.

Laura laughed. 'It's a kind of computer virus. Bryan got an email from the Poet. When he opened it, it loaded software onto his machine that gave the Poet remote access.'

'The Poet?' said Danny. 'Are you sure?'

'Looks like it,' Laura replied. 'My guess is he used it to dump all that vile crap on Bryan's computer then threatened to accuse him of being a pedo ... only he really was.'

'Really?' said Danny. 'Doesn't sound like the Poet's speed.'

'Bryan obviously knew how to encrypt files,' Laura explained. 'Why would he leave material like that openly available, especially when he had carefully locked other less awful shit away. Someone else put it there and it looks very much like it was the Poet.'

'Like I said before, the Poet could barely write an email,' said Danny.

'Well he wrote this one,' said Laura. 'And then, when he got into Bryan's computer, he cleaned out every other message referring to the *Redneck Airlift* project.'

'Did you say young Weezl was an IT student?' Danny said.

'Fuck,' said Laura. '*Of course*. You don't use your own computer to hack another computer, you hijack a third party.'

"So he hacked the Poet's computer and hijacked it to send Bryan the virus so he could upload kiddy porn,' Danny said, testing the theory.

'Why not just hack Bryan's computer?' Laura asked.

'Overkill seems to have been the kid's trademark,' Danny said. 'And maybe he knew Bryan was smart enough to spot the attempted intrusion.' A thought struck him. 'Should you be looking for another body?'

'We're not even looking for the girl anymore,' said Laura. 'Too hard, according to McCue. Otherwise I wouldn't be telling you all this. The good news is you can take down the *scene of crime* tape. Case closed, as far as we're concerned.'

Danny's phone rang. He looked at the screen. 'It's Rob, my agent. He might have something on Jackie Jazz.'

'Take it,' Laura said. 'I'll call you later if I hear anything. Oh, before you go, you need to have a word to Zan about the Hahn thing. It's not going to go away.'

A low mixture of a groan and a sigh was all she heard before the line went dead.

22

DANNY SAT nursing a bone china mug of chilli and chocolate herb tea – which, to his amazement, was quite drinkable. Zan sat opposite him sipping homemade sparkling water from a tall glass garnished with a slice of lemon. Again, perfectly okay, although Danny secretly ached for a tin mug full of hot English breakfast with too much sugar in it.

'We all know that even if you hate the script changes, when push comes to shove, you go along with them because that will get you to your next payday and you might get a chance to undo them,' Danny said, thinking aloud.

'And if you refuse, the studio will just put a new writer on it or shut the project down and write off their losses,' Zan concurred.

'Yeah, so you don't go to the barricades on script changes unless you want to wake up one morning and see a picture in *Variety* of the writer who got your gig,' Danny added.

They looked at each other, unable to make sense of what had happened. 'Run this past me again,' Zan said. 'What exactly did Rob say?'

'According to his contacts, Jackie Jazz sold a movie treatment of *Redneck Airlift* to a studio in Hollywood. There was a bidding war at the Cannes film festival and the price got silly. Three million US dollars.'

'Shit,' said Zan. 'Is he sure? Not even red-hot writers get that for a script.'

'It was a development deal,' Danny continued. 'Seed money for the script, plus studio space, offices, set-up crew. So imagine their surprise when the producer …'

'Jackie Jazz?' Zan speculated.

'The very same. He gets shirty about some script changes the studio demanded. The studio points to the contract and says if he doesn't accept reasonable changes he has to pay the money back.'

'So they cave in?' Zan asked.

'They say they'd rather pay the money back than make changes.'

'What?' Zan's voice dripped incredulity.

'I know. Never been known in the history of Hollywood. Apparently it's in *Variety*.'

Zan turned to her laptop and Danny looked around her flat while the cursor skipped across its screen. She must have a butler or a maid hidden in a cupboard, he thought. There wasn't a single stray cup, glass or magazine to be seen. All the flat surfaces that God intended for the storage of books, clothes and pizza boxes were clear and clean.

'Here it is,' she said, turning the screen toward him. '"Oz Execs Nix Big Flix Bucks", whatever that means.'

'Does it say why?' Danny asked, peering at the text.

'It quotes Jackie Jazz saying *the integrity of the project was paramount* and it was his duty to protect the original work,' she said.

'Well, he's like no producer I ever met,' Danny muttered. 'I mean, walking away from three million dollars on a point of principle?'

'So *Redneck Airlift* is dead?' Zan said, unable to suppress a smile.

'Why does that make you happy?' Danny said. 'I'm the one who should be gloating.'

'I'm … um … happy for you.'

Danny wasn't buying that for a second. He looked at Zan over the rim of his mug. She was staring at her computer screen, absorbing every word of the *Variety* story and smiling.

'Danny, I have a confession to make,' Zan said eventually, turning and lowering her eyes, but unable to suppress the beginnings of a grin.

Danny sat back in his seat. He smiled supportively, but the words *what fresh hell is this* scrolled through his mind.

'You know the perfect murder scene from your crime show?' she twisted her hair in her fingers. 'I kind of dropped it into *Redneck Airlift* for the boys.'

'You what?' This was not the confession Danny had been hoping for.

'They needed a cool way to kill a character and your script wasn't going anywhere and neither was theirs and I couldn't ask you ...'

'Because you had cut me out of the deal ...'

'Sorry,' she said, using her best big-eyed, fluttering-eyelash look.

'Just as well it's going nowhere.' Danny smiled thinly. 'Especially with all the media attention you've been getting.'

Zan pouted. 'Oooh, that reminds me. You're getting a bit of a negative backlash on the internet.'

'Me? Why? What did I do?'

Zan flicked open her laptop and tapped a key. An online news page popped up. 'SAS gunman a fake, says war hero,' she read the headline aloud.

'What's that got to do with me?' Danny asked.

'According to this, you claimed to be in the SAS and you shot Weezl.'

'What the fuck?!' Danny grabbed the laptop and started to read.

> *The ex-soldier who allegedly shot an intruder in his Kings Cross home lied about being in the SAS, according to a former special forces operative.*
>
> *Former Lieutenant Menzies McFadzean, decorated for his part in a daring raid against Taliban insurgents in Afghanistan, and now a bestselling military historian, says Danny Clay has no right to claim he is in the SAS and says police should look more closely at his claims he was defending himself from a terrorist revenge attack.*
>
> *'Danny Clay was an army engineer in Afghanistan,' Lieutenant McFadzean told OnlineToday. 'That's like a plumber*

with a gun. It makes me sick that every wannabe hero who ever put on a uniform claims they were SAS. We are an elite force of highly trained soldiers, and we deserve more respect.

'The police need to look a bit more closely at this. What was Clay doing with a gun? What was this young bloke really doing in his flat? How did he end up dead?'

Lieutenant McFadzean was taking a break from launching his new book, Taking on the Taliban, *the fifth in his series of true stories of life in the Australian Special Forces.*

'Taking a break, my arse,' Danny said as he slammed shut the cover of the laptop. 'He's using me to sell his books. And I didn't say I was SAS, I didn't shoot Weezl and I never said he was a terrorist.'

'Yeah, sorry about that.' Zan looked shame-faced. 'It was me who said you were special forces.'

'Special ops – close but fucking miles off. Now all the SAS and Commando boys are going to hate my guts too.'

'Do you and this McFadzean guy have previous …?' Zan asked, noticing Danny's clenched fist.

'He did one three-month tour in Afghan, got in the way of a bullet, won a medal and wrote a book about it when he got home. Now it's like every six months there's another book, at least half of which must be made up because he couldn't be on two different ops at the same time. And he shouldn't still be calling himself Lieutenant.' Danny realised his indignation was starting to sound more jealous than righteous so he took a couple of breaths.

'And …?' Zan prompted

'And one night he was big-noting himself at the North Bondi RSL – it's the sappers' unofficial watering hole – and I happen to know he nearly got his whole platoon killed when he insisted on posing for pictures on top of their Bushmaster.'

'You just had to put the record straight,' her voice dripped sarcasm.
Danny shrugged.
'And you got into a fight ...'
Another shrug.
'And you kicked his arse ...'
'He's a trained killer,' Danny protested. 'I had to defend myself.'
'Do you think you will ever grow out of this?' she asked. 'I mean, fuck, Danny. How old are you? Take up hang gliding or knife juggling if you need a buzz.'
'What do I do about this?' he tapped the laptop.
'What makes you think you can do anything?' She laughed at his naivety. 'It's the internet. It's a wild animal. Haters hate, believers believe. If you defend yourself you attract more abuse. If someone else defends you, you look lame. The trick is not to care.'
'What if I do care?' Danny wailed.
'Then you lose,' she said, placing a consoling arm around him. 'Okay, you could issue a correction. That might shut everyone who's shut-uppable. But the trolls and flamers will be creaming their pants at getting a reaction.'
'I could go after McFadzean?'
'Like that's not going to help him sell more books.' Zan smiled and shook her head. 'Just Trump it.'
'Meaning?'
'Create an alternative reality, then truly believe in it.'
He glowered at her, smarting from knowing he was wrong but not enjoying being told.
'Okay. And what's your alternative reality with the Hahn thing?' Danny asked. 'What is it you choose to believe?'
Zan put her head in her hands, frightened and vulnerable in a way that put a knot in Danny's chest.
'I did it,' she said to her knees.

The idea fluttered around for a moment before it settled in Danny's mind.

'You what?' he asked.

'I fucking did it,' she said in a forced whisper. And then it all came tumbling out. She couldn't have stopped if she'd wanted to. She didn't want to. 'I didn't mean to do it, but we were in the lift and he started sneering at me. I was a loser gook, my mother was a loser boat person ... I called him a racist and he said he had Asian friends and they were too smart to get into a fight they couldn't win. But we were stupid and ignorant and ... and then he said it wouldn't be enough to destroy Mum financially, he wanted to break her. He wanted to open the newspaper one morning and read that she'd killed herself. He said he hoped she did it by jumping off the balcony so he could find her body ...'

Zan took a breath and pinched the bridge of her nose, too late to stop the tears.

'So you decided to kill him, just like that?' Danny asked, quietly

'I didn't decide anything,' Zan protested. 'He kind of leaned over me, shouting in my face. I could feel the spittle on my skin and I wanted to back away but we were in a lift and I headbutted his chest and ... I guess I got lucky. He dropped.'

'What about the perfect crime?' Danny asked. 'That wasn't your plan?'

'There was no plan. It just happened. I wasn't thinking – I was running on instinct. Then I remembered it and thought, fuck it, I'll give him CPR. If he comes round, fine. If not, maybe better. But I knew I was covering my tracks.'

'Except you'd put that scene in *Redneck Airlift*,' Danny said, reminding them both

'Who the fuck knew?' She shook her head in disbelief at her bad luck.

'Hahn's family don't need any more encouragement to come after you,' Danny said. 'If they're anything like their old man, they can afford to lose better than you can afford to win.

'They have so much money,' Zan wailed. 'They'll crucify me.'

And Danny simply wrapped her in his arms and held her, little ripples of her emotion washing through him as she sobbed.

'It'll be okay,' he said, not believing it himself.

23

PADDY PICKED up his phone and punched the button that would have got him to Jasmina, had she not been at a Women in Hollywood brunch. He flicked through his cellphone for a number and dialled it.

'Mr Lootkin's office,' a woman said. 'How can I help you?'

'Put me through to Saul, sweetheart. It's Paddy Rosenberg.'

'Connecting you now, Mr Rosenberg.'

There was the briefest burst of AOR music, then a gruff voice came over the phone. 'Paddy,' it growled.

'Hey, Saul.' Paddy beamed. 'You are about to owe me big time. You know you were telling me about your TV show – the one called *Perfect Crime*? Well, I got you one.'

'What?'

'I got your perfect crime.'

'Where?'

'I was thinking about it, and –'

'Paddy, you know I love you,' Lootkin said, his voice like a cement mixer filled with gravel, 'but you've never had an original thought in your life. This is no time to be pullin' my wire. I gotta go.'

'No, listen,' Paddy insisted. 'I got it right here in front of me. In print. By professional writers. Almost.'

'Okay, you got my attention,' Lootkin almost purred. 'Tell me more.'

'Chick gives old guy heart attack by punching him in the chest with some judo-fucking-jitsu karate shit.'

'How … I mean … okay, but how is that a perfect crime?'

'Let me bring it over to you,' Paddy said. 'One thing first. Do you have an opening for a bright young associate producer with a college degree and scary street smarts?'

—

Danny glanced in the mirror, caught the look of concern in the hairdresser's face, and smiled. She was a tall, thin young woman with mischievous eyes, narrowed by concentration as she negotiated the fringe around the dressing on the back of his head. This was primarily a ladies' hairdresser, with tints and foils and blow-dryers whining away, which Danny preferred because it was cheap, fast and wasn't one of those man-scaping salons that seemed to be popping up on every corner. He didn't need to pay fifty dollars for a haircut in a faux barbershop that was nostalgic for a time he never knew and wouldn't have cared about if he had. It also wasn't a ten-dollar buzz-cut shop. He'd had enough of that in the army.

Only, that was pretty much what he was going for. He wanted to even up his hair, for sure, but mentally he was preparing for war. Exactly with whom and over what, he wasn't certain, but he wanted to feel ready, even if he wasn't.

'Are you okay?' the hairdresser asked, concerned. She'd told him her name was Patricia, and he knew she was a Northern Irish Catholic – the crucifix on a chain around her neck and the flattened vowels of the least tuneful of the Irish dialects gave that away. She pronounced Belfast *'Bulfaast'*, just like a British commando he'd met in Helmand. Toby was from Carrickfergus, just outside Belfast, so he would almost certainly have been a Protestant – or a *Prawddy*, as Patricia would have pronounced it.

'Just thinking,' Danny replied.

'About something that's making you angry?' She laughed.

'No, sorry, that's my thinking face.' He smiled. 'It's … it's a puzzle, that's all.'

'Oh, go on, try me,' she said. 'I love puzzles.'

Danny had been mulling over Bryan's suicide note, trying to make sense of it. He wasn't about to blurt all that out … but then he thought, why not?'

'Okay,' he said. 'What do you think when you see four Xs?'

'Four Xs?' she said. 'Like Four-X beer?'

'Say again?'

'Four-X beer. You must have heard of it.'

'That's it,' he said. 'It must have slipped my mind.'

It was the way she said 'four' that got him over the line. She pronounced it with a short vowel – '*for*' rather than '*fore*' … 'for exes' … for-ex … foreign exchange. And now the reference to 'The Producers' made sense too.

'How's that?' she asked, holding up a mirror so he could see the back of his injured head.

'Bloody brilliant.' He grinned, ignoring the now even more obvious dressing and barely resisting the temptation to dance her off her feet.

24

DANNY SEEMED to be intently studying the flight ticket that had just been handed to him, like he was in search of a mistake – window seat instead of the aisle, perhaps, or destination Las Vegas instead of Los Angeles. In fact, he was lost in thought. At least in the army you knew who you could trust and how much you could trust them. And you knew who was out to do you serious harm and why.

'So tell me your theory,' Rob said, keeping his voice low to avoid the attention of the diners around them.

'Huh?' Danny looked up with an automatically apologetic smile. A passing waiter paused before realising Danny wasn't trying to get his attention.

'You said you thought you knew what had gone down,' Rob prompted.

'Yeah, okay, it's complicated but hang in and you'll get it,' Danny said, folding the ticket into his jacket's inside pocket. 'And stop me if you think I've missed something ...'

Danny spread his hands on the table top, took a breath and was about to continue when Zan nodded pointedly in the direction of a mousey, overweight, middle-aged woman with badly dyed blonde hair, sitting at a nearby table. The woman was fiddling furtively with her smartphone while looking at them in that *I'm not looking at you* way.

Two bright flashes from under the table confirmed what she was up to and Zan shaped to get up, but Danny placed his hand on her arm as he got out of his own seat. The woman slipped the phone under her newspaper and laid her hand on it.

'Did you just take our picture?' Danny asked the woman.

'It's none of your business what I did,' she said with a defensive twitch, her lips visibly thinning.

'It kind of is if you took our picture,' Danny retorted. 'May I see?'

'Certainly not,' she snarled through pursed lips. 'It's private.'

'So was our conversation.' He smiled, deftly knocking her brimming coffee cup and spilling the contents into her lap. The woman shrieked and pushed back from the table as Danny handed her a napkin.

'You did that deliberately!' she yelled, as waiters rushed over with cloths and serviettes. 'That's an assault.'

The woman dabbed frantically at the milky mess spreading across her lap, and Danny slipped his hand under the newspaper, retrieved the phone and tossed it to Zan. She quickly brought up the pictures and deleted them from both the gallery and the trash file. She then ripped the back off the phone and pulled out the battery and sim card. By the time the woman realised what had happened, having been distracted by the rapid progress of warm coffee through her clothes, Danny was placing the constituent parts of her phone in a neat pile in front of her.

'You broke my phone!' she squealed, for the benefit of anyone within earshot.

'It's not broken,' Danny said, shaking his head. 'But it will be if you point it at us again.'

'You're that fake soldier, and that girl – she's a murderer,' she yelled. 'You are all criminals!'

'That's absolutely right,' Danny whispered. 'Think about that. You really don't want to cross us.'

The woman was about to say something else but thought better of it. Instead she jumped to her feet, pushed the fussing waiters aside, jammed the pieces of her phone into her fake Hermes bag and scuttled out into the street. She looked back briefly, then hurried purposefully out of sight.

'You two make a pretty impressive team,' Rob said with genuine admiration. 'We've got about fifteen minutes before the paps or the cops turn up. So what's your theory?'

'The clue is in this suicide note,' said Danny, pointing at the photocopy. 'He says to "watch The Producers". Now I thought at first he meant we should be wary of Hollywood producers. They can be heartless bastards.'

Rob and Zan nodded their agreement.

'But I think what he means is the movie, *The Producers*,' he continued. 'Gene Wilder and Zero Mostel, *Springtime for Hitler* and all that.'

'Of course,' Rob confirmed. Zan looked from one of them to the other. They might as well have been speaking Swahili for all the sense they were making to her.

'The basic plot is that these two Broadway producers realise they can make a fortune if they get different people to pay for half their stage production in exchange for a half-share of the profits,' Danny explained.

'They sell half-shares in the show to different investors over and over and get more money than they could ever make legitimately. But they need it to be a flop so no one will ask for their investment back. So they produce a musical that they think is a guaranteed failure …'

'*Springtime For Hitler*,' Rob repeated.

'But it turns into a raging success,' Danny explained. 'They can't pay the money back so they end up in jail.'

'Thanks, that saves me watching the movie,' Zan said, irritated more by their superior knowledge than the lack of a spoiler alert. 'But what has this got to do with Bryan and Marcus?'

'Jackie Jazz bought the script off Bryan, Marcus and the Poet – keeping me out of the deal, by the way …'

'You and me both,' Rob gently rebuked, adding, 'which might explain why we are still alive.'

'Yeah, maybe,' Danny continued. 'Anyway, they got a ridiculous amount of development money up front. But then the US dollar dropped dramatically against the Australian dollar.'

'Please, don't remind me!' said Rob. 'I've just had three projects put on hold because Australia is too expensive.'

'So,' said Danny, 'The three million US that they got was worth four million Australian. But now that is worth nearly four million in US dollars.'

Zan still looked puzzled so Danny took four dollar coins out of his pocket and stacked them in a neat pile.

'Let's say that last year those coins were worth a million Australian dollars each …' he said.

'You wish,' Zan mumbled.

'Or three million US.'

Zan and Rob look at him, curious.

'Then the Aussie goes up and the greenback goes down, and suddenly each of these is worth a million US.' He looked at them to check they were still getting it.

'So if they pay the money back before the currency shifts back to normal –' he lifted one coin off the top of the stack and slid the three remaining coins back towards Zan. '– there's your three million dollars back, Mr Hollywood producer.'

Danny held the fourth coin up triumphantly.

'And you get a million dollars for nothing,' Zan said. 'Is anyone dumb enough to fall for that?'

'Sounds like someone is,' Danny said. 'If they canned the project while the Aussie was still high, all Jackie had to do was pay back the money in greenbacks and he had cleared one million Australian in profits.'

'But if they made the movie, there's a very good chance Jackie Jazz would get nothing back,' said Rob.

'Might even lose money,' Danny added. 'He's betting that against a guaranteed million-dollar payday.'

'How could he be sure the exchange rate would move like that?' Zan asked.

'It already had,' Danny explained. 'I'm no expert but I know that occasionally you get these sudden currency shifts – one goes up in value and another goes down – and people panic and everything gets out of kilter. Then it calms down and it all moves back to the status quo, only more gradually.'

'So this happened *after* Jackie Jazz got the money?' Rob asked, rhetorically. 'I mean, there's no way he could have planned it, right?'

'Nobody can be that sure of how the markets will move, not so dramatically,' said Danny 'But this fell into Jackie's lap when he was playing big-shot Hollywood producer. He's an opportunist and he knew he had a limited time to make a killing before everything went back to normal.'

'So the Poet tells Bryan and Marcus they are going to get paid well but there will be no movie,' Zan said, more pieces falling into place.

'Forgetting that they're writers and they see this as their best shot at the big time, Hollywood and all that,' added Rob.

'"The Poet stole my dream",' Zan quoted from the suicide note.

'And that's when all the threats and the blackmail start,' explained Danny. 'It only works if everyone agrees. It's a pity Weezl wasn't as good at controlling his violence as he was at hacking computers.'

'For him too,' Zan thought aloud, then paused. 'What about the Poet?'

'Maybe he's in cahoots with Jackie Jazz,' said Rob. 'Lie down with dogs and you get fleas.'

'The Poet already had fleas,' said Zan. They all laughed, glad of the release.

'Sounds like he's been deemed surplus to requirements too,' said Danny.

'What do you mean "surplus to requirements"?' Rob asked.

'You know the Poet has disappeared?' Danny said.

'Disappeared?' Rob was clearly shocked.

'It doesn't look like it was voluntary. His house had been turned over, his passport and credit cards were still there …'

'There was blood,' Zan added. 'His blood.'

'Fuck!' Rob said, struggling to form anything more coherent. 'I … wh… the Poet?'

Danny and Zan nodded in grim unison.

'Okay, that settles it,' Rob said. 'You both need to get your arses on a plane to LA. Jensen has persuaded the studio he can't live without you. They are rolling out the red carpet. Flight, hotel, job – the works.'

'It still feels like I'd be running away,' Danny said.

'Tony Cufflinks is after your blood and Jackie Jazz thinks you shot his nephew,' said Zan. 'So I think running away is a pretty good option.'

Danny sagged, then slowly nodded his agreement.

'The Hahn family has the hots for Zan – and not in a good way,' Rob added. 'Conspiracy theories about both of you are burning up the internet and every tosser with a mobile phone is looking to put you on their Facebook page. Also, it's only a matter of time before someone realises Zan put the perfect murder in the *Redneck Airlift* script.'

'What?' Zan exploded. 'How did you know that?'

'Because I'm not a complete amateur,' Rob said. 'As soon as I heard about the script, I got a mate to send me over a copy.'

'Is it any good?' Danny asked.

Rob answered with a disdainful shrug. 'Danny … mate,' he then said, tapping the flight ticket. 'You need to take young Jensen's offer and get over there and hold his hand – or dick, or whatever. At least you'll be safe there. I'll use my contacts and hook you up with an agent. Go along to some meetings, antagonise a whole different set of producers; you've worn out the local guys. Take Zan – she could do to be somewhere else too.

'Now I gotta go,' Rob said as he got up to leave. 'Don't wait till it's too late. The escape hatch is there but it's closing.'

As Rob ran to grab a taxi that was delivering a passenger, Danny and Zan looked at each other, both knowing the decision they were about to make.

'I can't afford ...' Zan said

'I can trade in this –' Danny patted his pocket '– for a couple of premium economy flights to LA, if I use some points.'

She shrugged. 'I don't mind flying cattle.'

'Neither would I if I was five foot two.'

'What about somewhere to live?'

'They're paying for a hotel room. We can share. No strings.'

'That *is* a string.'

'Twin beds.'

Zan thought. 'What about work?'

'Bring your laptop. I hear they even have the internet.'

She wrinkled her nose at his sarcasm. 'Do you think the cops really suspect me?'

'We'll find that out at passport control.'

As Danny considered the appeal of this tactical retreat, a taxi pulled up at the kerb and a bearded man in a rumpled khaki photographer's vest got out, hoisting a large camera bag from the back seat.

By the time he had paid the cabbie and raised a huge Nikon camera attached to an impressively tumescent telephoto lens, the table previously occupied by Danny and Zan was empty.

25

A FEW streets away, Tony Cufflinks was having a few tactical thoughts of his own. Clay could not go unpunished, that was for sure. But the girl ... it seemed like she was a natural-born killer who had dispatched one guy with her bare hands and then shot Jackie Jazz's nephew in cold blood. He didn't know whether to put a hit on the girl or hire her. But she could be useful. This brothel Jackie Jazz had sold him wasn't the goldmine he'd been promised. Maybe he could make the final payment on the deal in something other than cash.

He reached for his phone as he watched one of his new girls on a monitor, inspecting her trick's rapidly shrinking penis under a light so bright Stevie Wonder could have seen it.

'Come on, love,' he said pointlessly to the screen. 'Before we have to send a search party for it.'

He turned his attention to the much smaller screen on his phone and, as he pressed the talk button, silently prayed that he was interrupting Jackie Jazz when he was somewhere exotic, doing something fantastic.

'Jazzman,' Tony said, lacing his voice with as much sympathy as he could muster. 'Sorry for your loss, mate.'

'Thanks, Tony,' came the voice from the other side of the planet. 'We weren't close but, hey, he was a kid. Made a few mistakes but he would have come right.'

'How's your sister?'

'She's in bits, of course,' Jackie replied.

'And the kid's girlfriend?' Tony said with a smile.

'What girlfriend? News to me. The family says he was a total loner. His mother worried about that.'

'That's what I thought,' Tony said, trying to suppress a smile. 'Does the name Danny Clay ring a bell?'

'Yeah, I met him a while ago ... ex-army.'

'You know your nephew was killed in his flat, right? And the cops think it was *his* girlfriend shot your boy. Vietnamese chick called Xanthe, lives next door. They made up the story about another girl.'

'Really? Why do they think it was ... what was her name again?'

'Xanthe Tran. They call her Zan. And it looks like she killed an old guy in a lift a couple of weeks ago too.'

'Fuck ...'

'Alan Hahn, his name was. Look it up on the internet.'

'I will.'

'H.A.H.N. Like the beer. Anyway, Jackie, I just thought I would pass on my condolences and give you the heads-up on who's in the frame.'

'Thanks, mate. I appreciate it,' Jackie replied. 'I'll get someone to look into it.'

'Okay, *ciao*, mate. And don't eat the yellow snow.'

'I'm back in LA now. Got some business to attend to.'

'Is this more of that movie festival bullshit?' Tony couldn't resist.

'Movie festival?'

'Toronto, Berlin, Cannes and Edinburgh. You get around.'

'Someone has done their homework,' Jackie replied, irritated.

'I don't get it,' Tony said. 'You like movies so much you travel all over the world to watch them?'

'Not to see the movies,' Jackie explained, trying not to sound patronising. 'To meet the stars. Mingle, press the flesh with Brad and George ... and their ladies, of course. There's worse ways of wasting money. I could get a yacht but I get seasick. So I go to film festivals.'

'Is this business?' Tony asked. 'And if it is, how come I don't know about it?'

'It's a hobby,' Jackie explained. 'All you need is a half-arsed script, a couple of famous names who haven't said no and you schlep around the festivals acting like you to have something to sell.'

'You need a script for that?'

'With a script you get accreditation,' Jackie explained, 'and that means invites to all the best parties with real stars and some of the finest *punani* you'll ever lay eyes on. And all gagging for it.'

'And you get this half-arsed script from writers?'

'Of course.'

'Had to pull any of them into line?'

'You mean the guys who died?' Jackie laughed. 'I'm new to this but I don't think killing writers is going to make me too many friends in the business. Although I gotta say, creative types, man oh man! You think the people we work with have issues?'

Tony decided not to tell Jackie that his nephew had been the prime suspect in the killing of Marcus.

'Okay, what's the real angle? How do you get the drugs into the country? Film canisters?'

'There's no drugs, Tone. Not on that scale anyway.'

'I'm going to send you links to some news stories,' Tony said after a brief pause. 'They have pictures of Clay and his girlfriend. Just in case you want to take it further. And if you need any help from my crew …'

'Thanks, Tony. Maybe I can put a smile back on my sister's face. *Ciao.*'

And that certainly helped a grin emerge from the middle of Tony's designer stubble.

26

ZAN NOTICED the two thugs in the reflection of a sunglasses display. She wasn't addicted to shopping by any stretch, but she enjoyed travel and loved gadgets and that was enough to send her on a last-minute retail expedition. There she was on the lower-ground floor of the Queen Victoria Building, a sandstone wedding cake in the city centre saved from demolition by rich Asian developers, who then turned it into an upmarket shopping centre popular with other Asians, rich and otherwise.

Zan had already bought her gadget – a clip-on loop for attaching her jacket to her bag – and was trying to find a style of sunglasses that she didn't already own (her other passion). In the ebb and flow of Japanese, Korean, Chinese, Singaporean, Thai and, yes, Vietnamese shoppers, the two big guys with olive skin and all-day five o'clock shadows were easy to spot. Even in the display stand mirror, in the sea of shoppers and commuters, they looked more massive and Mediterranean than usual. Their wrap-around mirror shades were hardly necessary three metres underground in subtle artificial light.

Zan instinctively looked around for Danny. He had gone to an electronics shop for some unspecified kit and they had agreed to meet up back at the flats. She abandoned her quest for the perfect sunnies, guessing she was more likely to find them in LA anyway. Zan waited until a babble of Chinese tourists passed the window, the group expanding and contracting as if they were connected by invisible elastic threads, then she slipped into their web and allowed them to propel her along. She felt like one of those Vietcong who got past enemy lines by floating under beds of water hyacinths as they drifted down the Saigon river.

She allowed herself five shopfronts before she turned around. It was a mistake. The guys had moved forward, peering into the shop window to see where she had gone. When one of them turned around and looked straight at her, eye contact gave her away. He tapped his mate on the shoulder and they started pushing through the crowds in pursuit.

Zan sidestepped the crowd that clogged the small escalator from the basement level to the lower ground floor and took the regular stairs two at a time. She was smaller and faster than the two men, which gave her a huge advantage as she dodged and weaved through the foot traffic coming through the broad tunnel from Town Hall Station.

Zan already had her transit card out of her wallet and ready as she approached the barriers at the station entrance, but the electronic reader didn't register. She tried again. No go. Then she noticed the 'out of order' sign scrawled on a scrap of paper and dangling from the only strip of tape still attached to the machine. As she moved to the next gate she looked back and saw two large, close-cropped heads bobbing though the crowd towards her.

The barriers opened with a thud and she was through, but she had lost a lot of ground. Her pursuers came through the adjoining turnstiles side by side and one of them sprinted towards her as she took the escalator down to platform five. She could tell, from the movement of people on the platform, that there was a train about to leave for the Cross. Her feet were going so fast down the moving steps Zan was sure she was about to go arse over tit, but she made it – just too late. The train doors shut in front of her and it pulled away.

She glanced back up the escalator. One of the thugs had stopped, allowing the stairs to carry him towards her at their own pace. Zan jogged down the narrow but briefly clear platform until she reached one of the up escalators. Looking back, she saw her pursuer speaking into his mobile. She launched herself onto the escalator, but it was a mistake. Thug number two appeared at the top. She turned around as his off-sider got on the stairs behind her. She was trapped.

The man standing at the top with his arms folded began smirking as she was delivered helplessly towards him. About two thirds of the way up the escalator Zan noticed that on one side of the stairway there was a small triangular gap where two escalators crossed over in a giant, moving X. She hauled herself onto the polished steel slope beside the moving balustrade, used one of the anti-slide bumps for purchase and rolled through, landing on her feet on the stairs moving in the opposite direction back down to platforms five and six.

She ran onto a train waiting on the other platform and watched with satisfaction as her pursuer passed by, trying to walk sideways down the relentlessly rising stairs as he peered through the opening. The train doors closed. She smiled and waved as it pulled out of the station and the confused and frustrated thug was whisked upwards out of sight. Exhilarated, and grinning from ear to ear, she suddenly understood what it was that drove Danny to take risks. She pulled out her phone and dialled his number.

27

THE THREE men in the corridor between Zan and Danny's flats, all of them dressed in black tracksuits with no obvious logos, nodded at each other. *Now*. It was 2.30am and there was a chill drifting in from the street. Two of the men stood erect and alert, one watching the street entrance, the other beside Danny's door, his ear cocked for the slightest sound from inside that might indicate their mission was about to change, probably violently. The third was stooped over the lock and handle of Zan's door, working in quiet darkness until a faint buzz broke the silence. Though no louder than an electric toothbrush, to the men guarding the empty hallway the sound was like a chainsaw.

The crouching man was using a battery-driven electric lock pick, the type that flicks the pins on locks to the open position. There was a click and the man stood up, turned the handle and pushed the door open an inch. He stepped back as the others unclipped torches from their belts, opened the door further and slipped noiselessly inside. One torch came on, then a second. The beams swept the room, revealing nothing and no one. All the furniture had gone, the computer and screen, all the pictures on the walls, everything.

There was an envelope on the floor. The first man picked it up and ripped it open. It was an acknowledgement from a real estate firm and a rental bond claim form. He crumpled it up and tossed it to the floor. The second guy returned from the bedroom.

'Nothing,' he hissed. 'And no one.'

His mate pulled out his mobile phone and typed, 'She gone. Moved out.' In fact, he typed 'she goon' but the recipient must have understood because moments later the screen lit up and the words 'Okay try Clay's place' appeared.

The lock picker took longer on Danny's door – partly due to the fact that there were two locks and one of them was a high security BiLock NG with the double-sided U-shaped key. The electric bump pick was no use and working the pins on both sides was a challenge. But the lock picker was a pro and he switched to two ground-down nail files he kept for just such an occasion. Four minutes later, after he had moved to more specialised hooks and levers, Danny's door swung open.

Again the lock picker stepped back and let the larger, younger men explore. They were on high alert. Danny was ex-military, they'd been told, and therefore a threat. He had humiliated Tony Cufflinks, so he was either stupid or fearless – possibly both. It didn't matter which to them: all they needed to know was that he was unpredictable but highly trained, a lethal combination.

The scene inside was the polar opposite of Zan's empty space. There was a lot of furniture – too much, in fact – and their torch beams picked out overstuffed boxes and small tables stacked upside down on larger tables. Just as it dawned on them that this was where the contents of Zan's flat had gone, one of them nudged an invisible length of fishing line. They could only just hear the faintest ping as a paper clip was catapulted through the air, releasing a spring switch.

A desk lamp came on, illuminating a small package in the middle of the room, propping up a large digital clock screen that flashed three times then started counting down in seconds from 1.00. As they looked closer, the men realised that behind it was a bundle of cylinders, larger than cigar tubes but smaller than toilet roll cores, wrapped in paper with spirals of electrical wire protruding from the top and running to the back of the clock.

'Fuck me, it's a bomb,' one of the men turned and said to the empty space that, until moments before, had been occupied by his mate. As the second man charged out of Danny's room, following his off-sider out towards the street, the lock picker peered into the flat and saw the screen, now showing 00.56 and counting. He closed the door firmly to make sure the blast didn't follow him. As he jogged to the front door, he promised himself that he would make one more determined effort to pay off his gambling debts and free himself from having to do jobs like this.

After all, he'd never been lucky, otherwise he wouldn't be in this mess.

—

At precisely that moment, somewhere over the Pacific, Zan was watching an action movie on her screen. Danny was looking at the credits of a wildlife documentary scrolling up on his. He smiled as he looked over and saw the somewhat clichéd digital readout of a ticking time bomb in her movie. The oldest trick in the screenwriter's book: set a deadline and find ways of stopping your heroes from making it. He wished he'd set up a web cam to record the moment someone discovered his IED, if indeed there were any intruders.

He smiled again as he thought how odd it was to hope someone might break into your home. But then everything was odd in his world these days. Who spends their last hour before an overseas flight cutting up cardboard tubes, wrapping them in gaffer tape and attaching wires? While Zan was tunnelling through cardboard boxes for clothes she had packed away but now felt she desperately needed, he had turned the last remaining space in his flat into a craft workshop. He smiled again, this time catching Zan's eye.

'You look happy,' she said, as she pulled back the earpiece of his noise-cancelling headphones, keeping one eye on the frantically implausible physical feats lighting up her screen.

Danny just nodded and smiled. Then he pressed the service button. This called for whisky and chocolate.

As he gently lowered the phone handset into its cradle, Paddy looked through the open door, down the corridor to the approaching security guard. The large, uniformed African American man was carrying an empty cardboard file box, as clear a confirmation of the content of Paddy's recent conversation with Jasmina as he could have wished not to see.

First there was the frantic call at 7am telling him not to complete the buy-back deal with the Australians. *Redneck Airlift* was getting a lot of traction on social media and agents for Tarantino, Brad Pitt and George Clooney had been calling, asking if the director, writer and leads had been locked in.

Since he was suffering a hangover from celebrating having clinched the sell-back the previous evening, Paddy had spent the next three hours trying first to raise the Aborigine and his writer – a man who dressed like an extra from *Casablanca* – and then trying to persuade them to accept a check for a full refund of the money they had just paid back to him, plus a cast-iron commitment to consider their reluctance to change the script.

Then there was a very uncomfortable meeting with the head of studio and the comptroller of finance at which the latter explained how the Australians had played the forex markets to take one million of their dollars out of the project without doing a thing – and they still owned the movie rights.

Paddy was then dispatched to offer them yet another deal, only at less favourable terms. The profit projections suggested it would be an expensive shoot but, at best, a modest success financially, despite the kudos it would earn for the studio. Oh, and the Australians had already made a million from it, so let's not be greedy. However, since in a previous phone conversation with the Aborigine, Paddy had referred to him as a 'mendacious cunt' (those words separated by a racist epithet) his chances of success proved to be as slight as his diplomatic skills.

Faced with a very public humiliation, the studio decided that Paddy should take the fall. They didn't want it to be too embarrassing – for them, not for him – so he was to be moved into a 'key role in an emerging sector'. When he got the call from HR, Paddy had persuaded himself that this was a real opportunity to show the full range of his true talents. His friend Mr Lootkin needed an executive producer for a new TV project, and Paddy was the perfect man for the job, given his recent input on *Perfect Crime*.

Paddy was wondering how awkward it would be to work alongside Jasmina again when she called, basically to gloat. The head of studio wanted someone with a firm grip on Paddy's slate of projects to slide into his seat and hit the ground running, she said, mixing her metaphors like a celebratory martini. They were swapping jobs. She was moving up to movies, he was sliding down to TV. Karma is a bitch, she told him. Karma is not alone, he thought, still smarting from being told after all this time that the Aborigine was actually from somewhere near India. What the fuck!

To make matters worse, Lootkin had called to say his first project for the oh-so-small screen was going to be with even more Australians – and right now Paddy fucking hated Australians with a passion. He bet the entirely unnecessary security guard now standing in his office was Australian. Okay, Paddy had another job in another building on the lot, but he still had to do the walk of shame, his superglued comedy trophy protruding from the box. Paddy consoled himself, as he always did, with the thought that at least things couldn't get worse, even though experience should have taught him that they almost always did.

28

THE QUEUES at immigration in LAX were less painful than the last time Danny had visited the USA. There were machines that read your passport, took your fingerprints and photograph and asked you relevant questions like whether or not you were smuggling drugs or explosives into the country.

'These immigration checks always make me feel guilty for stuff I know I haven't done,' Danny whispered to Zan as they stood in a queue, waiting to be assessed by a glorified ATM. 'It's like I accidentally swallowed six condoms full of cocaine and had forgotten until now.'

Zan shushed him. She had read all the warnings not to joke about bombs and the like, and assumed that extended to drugs and other contraband. Maybe Danny could afford to joke; at least *he* was tall and white. But she was short and Asian, travelling on a non-Asian passport. That alone was surely sufficient grounds for a full cavity search, she thought. As it turned out, the only thing that delayed them was a German who insisted on the staff disinfecting the glass cover of the fingerprint reader before he would remove the white cotton gloves he was wearing. Zan and Danny moved to another queue but only lost a few places.

'Germophobic German,' Zan whispered.

'Mysophobic,' Danny replied.

'What?'

'Mysophobic – an irrational fear of germs.'

'Why on earth would you know that?'

'*Celebrity Spelling Bee,*' Danny said with a deep sigh. 'Channel 8. This writing game isn't all award-winning drama series, you know. If you're good enough to last long enough you will find yourself working on the most awful shit.'

'What's the worst?' Zan asked eagerly. 'Or are they all equally bad?'

'*Surprise Wedding*, by a country mile.'

'No fucking way!' Zan said a little too loudly, attracting curious and disapproving glances.

'I wish,' Danny said. 'I really, really do.'

Having retrieved their luggage from the baggage carousel, which turned out to be less of a roulette wheel than Zan had imagined, they walked a little tentatively towards the Los Angeles morning. There is something slightly disconcerting about arriving before you have left, the fourteen-hour flight not quite compensating for the seventeen-hour time difference.

'Have you ever tried to explain the time difference to an American?' Danny asked, rhetorically, as they scanned the ceiling for a taxi rank sign. 'They can't grasp the concept that they are almost a day behind us. America is always ahead, in everything.'

Danny was turning their trolley in the direction of the taxi sign when Zan tugged at his sleeve. A bored young man in a suit and tie was holding up an iPad that said 'Mr Clay' in large letters over 'arriving from Sydney' in smaller text with 'Australia' squeezed at the bottom as an afterthought, just in case there was a Mr Clay arriving from Sydney, the small town in Canada.

'Mr Clay?' asked the young man as they approached. Danny nodded. 'Welcome to Los Angeles,' he continued, taking charge of the luggage trolley. 'My name is Brad. Please follow me.'

As they exited into the gritty morning sunshine, Brad pulled a cell phone out of his pocket and pressed a button, then stopped at the side of the kerb.

'How far is it to the car?' Danny asked.

'Oh, he'll come to us. There's a holding area across the way.' He pointed vaguely behind an airport building. It turned out Brad wasn't the driver; he was an intern and, as Danny and Zan learned on the way to their hotel, fresh out of university with a degree in film production. Now he was working unpaid for the studio for a year while he learned the ropes. Danny wondered aloud if he was happy with that, but Brad thought it was a fantastic system.

'I get the inside track on a full-time job in the industry,' he enthused from the front seat of the car.

'And it keeps the riff-raff out,' Zan opined with a smile.

'I'm sorry?' Brad said, his smile even more firmly in place.

'Only wealthy middle-class families can afford to keep their kids in chinos and loafers for a year, right?' she continued. 'So poor kids never have a chance, regardless of how talented they are.'

'Zan is a communist,' Danny said with a matter-of-fact smile.

Brad swivelled round with a grin that suggested he thought Danny was joking. Zan met his look with a toss of her hair.

'It's in my blood,' she said.

Brad turned back to the view out of the front window: five lanes of traffic in both directions. They were on the 405 heading for West Hollywood. Zan had been wide-eyed at the eight lanes of the 105; now she was in traffic shock. Thanks to a minor incident on La Cienega that was threatening to turn into a major hold-up, it took them the best part of an hour to get Le Montrose, a boutique hotel a block and a half from Sunset Boulevard. Danny had been here a few times before, but Zan was in full tourist mode, squealing with delight when she saw familiar landmarks.

'Look, that's where they have the Oscars,' she shouted as they turned off Wilshire at the Beverley Hilton. Brad squirmed, etiquette preventing him from correcting her.

The driver had no such qualms: he was getting paid regardless.

'Golden Globes, ma'am,' he murmured. 'The Oscars are held in the Dolby on Hollywood Boulevard.' With his down-home Louisiana accent, he held the 'ah' of boulevard in his mouth like it was a fine Scotch, letting it out slowly and richly, skipping the R.

'I thought it was the Kodak,' Danny said.

'It was but they changed the name,' the driver said with a chuckle. 'Kodak out. Dolby in. I guess they got themselves digitised.' He chuckled quietly several more times, his shoulders heaving. Danny just hoped he wouldn't choke and crash the car.

Le Montrose was the opposite of the concrete and glass monstrosities that pass for hotels in many big cities. Tucked on the corner of two leafy streets, its entrance had the feel of a country house rather than the temporary home of minor celebrities that was its main function.

'Welcome back, Mr Clay.' The receptionist smiled as he handed Danny two room keys. 'And it *is* twin beds?'

'Yes!' Zan said a little too quickly and loudly as she snatched a key out of Danny's hand and headed to the lift.

'Welcome back?' she said as Danny caught up with her. 'You must have made quite an impression when you were here last.'

'I'm on their system. There's a computer screen cut into the desk. They probably know more about me that I do myself. But I like it here – it's comfortable, not too flash. Discreet.'

The bellhop pushing the luggage trolley nodded to himself, feeling validated.

'What were you doing here?' Zan asked as the lift doors slid open. 'Working on a movie?'

'Kind of, but not writing. A buddy of mine from US drug enforcement was setting up a company to advise on action and war movies and TV shows. Set himself up as an armourer.'

'You were in the DEA?'

Danny laughed. 'No, we used to go on joint operations in

Afghanistan. We provided the backup and firepower, they provided helicopters.'

'The DEA were in Afghanistan?' Her incredulity rising.

'Opium. Where do you think the Taliban get all their money from?' Danny realised the bellhop was staring at him, awestruck.

'You might want to shut your mouth, son, before something flies in,' Danny said with a smile. The doors opened and the bellhop gestured them into a carpeted, timber-lined corridor discreetly illuminated by subdued lighting.

Danny had a ten-dollar note ready for the bellhop, avoiding the customary awkwardness of new arrivals who don't know whether or not, and how much to tip. The answer is yes, and two dollars per bag.

'You gave that guy ten dollars,' Zan protested. 'That would buy you a dinner in Saigon.'

'Well, if he ever goes there he won't go hungry,' Danny said. 'Look there's no minimum wage here. These guys live on tips.'

'He's probably saving up to be an intern at a studio,' Zan said.

The room was split-level with the beds on a raised platform at the back and a safety railing between them and the living area to prevent any broken limbs. The living area had a desk as well as a table and a modest bar kitchen area. French doors led to a small balcony with a view to LA city centre beyond. Danny was always struck by how remarkably low-rise Los Angeles was. The office blocks stuck up like stalagmites in the middle of endless suburbs of bungalows and walk-up apartment blocks.

'They've done the place up since I was here last,' Danny said, taking in the minimalist furniture and decoration. 'It was a lot ... um ... *cosier* before.'

'I like it,' Zan said. 'I don't do cosy.'

Zan pulled her head out of the minibar and tugged at a small cupboard beside it. It was locked.

'That's where they put the booze when people who don't want to be tempted check in,' Danny said. 'Saves them counting all the bottles when they empty then restock the fridge.'

'I didn't realise there were so many alcoholics in the world,' Zan replied.

'Then there's Muslims, kids, corporates on a tight budget!'

'On the subject …' Zan said, raising a chilled bottle of Heineken.

'It's only ten in the morning!'

'It's still 3am in Sydney,' she said with a mischievous smirk. 'It's a nightcap.'

'Okay,' Danny said. 'But let's go up to the roof. I haven't had any natural light since we left the Cross.'

Le Montrose's roof was in two sections: one had a small swimming pool – or a large plunge pool, depending on whether you were a 'swimming pool half-empty' type – the other was a full-size tennis court complete with ball serving machine.

The pool was surrounded by elegant sun lounges, day beds and cabanas, half of which were occupied by the same range of don't-look-at-me celebrities and look-at-me wannabes as you'd find at Uliveto Cafe in the Cross – only in more expensive clothes. A bar in the corner was closed, but a room-service waiter was doing a brisk trade in healthy juices. Even so, he didn't blink an eye when Danny asked for a whisky sour and a bloody Mary, and smiled when Danny added, 'Breakfast in a glass.' This was Hollywood.

Danny wandered over to the balustrade and looked out over WeHo, as the locals called West Hollywood. Los Angeles was a deeply shallow city, he knew, but that only meant nothing was too far from the surface. A clutter of low-rise rooftops extended all the way to the city centre skyscrapers and beyond.

Somewhere in there lay so many broken dreams that, someone once told him, they used them to pave the streets. He thought about Jensen for the first time since he and Zan had decided to flee Sydney and wondered if the young actor was about to become just another piece of roadkill, kicked to the kerb when his star faded – if it ever truly got to shine.

Zan had commandeered one of the tables clustered around the pool and had already fired up her laptop and logged on to the internet by the time Danny joined her.

'Oh shit,' she said, turning the screen towards Danny.

'Hoax bomb in fake soldier's flat,' screamed the internet news headline over a picture of Danny's home-made, hand-crafted 'time bomb'. The story went on to relate how the 'bomb' was discovered by a neighbour who had peered through the letter box after hearing 'suspicious ticking'. Neighbours were terrified, the yarn continued, and police were on the point of evacuating the entire street before a courageous police officer risked her life to investigate. Next to the piece was a picture of Laura with a caption quoting her saying, 'It could have been devastating.'

'Okay, why?' said Zan.

'Somebody must have broken in and then called the cops, in case anyone got hurt from a real bomb,' Danny surmised. 'Just because someone's a bad person doesn't mean they aren't a good citizen.'

'Neighbours heard it ticking ...' she said.

'There was no ticking. Someone broke in – which is why I put the bomb there.'

'Unbelievable,' Zan complained. 'This is meat and drink to those internet arseholes. It just doesn't make any kind of sense to me.'

'Hey,' Danny was suddenly slightly riled. 'You're the one who started this, telling people I was SAS.'

'And that makes this okay?' she said.

'Okay, look: I guessed someone was going to come after us – probably Tony Cufflinks, maybe Jackie Jazz – and I wanted them to know what they were dealing with.'

'You're just making all this up now,' Zan said, her teeth clenched behind lips that barely moved.

'No, seriously. Sure, this was a fake bomb, but they know what that means: I – *we* – are a force to be reckoned with. They'll think twice now before they send anyone else.'

'They don't know where we are,' Zan said. 'Wasn't that the whole point of coming here?'

'Someone knows,' Danny said, nodding towards a waiter approaching with a portable phone.

'Mr Clay?' he said, offering the device.

'Maybe,' Danny said with a half-smile. 'It depends.' But he took the phone anyway and said his name. Danny nodded and said 'uh-huh' several times, ending with, 'great, looking forward to it'.

He handed the phone back to the steward, along with a five-dollar bill.

'They want me at a read-through tomorrow for the Jensen thing. They've got a new producer and he wants to hit the ground running.'

'Let's hope he hasn't Googled you, Bomber Clay,' Zan said as she snapped the laptop shut. 'Now, you need to be fresh for tomorrow so I suggest another drink, lunch, more drinks, more food, then an early night.'

'Is that your cure for jetlag?'

'No, it's my cure for being around you,' she said as she drained her glass and waved it impolitely in the direction of a waiter.

—

Danny woke and dressed, his head filled with fur. He guessed that if hangovers were really a cure for jetlag, someone would have written a book about it by now. He left a note for Zan with a thumb drive attached. It contained half a dozen scripts and pitches, just in case he got a meeting with someone who cared. He asked her to find a photocopy place and run off some copies of each document.

Danny didn't want to risk waking Zan so he waited till he got to reception to ask them to call him a taxi.

'Wouldn't you rather take your car?' the concierge asked, catching Danny's look of surprise. 'The studio has given you a Prius. Should I have it brought up?' His hand was already hovering over the phone as Danny nodded. Three minutes later, Danny was slipping the car valet a five. He'd once wondered how much hotels paid their car jockeys, only to be told the car valets paid the hotels, they made so much on tips. He'd thought this was bullshit until he chanced upon two of them counting out their cash during a shift change. There were so many five-dollar bills on the table he thought he was interrupting a drug deal – until one of the guys tossed him his keys.

The address of BJF Studios was already punched into the satnav, and Danny wondered if this was one of those cars that would drive itself. He decided not to take any chances and steered it out onto the street, mentally repeating his mantra of 'tight and right' until he got used to driving on the 'wrong' side of the road again.

Danny pulled into the BJF lot and joined the visitor lane to the right of the security booth. There had been an internet alert overnight and, according to a sign on the gate, the studio was on code yellow: extreme care. He would discover later that code orange was 'no visitors' and code red was a complete lockdown. Most of it was for show. There is no business where the phrase 'time is money' is more true than in film and TV production. Osama Bin Laden would have to rise from the dead and stand at the gates in a suicide vest before a code red was even contemplated.

The reality for Danny was that he had to get out of the car – already suspect because it was a rental with no number plates – while one security guard checked the trunk and underside and the other copied details from the registration papers. Danny watched the man with the clipboard. He stood tall and seemed relaxed, but his eyes flicked from side to side, registering every movement in the background.

'Where did you serve?' Danny asked.

'Huh?'

'I did three tours out of Tarin Kowt,' Danny continued, wondering if he had misread the situation.

'Ah.' The security guy smiled. 'Two in Kandahar.'

'Good to be home, huh?'

'You betcha,' the guard said, tugging at his pale grey shirt. 'It would be nice to get out of uniform though.'

'At least you don't have to wear that damned body armour.' Danny smiled back.

'Not till the suicide blondes get crazy ideas,' the guard grinned, letting him know he was smarter than he looked. Getting an all-clear signal from his partner, he waved Danny through. 'You have a nice day, now.'

Danny joke saluted and drove on. Suicide blondes, he smiled to himself, dyed by their own hand. More importantly, he doubted if he would ever have to stop for a security search again.

—

Zan and her bladder woke up about an hour after Danny had left. It wasn't until she had visited the bathroom and sat down reading the note on the table that she remembered she was in LA. It wasn't until she was standing stretching in the sun on the balcony and heard a loud whistle from the street that she remembered she was naked. Now she was awake, scuttling back into the room in search of her clothes.

There they were, neatly piled on a chair. There was the bathrobe, dumped on the floor beside the bed. There were the rumpled sheets on both beds, and her underwear had been removed and folded on a seat, where it still lay. All of this suggested that whatever had happened between last drinks and lights out would have no lasting consequences. Phew!

Danny's note suggested she get breakfast in La Conversation on North Doheny. Le Montrose, La Conversation – what is this, the French quarter? Zan thought as she Google-Mapped the cafe and the nearest print shop. Great, they were in opposite directions. Danny raved about the *huevos rancheros* at La Conversation, but as much as she liked spicy food – because it was spicy, and food – it was a ten-minute round trip just to get back where she started. She was sure she could find a cafe on the way, but then Danny would want to know why she hadn't gone to La Conversation and they would end up going there at some other point when they didn't have time, like when they were on their way to the airport. So she might as well go anyway.

Fuck him.

29

'OZZIE, OZZIE, Ozzie,' said the plump, red-faced man with the dark wavy hair as Danny entered the writers room. This was where he'd be working on *Pretty Boy*, as his former lesbian police procedural series *Lady Cop* was now known.

Danny smiled and ignored the plump man, looking around the table for Jensen and catching his eye briefly. Jensen was already colouring, as young people tend to do a little too readily in embarrassing situations. He only had the vaguest recollection of having seen the kid before. A dazzling smile had Danny instinctively feeling his teeth with his tongue, convinced they must be covered in green fur.

Danny could see how Jensen might be the next big thing. He had that semi-androgynous look – the one that inspired Ellen DeGeneres to describe a young Leonardo DiCaprio as looking like a twelve-year-old lesbian. He was fine-featured but tall and lightly muscled, in a carefully ripped but spotlessly clean T-shirt, a baseball cap and shades. But that face ... that smile. Danny could see exactly what the network execs had seen, and if he could remember lines without tripping over his co-stars, so much the better.

'Come on! Ozzie, Ozzie, Ozzie!' the man said again, nodding and smiling. 'Your turn.'

'To do what?' Danny asked.

'Don't you say, "Oi Oi Oi"?'

'Apparently not.' Danny smiled then looked around the table. 'I'm looking for Mr Rosenberg.' He left it hanging.

'That would be me,' said the Ozzie, Ozzie, Ozzie man. 'Paddy Rosenberg, executive producer.'

'Well, Oi, Oi … veh,' Danny said, regretting it before the last syllable had left his lips.

Everyone around the table tensed but Paddy Rosenberg laughed uproariously. The others joined in. Danny noticed Brad, the intern, and smiled. Brad, whose whole life at this point depended on not offending anyone, allowed himself the slightest flicker of an acknowledgement. If he'd held a lady's fan he would have flicked it open to hide his expression while conspiring with his eyes.

'That's what I love about these fucking Australians,' Paddy said. 'They don't give a shit who they offend.'

It was a phrase that should have ended with a laugh or a smile at least. Instead it soft-landed in the melting tar pit of Paddy's career.

'Hi, I assume you're Danny, Danny Clay?' a strong-featured woman with wild red hair said from halfway down the long table. It was the first time Danny had really taken in his surroundings. It was a nondescript room with no windows but lots of air-con vents. There was no furniture except the basic boardroom table and a cabinet that looked like it might contain coffee and biscuits. Or not. There was a jumble of eight extremely casually dressed people – checked shirts and/or ironic T-shirts and deliberately torn jeans – ranged around the table, plus Jensen, Paddy and the red-head.

'Sorry, my name is Ciara,' she said. 'Spelled with a C, pronounced with a K. Ciara Parres. I'm the showrunner.'

She flashed one of those laser-light smiles that mean only Brits and Scandinavians can ever do historical drama. (We accept dragons and undead because the dentistry in *Game of Thrones* is almost credible.) Ciara gestured Danny to the only empty seat at the table.

'Okay, so we've had to make some changes, obviously,' she said lifting her copy of the script that was in front of everyone at the table, even

Danny. 'But if you have any questions, could you please take a note and leave them to the end of …'

'Sorry, did you say "had"?' Danny asked.

Ciara nodded, clearly wondering if she should.

'It's just, I thought this meeting was to discuss the changes we were going to make.' Danny said, as calmly as he could.

'Yeah, well, time's a-wastin',' Paddy replied, looking around the table for support that was not forthcoming. These guys were writers. Danny may have been a foreigner but he was one of their own.

'There were certain structural adjustments that had to be made anyway when we changed the gender and sexual orientation of the protagonist,' Ciara explained, her misty green eyes drawing Danny in.

He was almost convinced until Paddy piped up: 'Obviously, with the lezzo lead gone, or at least, having changed sex, his wingman had to be a wingwoman. Am I right or am I right?'

Danny felt his blood rising, ready to go to the barricades to get this obnoxious toad of a man to admit he was wrong. Even – no, especially – if he was right.

—

Zan had made it to La Conversation despite crossing the road looking the wrong way three times and, as a result, almost being run over once. In Sydney this might have prompted an outburst of racist road rage. In LA nothing says sorry quite like a cute, apologetic smile from a pretty girl.

The cafe was basically the front room of a French-style patisserie. There were half a dozen tables on the footpath with honey-coloured bent-cane and raffia chairs, and inside were twice as many made from dark wood. The décor, including Regency striped drapes covering the walls of the main dining area, was way too chintzy for Zan's minimalist tastes, but it looked like it could rustle up a decent breakfast.

Brightly lit cabinets with curved fronts presented an array of fantastically coloured, diet-busting baked treats, displayed as if they were jewellery. Zan scanned the extensive menu though she knew she would order the *huevos rancheros*, just to be able to tell Danny that she had. Next time, maybe, she would try some of the technicolour goodies in the cabinets.

The eggs and beans didn't disappoint and she set about task number two, printing out the scripts. Zan had changed the sim card in her phone while she sipped her second coffee and, just as she was leaving a message on Danny's phone – 'Hi, it's me, leaving my new number on your phone, call me' – she noticed a man who'd been sitting at a table behind her, getting up to leave. He was tall and thin and strikingly dressed in a beautifully tailored white linen suit and a cream-coloured Panama hat held in his hand, the ensemble completed by classic Ray Ban shades and light-tan cowboy boots, the heels of which added another inch to his already impressive stature.

Zan stared. There was something familiar about him. Was he a movie star? It was hard to tell. He mostly had his back to her as he weaved between the tables to the door, but when she did catch a glimpse of his face in a mirror as he smiled his goodbye to the waitress, he flashed one of those thousand-watt Hollywood smiles that were as genuine as the emotions behind them. The waitress picked up the cash left on top of his bill. Judging by her expression, the hombre in the linen suit had underestimated his obligations.

'*Señor?* Was everything okay?' she called out to his back in an accent that came from the other side of the Rio Grande, rather than the Left Bank of the Seine. The man waved his hand dismissively without turning around. She looked like she wanted to throw the handful of coins at him but the door had already closed.

'Tourist?' said Zan, like she hadn't just got off a plane.

'English,' said the waitress. 'Like you.'

'I'm not English.' Zan smiled – they both did, two strangers, either of whom could be from anywhere, including right here.

'He rich,' said the waitress. 'Plenty money. Usually a good tipper.'

'Maybe he's just having a bad day.'

'Now I am too,' said the waitress, juggling the meagre pile of coins in her hand.

Zan made sure her own tip was on the generous side, gathered her things and left. As she turned right and started walking back up North Doheny, a flash of white caught her eye. There, across the road, about fifty yards away, was the man in the white suit, talking into a cell phone. He turned away as she got near, sheltering his face from the dust and fumes of a passing truck. Now she was even more sure that she knew him.

The body language was very familiar, but she'd had a couple of decent glimpses of his face and his features didn't match anything in her mental card index. When she turned and looked back, he was getting into a large black Range Rover. He was somebody, all right, but she just wasn't sure who.

Zan shook her head and chided herself for being so easily distracted. She took care to look left, crossed a side street and marched off to the copy shop.

—

Danny had had a long day and it was only lunchtime. Every suggestion he made was dismissed by Paddy, often contemptuously. Danny was doing a lot of deep breathing and 'angry face' control. It didn't take long to work out that Paddy was a complete fool who covered his shortcomings, which were many and great, by bullying the people beneath him. He wasn't the first person like that who Danny had met – the army was full of them – but he was possibly the one least entitled to any sense of superiority. This man was a bucket of clichéd ideas that seemed to have no bottom, and Paddy had been scraping down there looking for it for a while.

He shouldn't really have been at the meeting: that was way too hands-on for most executive producers. But it seemed to Danny that he was trying to convince himself as well as everyone else that he was the smartest guy in the room. Jensen didn't really belong there either, but Ciara wanted the writers to get a handle on what would and wouldn't work with him. Being forced to eat so many shit sandwiches in front of a young man who clearly admired him was excruciating for Danny.

'Hey, how about the kid is on a deadline, like he's about to quit the cops?' Paddy suggested at one point.

'So this is his last case before he retires?' Danny said sarcastically, earning a murmur of suppressed laughter around the table.

'Yeah, exactly,' Paddy said with a look that silenced the sniggers. 'What's wrong with that?'

'Because he's a kid?' offered Danny, not trying too hard to mask the contempt in his voice.

'Okay,' said Paddy, trying to recover lost ground. 'It's his last case before he goes to college.' He smiled and nodded.

'So, now we're doing *21 Jump Street*?' said Danny.

'The Jonah Hill movie?'

'I was thinking more Johnny Depp,' Danny said, poking the bear.

'Excuse me!' Paddy said contemptuously, inadvertently sounding like Steve Martin (when he was still funny). 'I am good buddies with Jonah, and Johnny Depp was nowhere near that movie. Get your facts straight, Aussie,' saying it with a soft S rather than a hard Z.

'Whatever you say, boss,' Danny said, similarly sibilant and smiling thinly. The other writers were suddenly finding that their notepads and laptops required serious attention.

'It was also a TV show in the late '80s,' Ciara interceded. 'Launched Johnny Depp's career.'

'The Deppster did TV?' Paddy said, amazed. 'Who knew?'

Everyone else at this table, you fat fraud, is what Danny didn't say. Paddy picked up the script and pointed it in Danny's general direction.

'So this isn't even original,' he said, shaking his head. 'I should have guessed. I mean, Australia, right?'

'It's completely original,' Ciara jumped in. 'As much as anything can be. We're just telling the same stories in different ways.'

Paddy did not look convinced. 'Okay, forget the college idea,' he said. 'Not one of your best, Danny boy.'

Danny's features were totally impassive. He realised his angry face wasn't there because he had stopped thinking about the script and was now daydreaming about ways he could organise a slow, painful, humiliating and preferably public death for Paddy. Right now he was calculating the logistics of firing DVD discs with sharpened edges at him while he was spread-eagled naked on a giant wooden X on Venice Beach.

When Ciara called lunch Paddy disappeared with Jensen, and the other writers evaporated as if even talking to Danny would infect them with whatever it was that Paddy hated about him. Only Ciara stayed behind.

'Care to join me in the commissary?' she asked.

'It would be a pleasure.'

The BJF commissary was a huge room with vaulted ceilings in a brick-and-glass building that had once been a small sound stage, then an audio recording studio, then, briefly and unsuccessfully, offices. Now it was mostly white and brightly lit – unlike the adjoining a la carte restaurant next door, which was warmed by a subdued glow and even had linen on the tables.

'Don't look,' Ciara said as they passed the adjoining door. 'You'll see someone famous, and they'll see you and then you'll have to act like you didn't recognise them and they'll have to pretend they did recognise you.'

The commissary was busy but not packed, mostly populated by writers (scruffy insouciance, with battle-scarred satchels), secretaries (elegant efficiency and killer heels) and crew (jeans, checked shirts and tool belts for the men; black leggings, muscle shirts and tool belts for the women). There was a steadily moving line around the large circular salad bar.

'Try the Cobb salad,' Ciara said. 'It's been a staple here since Courteney Cox said it kept her thin through ten series of *Friends*.' She nodded at a Starbucks franchise in the corner. 'At least they've improved the coffee.'

'Jeez,' said Danny. 'How bad was it before?'

They paid for their food and found a table in the corner. 'Okay, what's your story?' Danny asked Ciara.

'My town, my studio,' she said with a wide Julia Roberts smile. 'You first.'

So Danny gave her the bullet points, in reverse. Jensen, TV, the army, TV before that. He threw in the murders of Marcus and Weezl as icing at the end. Ciara was literally speechless, her mouth slightly open, awaiting a forkful of salad that was wilting as its delivery was delayed.

'Are you okay?' Danny said, half-expecting her to jump out of her seat and run from the room. She shook herself out of her reverie.

'I was just thinking, if that was real, wow, and if you made it up, double wow.'

'It's real. And you?'

'Compared to that, I have nothing. I have never fought in a war, none of my friends have been murdered and I have never worked on a show called *Surprise Wedding*.'

'I didn't actually mention that,' Danny said, puzzled.

'I Googled you. You might want to get that updated. Your CV is a couple of killings short.' Ciara caught the brief flash of pain that crossed

Danny's expression. 'I'm so sorry,' she said. 'That was insensitive. They were your friends.'

'One of them was.' Danny was about to add Bryan's suicide to the mix but thought better of it. 'So tell me about you.'

'My name is Ciara Parres which a lot of people think is Mexican – as in Peres – but it is in fact German, and I also have a chunk of Irish in me, which is why I was called Ciara, but a lot of people mispronounce it as *"see-ara"*. So I called myself Ki for a while but some people thought I must be Korean – as you can imagine.'

She opened her hands to invite his gaze. Danny thought he had never seen a woman who looked more Celtic, but nodded as if he could see the Seoul in her features.

'I come from Richmond, Virginia, which was the capital of the South in the Civil War even though it's only a couple of hours' drive from Washington DC,' she continued, having taken a breath like a distance swimmer. 'I am a lapsed Catholic and recovering sitcom writer. Funny people are generally too fucked up for you to want to be around them when they are not being funny. I admit I have taken at least one job a while back that was offered to me because of a 'minorities support' policy – yes, they thought I was Mexican and they couldn't take it off me because that would also have been discriminatory.

'I got asked to run *Pretty Boy* because my post-apocalypse cable fantasy about a world run by cannibalistic women didn't get up but they liked my writing and, obviously, a contemporary ironic gender-bending procedural cop show was almost the same thing.

'I am single by choice. My friends say I am commitment phobic but the day I feel comfortable about farting in bed next to my partner, things have gotten way too cosy and I move on … that's if they don't.'

'Because of the farting,' Danny offered.

'Exactly.' Ciara laughed.

'And you go speed dating?' he suggested. Ciara raised her eyebrows and cocked her head. 'If I had put a stopwatch on that little spiel I bet it would have come in right on two minutes,' he said.

Ciara contorted her lips into a crooked smile and narrowed her eyes. 'I'm not going to answer that because I hate smug men. And how about you? Married, single or gay? Or any combination thereof?'

'Single. I guess I couldn't handle all the farting.'

Ciara's laugh was throaty and real, but it died when a fat shadow fell across the table and Paddy Rosenberg plonked himself in one of the spare seats between them.

'Glad to get you two together,' he said, sarcasm dripping from every syllable. 'Look, Jen has filled me in on your background, Danny.'

'Jen?' Danny thought.

'I have to say, the kid admires you – worships you, even,' Paddy continued. 'But it's going to take more than a schoolboy crush to keep your project alive here. This is the big league, buddy, and I have to say I'm not impressed with either your proposal or your contributions so far.'

Danny was about to protest, but Paddy raised a finger and shook his head.

'But it's your attitude that really shits me. You second-guess me on everything I say. Your ideas are clichéd and I get the feeling you are one of these writers who has never lived in the real world. In fact, I know all about you.' Paddy paused for dramatic effect. 'I spoke to my good buddy Jeff Neumann back in Sydney – oh, yeah, it's amazing who you get to know in this business – and he did not have a single good word to say about you.

'So I'm sorry, pal, but I've got my eye on you and I expect you ...' he turned to Ciara '... to ride him hard, see if we can get some value out of our investment.'

Paddy looked up as Jensen neared the table. 'Try the crème brûlée,' Paddy said, rising from his seat. 'They make it in the a la carte kitchen.' And with that he put his arm around Jensen's shoulder and guided him to the exit.

Danny thought of razor-sharp silver disks flying through the air in swarms, slicing through pudgy flesh, enough to hurt but not to kill … not immediately, anyway.

'Sorry about that.' Ciara put her hand on his.

'That's okay. This is only temporary torture for me. You have to put up with this after I've moved on.'

'Maybe not,' Ciara said with a wicked smile. 'One of the reasons Mr Rosenberg is being such an asshole is that his career is hanging by a thread.'

As they walked back to the former cottage that was their production offices, Ciara told Danny how Paddy had screwed up the *Redneck Airlift* deal at every stage, cost the studio a million dollars and lost the project as well. He'd been demoted from movies to the cable division and been replaced by his former assistant, who was telling friends she had a sexual harassment suit locked down and ready to roll if he so much as looked at her the wrong way again.

Danny decided not to tell her that Paddy was lucky – *Redneck Airlift* was probably what cost his friends their lives.

When Paddy and Jensen didn't show for the afternoon session, Danny and Ciara were both pleased: at least now they could get some real work done.

—

The waitress brought their mac and cheese, but even that couldn't make Danny smile. They were in Mel's Drive-in on Sunset, a diner straight out of the '50s. Formica-topped tables with chrome trims, mini jukeboxes in every booth: design that had looked futuristic until it suddenly looked retro, like how *The Jetsons* (the space-age Flintstones) now looked as prehistoric as their dinosaur-riding near-namesakes. With waiters in little white hats and a menu that read like cholesterol was yet to be discovered, Mel's was less restaurant, more time machine.

Even the music selection was at least half a century old.

'Did Daddy Bear have a bad day at the office?' Zan said from behind a mountain of veggie burgers, milk shakes, fries, salads and now macaroni cheese.

'Jeez, Zan,' Danny said. 'You're never going to eat all that.'

'I couldn't make up my mind,' she said, pointing to the stack of menus. 'And anyway, you're going to help me.'

'If I wanted to eat myself to death I'd have chosen somewhere less touristy.'

'You suggested here.' She sniffed. 'Is the food bad?'

'No, it's fine. Mostly good, sometimes great … but you have to be in the mood.'

'Not the mood you're in,' she said.

'I'm cool.' He forced a smile. 'Let's eat. Then we can go somewhere that doesn't serve authentic '50s coffee.'

Danny hadn't told Zan, but he had a feeling they weren't going to be in LA for much longer so he wanted to tick all the tourist boxes while they had the chance.

'Oh … oh … oh!' Zan said through a mouthful of corn chips. 'The weirdest thing happened today. I had breakfast at La Conversation, as instructed.'

'Was it good?' he asked, ignoring the jibe.

'Yeah, okay, it was fantastic,' she conceded. 'Anyway I saw this guy – tall, thin, in a white suit – and it was like I really knew him but I have never seen him before.'

'An actor maybe?'

'Don't think so. The waitress said he was English.'

'They have actors.'

'It was so weird,' she continued. 'But I can't have known him cause I was sitting right next to him and he would have seen me.'

'Get used to it. Around here you see people you think you know because you've seen them on TV,' Danny explained. 'And then there are the people trying to look like the people you've seen on TV. Was there anything else about this guy?'

'Amazing teeth that you could use to light a stadium, and one of those straw hats like … what is it … a fedora?'

'Panama?' Danny guessed.

'What else?' she prompted herself. 'Ray Bans and cowboy boots – and it all looked really expensive.'

'Okay, that narrows it down to about a million people.'

Zan slumped down and put on her pouty face, then she brightened, the way only she could. 'Now tell me about your first day at school,' she said. 'Did the other kids not let you join in their games?'

'Worse than that,' Danny said, momentarily distracted by a waitress delivering a tray groaning with fried food to a booth at which only two were seated, having slotted themselves in sideways like peas squeezed between the tines of a fork. 'The headmaster hates me.'

But when he looked back at Zan for a smile, her face was entirely obscured by a giant mushroom burger, dripping with cheese, that she was trying to bite through in one go. Danny sighed, retrieved a French fry from a model of a '50s Buick convertible and took a long pull on Zan's malted milkshake. This could wait. He didn't want to even think about his day.

30

'SO YOU don't know where Clay is?' Tony Cufflinks growled into the phone. 'Or the girl?'

'I honestly don't,' said the voice on the end.

'And what was with that fake fucking bomb? My guys nearly had a heart attack. One of them pissed himself, literally.'

'Oh, it was your guys?'

'Who the fuck else would it be?'

'I dunno. I guess he was sending you a message.'

'What message?' Tony barked. 'That he's going to blow me up?'

'Maybe that he knew you would come for him.'

'Well, I told him I would, so his detective skills are right up there with yours, Sherlock. Anyway, it was the girl I was after: hurt her and I hurt him, he said so himself. Two for the price of one.' Tony paused. 'So Clay didn't tell you where they were going?'

'Nope.' It was only partly a lie.

'How about if I told you he is in Los Angeles, right now?' Tony rolled his letter opener around the fingers of his free hand. There was a silence, but he was sure he heard the word 'shit' whispered.

'Los Angeles?'

'You know, mate, if you're going to keep holding out on me, we may have to renegotiate our arrangement, if you get my drift.'

'I'm not holding out on you, Tony.'

'Okay, so get me something I can use – like where he's staying, for a start.' And with that, Tony clicked off the phone, picked up the letter opener and stabbed the cover of a pornographic DVD. The knife went straight through, pinning a lingerie-clad female dwarf to his desk.

'You are well and truly fucked, sweetheart,' Tony said to the DVD cover, but he was thinking about someone else entirely.

—

Rob clicked off his phone. That was weird. Kings Cross cops wanted to know where Danny was staying in LA. He'd claimed client privilege, knowing it was bullshit – he was his agent, not his lawyer – but then they started in with the threats. Did he know this was a murder investigation? Did he know the penalties for obstructing the police? How long did he think he'd last in jail before he was pulling a train of Lebanese bikies?

'Calm the fuck down, officer,' he'd said, using the phrase least likely to calm people down. 'He's staying in Le Montrose in West Hollywood.'

Rob sat back in his chair, wondering if he'd done a good thing ... or something very, very bad.

31

DANNY CLICKED on the walkie-talkie: 'All clear, come on down.'

'Roger that,' said Billy the Kid, the APC driver and youngest man in the platoon.

Danny heard the roar of the M113 armoured personnel carrier's massive engine and saw the cloud of dust before he saw the vehicle. Designed to carry ten troops in full kit, plus a driver, it was the workhorse of the army. Soon it would be replaced by Bushmasters with their blast-deflecting under-carriages. But not soon enough.

The dirt road split into two narrow tracks, one a couple of metres higher than the other. Danny had just cleared the top road, reckoning the Taliban would more likely mine the lower track, as it looked easier to navigate.

Something made him look back. The sound of the APC – it was coming from the wrong place. It was too low. Billy had taken the lower track, the one they hadn't cleared. 'Come on down,' he'd said. It was a joke. Danny grabbed the radio and clicked the button.

It was like he fired the IED himself.

The pressure plate detonated the bomb right under the APC's sweet spot. The vehicle split in two. What was left of Billy the Kid was propelled upwards like a mortar of flesh, blood and bone.

Danny helped clear the area around the smouldering wreck. Mine detectors and prodders. Often there was a second device to get the people who responded to the first. Lucky there was no one else on board. Unlucky for Billy the bomb wasn't a couple of feet further forward or back.

Safe now, they were collecting: arms, legs, hands, a boot with a foot still in it, another one empty. Where was Billy's other foot? Scraps of camo cloth, hot metal. 'Got it, Sarge.' Found the other foot. All good. Billy in a bag. Platoon moves on.

Then Danny spotted something, grey-white, covered in dirt and flies. He moved over. *Stay away, Danny. Leave it, Danny. Don't look, Danny.* He picked it up.

Billy's brain. *Nooooo!*

Danny was woken by Zan sliding into bed beside him.

'You were having a nightmare,' she said.

He felt the cloth of her T-shirt against his perspiring back. Spoons.

'This is nice,' he mumbled.

'Try anything and you are a dead man,' she says.

'Does farting count?'

'Eeee-yeeew!' she says, but snuggled closer and they both fall asleep.

—

Danny didn't tell Zan about his dream; instead he explained what had caused it. His run-in with Paddy Rosenberg must have triggered all his alert responses. His therapist had said he should always talk it out. Zan was a good listener so she got the whole box and dice over breakfast, although for some reason he glossed over his lunchtime chat with Ciara.

Breakfast was *huevos divorciados* at Loteria, a Mexican food stall in the Farmers' Market. They had driven there because Danny felt they should use the car, but it took longer than planned due to early-morning traffic. After breakfast, Danny drove to the studio while Zan went off to explore the Grove, an open-air shopping mall with its own tram car that ran for all of two hundred metres between trendy stores like Gap and Crate and Barrel. She wanted to see the musical fountain where the illuminated water jets danced to a soundtrack, and American Girl, a store that sold clothes for little girls and identical outfits for their dolls. Zan did not believe either of these things could exist in a logical universe.

Danny was late for work, but the security guard waved him through and Ciara didn't seem to mind. He slotted straight into a discussion about how much violence they could show in the timeslot they were aiming for, and he was getting a handle on the difference between American and Australian TV's tolerance for everything from bad language to nudity when Paddy burst in.

'Clay, do you know where Jensen is?' he almost screamed at Danny. Paddy was clearly the worse for wear. He looked like he had slept in his clothes – which he had – and stank like a brewery drain. Unshaven and unkempt, he was a wreck.

'Should I?' Danny said.

'You're supposed to be looking after him,' Paddy said. 'Why else would we have flown you out here?'

Danny lifted his copy of the script and raised his eyebrows.

'Don't kid yourself. We've got writers – real writers – coming out of our collective wazoo,' Paddy said. 'With me,' he added, exiting to the corridor and expecting Danny to follow.

Danny closed his eyes, breathed deeply and looked at Ciara, the other writers avoiding eye contact. She barely shrugged. *What can you do?* Danny followed Paddy outside.

'Has he called you?' Paddy said.

'No. The last time I saw him he was with you.'

'Yeah, well, never mind that,' Paddy said. 'Look, there was a situation.'

'What kind of situation?'

'We went for dinner and a drink and I thought I'd take him to the Zebra Zone, you know, show him a good time,' Paddy explained, then said quietly, so no one in the next room could hear, 'A strip club.'

'You do know he's underage? For drinking in this state, and, I'd imagine, strip clubs?'

'Yeah, yeah, yeah,' Paddy said, dismissively.

'And you know Jensen is quite possibly gay?'

'Oh,' said Paddy. 'That might explain ... I got us lap dances. When I ... um ... was free, he was gone. I called his hotel this morning but he's not in his room.'

'He'll turn up.'

'We have a lunch. An important one. I need to get home and freshen up. I need you to find him, Danny,' Paddy pleaded. 'I need you to get him here by 12.30.'

'Oh, it's "Danny" now, is it?' He couldn't resist.

'Don't be a dick, Clay. This is a big deal for both of us. He's at the Chateau Marmont,' Paddy said. 'Get him here by 12.30. You'll be doing me a solid. And you might even save your own ass too.'

Danny watched him disappear down the corridor then went back into the writers' room to get his phone and car keys.

—

Jensen wasn't that hard to find. Sitting by the Chateau pool in board shorts, thongs and a Bondi Lifesavers singlet, he couldn't have looked more Australian if he had been wearing a hat with corks around it while hugging a koala.

'You scared Paddy,' Danny said as slumped back in a seat beside him. 'He left messages that you didn't answer.'

'He's a tool,' Jensen said, then caught himself. 'Sorry, is he a friend?'

Danny almost choked on his mocktail and shook his head.

'No, he's a tool,' he said as a cinnamon-coloured, lightly muscled young man pulled himself out of the water near Jensen and started drying himself languorously in front of them. He whispered something in Jensen's ear, smiled at Danny, wrapped the towel around his waist and wandered off to the change rooms.

'You need to do this lunch today, for my sake if not yours,' Danny said.

'Yeah, okay, I will – for you,' Jensen said. 'But I've got to tell you I am over this place.'

'This place?' Danny said, gesturing to their elegant surroundings, 'Or Paddy?'

'Aren't they all like him?'

'God, no,' said Danny. 'He's one of a kind.'

He could tell that Jensen had arrived at a decision many budding actors only reach after years of trying and failing. Danny felt responsible, culpable even.

'Listen, every week about a thousand people arrive in LA looking to make it in movies or TV. Probably more,' he said, feeling like he was in a quiet corner of the base in Tarin Kowt, a sergeant telling a young sapper why he hadn't made a huge mistake in signing up for active service. 'You are one of the lucky ones that isn't starting off as a waiter. Hang in there until you can't hang any more. This chance might never come around again.'

'You're just saying that to keep *Pretty Boy* on the slate.' Jensen was well and truly jaded, albeit extremely prematurely.

'No, mate,' Danny said. 'The show will either go ahead or it won't, regardless of whether you or I are involved. But you have scored a ticket to the dance. All you need to do is not step on anyone's toes.'

'Meaning?'

'Take every lunch that's offered to you. There's a golden rule in Hollywood – if they don't need you, they don't feed you. So when you get an invite, pull a chair up to the table and tuck in … in every sense. Like this!' Danny gestured over the pool. 'You've already got so much further than most people.'

Jensen looked around, realising that he wasn't doing too badly.

'By the way, Jensen, thanks for getting me over here,' Danny said. 'It's just what I needed.'

'You're welcome, but it wasn't me.'

Danny looked puzzled.

'Seriously, no offence, but I was ready to come on my own until Rob insisted I get you on the ticket.'

'I thought you …'

'Look, I'm really glad you're here,' Jensen said. 'Super-glad. I loved your script, I loved that you stuck it to Neumann, all that stuff with you and the guy who got shot. You're the real deal, Danny. But it's Rob you need to thank, not me.'

'I didn't stick it to Neumann,' Danny corrected. 'Only one winner in that fight.'

'Not what I heard. Anyway, it's great to have you around. And good to know your agent's looking after you.'

Danny was still considering this when Zan appeared. He'd texted her on the way to the hotel, just in case he needed backup.

'You gotta come and see this,' she said. 'It's the guy in the white suit I told you about, and you will never guess who he's talking to.'

'No, I'll never guess,' Danny said, irritated that his thoughts had been interrupted. 'Tell me.'

'Jackie Jazz,' Zan said. Danny opened and closed his mouth several times as he processed this information. He looked at Zan quizzically, but she nodded. 'It's him, for sure. I Googled him.'

'Are we good?' Danny eventually said to Jensen, but the younger man had already been distracted by the return of Cinnamon Boy, now dressed in khaki Bermuda shorts, boat shoes and a white, short-sleeved linen guayabera.

'I'll be there,' Jensen said. 'And let's catch up later, okay?'

'Sure thing,' Danny said. 'We're at Le Montrose, just a few blocks away.'

'Cool,' Jensen said, offering Danny a fist bump, a bro handshake and a shoulder hug. When in Rome, Danny thought as he briefly squeezed the younger man to his chest.

Danny nodded and smiled at Jensen's friend before following Zan to the Bar Marmont. It was all timber, velvet and subtle lighting, filling up with a shift change from late brunchers to pre-lunchers. A couple of half-familiar faces floated past, eyes bright and smiles switched permanently on as Zan guided them to a small table behind a pillar that doubled as a tall, elegant bookshelf. There were books everywhere. The bar looked like a licensed library.

'This is what they were going for at the old Bourbon and Beefsteak on the Cross,' Danny said to a quizzical look from Zan. 'They never quite made it.'

Zan gestured Danny to hush and lean forward. As he peered around the pillar, he caught the glint of a diamond in the ear of a dark-skinned man sitting in a horseshoe booth, facing a thin, immaculately groomed fellow in a white linen suit, who looked for all the world like a Southern gentleman. Two espresso coffees sat on the table between them, with a white panama hat to one side. The man in white was facing away from Danny, so he couldn't quite see his face.

'That's him, isn't it?' Zan whispered. 'Jackie Jazz?'

Danny looked again to make sure, then nodded.

'I checked on the internet,' Zan whispered. 'There aren't that many pictures of him.'

'No, there wouldn't be, but that's definitely Jackie,' Danny said. 'I met him a couple of times when we were researching a TV show.'

A waiter walked past the booth, carrying two glasses of white wine on a tray. The man in the white suit turned as he followed the waiter with his eyes, allowing Danny a three-quarter profile view of his face. There was a flash of those Hollywood teeth Zan had mentioned, and a sheen of make-up or spray tan around his chin.

'Yeah, the other guy looks familiar to me too,' Danny said softly. 'Must be a TV star. Afternoon soaps, maybe. Not A-list.'

A waitress brought two glasses of mineral water to Jackie's table.

Again, as she moved on to another table with a bloody Mary on her tray, the man in white's gaze followed her but stayed with the drink even after it had been delivered.

'Alcoholic,' Danny said. 'Recovering, probably. He's on coffee and water but he can't take his eyes off the drinks.'

Jackie Jazz's mobile rang, that old-fashioned *tring-tring*. As he checked the caller ID, a familiar voice rang out.

'*Ask not for whom the bell tolls, it tolls for thee*,' boomed the man in the white suit.

Danny and Zan looked at each other in amazement, then both peered around the pillar.

'Fuck me gently,' said Danny. 'It's the Poet.'

—

'The Mexican waitress at La Conversation said he was English – like me,' Zan recalled. 'She wouldn't know an Australian accent from an English one.'

Danny and Zan had retreated to a corner table. They had decided not to confront Jackie Jazz – he was an unknown quantity – but, as far as they knew, the Poet was still possibly a friend. Danny waited until he went to the gents' and followed him in, appearing behind him in the mirror while he washed his hands.

'Nice makeover,' Danny said to the Poet's reflection.

The Poet took a full three seconds to process this intrusion of his past life into his current one. His expression and the slight slump of his shoulders suggested disappointment that a fear had been realised, rather than shock that his worst nightmare had come true. 'I thought that was Zan at breakfast the other day, but then …'

'They all look the same to you,' Danny quoted back at him.

The Poet splashed water in his face, as if that would snap him out of this awful dream, and looked towards the door as he dried his face with a small towel from a basket beside the sink.

'Let me get rid of Jackie,' he said. 'You really don't need him to see you here.'

'Why should I trust you?' Danny said.

'Because I have to trust you,' the Poet replied. 'Have you got a mobile phone?' The Poet reached out and Danny hesitated for a moment then handed him his phone. The Poet punched in his own number and the phone in his pocket buzzed. 'There, we've got each other's numbers now,' he said. 'How about I see you later at the In-N-Out on Sunset? It's about ten minutes east, by car.'

'I know where it is,' Danny said, unable to keep the chill out of his voice. 'What about your friend?'

'Jackie? He's rented a house in the Hills. He's having a party tonight. Another one. I can pull out ...'

'Now that you're not drinking,' Danny said. Again, the Poet was taken aback, but less this time. His reservoir of surprise was getting low.

'In-N-Out about seven,' the Poet said, drying his hands. Danny opened the door, checked Jackie Jazz wasn't around, and exited, pausing at the bar entrance and signalling to Zan to join him outside.

Danny and Zan erupted into the sunshine, laughing at the ridiculousness of it all and half-running, like shoplifters trying not to draw attention to themselves and failing because of their efforts. If they'd been black and in a different city, someone would have called the cops – or just shot them, to be on the safe side. As it was, they were clearly the least cool people on Sunset Boulevard

It was gone 3.30pm by the time Danny had dropped Zan off at Le Montrose and got back to the studio, his head still spinning from seeing the Poet again. Paddy was back where he wasn't needed or wanted, a glowering presence at the head of the writers' table. He practically jumped out of his seat and headed Danny off at the door, steering him into a small kitchen off to the side.

'What did you say to Jensen about me?' he hissed through gritted teeth.

'I dunno,' Danny shrugged. 'That you were one of a kind. I remember saying that. Why?'

'He was very unhappy over lunch. Hardly said a word. It was embarrassing.'

'Maybe he was embarrassed at the thought of being taken to a strip club by a middle-aged man who should know better.'

'You turned him against me,' Paddy said, his eyes narrowing as he stepped back.

'No, mate, you did a good job of that yourself.'

'You think you are so smart. Maybe in Australia,' he deliberately made it sound like *'Orstrellier'*, 'but this is the real world and you are nothing here.'

'Is everything okay?' Ciara was at the door, looking concerned.

'I ... um ... I was just giving Danny some script notes,' Paddy said, holding up his copy of the script. It was heavily marked with lines, crosses and scribbles, as if a child of four had been let loose on it with a box of crayons and had worn every one down to a stub.

'Shouldn't I be getting these notes too?' said Ciara, entirely reasonably.

'It's more ... general observations,' Paddy backtracked. 'Man stuff.'

'Carry on, then,' Danny said. 'Maybe Ciara should hear this too, this man stuff.'

Paddy's lips goldfished for a moment, but somewhere in his brain, a response to weeks of humiliation was triggered.

'Okay, okay. You asked for it,' he said thumbing through the script. His face reddening with frustration, he clawed at the pages like he was trying to dig a shallow grave with his bare hands.

'Look, none of this is real. You are just making up shit that couldn't possibly happen.'

'Give me an example,' Danny said, becoming dangerously calm. 'Maybe I'll learn something.'

Paddy flicked through the pages again till he came to one with a large red X through it.

'Okay, this fight scene. It's impossible.' His fury was as visceral as it was unfocused. 'Have you ever been in a fight or do you just learn this stuff off TV?'

Ciara opened her mouth to speak but couldn't find the words in time.

'Which part?' Danny asked, his face as expressionless as a statue on a tomb.

Paddy pointed to some lines of big print – the instructions that went between dialogue.

'It says, *He grabs the smaller man by the throat with one hand, pushes him against the wall then lifts him upwards so he is barely standing on his tiptoes*,' Paddy read. 'That's just superhero bullshit. No ordinary human being could do that.'

Before he realised it, Danny had lunged for Paddy, grabbed him by the throat with one hand, pushed him against the wall, slid him upwards and held him there, with only Paddy's toes touching the ground.

'See, the thing is, I'm not lifting you, you're lifting yourself,' Danny said. 'It's a reflex action to the pressure of my hand.'

'You fucking fuck,' Paddy spluttered. 'Put me down. Put me down!'

'And I just have to apply a little more upwards pressure …' Danny said with a smile.

'Aaaaargh! You're choking me! Help! Security!'

'Danny … Danny!' Ciara was gently touching Danny's arm. He closed his eyes, released his grip and Paddy slid to the floor.

'You are fucking finished in this town, Clay,' Paddy squeaked as he got to his feet.

'And you are a racist, sexist, talentless cunt,' Danny said. 'Now get the fuck out of here before I show you how someone who's never been in a fight snaps an idiot's neck.'

That earned an eye-roll from Ciara as she followed Paddy to the door.

'You'd better be gone by the time I get back, or I will have you deported, you sonofabitch Australian piece of shit,' Paddy hissed as he scuttled away. Ciara pointed to Danny's chair and nodded authoritatively before racing down the corridor to catch up with Paddy.

Danny returned to the writers' room and slumped in his seat, letting the buzz reduce to a gentle hum. Then one woman with a headful of greying curls, whose name he thought was Laurie, stood up and started to applaud. He thought she was being sarcastic until, one by one and then all together, the other members of the team stood up, clapped their hands and smiled. Danny smiled back. It felt good – even though he knew this round of applause could be the curtain call for his time in Los Angeles.

—

It was 6.45pm when Danny and Zan remembered they were supposed to be meeting the Poet at 7. But, then, they'd had a few distractions. Danny had spent a pleasant afternoon hearing Paddy Rosenberg stories from the other writers. First it was their own experiences, then the stories they'd heard from people they knew, then friends of friends. Each time, naturally, they became more outrageous and less believable, but nonetheless true. Paddy was a legend in Tinseltown, but not in the way he hoped or imagined.

Eventually Ciara came back, accompanied by the security guard Danny had connected with the previous day. The guard half-smiled, nodded, then resumed his look of professional disapproval.

'Danny, we are going to have to ask you to leave,' Ciara said.

'What kept you?' Danny said, gathering up his script and his laptop.

'I'm afraid the script is studio property,' Ciara said, holding out her hand.

'Even though I wrote it?'

'Even though.'

Danny handed it back to her. 'Going to erase my hard disk too?'

The security guard coughed to get Danny's attention. 'Sir, you may not remove any items of stationery that are the property of BJF Studios, including but not limited to paper, fastenings, writing instruments, writing material, recording devices, recordings or portable computer memory sticks or disks,' said the security guard.

'Jeez,' Danny said, opening his bag to show it contained only his laptop. 'I feel like I've been Mirandised.'

'It's just office stationery, sir,' the guard replied. 'You've only been Stapled.'

Danny noticed the flicker of a smile on the guard's face, then, out of the corner of his eye, a couple of writers making notes.

'Danny, I'm sorry ...' Ciara said. 'Do you have an agent?'

'Not here,' Danny said, unsure. 'Why?'

'You need someone who knows the system,' she said. 'Paddy will drop the complaint, for sure, but you should be paid out.'

'Paddy's made a complaint?'

Ciara rolled her eyes in a way Danny was beginning to find attractive.

'Oh, and the studio will not be paying your hotel bills after tonight.' She handed Danny a business card. 'Call me. Any time, okay?'

'Okay,' Danny said, pulling his jacket off the back of his chair.

The security guard gestured to the door. Danny gave a little wave to the writers and a couple waved back.

'I'm gonna need your car keys too, sir,' the security guard said.

'What's your name, chief?' Danny asked as he passed over the keys.

'Curtis,' the security man said. 'Curtis Brown.'

The name rang a faint and distant bell with Danny but he shook it off.

'Curtis, do you know a guy named Hume – ex-DEA in Afghan?' Danny asked. 'These days an armourer for movies.'

'Hume?' Curtis laughed. 'That hard-ass? Everybody knows Hume. And he's a lot more than an armourer now.'

'Do you have his number?'

'Not on me, but I can get him to call you,' Curtis said as they walked out into the sunshine. 'He's on the set right now. I'll see him when he checks out. Give him your cell, if you like.'

Danny scribbled his number of a scrap of paper and handed it to Curtis.

'You know plenty of people here are pissed with you?' Curtis said.

'I didn't realise Rosenberg was so popular.' Danny was surprised.

'He ain't.' Curtis chuckled. 'But you just made it harder for them to fire his sorry ass.'

They were at Danny's car and he realised he no longer had the keys.

'How am I going to get back to the hotel?' Danny asked.

There was a roar of a big diesel engine as a huge day-glo-orange Humvee roared into view.

'Ask and ye shall receive,' Curtis said, stepping onto the road and raising his hand to halt the vehicle. 'This is your boy Hume now.'

By the time Danny had climbed into the passenger seat of the Humvee, he and Hume had hugged, bumped fists, hugged again and slapped each other's backs so often Danny was beginning to wince in anticipation of the next display of affection. As they drove back to Le Montrose, Danny gave Hume the bullet points of his current predicament, and Hume had brought him up to speed on his burgeoning business as a supplier of all things military to the movie business.

'Remember that old car yard I bought in Industry?' Hume asked. 'It looks like a staging depot in a war zone. I got tanks, troop carriers, choppers, Humvees. Man, I could invade a small country.'

The City of Industry was a low-tax zone for businesses, tucked into the south-east corner of greater Los Angeles. Few people lived there and it even had its own fake McDonalds, used exclusively for shooting commercials and scenes in movies.

'The GM dealers gave me this pimpmobile as a thank you for all the business I sent their way. I think they couldn't sell it but, hey, it fits right in at the studios so I'm not complaining.'

There was a momentary silence as they both thought about how they'd met and what had brought them here.

'Brother, a lot of this is down to you,' Hume continued with a sincere smile. 'If you hadn't hooked me up with all those connections, I would be trading shifts with good ol' Curtis, back on the security gate.'

'He seems like a good guy,' Danny said.

'One of the best,' Hume replied. 'He worked for me for a while but it was like ripping scabs off all his wounds, being around all that hardware. I use ex-military whenever I can. They know their way around the equipment – mostly maintenance and changing the paint jobs, depending on which side we're supposed to be on, in whatever conflict. But for some of them it's just too much like the real thing, so I try to get them work around the studios.'

Danny looked at his friend as they drove up Avenue of the Stars, heading for the hotel. Hume was about six-three, with spiky blond hair, a couple of notches above a number-two scalp scraper. He looked fit and tanned, without a hint of excess fat. His square jaw supported an easy smile that set off deep blue eyes. You'd swear they were coloured contacts if you didn't know that vanity didn't run strong in Hume, although he clearly took care of his appearance. The muscle shirt, camo pants, combat vest and Merrell hiking boots were his work clothes, although Danny guessed he wouldn't dress that differently at home.

'Still working out?' Danny asked.

'Gotta go harder as you get older,' Hume said. 'Ease off and you are on a slippery slope, man. Especially in this town.'

Danny and Hume had already agreed that he and Zan would move into Hume's house in the Hollywood Hills as soon as they checked out of Le Montrose. Now that Danny had remembered their meeting with the Poet, Hume had offered to pick up Zan and drive them to In-N-Out. He stopped his massive orange truck just behind the car valet parking area outside the cobbled entrance to the hotel, got out and leaned against the passenger door while Danny went inside to get Zan.

When they came out, Zan stopped in her tracks. At first Danny assumed it was the truck, but then he followed her eye line to Hume, who had stood up at their approach.

'Well ain't you the cutest little thing that didn't drop out of a Christmas cracker.' Hume grinned at Zan. He had a mid-west drawl that he frequently enhanced for effect. 'Danny, you dog, you didn't say …'

'Oh, we're not an item,' Zan quickly interjected. 'We're just friends.'

'My, oh, my, you are losing your touch, old buddy,' Hume said with a laugh. He ushered them into the vehicle, helping Zan with the high step.

'Did you know we had a tail?' Hume asked, looking into the rear-view mirror once they were all seated and belted. Danny looked over his shoulder down Hammond Street. There were cars parked both sides. 'Black Escalade with tinted windows,' said Hume. 'They'd been following us since Avenue of the Stars but they got locked up in the lights at Wilshire and Santa Monica. Even so, here they are again – they must know where you live.'

Danny twisted around in his seat for a better look.

'Two brothers, got out when you did,' Hume continued. 'Got back in as soon as they saw I wasn't going anywhere.'

'Shit,' said Danny, his eyes still on the large black SUV.

'Want to lose them?' Hume asked.

'Why not?' Danny said.

'This ridiculous truck is not the fastest or least conspicuous vehicle around,' Hume said, getting out. 'We're gonna need some assistance.'

Danny watched as he chatted to the car valet in Spanish and handed him some money.

Hume swung back into the Humvee, moved forward then stopped, watching in the mirror as the escalade pulled out from the kerb. Moments later the roller gate of the parking garage slid up and a large BMW saloon car came out, got halfway across the road between the Humvee and its tail and seemed to stall, blocking the road. As Hume pulled away, the Beamer's driver got out and popped the hood.

Hume took a left into Phyllis as the passenger of the Escalade ran towards the Beamer, remonstrating and gesticulating at the car valet. Now out of sight, Hume turned left and left again so they were now on Cynthia, crossing Hammond behind the blocked street. As luck would have it, a FedEx truck had come up behind the Escalade and now it was well and truly stuck. The BMW was moving back into the garage entrance, pushed by the valet and two large black men in dark suits.

Seconds later Danny, Zan and Hume were on San Vicente, heading up to Sunset for their meeting with the Poet and who knew what.

32

THE JAILS of the world are full of decent cops who took a small gift from someone they shouldn't have, thought Laura. A bottle of red wine – a token of thanks for a problem solved – is no big deal until a favour is asked in return. The cop declines, and the voice at the end of the phone suggests he or she looks at the bottle more closely. This is no ordinary thirty-dollar plonk; it's a 2011 Grange, eight hundred a pop.

The cop then has a choice: fess up and risk losing their job, or perform the tiny favour the criminal wants and risk everything, including their freedom. How tiny? A car rego check, perhaps, revealing the owner of a suspicious vehicle seen prowling Tony's streets. Or a quick look on the computer to see if a prospective employee has a worse criminal record than they are claiming.

It's all small beer, but once you've crossed the line you are forever on the wrong side. And history tells us that for those who take the second option it's not the crime that gets you, it's the lies you tell to cover your tracks. And the further over you go, the higher the stakes get.

In Laura's case, it hadn't been a crime – more of an indiscretion, really. It was a Christmas party at a hotel ballroom and one of her bosses, a station commander and a mentor of hers, had booked a room upstairs rather than run the gauntlet of his own Random Breath Test units. His wife was away visiting her sister overseas and the mutual attraction that he and Laura had successfully suppressed for three years was unleashed, thanks to copious amounts of alcohol and a feeling of inevitability.

Unfortunately for both of them, through a network of company trusts, ghost directors and frequent name changes, the hotel belonged to Tony Cufflinks, and he'd made sure his staff directed any senior police officers attending the party in its ballroom to one of his 'special' rooms.

It was two days later when the package arrived at Laura's flat. It contained a computer thumb drive and a mobile phone. The memory stick carried a compilation video shot from several angles of everything she and the commander had done in the hotel room, plus security footage of them entering and leaving the same room separately. Together would have been noteworthy, but separately made it suspicious, revealing awareness and intent. Some of the rest of the tape Laura didn't remember; most of it she didn't watch.

Laura simply sat and stared at the phone for a whole day as it lay on her sideboard like a threat. On day two it buzzed and the name 'Tony' appeared on the screen. He wanted a chat. The deal they struck was that she would feed Tony titbits of information provided he left the commander and his marriage alone.

Laura and Tony had had a lot of chats since then. As far as she could tell, he had kept his side of the bargain and it had all become slightly irrelevant since the commander's wife had caught him in flagrante with their dog-walker and was now grinding his bones through the proxy of divorce lawyers. But Laura had already crossed the line. That bell could not be un-rung.

As for the information Laura gave Tony, mostly it was low-level stuff about his criminal, and occasionally legitimate, rivals. Often it was a two-way street. He would tell her about who was getting an illicit shipment from where, information she would pass on to detectives. She would tell him about which of his clubs were under scrutiny, convincing herself that if she had succeeded in shutting down some drug deals she was doing good police work. Of course she knew that was bullshit, and her sense of unease was growing.

She had asked him to meet her face to face — secretly, as this was not a good look in either of their worlds. They chose Harry's Cafe de Wheels in Burwood, a bizarre, pagoda-like building just off the linear car park they call Paramatta Road. Laura, blending in with the truckies and soccer mums in her jeans and hoodie, was more tense than she'd thought she'd be. Tony, looking totally out of place in his cashmere coat, was surprisingly relaxed.

'This Australian food …' he sighed and shook his head. 'What's wrong with a good bowl of pasta? Puttanesca. *Bellissimo*.'

Laura smiled economically. This was less of an intro to what she wanted to say than she'd been hoping for.

'You know where puttanesca comes from?' he asked. She shook her head.

'Puttana, the prostitutes,' he explained. 'Olive oil, chilli, garlic, anchovies, capers. They say it's so the customers could find the hookers by following their noses.' He laughed and shook his head. 'Nice story but it's a dish they could cook quickly and eat between clients … and get the taste of the previous guy out of their mouth.'

'I can see why you'd like it,' Laura said mischievously, before adding 'I mean, cutting the time between clients.'

Tony's demeanour changed, slightly but perceptibly. He spread his large hands on the table and leaned in to Laura. She detected a whiff of breath mint.

'Now please tell me why you want to end our little arrangement,' he said. 'One that has been so mutually beneficial.'

'These are my friends,' she said. 'That's different.'

'To you, maybe. Not to me,' he said. 'It's all just business.'

Laura shook her head. 'I'm done. The commander's wife has left him now so there's no marriage to threaten any more. They won't sack him for shagging a fellow officer.'

'But what about you?' Tony smiled, sounding concerned for her welfare. 'You are, by any definition, a corrupt cop. You can't be half pregnant.'

'I'm quitting anyway,' she said. 'All you've got on me is an exchange of information. I never took a bribe. I never got a direct benefit. All I did was make some bad decisions.'

'Ain't that the truth.' Tony laughed, then his face darkened. 'Do you really think you're the only snitch I have in that station?'

The thought had never occurred to Laura but now that it did she could feel the bile rising in her throat.

'And do you think you're the only police officer who knows their way around a computer?' he continued. 'What's the penalty for a cop who conceals or destroys evidence? I'd imagine it would be particularly tough for a pretty girl like you in jail. But that's just the least of it, isn't it Laura?'

As Laura tried to think who the other informer – or informers – might be, Tony put his hand in his pocket, took something out and rolled it across the desk towards her. At first Laura though it was a Malteser. Then, as she caught it before it dropped into her lap, she realised it was a paintball.

'Now, I need you to find out where your friends are staying in Los Angeles,' Tony hissed. 'Then, maybe then, you can abandon this career that, let's face it, is not ideal for someone who makes so many bad choices.'

She was thinking about the potential cost of betrayal to Danny and Zan, not to mention herself, when her phone buzzed. It was an email from Danny.

—

Danny used Hume's binoculars to watch the Poet, who was sitting in In-N-Out, from a doorway across Sunset. Hume was driving his disco truck to meet one of his men and trade it for something less attention-seeking.

The Poet seemed calm but alert, facing the door and looking up whenever anyone new entered, but not any more than you would if you were on a blind date, Danny thought. Zan was across the road in an iHop, a twenty-four-hour diner best known for its breakfasts, waiting for the all-clear from Danny. While he had his eye on the Poet, she had hers on a cross between a waffle and a croissant laced with salted caramel and banana.

Eventually, the Poet became a bit more agitated and got up from his seat. Danny thought he was going to leave, but he was only rising to order at the counter. Betraying your mates must work up an appetite, Danny thought. Moments later there was a tap on his shoulder.

'Looks clear,' Hume said, reaching out for the binoculars. 'I got your back.'

Danny nodded and shrugged into his jacket, a cool breeze having worked its way up from the ocean towards the hills that started just half a mile away. The In-N-Out had a similarly garish retro look to Mel's, without being quite so over the top or touristy. Its Protein Burger, with lettuce replacing the bun, was understandably popular with the permanent dieters of LA.

'Double-double with fries,' the burger flipper at the counter called out, and the Poet rose to collect it. By the time he got back to his seat, Danny was sitting opposite.

'Hungry?' Danny asked.

The Poet looked him in the eye and then offered him a French fry without smiling. Danny declined. Instead he reached out his hand.

'Your mobile …'

'What?' the Poet said. 'Why?'

'Your goons nearby? Waiting for a signal?' Danny said.

'What goons?' the Poet looked genuinely surprised, not to say alarmed.

'The two heavies who tailed me from the studio? Are they still around or can't you afford the overtime?'

'My dear fellow,' the Poet protested. 'I wouldn't …'

'Phone!' This time Danny's voice carried just the right mixture of authority and threat. The Poet meekly slipped his mobile phone out from an inside pocket in his silk-lined suit.

'Danny, my dear chap, I honestly don't know what you're talking about,' the Poet said, overdoing the sincerity.

'They knew where we were staying. Caught up with us there. How did they find that out?'

There was a brief flicker of panic in the Poet's eyes. Danny had seen it before in 'fighting age males' during stop-and-searches, particularly when he brought out the spray that revealed whether or not they had recently handled explosives.

'You are working for Jackie Jazz, right?'

The Poet nodded. '*With* him, rather than *for* him.'

'And Jackie was behind Bryan's and Marcus's deaths?'

'What?' the Poet almost shrieked. 'Fuck, no! We thought it was you!'

'Me?'

'Well, not you, but Zan.'

'Hang on. You thought Zan was responsible for Bryan and Marcus?' Danny asked.

'Well, she killed the guy in the lift. And Arana ... whatsit. Jackie's nephew.'

'Weezl? It was his girlfriend who killed him.'

'Jackie says his nephew didn't have a girlfriend. By the way, I wouldn't go around calling him Weezl in front of Jackie if I were you,' the Poet said. 'Anyway the cops are hot for Zan on this – which is why you left Sydney.'

'It wasn't Zan.'

'According to her,' the Poet said. 'Somebody in Sydney has an inside line to the cops and he is telling Jackie that she is the main suspect.'

'Tony fucking Cufflinks,' said Danny. 'He's doing it to get at me. Give me a second.'

Danny got up and pocketed the Poet's phone with an unapologetic smile. Then he went to the window and looked straight at one of the few doorways on that stretch of Sunset that were even remotely in shadow. Hume emerged from the darkness and gave him an 'all clear' signal. Danny texted Zan on his own phone then sent another, longer message before returning to the table.

'You're showing your age,' the Poet said. 'The young folk wouldn't even excuse themselves before using their phone at the table.'

'I'm just an old-fashioned guy,' Danny said, then noticed the Poet stiffen, alarm in his eyes. Danny looked over his shoulder, expecting to see the heavies from earlier. It was Zan.

'Well, look at you,' she said, as she slid onto a stool beside Danny. 'Forgive me if we don't hug but I don't like getting too up close and personal with killers.'

The Poet covered his face with his hands, ran his fingers through his carefully coiffed hair and shook his head.

'The Poet says he and Jackie Jazz weren't behind Bryan's and Marcus's deaths,' Danny explained. 'They think it was us.'

'What? That's bullshit!' Zan exploded.

'Yeah, but unless the Poet here is a better actor than he is a writer – which, admittedly, wouldn't be hard –' the two men traded exaggerated sneers '– I reckon he's telling the truth.'

Danny's phone buzzed briefly and he checked the screen.

'You got your laptop?' he asked Zan.

'Of course,' she said, patting the small Crumpler shoulder bag by her side.

'Fire it up. I'm sending you something.'

'Right away, Mr Clay,' she mocked in a sugar-sweet American accent. 'Now, can I get you gentlemen a coffee or a cold beverage?'

The Poet was about to order a drink but Danny shook his head. Zan pulled out her laptop, actually a Microsoft Surface with a clip-on keyboard. She switched it on and started searching for a wi-fi signal.

'Okay,' Danny said to the Poet. 'Let's assume you guys had nothing to do with Bryan or Marcus ...'

'We didn't,' the Poet said, matter-of-fact.

'And we say we didn't either.'

'We didn't,' echoed Zan, briefly looking up from her screen.

'So who the fuck was it?' Danny said. The Poet shrugged, Zan watching him for a tell.

'We know about the foreign exchange scam,' Danny said.

'Hardly a scam,' the Poet replied. 'Just smart business.'

'And Bryan's suicide note said you stole his dream.'

The Poet was rocked. 'There was a suicide note?'

'Came in about a week ago,' Danny said. 'That's snail mail for you.'

'I stole his dream?' the Poet said, his brows furrowed.

'Our thinking is Bryan always wanted to write a Hollywood movie – don't we all – and your forex venture killed it,' Danny said.

'I can see why you would think that,' the Poet said, 'but Bryan had given up on the whole Hollywood thing. He knew it was a poisoned chalice ...'

'Ain't that the truth,' muttered Zan.

'No, his dream was to buy a little house in the Blue Mountains, where every so often he could escape from Emma and the kids and just write,' the Poet explained. 'That was his dream.'

'That's right,' said Zan. 'I remember him saying that a couple of times. All he needed was a deposit and Airbnb would do the rest.'

'And you just remembered this now?' Danny complained.

Zan winced her *sorry*. Then, lamely, 'People can have more than one dream.'

'But how did I kill his dream if I was getting the money for him?' the Poet asked. 'There was never any doubt that Jackie would pay us our full share.'

They looked at one another, hoping for a clue. Zan's laptop pinged.

'Is that my email?' Danny asked.

Zan nodded as she flicked her delicate fingers over the laptop's screen.

'Show the Poet the video,' Danny said.

Zan turned the screen around so the Poet could see it. It was video clips sent by Laura from her computer showing Chita just after the shooting and the previous night, albeit indistinctly, in a reflection in the window of the roadhouse in Glenrowan.

'That's Weezl's girlfriend,' said Danny. 'The gloves she dropped in the bin were covered with gunshot residue. Very few people ever saw them together and, as you can see, she used disguises and kept her face away from security cameras.'

He spread his thumb and forefinger over the image of Chita in her wig and face mask, not that it offered any kind of calibration.

'She's way too tall to be Zan, even from that angle, and now she has disappeared off the face. Kind of like you did.' He eyed the Poet defiantly. 'Satisfied?'

The Poet nodded, clearly already wondering how he was going to frame this for Jackie.

'Now tell us why *we* should believe *you*,' Danny said. 'I mean, her co-pilot was Jackie Jazz's nephew, after all, and the Jazzman is in this right up to his diamond-studded ear.'

'Jackie Jazz is one of those people you don't ask too many questions,' the Poet said, shaking his head. 'He works on a "need to know" basis. I work on a "don't want to know" basis, so a lot falls through the cracks.'

'And what happened to you?' Zan asked, looking him up and down. 'It's like your brain had a body transplant.'

'Okay, but we're going to need a drink,' the Poet said, pulling money out of his pocket and turning to the counter to order milkshakes all round. They had finished them long before the Poet had finished recounting what had happened after he left Marcus in the pub in Paddington.

News of Marcus's death had been quickly followed by instructions from Jackie Jazz to make his way to a Sri Lankan restaurant in Melbourne. From there he was taken to a hotel near the airport – at gunpoint – while Jackie's henchmen faked a violent abduction from his house, using blood drawn from his arm with a syringe. He winced as he recalled the moment they took it. They were not experts with needles. He stayed at the hotel for three days and was given a new identity, including a fake passport, a haircut and shave, some new clothes and an air ticket to Bangkok.

'Why all the cloak and dagger stuff?' Danny asked.

'Jackie was freaked out by Bryan's suicide and Marcus's death,' explained the Poet. 'He genuinely didn't know who was behind it, or why.'

'And why you?' Zan added, making no effort to conceal her scepticism that the Poet would be worth all the effort.

'Well, I'm not naive enough to think it was the love of his fellow man or even concern for my welfare,' the Poet replied. 'My best guess is that Jackie was fiddling the finances on the script but knew it could all fall apart if anyone got suspicious and started looking too closely.'

'Credibility,' Danny agreed. 'When studios are throwing millions of dollars around they can get spooked by little things ... like all the writers on a project being dead.'

'And Jackie's past wouldn't stand up to a closer look,' Zan added.

'Also, he thought he could get the project back and sell it again, if he had a writer on board,' the Poet added.

'Preferably one who wasn't a shambling drunk with a smile like an earthquake in a graveyard,' said Zan.

The Poet held his hands open. 'It works for me.'

'So he put you in rehab?' Danny asked.

'Not quite. He booked me into a nice hotel and paid for a good tailor and a great dentist,' the Poet explained. 'By the way, it's weird over there in Thailand. The clinics are pristine – all shiny and white – but the nurses wear tiny uniforms like they were bought from a sex shop. Bizarre. I didn't know if I was in a hospital or a brothel.'

'The results are impressive,' Danny said, earning a dazzling smile from the Poet.

'A few crowns, a couple of implants and a heavy duty scrape and polish and I could do toothpaste commercials,' he said. 'Hurt like buggery at the time, though.'

'And the drinking?' Zan asked.

'I don't want to get all preachy and self-helpy,' the Poet said, looking almost sheepish. 'But I always knew my drinking was holding me back. And how many times in your life do you get the chance to start afresh? Clean slate. New identity. Plenty of money. So I made that decision myself.'

'How's it going?' Zan asked.

The Poet smiled wryly. 'Easier than I thought. I was lucky. It turns out alcohol was a choice for me, rather than a need. Just think if the boys could see me now.'

The boys. Bryan and Marcus. Zan squeezed the Poet's arm.

'Okay, Poet, at the risk of ruining this tender moment, you need to tell Jackie to back off,' Danny said. 'No more tails. No more threats.'

Zan sniffed as she pulled a tiny red-and-black thumb drive from the side of her laptop, clicked its cover into place and handed it to the Poet.

'The video of Weezl's girlfriend, from the cops,' she said. 'It's all on there.'

'Okay,' said the Poet, hesitantly. 'But now I need you to tell me what happened after I left. I have no fucking clue except that Jackie's nephew and Marcus are both dead.'

Danny's phone buzzed. It was a text message from Hume: 'All Clear?'

'AOK,' Danny typed, then, 'coffee?'

'Ihop in 5,' came the reply.

'First thing I do when I get back to Sydney is line up some espressos,' Danny said as Hume topped up his cup from the bottomless jug. 'Get my taste buds back.'

'Quit bitchin' and drink, you pussy,' Hume said. Danny noticed that Zan seemed to be edging closer to Hume on their side of the booth. Danny smiled.

They had intentionally freaked the Poet out, introducing Hume to him as ex-DEA, rather than an ex-combat buddy of Danny's – or, indeed, a movie armourer. Once the Poet was over his shock, he was terrified Jackie Jazz might make some sort of connection. When they had calmed him down, they filled him in on all that had happened, including the news that Weezl had accidentally killed Marcus, and that was after accidentally prompting Bryan to take his own life.

'Then he accidentally got his girlfriend pissed enough for her to shoot him?' Hume said. 'Don't you have any professional criminals down there? We could send you some. We got plenty.'

Zan seemed to find this hilarious, punching Hume on his well-defined bicep. Danny gave her a *what are you doing?* look. Zan replied with a *what's it to you?* toss of her hair.

It was still early in the evening so there were families and tourists at the big tables in the central area, all rubbernecking like crazy to see if anyone famous was there. But the shift change to clubbers, drunks, quasi-incognito movie stars and other night people wouldn't be for another couple of hours.

Hume suddenly became very professional, moving cups and condiments around the table top, like he was planning an operation.

'So you guys didn't kill the writers or the Weezl kid,' he unnecessarily confirmed with Danny, moving a cup and spoon to the edge of the table to signify their demise. Danny added a sugar packet.

'Weezl,' he said with a half-smile.

'Oooh! Which one am I?' Zan demanded.

'You're the pepper, baby,' Hume said with a grin that she reflected straight back at him. Danny shook his head and sighed.

'And your guy says he didn't set his boy onto your friends?' Hume asked the Poet.

'He was having kittens when Bryan and then Marcus died,' the Poet said. 'It threatened to blow the whole deal. That's why he got me out of there, before the killer could get to me. He didn't even know his nephew was involved until he heard he had been shot.'

'That *is* weird,' Danny said. 'Do you believe him?'

'One hundred per cent,' the Poet said. 'The nephew had approached Jackie some time before about getting involved in his, you know, "business".' He hooked his fingers into air quotes. 'He was entertaining some fantasy that he was going to be a crime writer. Said an agent had told him he needed some real-life experience. Jackie told him to go away and grow up.

'I was there one time they met, and I saw it with my own eyes. Jackie thought the guy was a liability – and he didn't want any grief from his sister. These criminals are more frightened of their own families than they are of the forces of law and order.'

'Do you think Weezl was acting alone?' Zan asked. 'I mean, why would he be? He did mention his uncle when Danny was … um … questioning him.'

Hume looked over the top of his coffee mug; he knew exactly what that meant.

'My guess is that there was someone pulling the strings,' Danny said. 'But, if it wasn't Jackie, or Tony Cufflinks for that matter, "who" and "why" are the questions.'

'We were a very tight little group and mostly flew under the radar,' the Poet said. 'Nobody had any idea what we were doing.'

'Tell me about it,' Danny said, frowning at Zan. She answered with a guilty smile.

'Until y'all started getting yourselves killed,' Hume interjected. 'So who was in this tight little group, exactly?'

'Zan and I, of course,' the Poet said, 'Bryan, Marcus and Jackie.'

'You were part of this, sweet thing?' Hume asked Zan, incredulous.

'It was a cash job, formatting and editing,' she replied. 'I did the work, got paid and that was it. I wasn't really part of it after that.'

'Even so, Zan was very nearly victim number three, the night Marcus was killed,' Danny added. 'And we know Weezl was just trying to scare people into changing their minds. From what, to what, and for who is the question.'

'If everybody was onside with the plan, who wanted to stop it?' asked Hume.

'Paddy Rosenberg?' Danny offered. 'He was the original EP.'

'Rosenberg?' Hume laughed. 'The fat fraud couldn't organise bagels for a bar mitzvah. And he clearly knows bagels.'

'He couldn't wait to take the money back from us,' the Poet said. 'I was at the last meeting with him. I had to sign a letter agreeing that I had no further claim against the studio.'

The table was briefly a small island of silence in the chatter and clatter of the iHop.

'If what you say is true, there must have been someone else,' Danny said. Again, there was that flicker of guilt in the Poet's eyes. He leaned forward.

'There was another person, but I never met him or her,' he said. 'A kind of fixer. Jackie referred to him – I always assumed it was a he – as "Twenny".'

'First name or last name?' Hume asked, already tapping the name into the search engine on his phone. 'And how do you spell it?'

'No idea. The name could be Twen for all I know.'

'Sounds Asian,' Danny said.

'No, it doesn't,' Zan said, snorting.

'All I got here for "Twenny" is a health snack,' Hume read from the phone's screen 'and idiots wasting their brain cells debating how you pronounce two times ten.' He tapped again. '"Twen" gets me a German TV show from the '60s.'

'So what was this Twenny's role, exactly?' Danny asked.

'I don't know,' the Poet said. 'As I explained previously, Jackie is not what you would call "loose-lipped". It was a mention in passing now and then, but otherwise he was quite secretive. He did once say that Twenny's connections had come through. But that was it.'

'Come through for what? When?' Danny asked.

'This would have been before the movie was sold, and I have no idea what the rest of it was about,' the Poet said. 'You have to understand that Jackie liked to keep everyone separate. I dealt with Zan, Bryan and Marcus, and he dealt with me. It's how they work in that world.'

'Everyone in their own little cells, like terrorists,' said Danny.

'And drug dealers,' said Hume.

'Well, the latter does seem to be one of Jackie's major sources of income,' the Poet confirmed, slightly put out to be bracketed with criminals and suicide bombers.

'When he's not pretending to be a movie producer,' Zan added.

'He is single-minded, ruthless, greedy and a bully,' said the Poet. 'So even if he's pretending, he has the complete skill set.'

The others nodded and smiled.

'Okay, Poet,' Danny said. 'Like I said, you need to tell Jackie to back off. We didn't kill his nephew and we'll take your word that he had nothing to do with the kid coming after us.'

The Poet nodded, fishing out the thumb drive Zan had given him earlier, to show he still had it.

'What are you guys going to do now?' he asked Danny.

'You can't go back to the hotel,' Hume said. 'Not until we know those goons are back in their cage.'

'Sorry.' The Poet shrugged. 'I had no idea.'

'Are they Jackie's people?' Danny asked. 'Or Tony Cufflinks's? Or this Twenny guy's, whoever the fuck he is?'

'Tony told Jackie that Zan killed Weezl,' the Poet counted the connections off against his fingers, checking. 'Shortly after that, Jackie was making calls that he didn't want me to hear. It's a reasonable assumption that they are his henchpersons.'

'When will you be able to get to him?' Danny asked.

'Tomorrow at breakfast,' the Poet said. 'We have a meeting with BJF.'

'Finalising the pay-off?' Zan asked.

'*Au contraire*,' the Poet said, raising an eyebrow. 'They now want to buy the script from us again. For less money than before, of course, but still, another payday.'

Danny and Zan looked at each other. Hume caught it but said nothing.

'We're talking about *Redneck Airlift*?' Danny asked.

'The movie that refuses to die,' the Poet said. 'And on that note, I had better get back to the hotel before my absence is noted. Jackie likes people to be where he expects to find them.'

The Poet picked up his Panama hat and held it in one hand. His new-found manners would not permit him to don it until he was outside.

'Okay, you two are coming back to my place,' Hume said to Danny and Zan, who brightened visibly.

'Oh, and where do you live?' the Poet asked instinctively. Then, 'Sorry, no, I don't want to know.'

'No, you really don't,' Hume growled, and Zan sighed and looked at him with great big eyes.

33

THE FIRST thing any visitor ever noticed about Hume's house in the Hollywood Hills was the driveway, a tiny track on the apex of a hairpin bend. It was fine for coming up the winding road from Mulholland – a simple right-hand turn. But most drivers were immediately aware that when it came time to head back to the city, exiting left would require them to summon all their skill and nerve. Thankfully beyond some bushes a large turning circle with parking for several cars had been cut into the hillside.

The house itself opened from an unprepossessing gate and door to what was basically an open deck that stretched out over the ravine on steel stilts and beams. Timber floors and sliding glass doors gave it the look of a city apartment that had been transported to the hillside.

Down below, a kidney-shaped swimming pool hugged the contour of the gully. Beyond that, scrub disappeared into the darkness and, way past that, glowing down on the fortunate and less so who'd been drawn like moths to its flame, was the Hollywood sign.

'Wow,' said Danny. 'I should have gone into business with you.'

'Ah, it didn't cost as much as it should have,' Hume confessed. 'It was part of "proceeds of crime" seizures from a major-league drug dealer called "El Gordo" Guiterrez. He's now ticking off thirty years in prison. If he survives that, he'll be on a plane back to Colombia. El Gordo let it be known that he would reach out from prison and punish anyone foolish enough to purchase his home in his absence – even though his chances of ever living here again were somewhat less than zero.'

'So you got it cheap?' Zan said, awestruck but glancing nervously out into the darkness.

'Basically just had to pay the back taxes on it so the DEA could get it off their books. After twelve years in the Drug Enforcement Agency I've had more credible threats than the last ten presidents of the USA combined.

'Then I visited El Gordo in jail and told him it was easier for my people to get to him than it was for his to get to me. I even suggested he pay someone to guard me because if anything happened to me ... Well, let's just say the first response would be to make sure me or my buddies didn't miss the obvious.'

'I think it's kind of cool,' Zan said, looking at the designer furniture, which was like her own only much more expensive. 'Did it come furnished?'

'Hell, no.' Hume laughed. 'You've never seen so much carved timber, leather and gold this side of a pirate movie. I sold it to a set designer. He calls it his Scarface Collection. But that's the power of cocaine: fucked up dreams and the money to make them real.'

'You've done a nice job with it,' Zan said.

'Why, thank you, little lady,' Hume drawled. 'Don't let me forget to show you the torture chamber and the escape tunnel.'

Zan giggled but Hume winked at Danny – he wasn't joking. El Gordo had specific needs.

Later that night, as they sat around drinking their way through Hume's collection of exotic whiskies of the world, they speculated on who or what Twenny might be.

'What was that look?' Hume finally said.

'What look?' Danny replied, although he half-knew the answer.

'When your poet friend mentioned the movie – what was it? *Redneck Airship?*'

'*Redneck Airlift.*' Zan giggled and leaned against Hume, less drunk than she looked but still a bit pissed. '*Redneck Airship* is the sci-fi sequel.'

'It probably will have a sequel the way it's going,' Danny mused. 'Fucker refuses to die.'

'Okay, tell uncle what the problem is,' Hume said persuasively. 'Uncle can't help if uncle don't know.'

Danny looked at Zan for approval and she answered with a *whatever* sigh and a thin smile. So Danny told Hume the whole story, including Hahn's death and how the perfect crime in the movie might give people ideas that Zan had killed Hahn rather than tried to save him.

'You know that puts you in the frame for your friends too?' Hume said after a moment's thought.

'Oh fuck, don't you start!' Zan protested.

'No, he has a point,' Danny said. 'We've been looking for someone with a motive for killing the writers of a movie …'

'And it's me,' Zan wailed.

Hume put his big, muscly arm around Zan's shoulder, comforting her like a gorilla with a child who's fallen into its enclosure. Danny rolled his eyes, almost expecting – no, hoping – to hear a shot from a zookeeper's tranquiliser gun.

'Actually,' Danny said to Zan. 'You would have wanted the movie stopped. Our killer clearly wanted it to go ahead.'

'Only nobody knows that except us,' Zan said bleakly.

'Well, it seems the asshole's prayers have been answered,' Hume said. 'The Lord moves in mysterious ways.'

'Spoken like a true atheist,' Danny said. 'So how do we stop it? Short of increasing the body count?'

Hume thought for a moment. 'Injunct the fuck out of it,' he eventually replied. 'You two are semi-connected. File a legal action against Jackie Jazz and BJF saying you want a share of the money from the last round and more from this round.'

'We don't really have a claim, though,' Danny said.

'Facts are snow on water when it comes to the law,' Hume replied. 'You have a credible position. Just saying the words "court action" will scare most studios off, especially with this project's history. A lawyer's letter could do it, followed by dropping a dime on *Variety*. Mentioning two dead writers and a terrorist connection …'

The outrage flashed in Danny's eyes, Hume held up his hands in surrender.

'I'm just sayin',' he continued.

'You think that would scare them off?' Danny asked.

'The completion guarantors? The talent? They would run a mile.'

Danny's wristwatch buzzed. It was 11pm: six in the morning in Sydney. Zan was fighting sleep, and losing. Hume yawned and stretched. Danny excused himself while he walked out onto the blue painted timber terrace.

As soon as he had stepped outside and closed the door, Zan seemed to rouse herself from a semi-slumber. She sat up and looked at Hume, but hesitated before speaking. He tilted his head to one side, inviting her to continue.

'You knew Danny before,' she said. Hume nodded and stroked his chin, wondering where this was heading.

'In the army?' Zan continued.

'He was in the army,' Hume confirmed. 'I was with the DEA but we did a whole stack of batshit crazy ops together. Why do you ask?'

'Is he gay?'

Hume hesitated for a second, then the smile forming on his lips exploded into a full-throated laugh. Zan shushed him and looked outside to Danny on the terrace. But the bulletproof windows also blocked sound and he continued talking into his phone, untroubled.

'I'm pretty sure on God's great gauge of gayness, Danny's needle is on the wholly hetero end,' Hume said. 'But, once again, why do you ask?'

'Look, I'm not exactly ugly,' she ventured.

'You most certainly ain't, little lady,' Hume said with an easy smile.

'And he obviously cares about me.'

'Copy that,' Hume said.

'So why hasn't he …' the words she was seeking failed to materialise.

'Jumped your bones?' Hume offered, in a tone as innocent as if he was suggesting a second lump of sugar for her tea. 'I'm guessing that's the issue.'

'Yeah, something like that,' Zan shook her head. 'It doesn't matter whether I play hard-to-get or come-and-get-me, there's nothing there.'

'Except he's possibly the best friend you'll ever have?' Hume said.

'You think that makes it any easier?' Zan asked.

Hume sighed, wondering if what he was about to tell Zan would be betraying Danny's trust. He looked out on the terrace where his friend was in animated conversation and then back at Zan, a picture of frustration and distress.

'Okay, you know people who don't give a shit what happens to anyone as a result of their actions?' he asked.

'Do I ever,' Zan said with raised eyebrows.

'Well, Danny is the opposite. He cares too much. Not only that, he takes responsibility for anything that goes wrong with anyone he feels responsible for.'

'I don't get how that's a problem,' Zan said. 'And I don't get how that's got anything to do with me.'

Hume hesitated again, but continued.

'If a young grunt in his patrol did something stupid, maybe almost got himself killed, Danny would beat himself up about it, like it was his fault.'

Zan shrugged. She still didn't get the connection. Hume sagged slightly, knowing he was going to have to open up the whole Pandora's box marked 'Danny Clay'.

'He used to be married, did you know that?' Hume asked.

'No. Wow! He never said.'

'She was a nice girl, smart as a whip and twice as scary,' Hume explained. 'Her name was Melissa. Blonde with freckles, would have looked at home on a surfboard, and almost as cute as you.'

Zan gave him an *aw, shucks* look.

'But she couldn't handle the way Danny put the blame for everything on himself,' Hume continued. 'She told me that last time I got back from Afghan, in a lot of late-night phone calls.'

'She called you from Australia?' Zan asked.

'Uh-huh,' Hume nodded. 'She was desperate. They were falling apart but everything she did or said seemed to make it worse. It was like she'd lost the right to screw up, because he put it on himself. And she couldn't get mad at him when he screwed up because he just ripped himself apart. There was no room for either of them to have all the normal fuck-ups that people have.'

'What happened?'

'She just left. Like, totally. No forwarding address, no "I'm all right" emails, just gone.'

'Nothing?' Zan was appalled that Danny could be abandoned like this.'

'There was a note,' said Hume. 'Something like, "Someday you'll find a woman who can deal with your shit – I don't have the strength or patience."'

'Ouch!' said Zan. 'Where is she now?'

'Running a bar in Bali, last I heard,' Hume said. 'He still having the nightmares?'

Zan nodded. Hume shook his head sorrowfully.

'Babe, I can see he loves you to pieces but I truly believe that means he'll never make a move. I ain't no trick cyclist, but he doesn't think he could handle it if you got together and then he lost you down the track.'

Hume and Zan looked out to the terrace where Danny was on his call, smiling then frowning. They smiled at each other, then both slumped back on the sofa and sank deeper into their thoughts as sleep snuck up on them.

—

Earlier, when Danny stepped out of the room, having been alerted by the alarm on his watch, he hit speed dial and woke a very grumpy Rob to find out if he knew any fixer called Twenny operating in Sydney, LA or preferably both. Rob was a blank, and irritated at being disturbed at such an early hour. His demeanour didn't improve when Danny told him he had been sacked from *Pretty Boy* and Jensen was about to jump ship too. 'I only ask you to do one thing …' Rob began.

'What was that?' Danny asked.

'Not fuck up,' Rob said. 'And no sooner do you hit the tarmac at LAX than you get fired and Jensen is up to his nuts in a Latino pool boy and getting ready to jump off the gravy train.'

'Nice turn of phrase you've got there, Rob.'

'Well, what the fuck, Danny? You're turning into a one-man disaster zone.'

'Hey, we met the Poet,' Danny said, by way of a distraction, looking far across the valley to the Hollywood sign stretching away from him on a thirty-degree angle.

'What?'

'He's amazing. Like the second half of an extreme makeover show,' Danny said. 'We didn't recognise him at first.'

'But it's definitely him?'

'Oh yeah,' Danny said. 'We spent a couple of hours with him. And he doesn't have a clue who was pulling Weezl's strings.'

'Jackie Jazz, surely.'

'You would think, but the Poet says no. Even though he had a couple of heavies follow us to our hotel.'

'Jesus!'

'Yeah. We lost them along the way but they got there anyway.'

'Fuck, that's scary,' Rob said.

Yes, it is, Danny thought as he watched a snake of tail-lights wriggle its way down Mulholland to the 101.

'Hey, Rob, do you know any showbiz lawyers here?' Danny asked.

'A couple. Why? Who did you punch?'

'We're going to injunct *Redneck Airlift*,' Danny explained.

'The movie? I thought that was dead,' Rob said, incredulous.

'It lives, my friend,' Danny said. 'And I have to find a way of putting a stake through its heart.'

'You can't afford to take on a movie studio,' Rob protested. 'And why would you, anyway, for fuck's sake?'

'The scene with the perfect crime, remember? That would put Zan in the frame for both Hahn and Weezl. And Hume reckons just a lawyer's letter and a well-timed piece in *Variety* will kill it stone-dead.'

'Hume? Do I know him?'

'I must have told you about him,' Danny said. 'Ex-DEA. Met him in Afghanistan. He knows the business here. He says people are already nervous about this movie.'

'Okay, I'll text you some lawyers' names and numbers,' Rob said, but then paused. 'Hey, Danny, it sounds like this could get messy. Are you safe there?'

'Never been safer. We're staying with Hume,' Danny said. 'He even scares me.'

'Okay, if you're sure.'

'And you have no idea who this Twenny is?'

'No bells are ringing, Danny boy,' Rob said. 'If I think of anything I will let you know. Stay safe. And thanks for waking me. Now I have no excuse not to go to a fucking spin class and be screamed at by a lesbian with no tits and a voice like a rusty bandsaw.'

'Have fun,' Danny said.

'Go fuck yourself,' Rob replied and hung up.

When Danny went back into the lounge, Hume and Zan were snuggled up on the sofa together and snoring in perfect, syncopated harmony.

Danny's phone pinged. It was a text message from Ciara telling him to come to her house the next morning and bring any other scripts he might want to show her. Danny Googled the address she had provided and saw it was just a mile away, albeit via circuitous, snaking roads. He wasn't sure exactly why Ciara needed to see him, but he'd go. He wasn't completely done with this town, Danny thought as he shuffled through to the bathroom, and maybe it wasn't done with him.

34

HUME'S HOUSE was echoing to the sound of wire on crockery when Danny got up in search of the kitchen. He followed the sound behind a false wall bearing a massive abstract oil painting that looked too tasteful to belong to anyone whose last full-time job had been blowing up opium presses in Afghanistan. There he found a fully equipped but discreetly hidden stainless steel kitchen that would have done a small cafe proud.

A slim Hispanic woman in her mid-thirties turned and greeted him with a warm smile.

'*Buenos dias, Señor Clay,*' she said.

'*Buenos dias,*' he replied, unconvinced by his own accent.

'*Huevos?*' she asked, nodding towards the bowl of eggs and milk that he had heard her beating.

'*Sí,*' he said, gaining confidence. '*Por favor.*'

'Your Spanish is very good,' she said with a laugh, in perfect Valley, her dark eyes accentuated by her thick black hair which was scraped back and tied in a bun.

'Not as good as your English,' he said with a smile.

'*Señor* Hume has arranged cars for you.' She nodded towards the worktop where, next to a pot three-quarters full of hot coffee – stewed, Danny thought – he found two sets of car keys each with a note. There was a Prius for Zan and a Porsche SUV for him. Hume was clearly doing well hiring out his war toys.

For you, sweet thing, Zan's note read. *You behave now!*

And in case there was any doubt, Danny's note had his name scrawled in block letters at the top. *Dan, my man,* it read, *Gotta go and fight the good fight (again) but at least this time nobody comes home in a box. Take the car if you need it. See you some time after seven.* Vía con dios. *P.S. Her name is Bel and you gotta have the eggs.*

'So, Bel?'

'*Sí, Señor Clay?*'

'You are Hume's …?'

'Housekeeper,' she said with a grin.

'Of course,' he smiled.

'*Por supuesto,*' she translated, handing him a plate of eggs, beans and tortillas, the aroma of chipotle transporting him to a place he'd never been but that, strangely, in that moment, felt like home.

—

It was the sound of vacuuming, rather than cooking, that roused Zan. She awoke in a king-size bed that had barely been disturbed on one side let alone both. She looked down. She was wearing a T-shirt about twenty sizes too big for her, advertising the first series of *The Wire*. 'Listen Carefully,' the logo said. Fuck – was that advice a little too late in getting to the arrivals gate? Zan pulled her knees inside the T-shirt and went into a full-body cringe as the jigsaw memories of what had happened the previous night fell into place.

She and Hume had fallen asleep on the sofa then he must have roused first because when she woke up she was being carried through to a bedroom. She pretended she was still asleep as Hume laid her gently on top of the bed. She heard him opening and closing drawers then leaving the room. She opened an eye and saw the T-shirt she was now wearing and a towel lying on the corner of the bed. What a gentleman, she thought.

She quickly stripped, put on the shirt and then crept through to Hume's bedroom. Gently opening the door and closing it behind her so as not to wake Danny, she was just adjusting to the darkness when a light went on full in her face. She realised she was staring down the barrel of a large silver automatic pistol, held in both of Hume's giant paws.

'Sorry, Honey,' Hume drawled as he lowered the gun, 'I guess I'm not used to visitors.'

'That's okay,' she said as she caught her breath and advanced on the bed, a massive affair with black-and-silver linen to match its velvet-and-steel headboard. 'I'm ready to feel protected.'

Hume laughed as she lifted the corner of the sheet.

'You're welcome to join me, sweet thing,' he said with a grin. 'But to be honest, I prefer to share my sack with members of my own club, if you get my drift.'

Now, alone in her bed, Zan groaned to herself. She would have to get out of the house without seeing him. Or Danny. So that's what all the *what the?* looks had been about. Danny could have said something. Hell, Hume could have said something when she was asking if Danny was gay. Now she had to get to the airport and take the next plane to anywhere. Or kill herself, which would be easier.

Or have breakfast and deal with it. As usual.

She looked at her clothes, strewn on the floor, and remembered that her and Danny's luggage was still at the hotel. Great. An excuse. She made a silent prayer to all the gods she didn't believe in that it wasn't Hume or Danny wielding the vacuum cleaner, and started to get dressed.

—

There was a clipboard on Danny's place setting, between a modern, but not too modern, knife and fork, book-ending a kind of loosely woven coloured raffia. A glass of orange juice sat untouched and a suggestion of steam rose from a mug of coffee. Danny sniffed. Real coffee. It smelled like the start of a good morning.

'Read it,' Ciara said from the other side of the table. They were on her verandah. The crisp early sun was just starting to lose its daily battle with the LA traffic fumes, but it felt good on his face. The view wasn't as good as Hume's, but it would do. Danny looked at the clipboard. A check with a two, a five and three zeroes before the point partially covered a letter he could tell at one glance had been written by a lawyer.

'Just tell me what it says,' Danny replied, trying to keep the resignation out of his voice. Ciara looked at him and shrugged.

'Okay, you sign off all direct involvement in *Pretty Boy* but you will receive all residuals as if you were still the creator ...'

'I am,' said Danny.

Ciara raised an eyebrow. 'As if you were still the creator,' she repeated, reading from her own copy. 'Then there's some legal blah that basically tries not to say they hate Paddy even more than you do so they are cutting you a break, the incident in the kitchen will be forgotten and you get everything you are entitled to and more.'

'It's not going ahead, is it?' Danny asked, meaning the TV show.

'Not a chance in hell,' she replied.

'So this,' he said, tapping the check, 'is it.'

She nodded and he suddenly realised she was more smartly dressed than he'd seen her at work: crisp white cotton blouse, smart skirt, jacket over the back of her chair. He guessed it wasn't for his benefit.

'Job interview or funeral?' he asked.

'Just in case this does go the same way as everything else involving Paddy, there's a couple of studios that want to talk to me about script development,' she said, almost guiltily, then she nodded to the stack of print-outs he'd brought. 'Thanks for those, by the way. Just what I need.'

'You're welcome,' he said. 'But if you were looking for ballast for your shoulder bag, you just needed to drop into a Starbucks. Those places are stacked with writers.'

'Does anyone else find this self-deprecating shit annoying?' Ciara frowned. 'Or is it just me?'

Danny resisted the urge to say 'sorry', guessing that would make things worse.

'So, what happens if I don't sign the letter?' he said, anxious to change the subject.

'Then you don't get your pay-off or your bonus,' she said, almost officiously.

'What bonus?' Danny replied, glancing at the document and peering at the dense type.

Ciara turned his swivel seat around, hitched up her skirt and straddled his lap, facing him, cowgirl style.

'It's not the trail of dead people you leave in your wake,' she breathed. 'It's not the fact that are single and not gay, your cute accent or the first wisps of grey hair in your temples …'

Danny instinctively touched the hair above his ears.

'It's not even the fact that you can write and you're funny,' she continued. 'Or that you're just passing through.'

Danny briefly noticed lacy French knickers, the crotch of which she deftly pulled to the side.

'But put all that together …'

'I might not be passing through,' Danny half-protested.

'Just shut the fuck up,' Ciara breathed in his ear as she tugged at his zip with one hand and unbuttoned her blouse with the other.

The phone in Danny's bag buzzed then stopped. By the time it beeped to tell him a message had been left, he was too busy collecting his bonus to care.

35

DANNY COULDN'T get the hands-free connected – he didn't even know if you could do that in this car – so he was working the buttons on his phone at every traffic-light stop, painfully aware that now was not a good time to get pulled over.

After, when he'd checked his phone to see who had been trying to interrupt his tryst with Ciara, he'd found two messages from Jensen.

The first said: 'On way to your hotel, see you soon.'

The second said: 'Get here now, man. Serious shit going down.'

His first call, to Jensen, established that the actor had seen Zan attack someone outside the hotel before driving away with two large men in dark suits. The second, to Hume, established that he was on his way too.

Jensen was almost hysterical when Danny pulled up in front of the hotel. He was sitting on a low stone wall near some shrubbery and was visibly shaking.

'Weirdest thing I ever saw, dude,' he told Danny between sips of water from a plastic bottle. 'She was like talking to these three guys and then she just like nutted one of them and he went down like a sack of potatoes.'

'Nutted him where?' Danny asked.

'Right over there,' Jensen replied, pointing across the road.

Danny couldn't suppress a smile. 'No, I meant where on his body,' he explained.

'On his chest,' Jensen said, pointing at his own sternum. 'But he dropped like she'd chinned him.'

Hume rolled up and stood behind Danny, acknowledging him with a nod, then listening.

'Then she and the other dudes just got in their car and drove off,' Jensen continued. 'Then the guys from the hotel came out with a portable heart starter machine —'

'Defibrillator,' Danny offered. Jensen looked at him like he was speaking Klingon.

'And then an ambulance came,' he continued. 'I was going to get them to call the cops but ... you know ... she is your friend. And they said it was a heart attack, so ...'

Danny nodded his thanks and squeezed Jensen's shoulder. He could sense the kid was already mentally booking his flight back to Sydney.

'These guys, can you describe them?'

'Two of them — the guys she drove away with — were big, dark skinned, like Islanders. Dark suits. Like the Blues Brothers. The guy who got headbutted, he was a tall, skinny dude in a white suit.'

'The Poet,' Danny said to Hume.

'I'll go and talk to the car-hops,' Hume said, turning towards the garage. 'You ask inside what happened with your Poet buddy.'

The receptionist was a tall, fit-looking thirtysomething with a Freddy Mercury moustache framing designer stubble on angular cheekbones. A study in reassuring calm, he hadn't seen the incident but had taken care of the aftermath.

'We are trained for it — hotels in this area get a lot of that — but the machine does most of the work.'

'Get a lot of what?'

'Heart attacks. I'm told he was involved in a confrontation with your ... um ... roommate, and then he had a seizure and fell to the ground. That's when we were alerted and called an ambulance immediately.'

'Where is he now?' asked Danny, who had a pretty good idea what had caused the 'seizure'.

He gave Danny the hospital name. 'It's not too far from here.'

'Was he alive when he was taken there?'

'Oh yes, very much so. Those machines are little miracle workers.' The receptionist smiled. 'He seemed more concerned about a tear in his jacket than his heart.'

Danny joined Hume outside as he was finishing up with the car valets, speaking Spanish so fluently that Danny didn't have a hope of catching more than the occasional word. One of them was *corazón,* the other *cabeza*. Heart and head.

'It seems Zan came out of the hotel and walked over to where the Poet was talking to two guys,' Hume said, turning to Danny. 'They exchanged words. She headbutted the Poet in the chest and down he went. Zan and the big guys got in their car and drove off, leaving the Poet in the dirt.

'The car-hops wrote down their plate.' Hume handed Danny a scrap of paper with a number scrawled on it. 'You know, good buddy,' Hume continued, 'as exciting as this all is, I think we should just hand this over to the cops, for everyone's sake.'

'Can't,' Danny said. 'Zan has form, remember?'

'Oh, the guy in the lift,' Hume said. 'I get it.'

'I think the goons who drove off with Zan belong to Jackie Jazz,' Danny said.

'Looks like it,' Hume replied. 'The car-hops were a little hazy on whether she got in the Escalade willingly.'

'It's amazing how willing you can be when you've got a gun pointed at you,' Danny said. 'Let's go see what the Poet knows.'

'Hey kid, can you drive stick?' Hume asked Jensen, who was hovering nearby looking lost. Jensen nodded, and Hume tossed him his car key. 'Get yourself back to your hotel then call the number behind the sun visor. One of my guys will come and pick it up.'

Jensen was nodding and smiling until he realised Hume was talking about the Hummer. By the time he had formed into words the facts that a) he had never driven in America, and b) he had never driven anything that big, Danny and Hume were already in the Porsche and peeling out from the sidewalk like TV cops on a mission.

—

It wasn't a calculated attack that had dropped the Poet. Zan had lashed out in frustration and fury and got lucky – or at least, that's what she told herself. What was it that golfer said? 'The more I do this, the luckier I get.' Something like that. Anyway, while the Poet was gasping on the ground, one of the heavies pulled a gun and jammed it in Zan's ribs, and it was game over. They made her lie down on the rear floor of the SUV, and now she was …? She genuinely had no idea.

The Poet. That slimebag. He'd called her over when she came out of the hotel and then the two thugs appeared from nowhere.

'Jackie Jazz wants to speak to you about his nephew,' the Poet had said. Zan, puzzled, asked him why. Hadn't he seen the video? Then she saw that look on his face. That pathetic, familiar *I got drunk and screwed up* apology for an apology.

The previous day's events had proved too much for the Poet's new-found resolve to stay sober. One drink too many, ten drinks too few. By the time Jackie's men had woken him up, Jackie was already gone for the morning, leaving instructions. Once Zan had been prodded into the vehicle they drove off, leaving the Poet gasping in the gutter like he was nothing. The thugs had argued about whether they should hang around but decided the boss would not want them to lose Zan or to come back with a dead body, and they weren't taking him to the ER with a hostage in the back.

About an hour later they were pulling up at some tall gates. Two sets. Plenty of clanking and rumbling and, looking up from where Zan lay on the floor of the Escalade, a glimpse of razor wire on top of a chain link fence. They drove around the side of a building – she guessed it was a house – and, as they pulled her out of the back of the vehicle and just before they pushed her down steps into a side door, she'd noticed a couple of guys in combat fatigues carrying stubby machine guns, probably Uzis.

Now she was in a cellar and able to see everything that was going on. This was not a good sign, she told herself. She could clearly see the faces of her abductors, which meant they did not expect her to be identifying them to the cops any time soon. Or ever. One of them, a giant, was already making plans for her last few hours. As soon as they had used cable ties to secure her to a tubular-steel and plywood office chair, he was at her, pushing his groin against her shoulder, rubbing his crotch and giggling.

'Leave her, Sammy,' the other one said. 'I'll go and get the boss.'

But as soon as he had gone, Sammy was back, pulling down the zip of her hoodie, and looking down the front of her sports bra. She wriggled and twisted but he grabbed her shoulder in his massive paw and held her still. Then he slid his other hand inside the right cup of her bra, his meaty fingers searching for her nipple. Just as he found his target, Zan sank her teeth into his ample forearm, biting hard until she could taste blood then holding on and pulling as if her true intent was to rip out a tendon. Which it was.

Sammy roared and jerked his arm away, then looked in horror at the blood oozing from two rows of perfect bite marks.

'You fucking …!' was all Zan heard as his massive fist jolted into the side of her head, propelling her into welcoming velvet blackness.

—

'You don't seem pleased to see us,' Danny said. 'Maybe we should have brought flowers and chocolates.'

'Not pleased' didn't cover it. Panicked, guilty and desperate were the emotions flitting across the Poet's face, especially when Hume closed the door to the private room and adjusted the little venetian blind covering the observation window. Getting in had been a potential obstacle but Hume had it covered. He still had his DEA badge and ID and simply asked if Mr Marvell – taking care to pronounce it Mar-*vell*, which may or may not have been correct but implied superior knowledge – was up to being questioned about the attack.

Danny stayed quiet, guessing there weren't too many Australian cops in the DEA or LAPD. The nurse said they'd just got there in time. The nurses had been told to check Mr Marvell's vitals one last time then release him if everything was okay.

Danny and Hume worked briskly and wordlessly, a state that seemed contagious. The Poet watched in stunned silence as they went about their business. Hume switched off the monitors to which the Poet was wired up, as the readings were already rocketing towards alarm levels. Danny raked through the drawer in the side table, at first finding nothing of interest except the thumb drive Zan had given the Poet.

Finally the Poet spoke. 'Hey!' he said, his voice rising. 'Nurse! *Nu–*'

His cry was cut off in mid-vowel by the insertion into his mouth of a flight sock, used to ward off thrombosis in the legs of frequent flyers and hospital patients. The poet reached for the alarm button but Hume pushed him back onto the mattress. Danny found what he was looking for: the restraints used to subdue violent patients. He and Hume worked quickly together, and before the Poet even realised what was going on he was strapped to the bed by his wrists and ankles.

'Okay, Poet, we don't have much time so we are going to cut the preliminary chit-chat and get straight to the part where we scare the shit out of you, and you tell us everything you don't want us to know,' Danny said.

The Poet looked, wild-eyed, from Danny to Hume and back again.

Danny spotted a trolley with electric shock paddles parked in the corner of the room. 'Crash cart,' he said to Hume, nodding in its direction.

Hume wheeled it over, located the power switch and clicked it on. The whine of the capacitors charging up prompted another wave of panic on the Poet's face. Hume ripped open the front of the Poet's gown and placed the paddles on his chest. The Poet shook his head in desperation, his eyes pleading with them as he tried to force the words 'no' and 'please' through the elasticated fabric filling his mouth.

'Are we good?' Danny asked the Poet. 'If we are, nod, and I'll remove the gag. But if you try to call for help, Hume is going to push that red button.'

Hume indicated the button with an elegant flourish, like a gameshow hostess showing off a prize.

The Poet nodded, and Danny removed the sock from his mouth.

'Fuck sake, you guys … I just had a heart attack!'

'No, you didn't. Your heart stopped beating briefly and we know why,' Danny said. 'Now where the hell is Zan?'

The Poet thought for a moment, then shook his head.

'Sorry, Danny, it's more than my life's worth.'

'Really?' Danny said. 'Let's test that theory. Hey Hume, how high does the voltage on that thing go?'

Hume peered at the scale on a dial.

'Looks like 200 volts to 1000,' he said. 'What do you think?'

'Split the diff and set it at 600, see what happens.' Danny said. 'And don't forget to shout "clear" before you press the button.'

'Roger that,' Hume said and started to fiddle with the controls.

'Okay, okay,' the Poet said. 'She's at Jackie Jazz's place, out past Sleepy Valley.'

'Is that even a place?' Danny asked. Hume nodded.

'It's off Spade Spring Canyon Road,' the Poet continued. 'It's a veritable fortress. Like a prison. Except it's the bad guys who have the guns.'

'So why did Jackie Jazz take Zan?'

The Poet's eyes flicked involuntarily towards the thumb drive. Danny caught the look and made the connection.

'You piece of shit. You didn't show him the videos.'

'I was waiting for the right time.'

'Press the button, Hume,' Danny said. 'Press the fucking button.'

Hume rolled his eyes but, even so, the Poet looked terrified.

'You could trade her for dropping the legal action,' he said.

'What legal action?' Danny asked.

'Your threat to sue for a slice of *Redneck Airlift*. Sign off your rights, show him the video, and he'll probably give you Zan back.'

'Probably? Thing is, Poet, I don't believe your credit with the Jazzman is as high as you think it is,' Danny said. 'Otherwise, why would you have been left to die like a dog in a ditch?'

It was clearly not the first time this had occurred to the Poet as his face crumpled under the weight of the truth.

'Take me with you,' he pleaded. 'Let me make it up to you. I don't want Zan getting hurt any more than you do.'

Danny wasn't buying it and Hume didn't look convinced.

'I can show you exactly where she is,' the Poet said.

Danny and Hume looked at each other. It wasn't the dumbest idea they'd heard that week.

'All right,' Danny said, holding up the thumb drive. 'But you need to give us Jackie Jazz's email address.'

36

THE FIRST thing Zan noticed when she came to was that the front of her shirt was wet. She'd been unconscious when Jackie Jazz threw a jug of water in her face to wake her up, so she could only be sure of the consequences, not the action. Then there was the voice, a rich baritone with a cultured Australian accent asking questions to which she didn't know the answer.

'What the hell were you thinking?' it said. 'How many times have I told you not to damage the merchandise?'

She opened her eyes reluctantly and the scene swam into view, like a watery video on a computer screen that suddenly gets a boost in bandwidth. The voice belonged to Jackie Jazz but the questions weren't directed at her. Instead they seemed to be aimed at Sammy, her molester, who was slumped against a wall bleeding from both his nose and his arm. This confused Zan because she remembered the arm – she could still taste it – but the nose?

'Boss, she's awake,' her other abductor said from the shadows. Judging by the way he was rubbing his knuckles, he was responsible for Sammy's facial injuries.

'Get him cleaned up, Kato,' Jackie said, gesturing to Sammy. 'I need to have a private chat with Ms Tran. Does he need a rabies shot, Xanthe?'

Jackie laughed and Zan was spooked that he knew her name. Sammy gave her a poisonous look as he was ushered out of the room by Kato.

'Why am I here?' Zan asked.

Jackie thought for a moment.

'Mainly because you killed my nephew,' Jackie said, suddenly serious. 'And partly because you and Mr Clay are fucking up my business.'

'I didn't kill Weezl,' Zan said.

Jackie sucked air noisily through his teeth.

'Ignoring the fact that I don't like my nephew being referred to by his unfortunate street name, even if he did choose it himself,' Jackie said, 'I have been informed that you killed Mr Hahn, you may have killed the Poet and you took a sizable chunk out of my second-best henchperson. I'd say you've got what it takes.'

'So ...?' Zan said, defiantly.

'So, once we have persuaded Mr Clay to assist us with our business venture, I'm afraid you have to be punished.'

'You're going to torture and rape me?' Zan asked, like she was talking about a parking fine.

'Good God, no,' Jackie spluttered. 'What kind of animal do you take me for? I'm not even going to let Sammy touch you. No, no, no, my dear. When you have served your purpose, I'm going to kill you.'

She looked at him blankly.

'It's a family thing – nothing personal,' he explained

Jackie Jazz's phone rang. He looked at the screen, smiled and showed it to Zan. It read, *The Poet*.

'Speak of the devil,' Jackie said, touching the answer button. 'Andrew, you're alive. How ...'

It was clear from the look on Jackie's face that it wasn't the Poet on the other end of the phone, a fact that was confirmed when he said 'Clay?' and walked into the corner of the cellar, his back to Zan. She couldn't hear what Jackie was saying and, in fact, he seemed to be doing more talking than listening. She realised there was limited time for her to shout a coherent warning before Jackie ended the call. But she had to give it a shot.

'Tethered goat!' she called out. 'Tethered goat!'

'Tethered goat?' Jackie Jazz said, so surprised that for a moment he forgot to switch off the phone and inadvertently relayed her warning to Danny. When he did hang up he turned to Zan, puzzled. 'Did that mean what I think? You're saying that you are bait?'

Zan nodded and shrugged. There wasn't much point in denying it, especially since she couldn't think of any other reason for saying it.

'Don't you think Clay would have worked that out for himself?'

Another shrug.

'You really are a deeply strange young woman.'

Zan took it as a compliment and smiled.

—

It took Hume about an hour to drive to Sleepy Valley, taking the 405 to Sylmar, then sliding over from Antelope Valley Freeway to the Sierra Highway at Humphreys. It was approaching 7pm so traffic wasn't exactly thinning, but at least it was moving. Danny called Jackie on the Poet's mobile phone and heard his muttered threats before Zan shouted her cryptic warning, helpfully repeated by Jackie Jazz.

Once they were off the main highway, they followed a series of turns, taking them further into the hills on increasingly narrow tracks. There was a glow from artificial lights on the other side of a rise ahead, and the Poet, who to this point had been sitting silent in the back, told them to pull over and kill the lights.

'Stay in the car,' was all Hume said over his shoulder as he and Danny got out. They clambered up the side of a grassy bank, loose soil and stones occasionally slipping from under their feet. As they crested the rise and saw the compound in front of them, Danny lay flat and let himself enjoy the rush. He could see the clear shapes of one central building and a couple of outlying constructions, probably garages and sheds. A swimming pool, lit in iridescent blue, ran down one side of the house. A tennis court sat in semi-darkness at the back.

Hume handed him night vision binoculars. Now Danny could see several vehicles, including a black Escalade, parked at odd angles around what must have been the main entrance. Large red signs in English and Spanish warned that the three-metre-high chain link fence, topped with coils of razor wire, was electrified. Movement below one of them alerted him to a coyote pulling at the corpse of a racoon. He guessed racoons couldn't read either language.

Danny scarcely needed the night vision facility on the glasses. The area around the house was floodlit all the way up to the fence and beyond. A double-gated 'airlock' arrangement was designed to prevent anyone tailgating a vehicle in or out. The fences, gates and cameras created an impression of such security that it looked like the place was more designed to keep people in than prevent intruders from entering. That was enhanced by figures dressed in black combat fatigues and beanies, carrying small machine guns.

'At least three of them, maybe four,' said Danny. 'Looks like they're expecting company.'

'Drug house,' Hume murmured. 'But not one I'm familiar with. Must have been built after I quit the agency.'

They scrambled and slid back down the hill to the SUV. Hume started the engine. On the way there he had spotted an overgrown farm gateway set back from the road. He drove slowly on parking lights until they found it and then took the SUV as far into the scrub as he could, turning it around so the rear reflectors wouldn't give their position away to passing drivers heading to the house.

Hume got out and, using the vehicle's hood as a desk, quickly got to work with his laptop and phone. Danny took the opportunity to grill the Poet and find out everything he knew about the house and the people in it, which wasn't much. He clearly took his 'don't want to know' philosophy seriously. He was more forthcoming about who had tipped him off about Danny's plan to stop *Redneck Airlift*.

'Twenny,' he said. 'He called Jackie last night and Jackie got me to find out if you had cleared your hotel room yet. When they said someone was coming to collect your stuff, his goons and I drove down and waited. When Zan saw me with the heavies, she just lost it and tried to kill me.'

'I don't think she was actually trying to kill you,' Danny said.

'You're not the one who ended up in hospital,' the Poet replied.

Having made several phone calls and sent a series of texts, Hume swung his large frame back into the car. 'Tell me about "tethered goat",' he said.

Danny explained how he had once outlined the tethered goat military tactic to Zan. A lightly-armed, poorly defended outpost – something like a supply base or a maintenance depot – was positioned to draw enemy attackers out so they could be mopped up by covering patrols. It was like hunters in India would tie up a goat to attract tigers so they could shoot them. Then they would feast on the goat anyway.

'It didn't matter how many times I told her there was no goat, she obsessed about it,' Danny said. 'I know she's vegetarian and an animal activist but I think she was taking the piss. "Poor goat," she would say. "The goat always ends up dead."'

'So she wasn't telling you she was bait,' Hume said. 'She was telling you that she is going to die anyway.'

'He *is* very pissed off about his nephew,' the Poet said.

'No fucking thanks to you,' Danny murmured, turning around in his seat to fix the Poet with a glare. Hume's laptop burped and he opened the screen. A couple of clicks and he was looking at a detailed plan of the outside of the building they had just seen from the hill.

'Local council building consent for electrical installations,' he said. 'Their computers are usually less secure than City Hall.'

Hume and Danny scanned the plan. Danny pointed at the outline of a much smaller building outside the perimeter fence but still connected to the mains supply from the house.

'What's that?'

'Well, it looks like a boathouse, but there's no water,' said Hume. 'Or a gatehouse, but there's no gate.'

'Normally you would think it was a power junction box, but the power comes in here –' Danny pointed to the opposite edge of the screen, '– and goes out here –' following the line to the mystery building. 'I'm going to go take a look.'

'While you're gone, I'll see if I can jog Rhymin' Simon here's memory, see if we can't find out who this Twenny guy is,' Hume growled.

'Oh, I know who he is,' Danny said. 'I'm just not sure that the Poet doesn't know. See if you work that out.'

The Poet didn't respond except to sigh deeply from the darkness of the rear seat. Danny slipped out of the car and disappeared into the night.

'I need to pee,' Zan said, and Kato groaned softly as he looked up from his *Hunger Games* novel. This was not in his job description.

'Like, now!' she said.

'So pee,' Kato replied.

'You really want to be locked in this airless room full of the stink of piss?' Zan asked.

'I'll take her,' Sammy said, rubbing his forearm.

'Will you, fuck,' said Kato. 'Keep your gun on her and if she even looks at my chest, shoot the bitch.' Then an afterthought. 'And try not to shoot me.'

Sammy pulled out a pistol from his belt and racked the slide, pointing it at Zan.

'That's a bit girly for you, isn't it?' she said as Kato cut the cable ties around her wrists. He looked up at her quizzically. 'Not you. Sammy. That looks like a Ruger LC9.'

Sammy looked at the gun and then at Zan. *How did she know?* Zan smiled. Research for countless cop shows and movie scripts, where every handgun was either a Glock or a Magnum, had given her a passing knowledge of popular firearms. The Ruger was an informed guess based on its size.

'That's a bit, umm, dainty for a big boy like you, isn't it?' she continued. 'I'd have thought you'd have gone for something a bit more … manly. The guys outside have Uzis.'

Sammy looked at her and then at his gun.

'Hey, I get it,' Zan continued. 'You know you're not gay, no matter what other people think.'

'I thought you needed to pee,' Kato said, pushing Zan towards a grey painted steel door.

'You can watch, if that's what floats your boat,' she said to Kato, but it was Sammy who looked up.

She didn't know why she was winding Sammy up. Revenge? Unsettling him to keep him off balance? All she knew was that if Danny had the Poet's phone, he had the Poet, and it would take him zero seconds flat to find out where she was being held. Anything she could do or say to delay her captors working that out – if they hadn't already – had to be worth a try.

Kato said nothing but turned the handle and pushed her in, closing the door behind her. Zan thought he was being a bit slack until she looked around and realised there was no lock on the door and no way out.

A small metal grill with fixed louvered slats let air in and out, and Zan thought if only she'd had her trusty Swiss Army knife and a couple of hours to spare she could have removed it. But the hole would have been too small anyway, even for her.

As she sat looking around the empty concrete box, her predicament seemed hopeless. Even Danny couldn't get out of this. Stainless-steel sink, stainless-steel toilet (with no seat). There was nothing to break or bend, to use as a tool or a weapon. She looked again at the too-small, too-fixed air vent and smiled as she was struck by a thought. She started unzipping her hoodie.

—

Danny was skirting around the compound, moving through the scrub to the south and east of the main house, stopping every so often to check where the mystery building might be. The sound of engines and slamming doors drew him to the edge of a clearing where he could see cars being backed up to the main door of the house and cardboard boxes being loaded into them. He was alarmed at first, but there was something about the leisurely pace of the guys loading the vehicles that told him this was preparation for a later departure, rather than a sign that they were about to cut and run.

He merged back into the shadows and only took a few more steps before he almost walked into the wall of the building he was looking for. It was smaller than he'd thought it would be, about double the size of an outside toilet. There was one small window and a heavy metal door on the opposite wall. Risking his torch, he looked inside. The door was locked from the inside with a large but simple bolt.

There was a painted metal plate in the floor, about sixty centimetres square, with external hinges and a recessed handle: some sort of inspection hatch. The sound of footsteps dropped Danny to his haunches. He realised the nearest part of the fence was just a couple of metres away and there was a guard patrolling inside the perimeter, sweeping the fence with a powerful torch. Danny eased back round to the far side of the small block, but the rustle of leaves and gravel had the guard's torch beam whip around in his direction.

'Who's there?' the guard shouted, disturbing a large ginger cat, which shot out from under a bush and disappeared into the night. 'Fucking cats,' the guard called after it and moved on. But as he swept the scrub one last time with his torch, Danny noticed a shape beyond a bush.

Waiting until the guard was out of sight, he crawled through the undergrowth until he found himself looking at a dark-green camouflage net. Danny lifted a corner, uncovering a shiny new Jeep Wrangler inside. Further investigation revealed the keys were in the ignition and the vehicle was pointing straight down a narrow cut in the woods. This was an escape route, which meant …

Danny looked back at the dunny-shaped block and followed a line through the fence and up the hill to a windowless extension that had been built onto the back of the main building, a couple of metres down the slope. If the dunny block was the exit of an escape tunnel, then the box-like extension at the top of the hill was probably its entrance.

Sure enough, off to one side there was a tube-like concrete shape that came out of the side of the building and disappeared into the ground at an angle of about 45 degrees. And then he noticed something that made him creep a little further forward. There was a small, squarish air vent, and something was squirming out it. Narrow at first, it looked like a snake, but then it got wider and suddenly it was round, followed by another round shape, like a figure eight.

Danny switched on the night vision binoculars, focused them and smiled. It was Zan's bra.

37

THERE WAS another vehicle parked next to the Porsche when Danny got back to Hume's position. He hesitated, waiting until he was sure Hume hadn't been bailed up by Jackie Jazz's men. Then he recognised his friend's voice and shape in the gloom.

'Come out, Danny,' Hume said. 'You're crashing around there like a fucking rhino.'

As he got closer, Danny could see Hume was talking to an equally tall man dressed in black combat gear.

'Danny, this is Jace,' Hume said. 'He knows you but you don't know him.'

Jace nodded a reluctant greeting without meeting his eye, and Danny was immediately transported back to holding areas, where special forces troops would come through so exhausted, or wired, or both that they couldn't even remember the fake names they had been given to protect their families back home. Or something like that. Danny suspected it was mostly to enhance the sense of 'them and us' that made it easier to do hideous things to other human beings.

'They're getting ready to move,' Danny said, eager to debrief. 'But I don't think it's tonight.'

'A convoy of cars coming out of the hills at night would have cops all over it before they reached the city limits,' Hume said. 'Once the morning rush starts they can just blend in.'

Danny thought for a second, not wishing to seem foolish, but ploughed on. 'That comment you made about how your house had a torture chamber and an escape tunnel for the drug guy. Was that true?'

'The tunnel sure was. How the blood got on the walls of the wine cellar is anybody's guess,' Hume said. 'Why do you ask?'

'Is that common? The tunnel thing, I mean,' Danny asked.

'Mexicans drug lords love their tunnels,' Hume said with a laugh. 'El Chapo had a tunnel out of his prison and another one out of his safe house and all the way across the border to Mexico on a motorbike on a rail. Sonofabitch got away without ever seeing the light of day.'

'We used Mexicans for tunnels in 'Nam, because they were small,' said Jace, who was much too young to have been there, except as a tourist. 'Guess they got a taste for it.'

Danny explained his theory that the outhouse was the escape end of a tunnel, with a getaway car sitting just a few steps away, ready to go. He also told them how he knew Zan was alive and in the room at the other end of the tunnel.

'What do you need?' Jace asked.

Danny gave him a verbal list of the equipment he thought he might find useful: glass cutter, small hacksaw, a square of aluminium foil and a fishing rod. Jace, without batting an eye at the bizarre selection, went to his truck and came back with a full set of black combats, night vision goggles and the other gear. A long whip aerial and some fishing line substituted for the rod. Danny held the aerial at arm's length and decided it would do the job, then he, Jace and Hume crowded around the laptop to start formulating a plan.

———

On the other side of the house from where Zan had used her underwear to signal her position, Jackie Jazz had a problem. The images on his computer screen confirmed two things: his nephew did have a female companion after all, and she was probably at the very least there when he was shot.

The Vietnamese girl's story, as outlined on the email Clay had sent along with the video clips and pictures, was starting to stack up. A twinge of irritation at Tony Cufflinks for having led him into this blind alley was exacerbated by the thought of how completely he had been played. Even this hideaway had been organised by Tony through a 'friend of the family'.

What really pissed him off was Tony's assumption that in anything Jackie did to make money anywhere in the world, Tony had to get his slice. They should call him Tony the Taxman, he thought. This business with the foreign exchange had been a straightforward cash transaction weighted in his favour: the Australian dollar was weak against the greenback when the studio sent the money, then suddenly it was strong and he stood to make a profit just by paying the original stake back. This situation, he'd guessed, could not last forever and he'd had to move quickly.

None of it had been planned, of course – if he could predict the movements of the money market so accurately, he wouldn't need to run girls and drugs. And he hadn't been lying to Tony when he said the movie game was more of a hobby than anything, a fun way to gain access to real stars and celebrities. Jackie simply knew an opportunity when he saw one.

And yet ironically, now that *Redneck Airlift* was about to pay off in unexpected ways, the studio wanted to buy it back from him again. Someone was queering his pitch.

He was pretty sure it had Tony Cufflinks's paw prints all over it. The Kings Cross crim had gone to great lengths to put Clay and Zan in the frame, when he must have known it probably wasn't them. But what was his angle? And what did he stand to gain by threatening Jackie's writers, causing the deaths of two of them? That part just didn't add up in any logical way.

Now, also thanks to Tony, he had the additional problem of Zan, who may have assaulted the Poet – although that was nothing compared to what Jackie planned to do – and had seen his cocaine smuggling operation. Then there was Clay, who sooner or later would persuade the Poet to give up their location, if he hadn't spilled his guts already. Jackie switched off the ceiling light and, illuminated only by the laptop, looked out into the night. Was Clay already out there?

Back to his immediate problem. Killing someone as revenge for the death of a family member was one thing, but the cold-blooded murder of a mostly innocent civilian was another entirely. And then there was the potential loss of the money for the movie. And then there was the shipment of cocaine sealed in DVD cases. At least he could thank that dinosaur Tony Cufflinks for giving him the idea when he was jabbering on about film canisters. Five hundred remaindered copies of *The Black Dahlia*, locked, sealed and shrink-wrapped. Jackie really didn't want to draw any unwanted attention to his little operation.

Even if he was up for it, icing the girl wouldn't solve the Clay problem. In fact, it would only make it worse. Killing both of them and disposing of their bodies might be beyond the capabilities of his hired morons and, in any case, it would escalate this problem to a level at which he didn't want to operate, especially in a country that still had the death penalty for murder. But letting them go risked both his business enterprises. He needed leverage.

What he couldn't understand was why Zan and Danny were so hell-bent on stopping *Redneck Airlift* from going into production. There was only one thing for it: he would have to read the damned script.

—

Thirty minutes later, Jackie stomped down the steps to the cellar carrying the script, folded open halfway through, and his mobile phone. The rest of the house was all white walls and carved oak, like the set for a movie about Mexican drug kingpins, but the cellar was light grey concrete and stank of fear. All three of its occupants were dozing but snapped awake and alert as soon as the heavy door to the rest of the house slammed shut behind Jackie. He walked straight up to Zan, swiped his iPhone into life and pressed the record symbol.

'Tell me about the perfect crime,' he said, holding the phone closer to Zan. 'Tell me about the old guy in the lift.'

'Fuck off and die,' Zan said.

'I could fuck off, as you so charmingly put it, but you'll be the one who dies.' He laughed. 'Eventually. When Sammy here is finished playing with you.'

Both Zan's and Sammy's eyes widened at this, albeit for different reasons.

'So tell me everything,' he said.

'Why?' she asked, puzzled. 'What's it to you?'

'Insurance. I've never killed a woman. I don't really want to start with you if I don't have to.'

Zan sat silently for a moment, not keen to play Jackie's game – not even sure what it was that he wanted. Then she realised that at least she could buy some time.

'You want me to confess?' she said.

'I want every detail. The truth and nothing but. Don't leave anything out. It needs to be something you don't want anyone else to hear – especially the cops.'

'Pull up a chair,' Zan said.

Kato surrendered his seat to Jackie and then gestured to Sammy to relinquish a square yellow pressed-metal stool. The pecking order well and truly established, Zan began. 'Okay, Alan Hahn was a very rich man who wanted to enclose a balcony on his apartment in my mother's building …'

—

Danny felt excited, for sure, but the one overwhelming sensation was comfort. The combat fatigues weren't a perfect fit but they were no worse than army-issue. The sapper's tool belt felt snug and secure and the helmet, with clipped-on night vision goggles, felt like home. All that was missing was his assault rifle, but for reasons Hume could not comprehend, Danny had drawn the line there. 'If I go in there with a gun, there will be shooting,' he said.

'That's the general idea,' Hume muttered in reply.

Danny compromised and slipped a Colt automatic into his side-arm holster. His plan was simple: infiltrate the house via the escape tunnel, locate Zan and extract her by the same route. Easy as that. He had already cut the pane of glass, used the aerial and fishing line to snare the end of the bolt and pulled it open. Now inside the block, he was cutting through the retaining pin on the hinge of the hatch on the floor.

The mini hacksaw was basically an S-shaped handle into which one end of the hacksaw blade slotted while the free end was gripped by a screw. It was a cheap mild steel bolt, and the hacksaw cut through it with ease while Danny sat on the hatch cover to deaden any sound. Once the pin was cut and driven back through the hinge, it was easy enough to free the cover, pull it away and see the small ladder that led to the tunnel itself.

The tunnel was surprisingly high and wide. Not quite large enough to walk through fully upright, but you could move quickly enough – at a stooped jog. The walls were rough but sealed with cement so there wasn't much dirt or debris. About a hundred metres in there was a set of steps up to a plain domestic door. Danny could hear muffled voices; occasionally there was a deeper male voice, responding in monosyllabic bursts, but mostly it was Zan's familiar lilt.

There was no light escaping around the edges of the door, so Danny reckoned that would work both ways. He used his head light to scan the door and saw a simple cylinder lock handle with the keyhole on his side of the door. He worked his lock picks carefully and silently, switching off his headlight before moving the final tumbler into place and turning the handle. With the gentlest of clicks, the door was free.

Danny turned the handle back then retreated down the tunnel to the exit block. Removing the bare lightbulb, he pushed a small square of aluminium foil into the socket and replaced the globe. He turned on the power and there was a flicker and fizz and then nothing. He looked around the corner of the block. The entire compound, including the house, was in darkness. He had blown the fuses. Thank God for a cheap wiring job, he thought.

Back in the tunnel, headlight on, Danny raced up the slope and the stairs to the room door. He could hear shouts inside. This was his chance. He opened the door and threw in a smoke bomb followed by a concussion grenade. Zan would forgive him once her ears stopped ringing. Danny quickly closed the door and felt the blast through the handle.

He waited five seconds for the smoke to fill the room, then switched his goggles to infra-red, expecting to open the door and see several human shapes, one of which would be much smaller than the others. Instead, the only heat sources were the two bombs he had just detonated, glowing on the floor.

Suddenly the lights came on, presumably when someone reset the trip switch for the whole building, and an extractor fan pulled cones of fumes towards one wall. Danny flipped the goggles up and looked around. All he could see were a table and boxes of DVDs. It was only when he lifted a cover and white powder trickled out that he realised what was going on. Danny was distracted by his discovery, moving closer to check, when a door in the far wall opened to reveal three male figures, backlit brightly from the hallway, the two at the front holding guns.

'Hello, Danny,' said Jackie Jazz. 'All you had to do was knock.'

Danny was about to pull his pistol when one of the men raised his gun and fired a short burst of bullets.

—

Up on the rise overlooking the compound, Hume and Jace tracked Danny down towards the exit block, mainly through the movement of bushes and the occasional shadow. Once he was at the block, they made their own preparations, hurriedly but efficiently, just in case things didn't go as smoothly as they hoped.

Precisely thirty minutes after Danny had left their side, all the lights went out in the compound, as planned, and shortly thereafter they heard the thud of the concussion grenade, as expected.

They waited for signs that Danny and Zan were on their way back, just in case they were required to create a distraction. Instead, the lights came back on again and they heard the burp of an Uzi from inside the house.

Sammy was bored shitless. This Asian chick was going on and on about her mother and an apartment building and some trick she'd been taught at her gym, and Kato had taken his stool so he had to stand or sit on the floor. Fuck it, he thought and wandered out to talk to the Mexicans. Jackie said they came with the house – to protect whoever was renting it – but Sammy knew they were also there to make sure guys like him didn't steal anything, and to keep an eye on the product.

The chick was right: they had Uzis. He'd never actually seen one before and asked the Mexican if he could hold it. He said okay. And then the lights went out and the Mexican was running for the fuse box and then there was a fucking explosion, and another, louder, and the next thing Sammy knew he was at the door of the packing room and there was a fucking ninja in there and he lifted the gun to cover him and the fucking thing went off.

A neat row of bullet holes ran up one wall and into the ceiling.

'There goes the rental bond,' said Jackie, joking but not smiling.

Jackie's problem wasn't so much doubled as squared now that he had Zan *and* Clay. Clay had seen the drugs, but if he wasted him Zan would know and she didn't seem like the type who could be easily intimidated into silence.

At least he knew who was responsible – albeit indirectly – for the deaths of the two writers and his nephew: Twenny, that cocksucker.

While Jackie was trying to work out what to do with his unwanted guests, Clay had laid it out, his theory. Twenny would have got his share of the profit when *Redneck Airlift* was sunk, but he didn't want the money. This was his ticket to Hollywood, the big time that he dreamed about every time he watched *Entourage* or *Californication* on TV.

So there's this kid with criminal connections who wants to be a crime writer and Twenny tells him, okay, by way of research, how about you hack into this guy's computer and heavy these other two people to make sure the movie goes ahead. Only the kid – Jackie's nephew – puts kiddy porn on the computer of a guy who is already crippled with guilt. He tops himself.

Then he overdoes the violence and kills the second guy. Then he gets himself caught by Clay and shot by his own girlfriend, who is a bigger psycho than everyone else put together. And all of this is too ridiculous not to be true.

Jackie was genuinely wishing he had more options, because Clay was a truly interesting guy – and boy, could he tell a story. If only he hadn't broken into the room next door to where they were holding Zan, this could all have turned out so differently. Jackie allowed himself the briefest fantasy. The three of them would make a great team. Clay could be his bodyguard and writer, and the girl – come on, she was worth the price of admission on her own.

But that wasn't going to happen. Jackie knew that. He also knew Clay was stalling for time, staving off the inevitable. And hell, why wouldn't you? At least he wasn't pleading and crying, making his last moments on the planet embarrassing for himself and everyone around him. But there was a question niggling at the back of Jackie's mind, like a bad heckler at a stand-up comedy show.

'Hey, Zan,' Jackie said. 'We were interrupted and I still don't get it. You punch the guy in the chest, stop his heart. Correct?'

'Headbutted, to be exact,' Zan confirmed. Danny looked askance.

'So how is that the perfect crime?' Jackie said. Danny and Zan looked at each other and she nodded.

'Because,' Danny said, 'When she's doing CPR – looking like she's trying to save his life – she's covering the bruise from the initial blow.'

'Oh, I get it.' Jackie smiled. 'Cute.'

Outside the window, the black night sky turned bright orange.

—

The way Hume would tell this, as the story spread and grew over the coming months, there was more equipment and fewer men, until it was just him and Jace. In fact, Jace had his whole props crew of six with him and they set up the lights, the loudspeakers and the finishing touch: forty-two cardboard shooting-range targets shaped like men with guns, which they ranged across the ridge above the compound. Hume fired the flare.

That got everyone's attention – that and the silhouettes of armed men on the horizon. Normally Danny would have questioned the tactical wisdom of back-lighting your troops so they showed up in the darkness. He might also have doubted the efficacy of a recording of a helicopter, albeit played over massive rock-concert speakers. But it seemed to work.

Hume used a loud-hailer to inform the occupants of the house that they were surrounded by DEA officers and they should lay down their weapons and surrender. One of the Mexican guards fired impotently towards the targets before he and his colleagues all melted into the darkness. Evidence of their successful escape came less than sixty seconds later with the sound of a Jeep roaring off into the trees below the house. Was Jackie Jazz in it? No one knew, but Zan was sure he had followed the Mexicans into the tunnel. He was certainly nowhere to be found when the real DEA turned up later.

Sammy and Kato surrendered to Hume and Jace when they appeared in the doorway in full SWAT gear, uniforms left over from a recent episode of a cop show they'd worked on. This gave them a problem, as they didn't really have facilities for taking prisoners. In the end they secured them with cable ties, locked them in the room with all the cocaine and called the DEA.

When Sammy was face-down on the ground, his hands behind his back, Zan took the opportunity to deliver a flurry of hefty kicks to his ribs until she was picked up and carried away, still kicking, by Hume. A last-minute rethink had them park the Poet there too. He and his new identity could take his chances with immigration. Hume would brief his former DEA colleagues once they were well clear of the compound.

'So, who is Twenny?' Zan asked as she sat on Danny's shoulders to retrieve her bra from the outside of the air vent.

'You know the rapper, Fitty?' Danny asked.

'Fifty Cent?' she replied. 'Left a bit … He's a movie producer now.'

'That's right. So if Fitty is Fifty Cent, what does that make Twenny?' Danny said.

'Twenty cent?' said Zan.

'How about twenty *per* cent?'

'Ohh. Mr Twenty Per Cent,' she said, getting it, and then shocked when she realised the implications. 'Rob? How long have you known?'

'Only since the Poet told me they would trade you for my agreement not to sue over the movie,' Danny replied as he lowered Zan to the ground and tried but failed to look away as she put her bra back on. 'Rob was the only one I told. He was the only one who could have told the Poet. He is Twenny.'

'And all that stuff you told Jackie, about his nephew?'

'Mostly speculation, but the Poet filled in some of the blanks on the way up here. Weezl wasn't a wannabe criminal, he was a wannabe writer.'

'Like the world needs more of those,' Zan said. 'And the Poet, he knew Rob wanted to make sure the movie went ahead?'

'Only as much as his "I don't want to know" philosophy allowed,' Danny said. 'He was just riding his luck. He asked Bryan and Marcus to agree to the movie being abandoned, they went with it and that was fine until Rob got Weezl to send a fake email from the Poet, telling Bryan to back out of the deal and make sure the movie went ahead, or find himself in a world of paedophile pain – so when he died he still believed the Poet had "stolen his dream" of getting out of the business and finding some peace.'

'So the Poet wasn't involved in the Weezl stuff?' asked Zan.

'I don't think so. He says not. But he could have given the rest of us a heads-up that there was more to Bryan's and Marcus's deaths than met the eye.'

'And Rob?'

'He wanted us out of Sydney because we were the only ones left who might connect him with Bryan, Marcus and Weezl,' Danny said. 'It would never have occurred to him that we would cross paths with the very people he wanted us to avoid.'

'You wouldn't want to be in his shoes,' Zan said. 'Not with Jackie Jazz out there, roaming around, pissed off at anyone and everyone who ruined his plans.'

'And Tony Cufflinks is looking for someone to hurt.'

Zan and Danny looked at each other, their faces half-lit in the flat white light leaking from the scene-of-crime lamps. That included them too.

38

IT WAS only two days before *Variety* ran the story of how *Redneck Airlift*'s producer was an Australian drug dealer and there were three suspicious deaths associated with the project. After that, the movie was so dead it couldn't have been revived as a zombie flick.

Hume did okay though. Jasmina put him in a room with some writers to create a script about a movie armourer who turns out to be an undercover cop – it would be like the *SFX* films, only with more guns. Hollywood loves Hollywood and Hume loved the idea. He'd get a double payday through the contract to equip the production.

Ciara called Danny to tell him she liked one of the TV scripts he'd left her and that she had her new studio's backing to shoot a pilot. Disappointingly for Danny it was *Crossfire*, Laura's script. Danny called Laura with the news on the same day she had finally decided once and for all that being a cop wasn't a good career for her.

Paddy Rosenberg was producing a bizarre medical gameshow called *What's Your Problem?* which was already getting horrendous reviews before a single episode had aired. Then Paddy was overheard propositioning an intern who was the adopted daughter of one of the network's senior executives, and it was cardboard box time again.

After being tipped off by Danny, via Laura, Detective Inspector Bill McCue turned up at Rob's office. A week earlier Rob had agreed to an initial interview about the deaths of Bryan, Marcus and Weezl, but McCue found the rooms locked and empty. Rob had flown to Singapore and thence to an unspecified Asian destination. His bank accounts, including trust accounts for his clients, had all been emptied. He wasn't coming back any time soon. In fact, months later, he would be lured to a meeting with film financiers in a hotel in Penang, Malaysia. He would never be seen again.

Danny and Zan had been hanging out in LA with Hume for a few days, wondering what to do next, when Danny got a message from Brendan Willis, a former sapper living in Vũng Tàu, south of Saigon, who had gotten himself involved in a very messy property deal with his Vietnamese wife and her brother. He thought his life was in danger and he knew if he left the country he'd never get back in. He'd lose everything. If Danny had the time, he had the money to pay for a little technical assistance and some moral support.

That night, Danny and Zan were watching TV when a promo for a new show called *Perfect Crime* was aired. It opened with a young woman giving an older man CPR as he lay on the floor of a lift. Suddenly a trip to Vietnam seemed like a terrific idea for both of them. Zan would be the ideal assistant-cum-interpreter and fixer.

Laura was being hassled by Tony Cufflinks for information on Danny's movements. He was threating to spill the beans to her soon-to-be former employers if she didn't get him something usable, and fast. Tony was particularly stressed because of rumours that Jackie Jazz had taken a contract out on his life – for which he blamed Danny – and he certainly wasn't happy about Laura's imminent career change. Two nights before she was due to fly to LA to take up her new life as a screenwriter, Laura told Tony that Danny and Zan would both be at her farewell drinks at the Soho Bar. Tony decided he should be there too.

As Tony and two of his thugs reached the entrance of the club, they were met with a fusillade of paintballs, fired by Laura from a nearby roof. When Tony dropped to his knees, clutching his chest, Reuben the doorman stepped forward to reassure him it wasn't real blood. But it was a real heart attack, and soon he was really dead.

In fact, Danny and Zan were several thousand kilometres away in Tommy's Bar in Vũng Tàu, waiting for Brendan Willis. They were checking the memorabilia on the walls, from posters of Aussie Rules teams to black-and-white pictures of too-young men sweating in battlefields too far from home, when a teenager skidded his Honda step-through to a halt outside the door and ran in.

'Mr Bren, he is …' he began in broken English, before spotting Zan and switching to Vietnamese.

'Brendan is in hospital,' Zan translated for Danny. 'They think he's been poisoned.'

The messenger looked at Danny then stepped back, alarmed by the X etched on the Australian's features that gave him a look of barely contained fury.

'Your boyfriend, is he angry?' he asked.

'No, he's just thinking,' she replied. 'And he's not my boyfriend.'

THE END

ACKNOWLEDGEMENTS

I would like to acknowledge Australian sappers (army engineers) past and present whose true stories provided me with material for four previous books, as well as Danny's nightmares.

I want to thank my tutors at Swinburne University who allowed me to start this novel as part of my MA submission, and my agent, Fiona Inglis of Curtis Brown who encouraged me to keep going.

Thanks to Martin, Keiran, Emily and, especially, Ruby at Affirm Press for taking a punt. Thanks also to The Inspector for leading me up some of Kings Cross's darker alleys and to John for explaining the difference between organised and disorganised crime.

Finally, thanks to Lily (Ly) Phan for not being Zan and to Sue Williams for supporting me for half my life, regardless of my ridiculous plans and dreams.